The Curve of the World

Advance Praise for The Curve of the World

"*The Curve of the World* is Vonda McIntyre's last gift to us, and it is magnificent. In this alternate history of the ancient world, where Minoans build a globe-spanning trading community, Vonda has taken up the challenge of her good friend Ursula Le Guin and become a dreamer of a wider reality, creating a glorious vision of a working world in which global commerce and fairness are not a contradiction in terms. The Curve of the World is the sum and summit of all Vonda McIntyre was as a writer and as a human being."

—Nicola Griffith, author of *Ammonite* and *Hild*

"Vonda takes us from the known world, a world with known dangers and known comforts, into the unknown, the wild but civilized West. As she herself looked ahead to the journey from life into death, she opens to us a world filled with unrealized possibilities. This is a marvelous book of the civilizations that could have been."

—Eileen Gunn, author of *Stable Strategies for Middle Management* and *Questionable Practices*

"*The Curve of the World* is full of daring, and rich and rare invention, but feeling true, as far as can be known, to the mysterious, apparently/probably women-centered, ancient Minoan culture. I loved the giving of beautiful gifts, between chance voyagers meeting on the ocean. So much better than mere trade. A wonderful book."

—Gwyneth Jones, author of *Life* and *Bold as Love*

"A vivid, luminous novel. As Minoan traders travel the ancient world, McIntyre brings to richly imagined life six distinctive cultures of antiquity, all touched with magic. The characters are so real that I could see, feel, even smell them, and I passionately wanted each to succeed at their various quests. The Curve Of The World is a wonderful capstone to a storied career."

—Nancy Kress, author of *Observer*

"I loved this book! It's a glorious adventure with a heart as big as the world! Iakinthu Gephyra is a diplomat, trader, explorer, and the 'bridge between people' who strives to understand and accept cultures that are not her own. To find the family of her adopted child, she sets forth on the most difficult voyage her people have ever undertaken, sailing beyond the Sunset Sea and across the Nameless Ocean. A fascinating exploration of culture, family, and identity, about finding your way and discovering where you belong."

—Pat Murphy, author of *The Adventures of Mary Darling* and *The Wild Girls*

The Curve of the World

Vonda N. McIntyre

Seattle, WA

Aqueduct Press
PO Box 95787
Seattle, Washington 98145-2787
www.aqueductpress.com

Library of Congress Control Number: 2026933383

ISBN: 978-1-61976-280-0

First Edition, First Printing, May 2026

Cover Illustration courtesy Ruby Rae Jones

Book design by Kathryn Wilham

Printed in the USA by Bookmobile

In Memoriam
The Chimacum People

Publisher's Note

The Curve of the World is Vonda N. McIntyre's final novel. When she died in 2019, the manuscript was complete. Judging by the file name, the manuscript she left was in at least its fifth iteration. She bequeathed it to Clarion West, an organization dear to her heart, and Clarion West hired agent Jennie Goloboy to represent the novel; Aqueduct Press acquired it through her.

Not all readers will realize that the publication of a book involves more than simply printing copies of a manuscript accepted for publication. At every stage, the author engages in a collaborative process that aims to make the author's work the best that it can be. And so, once Aqueduct decided to publish Vonda's novel, we knew that we would need a writer to stand in loco Vondae to engage in that process. Clarion West hired the highly accomplished Nisi Shawl to do just that.

The collaborative process in bringing *Curve* into the world principally involved four people: Nisi Shawl, Debbie Notkin (whom Vonda wished to copy-edit her book), Kath Wilham, and me. Kath made the first pass, correcting obvious typos and marking the ms with queries in the margins anent variant spellings, inconsistencies, and occasional awkward diction. I then did a thorough line edit and raised more questions, the sort I would ask any author, some of which I knew would require judgment calls, and addressed Kath's queries. Nisi then addressed my line-edits and our queries as well as adding new queries before sending the file back to me. Throughout, Nisi and I had numerous Zoom conversations to supplement the discussion taking place in the manuscript's margins. When we'd resolved most of the issues raised in the queries, the file went to Debbie Notkin, who copy-edited the manuscript and contributed to the discussion in the margins as well as a few new queries. Nisi then addressed Debbie's edits and comments, had another discussion with me on Zoom seeking to resolve the remaining unresolved queries, and sent the file on to Kath for typesetting.

Our concern throughout was to be as faithful as possible to Vonda's intentions. Nisi's constant goal was to preserve Vonda's voice, while my primary concern was determining which stylistic prose habits in the ms were tics (i.e., scaffolding for the writing process that needed to be removed before publication), and which were intentional. This was particularly tricky for me because the narrative form and style of *Curve* mark a departure from the standard narrative forms and styles dominating fantasy and science fiction, which meant that some of those stylistic habits preoccupying me were likely intentional. All such calls ordinarily would be made through author-editor discussion.

The four of us have done our best to serve the novel as well as to preserve Vonda's voice and intuit her intentions. This final work by Vonda is bold, confident, and innovative, helping us to imagine what humans from a spectrum of cultures can be to one another. It is my pleasure to be publishing it.

L. Timmel Duchamp, December 2025

Contents

I
Home Waters

Chapter One

In the full of the Moon, a fire blazed between the horns of the mountain. The Moon rose over them in a night sky black and clear and deep, and paved in stars. The fire's sparks reached to join the gleaming path.

A branch exploded in the flames, spraying a shower of embers. The embers died, their sharp smoke drifting into the soft, warm air. The adults gathered, circling the fire, carrying armsful of golden lilies or sprays of lavender. Their long, tiered skirts and bare feet brushed the ground. Sealstone bracelets and gold earrings caught the starlight, the firelight, the light of the Moon.

The moonlight wove silk around the deep cleft in the mountainside and clothed Rhenthizu in silver as he stepped from the cave.

Iakinthu took Rhenthizu's hand and drew him into the circle, into the center, into the light. The boy gripped her fingers but followed without hesitation, his natural dignity obscuring his apprehension. He held his head high. The silver of the Moon gave way to the gold of firelight against his skin. His scalp was shaven, except for his long straight child-locks; his hair never would form proper curls. Spots of scab covered his knee, like any boy's; a scraped knee hardly counted as a blemish, compared to the scars on his back from the bad times before he became Iakinthu's given child.

Iakinthu brought Rhenthizu to the Eldest Daughter. The daughter's companion snake coiled around her arm, curved toward the tempting heat of the fire, returned to the secure warmth of her body. Its tongue flicked; its scales glimmered in starlight.

Iakinthu and the Eldest Daughter smiled at each other, sharing their joy. The Eldest Daughter kissed Rhenthizu's forehead. One of her sisters brought an ancient nippled ewer with a bird-woman's head, painted with flowers. The Eldest Daughter accepted it reverently and raised it above the boy. Iakinthu helped her tilt it. Oil infused with lavender and gold dust gushed from its mouth, releasing a sharp resinous scent. The oil ran through Rhenthizu's child-locks, down his cheeks, onto his shoulders, down his chest and his back, over his sex. Firelight gleamed on his skin, reflecting from the flecks of gold, anointing him.

Iakinthu guided him to face the fire. He gazed into it, hypnotized by the ceremony, the blaze, the night's breeze. Breaking his stillness, he leaned toward the fire and flung an offering into it; the tiny clay sculpture vanished into flames and ashes before Iakinthu could make out its shape. She should leave him the secrets of his deepest wish, but Rhenthizu was her given child, and she wondered what he most desired.

He straightened, squared his shoulders, and drew his hand from hers. He was ready.

Standing behind him, Iakinthu drew a new obsidian knife from the sheath tucked into the cincture of her skirt. The black blade held an edge so sharp it gleamed transparent gray.

Carefully, delicately, Iakinthu grasped the end of Rhenthizu's forelock and drew it taut. He arched his neck, tilting his head back so she could reach him. She shaved the forelock close, careful of his skin. The knife parted each strand of hair with barely a touch. His forelock came free. She flung it into the fire. It sizzled and disappeared, leaving only its sharp scent.

She shaved his other child-locks. When she finished, the Eldest Daughter smiled again. All the adults together gave a single, quiet sigh. Iakinthu threw the knife into the fire; it stuck upright, reflecting the flames, unchanged.

Rhenthizu faced Iakinthu. Sleeping in the mountain, joining the adults, surrendering his child-locks, he had taken up the rights of a young man.

Each of the adults crossed into the circle to kiss Rhenthizu on his forehead and fill his arms with lilies. He accepted their blessings, his eyes shining.

Approaching him last, Iakinthu drew him down and kissed his forehead. The perfumed oil, warmed by his skin, touched her lips with the essence of lavender.

When did he grow taller than I? she wondered. *I knew he was taller than I—did I think of it before this moment?*

"You're my family's given child," she said. "Before I give you back to your mother, I give you back to yourself."

She kissed him again.

The ground trembled. The hollow of the mountain held the rumbling of the earth, concentrated it, extended it with echoes. Iakinthu imagined her feet sinking into the ground, steadying her. She dreaded another strong earthquake, the cruel disruption of the land, thunder and lightning out of nowhere, out of the ground where it never belonged. Sometimes, to this day, she lay waking in the dawn light and thought she felt the quivering of the world.

The trembling subsided with a final sharp shake. Iakinthu rubbed her arms, chilled despite the warmth of the night.

Rhenthizu stared at the cave, his eyes wide and horrified. Lilies spilled from his hands. Iakinthu touched his cheek and turned him to face the fire again.

"Our mother's companion is angry," whispered the Eldest Daughter, gazing toward the cleft in the mountainside. "Angry that you've joined us instead of him."

The shock left Rhenthizu's face, and he smiled.

"Go ahead," Iakinthu said. "Go down the path, and we'll follow. Your friends are waiting."

He gathered the lilies in one arm, touched his fist to his forehead to salute her, then wiped the oil from his brow. She stepped aside, opening the circle for him. He stepped over it and strode away, all apprehension and anticipation. Streaks of golden oil gleamed along his back, obscuring the scars. He vanished into the darkness. Lilies scattered after him, bright against the ground.

The adults danced around the fire, faces raised to the glow of the night sky.

Iakinthu and the Eldest Daughter shook the ancient ewer over the fire. The last drops of oil popped and smoked; Iakinthu wafted the scented smoke around the Eldest Daughter, around her own face, toward their dancing companions. When the scent faded, the Daughter lit new torches.

The dance ended.

Kilinkizu, as familiar to Iakinthu as a granddaughter, yet unfamiliar in her skirt and tight open vest, her palms patterned with henna and her ears and cheeks bright with rouge, slipped from the group of dancers. She poured water onto the fire. Smoke and steam billowed; the fire died. When the air cleared, Iakinthu glanced into the ashes. In and around the firepit lay hundreds of small sculptures, some roughly made, some exquisite, whole and new or ancient and broken: tiny bulls, lily flowers, oil flasks; a sculpted hand or foot, a leg, an eye, each a wish for help, for wealth, for health. Rhenthizu's offering tumbled indistinguishable among them. A million shards of burned terra-cotta, crumbled, shattered clay, bits of cracked bronze, small solid puddles of gold and silver, spread across the firepit, the remnants of timeless ceremonies and private meditations.

The wind rose, swirling puffs of dust, clinking together bits of burned clay. The adults hurried from the cleft of the horns of the mountain, for the wind could quickly turn cold and relentless. Slipping into their sandals,

Iakinthu and the other companions of the Eldest Daughter entered the shelter of the cypress forest. The treetops whipped and whined.

The Eldest Daughter slipped her hand into Iakinthu's and squeezed it gently. She put aside her aspect and once more became Iakinthu's young friend Maranti.

"A good sign," Maranti said.

"The earthquake?"

"His anger. It was a sign that Rhenthizu is a good man. Can he draw a good man to his bidding?"

"It was only an earthquake," Iakinthu said. "Can an earthquake decide if Rhenthizu is a good man? Only Rhenthizu can do that."

"You're so admirable," Maranti said. She laughed. "And such a radical!"

"I say what I see."

Behind them, Maranti's companions laughed and chatted and spun in final echoes of the dance. The torches sparked and smoked; the wind threw moving shadows far down the path.

"I wish I were still a young woman new-made," said one of the companions. "Just for tonight."

Maranti giggled. She never giggled in her Eldest Daughter state. "I wish I were, too," she whispered to Iakinthu. "I'd be waiting with the rest at the foot of the path."

"Join them," Iakinthu said. "You'd honor Rhenthizu. He might please you."

"A year ago…" Her voice trailed off wistfully.

A year ago, she had been only Maranti; a year ago the Idaeans ended their mourning for the death of the previous Eldest Daughter. To take the ancient one's place, they chose Maranti, a new-made young woman herself.

"May I run around in the fields at night, as Eldest Daughter?" she said. She plucked at the highest flounce of her skirt, a purple deeper than wine, and chose a trivial reason to remain behind. "I might spoil my skirt, after you went to such trouble to bring me Egyptian linen."

Iakinthu smiled to herself. Maranti was very young to be Eldest Daughter, the youngest in generations. She had reason to protect her dignity. But she should keep her right to pleasure.

"You may leave your skirt in my care," Iakinthu said. "And your snake. As to running around in the fields at night, with a young man new-made, who has more right than Eldest Daughter?"

Maranti hesitated. Kohl enlarged and brightened her dark eyes; her flush lit her goldstone complexion. She giggled again, handed Iakinthu her companion snake, and fumbled at the complex knot of her girdle. Iakinthu handed the ancient nippled ewer to Kilinkizu, let the snake coil around her arms and over her shoulder, and helped Maranti take off her skirt. She drew out the hairpins and the long strand of freshwater pearls that Aranthau had brought from Hind. She let Maranti's hair fall loose and long down her back. In loincloth and jacket, her hair curling and streaming behind her, Maranti ran down the trail, as sure-footed as a young agrimi.

Dawn brightened the inner windows of the light-well and the wide unshuttered outer windows, reflecting white from the walls of Kunusu, the harbor-on-land, the great labyrinthine building that stored the year's harvest, sustained the community's artisans, and gave focus to the celebrations of the seasons.

Iakinthu's family held an apartment in the land harbor. The plaster walls displayed the accomplishments of generations. In the luminous liquid light, Iakinthu imagined that the painted figures moved and played, the lily buds opened and bloomed, and she danced again with bulls.

She lay wakeful in her bed, pleasantly cool beneath a light cover of fine linen. All around her, the members of her household slept and sighed, snored, softly farted. Nearby, Kilinkizu pulled the bedclothes over her head, covering her unusual light brown hair, hiding her eyes from sunrise.

Neinthi's little Phialta climbed down from the children's pallet, scampered across the floor, and clambered into bed with Iakinthu for his morning cuddle. She stroked the soft stubble on his scalp between his child-locks and put her arm around him; he snuggled close, smiled blissfully, twined the long plait of her hair in his fist, stuck his thumb in his mouth, and went soundly back to sleep.

The door creaked open. Rhenthizu slipped into the sleeping room, bringing with him the heady scent of lavender oil and sweat, of meadow and cedar forest. Bits of leaf and grass and dirt clung to him. He closed the door. When dawn light fell on his face, his expression of wonder and joy reminded her of her own rite of passage. It reminded her of the following spring, too, when she was a young woman new-made, and she waited with the others of her age at the foot of the pathway, eager to welcome childhood friends to adulthood.

She wondered if Maranti had found him.

Rhenthizu silently crossed the floor, moving easily between the pallets in the dim light. He knelt beside Iakinthu and touched his fist to his forehead. Rouge and kohl smeared his face, his throat. Iakinthu raised herself on one elbow and leaned over Phialta to kiss Rhenthizu's cheek.

"You'd better wash before you sleep." She smiled. "Could leaf mold in bed be comfortable?"

He brushed at his shoulder. Bits of dirt and broken leaves scattered to the floor and stuck to his fingers. "Did I notice it, in the meadow?"

"It's different, in the meadow."

He rubbed both hands over his shaven scalp.

"Will you grow your hair?"

"Maybe I will."

"You begged to, when you first came to us."

"I remembered…when I was little…we all had long hair. I thought… my—" His voice dropped to a whisper. "—Could my father recognize me if I had only child-locks?"

Iakinthu shook her head fondly. She was glad Rhenthizu trusted her enough to talk about such a delicate subject. One of Rhenthizu's strange ideas, left over from his distant home, was that his father could recognize him at all. That any sire could recognize any child as his own, for certain sure. Though they cautioned him about giving offense to others, her family tolerated his strange ideas as they would tolerate the strange ideas of any given child. Besides, her family sprouted radicals, like Iakinthu herself, every other generation.

Can anyone call me a radical, though, she thought, when I offer to fulfill an ancient tradition for my given child, whatever the cost in time, and danger?

Phialta snuffled again in sleepy protest; Iakinthu lay down so the child could snuggle; she pillowed her head on one arm. With her free hand she brushed away a bit of broken leaf from Rhenthizu's shoulder. The musky scent of sex and the tang of lavender oil clung to him. Beneath the stronger scents, Maranti's rose perfume graced his skin like gold dust.

"What would you say to this person, if you saw him?" she asked. "What would you say to your mother?"

He hesitated. "How can I know? I barely remember them. Can I let myself believe I'll ever see them again?"

"Have I ever broken a promise to you? I've promised to give you back to your mother."

His life would have been easier, Iakinthu thought, if he had been stolen away much younger. If he had been stolen as a baby, and rescued as a toddler. Would a baby fight so hard against captivity? Would a baby be beaten and scarred?

Perhaps it would, she thought; why would his captors hesitate to strike a baby, if they would strike a boy? She rejoiced in the capture of every pirate boat she had taken, every pirate crew her companions had destroyed. Who knows what the pirates might do to a baby? They had left the captured boy scarred. They might have given the infant death.

"You've told me only truths," he replied. "And you gave me back my life."

"You're a young man now," Iakinthu said. "I think of you as my own, but you're my given child. My obligation — my wish — is to return you to your born family. To your mother."

"Can she be alive?" he said softly, more to himself than to her.

"Of course she could. She must be younger than I."

"It's so far."

"It's far. But, Rhenthizu, you made the trip. It's a long voyage, but —"

"It was horrible," he said. He shivered suddenly, though the day already promised to be bright and hot.

Iakinthu drew him toward her, moving herself and Phialta over to make room for him.

"The dirt..." He said. "The leaves..."

"I've had dirt and leaves in my bed before," she said. She laughed at his shock, laughed at his surprise that she might ever have dashed naked through the woods to tumble in breathless passion among leaves or new grass. She had made love in many places besides her bright private chamber. Of late, her private chamber had lain empty. Aranthau, her companion of many years, was away, and she had been too busy to choose a casual lover.

The sleeping room was a place for companionable huddles, for cuddling, for sleeping with a lover after making love, even for sleeping alone. Rhenthizu, Iakinthu thought, needed a cuddle.

Rhenthizu crept in beside her. Phialta, who adored him and followed him around and imitated his every move, snuggled contentedly between them.

"It was a horrible voyage," Iakinthu said. "Of course it was. You were with horrible people! But the return — with friends, with me, with my companions, in *Flying Fish*... Difficult? Perhaps. But horrible?"

"Could I retrace the voyage?" he said. "Did I ever know what land we were in, what rivers we crossed?"

"You lived beyond the Sunset Sea."

"Yes. And the land beyond the Sunset Sea is too wide to imagine. So many different people live in it — can I even remember the villages I passed through? How will we find my born family, among so many?"

He had come to her naked, lacking any talisman naming his mother or any bit of jewelry she could trace to his distant village, as in a fireside story. He had come to her with only the scars on his back… And the languages he spoke.

"By your languages," she said. "The people beyond the Sunset Sea speak different tongues — are they any different from the people of the islands and the people of the mainland? Do you remember Uinthi?"

"Of course. I followed Uinthi around like a puppy. You and Uinthi were the only people who learned my language."

Iakinthu switched from Idaean to Rhenthizu's boyhood language. "Uinthi, my given child, returned to the Maisusutha and promised to search for people who speak your language."

"In my village, the sun set in the Untamable Ocean!" Rhenthizu exclaimed. "All the way around the world!"

"Halfway," she said, smiling. "To the other side, indeed." She stroked his shorn scalp. "You're my given child. It's proper for us to accompany you to your born family, your born people, so they may see that we love you and value you. So we may share their pride in you."

He drew his eyebrows together, uncertain. Iakinthu wondered if he would tell her his true wishes, or try to please her. His diffidence flawed him; he lacked the proper arrogance of youth, and that distressed her.

"Would you be angry," he asked, "if I decided to remain a member of your family, and stay on Fair Island?"

"Angry!" she exclaimed. "It's my dearest wish that you return to us, to become Gephyra between your people and Idaeans."

"Everything's different," he said. "Did it seem real to me, before last night?"

"Everything's different," she agreed, "when you make the passage from boy to young man new-made."

"And so we must make the voyage," he said.

"Yes, she said. "We must."

All around them, her companions and the other members of her household were stirring, waking, yawning, leaping up.

"Go to sleep," Iakinthu said gently.

She slipped out of bed, bringing Phialta with her.

"Rhezizu!" he said, protesting.

"Let your brother sleep, my dear," Iakinthu said. "And Rhenthizu will see you later. Go to your grandmama, now, and ask her for milk and honey."

She gave him an easy push in Neinthi's direction; he scampered off toward his grandmother, who was just beginning to stir.

Iakinthu put on a loose robe of pleated linen. The Egyptians had some good ideas about clothing, about comfort.

Iakinthu's stomach growled; she wanted milk and honey, too. She drew the bedclothes up around Rhenthizu's dirt-smudged shoulders, tucked him in as if it were yesterday and he were still a boy, and stroked the stubbly place over his ear where she had shorn away his child-locks.

Thick, sweet honey melted into sharp, cool yogurt. Iakinthu liked the way the textures separated and then combined on her tongue, the sweetness dispersing the tartness as the honey dissolved. She sat in a camp chair on the balcony, eating breakfast. Phialta chewed on a chunk of fresh bread, honey smearing his cheeks. Nearby, Kilinkizu grilled cheese on the brazier.

The sun rose higher, leaving the deep balcony in shade. The sky glowed such a transparent blue that Iakinthu imagined she could see the stars beyond the color, like fish in clear water.

Kilinkizu brought her bits of cheese. The burned brown grill-marks still smoked. Iakinthu picked up a morsel, juggled it cool, and bit through the chewy surface. She savored the salty, slightly greasy taste.

"Thank you."

Kilinkizu touched her fist to her forehead.

A messenger came running in, child-locks flying, her short kilt tucked up around her brown legs.

"Iakinthu Gephyra," she said, breathless, "will you bathe with Eldest Daughter?"

"I will," Iakinthu said. "Will you share our breakfast?" She gestured to the yogurt, the honey, the cheese.

The messenger swirled her finger through the honey, sucked it off her finger, grabbed a slice of cheese with her sticky hand, bit into it, mumbled her thanks around the mouthful, and ran away to deliver Iakinthu's reply.

Iakinthu rose, stretched, and strolled from the shaded balcony to the dim sleeping room. All the pallets had been rolled up and put away except the one where Rhenthizu lay.

She wondered what Maranti—Eldest Daughter, the messenger said, bringing an invitation of official importance—wanted to tell her. She wondered what had happened last night.

In her household's bathing room she splashed warm water on her face and washed away the last traces of rouge and kohl.

The drain ran slow, leaving streaks of black and red in the ceramic basin. Kunusu was old; the new hot-water reservoirs sometimes overwhelmed the drains of the harbor-on-land. The enormous black pots, squatting on the reinforced flat roofs, soaked up sunlight and dispensed hot water direct to the basins and baths. They saved many fires and much carrying of water. The younger people thought hot running water as ordinary as cold, but Iakinthu still considered flowing hot water a luxury.

I am old-fashioned, she thought, smiling to herself. An old-fashioned radical.

When Iakinthu came out of the bathing room, Kilinkizu waited with a good flounced skirt and an open vest, and the silver mirror in its padded cloth bag.

"Let me help you dress, Iakinthu Gephyra," she said.

"My dear, do I need help to put on a kilt?" Iakinthu wished Kilinkizu would stop trying to serve her. Kilinkizu was a member of her household, an adult with the honored status of given child, a numerator whose knowledge benefited Iakinthu's family and the whole community. Yet when Iakinthu served her in turn, Kilinkizu grew shocked and unhappy.

"You're going to see the Eldest Daughter!" Kilinkizu exclaimed. "How can you wear a kilt?"

Iakinthu put the mirror away without taking it out of its covering.

"How can I look at myself when I've been awake most of the night?" She smiled and took the skirt from Kilinkizu, shook it, and refolded it into the clothing trunk. She chose a kilt instead, one painted with red leaves and yellow lilies, and her second-best closed jacket. Ever since she had borne a child, she had found the closed jacket more comfortable than the formal open vest, which she thought more suitable for a woman of Kilinkizu's age.

"It conceals your beauty," Kilinkizu said.

Iakinthu took Kilinkizu's hand, pressed it to her breast, pressed it to her lips.

"If I dress formally, I'll be late. Should I put on clothes I'll only take off, to bathe with a friend?"

"Your position —"

"My dear one, my position is secure. If I wear homespun instead of Egyptian linen, will people say, 'Look at Iakinthu — she must be poor'?" Iakinthu smiled, for she had been a part of Idaean politics since long before Kilinkizu came to her family, since before Kilinkizu was even born.

"They might."

"They say, 'Look at Iakinthu. Does she adorn herself?' They'll say, 'Her people eat well, her people have good clothes, her people live well.'"

"They might think we're rustics, with no one to serve you."

"They'll think I've taken up the habits of pirates, if I treat you as a servant," Iakinthu said. "If they regard us in Kunusu and say, 'Look—they're from Fair Island,' why should we be anything but proud?"

Kilinkizu gave up her objections. Iakinthu wrapped the kilt around her waist and knotted its belt. She allowed Kilinkizu to hand her the jacket. When she had put it on and fastened it, glad of the support for her breasts, she turned to her younger companion and arranged the errant curls of her bright hair so they fell perfectly in front of her ears. Iakinthu placed her hand against Kilinkizu's fair cheek. Kilinkizu stood nervously beneath her hands, like a bandit's frightened, beaten horse.

"You're a member of my family, and beloved."

Kilinkizu nodded without speaking, biting her lip, gazing down at Iakinthu. Iakinthu shook off the feeling of discomfort, her response to Kilinkizu's strange light eyes. She kissed Kilinkizu's forehead, picked up the woven basket in which Maranti's snake coiled, asleep, and strode from the apartment onto the balcony.

Balconies surrounded the living quarters of the harbor-on-land, shielding and shading the rooms from the heat of day. Beyond the shade, beyond the elegant columns that tapered inward to their bases, the sun shone bright and hot on the stone paving. The cypress trees stood silent in the still air.

On the ground level of the complex of buildings, the clink of hammers and the grinding of small drills, the rasp of saws and the rhythmic thump of kick-wheels interrupted the morning's silence. The artisans had finished their breakfasts; the workshops had come to life.

Iakinthu passed a painter touching up the wall with a yellow brush, taking away new cracks and flakes that marred a plaster fresco of blooming lilies.

The paintings often cracked when the ground shuddered. Many generations past, and more than once, the ground had shuddered and destroyed the harbor-on-land entirely. Each time the people built it anew, and better. But the renewal came at great cost in effort and treasure and attention, in famine and poor harvests if the storerooms and seed grain were lost, and most of all in the people hurt and killed during any tantrum from beneath the earth.

Earthquakes plagued Fair Island even worse than they afflicted the island of Idaea, on which Kunusu stood. Iakinthu had been caught in those earthquakes herself. They were gentle compared to the great quake of a thousand years ago. It had destroyed much, yet saved everything.

The painter greeted Iakinthu; she returned her salute with a smile.

A staircase led from the balcony to the next lower level, deeper and farther into the complex. Iakinthu strode down the cool stone slabs. Familiar with her route, she hardly hesitated when she moved from dazzling light to the dimness of the interior. Her sandals fit the depressions worn into the rock as she followed the path of centuries of inhabitants.

The inner courtyard blazed with sunlight. Iakinthu kept to the shade of the walkway on the courtyard's long side, enjoying its coolness. She took a deep breath of fragrant fresh air, preparing herself for the Eldest Daughter's receiving room. Reluctantly, she left her sandals with the other pairs at the edge of the path.

She stopped in the wide doorway, blinking in surprise.

The Eldest Daughter's apartment used to be crammed to the ceiling with the accumulation of decades of gifts and possessions, pottery and jewelry, sculpture and clothing, morose exotic animals snarling and scratching and pooping on the floor. The smell of animal droppings, masked with a hundred different perfumes, had oppressed the air. Visitors, barefoot by tradition, stepped cautiously across the obscured designs. Now, painted gryphons flanked the chair of the Eldest Daughter, the new brushstrokes on the plaster so deep and vivid that the creatures might have breathed. The whole apartment had been cleaned out, freshly plastered, and painted. Striped dolphins frolicked on the floor, their sleek flanks as blue as the sea.

Maranti sat playing with her eldest sister's child, a sweet little boy who grasped at her sealstone bracelets. She caressed him and made faces at him till he laughed. She glanced up, saw Iakinthu, and laughed as merrily.

"You look surprised!" she exclaimed.

"You've changed the apartment since I went to Egypt."

"Yes. Now you may cross the floor without watching every step."

Iakinthu did so, glad of cool painted plaster rather than fetid animal droppings beneath her bare feet. She strode across the painted dolphins, stepping from one curved back to the next, as if the creatures would carry her through the room.

Iakinthu brushed her fingertips across the dark fuzz of the little boy's hair and kissed Maranti's cheek. Maranti had washed off her cosmetics, all her kohl, all her rouge. Her palms were patterned with last night's henna.

Her light, rose-scented perfume hung gently around her. She wore a skirt and cincture and an open jacket. She seldom wore an informal kilt these days.

Maranti nodded toward a wicker chair, placed more conveniently for conversation than the ceremonial stone benches along the walls. Iakinthu settled into it.

"The beasts—?"

Maranti gestured—as far as she could while the baby clutched her bracelet—to the gryphons, the dolphins, the swallows dancing together near the ceiling.

"Painted beasts are enough for me," she said.

"Except for this one," Iakinthu said, handing Maranti the snake basket.

"Except for this one." Maranti accepted the basket, raised the lid, stroked the smooth coils of her companion snake. "As for my predecessor's pets, those who could live free, I freed; those who might die, or who might be a danger, I returned to her family."

"A danger? That feeble toothless old cheetah?"

"It loved her, my friend, and pined for her, and followed her. When its bones are clean, I'll bury them beside hers."

Iakinthu had always felt sorry for the cheetah, a gift of Pharaoh to the previous Eldest Daughter. If it had loved her, it was the first cheetah of Iakinthu's acquaintance who harbored deep feelings for any human person.

"And the other gifts?"

"I sent them back to her family, of course."

"That was generous." The gifts to the Eldest Daughter belonged by right to the person who carried the Eldest Daughter's aspect.

"Could I keep them?" Maranti said. She gave up being serious and giggled. "Oh, Iakinthu, stop it! The poor old woman filled her rooms with trash and with treasure, and I wanted none of it. I could hardly move! Or breathe!"

Iakinthu remembered last spring's visit, the last time she had been in the Eldest Daughter's apartment, when Maranti, newly elected, saw it for the first time, refused to cross its threshold, and expressed astonishment that any of her predecessor's companions would enter it.

"Did she and I agree on everything—"

"On anything?"

"But I loved her when we were young. She changed… Slowly, over years. Finally, she lost herself. I lost her. When she died, I already had mourned her."

"I sent her family the treasure to ease the grief of their loss. But they must also take the trash, and do with it what they please."

Maranti's gesture would help ease the family's loss of prestige. The position of Eldest Daughter seldom passed by heredity. Even the relatives of Maranti's revered, then wandering, predecessor knew the position would go to someone outside their line.

"I believe she kept every gift she ever received as Eldest Daughter," Iakinthu said. "Every screeching bird or shedding rodent, every shitting monkey—"

"Be fair. She had only the one monkey."

"My dear, she had several, but they grew old and died before you were born. The last one was so lonely, it tried to play with the cheetah. They stumbled about in the pathways, knocking over trash and treasure alike. The monkey was lucky the cheetah had lost its teeth."

Iakinthu flung up her hands, recalling long years of exasperation, of trying to believe everything was well with her old friend and political adversary.

"I'm glad to see this floor again," she said. "I've missed the dolphins."

"They were rather deeply buried," Maranti said. "But, see, a great deal of scrubbing, some fresh plaster and paint—and the memories of our elder artists."

Maranti's nephew tired of seeing her attention elsewhere. He jammed a stone from her bracelet into his mouth and gummed it happily. Maranti gently disengaged the stone and handed him a crust of bread to distract him.

"He's teething," she said. "If I let him chew on stones, he'll ruin his teeth... But I think he likes the taste of carnelian."

The baby boy dropped the crust of bread and reached for Iakinthu's sealstones, one of which, her favorite gryphon, was carved from fine carnelian.

"Ah, my dear," she said. "Leave my poor gryphon."

Maranti's mother Gientiia hurried in, twisting her long thick silver hair into a knot at her nape. She gathered up the little boy; once again he allowed himself to be distracted.

I wish my grandchild had been as tractable! Iakinthu thought, a little envious. Issiia had been a colicky baby, and from her infancy had known what she wanted and demanded it.

"Come back with me," Gientiia said. "Silly boy-child, poor boy-child, poor sore teeth." She gave him a roll of felted wool. He fussed, grabbed the wool, and chewed it.

"Good morning," Gientiia said to Iakinthu.

"How are you?" Iakinthu replied.

"I'm well, the children are happy, and this boy's mother is halfway to Alashya to trade for copper."

"I wish her great success," Iakinthu said sincerely.

"What of Issiia?"

"Visiting her mother, on Fair Island."

"Did she like Egypt?"

"It entranced her," Iakinthu said.

"Of course it would," said Gientiia, with a bit of envy, "since your family traces its roots there."

Iakinthu smiled politely. She thought Issiia enjoyed Pharaoh's court far too much.

"What next for her?" Maranti asked.

"She goes with Kilinkizu." And will benefit from much plainer living, Iakinthu said to herself.

"What an adventure!" Maranti said, her tone quite sincere. "I'm envious. Iakinthu, you promised me an adventure."

"Can you cast another net into the sea?" Iakinthu said.

"I'm a woman of many nets." Maranti said again. "You promised me an adventure."

"I hope Issiia looks upon this as an adventure," Iakinthu said. "It's less so for my daughter. Did I give Omempau a sister, a brother, to share her responsibilities? She wishes Issiia would stay and learn the family business."

"Issiia!" Maranti exclaimed. "Would Omempau take your granddaughter from you?"

"She understands Issiia's path," Iakinthu said. "But she wishes it were different."

Maranti kissed her nephew and her mother, rose, took Iakinthu's hand, and led her from the apartment.

Unattended, Iakinthu and Maranti took off their clothes in the anteroom and descended the long staircase to the bathing chamber. Sunlight sparkled from the alabaster walls, fading as they moved into cool dimness. The stone floor gleamed with the patina of a millennium.

Iakinthu shook fresh sand onto the stone, scattering it evenly to improve their footing. Maranti poured oil from a bird-beaked ewer onto a large sea sponge. The oil, its thick green scent lightened with costly wild-rose essence, dripped over her hand and down her arm. She stroked the cool oil along Iakinthu's shoulder blades and back, down her arms and over her collarbones, and followed the deep scar that crossed her biceps and her left breast.

Iakinthu closed her eyes, enjoying the rough sponge, the smooth bathing oil. Oil flowed down her legs and onto her feet. She rubbed the calf of her left leg with the top of her right foot, spreading the oil upward to keep it from going to waste on the stones and sand.

"Let the ground have its share," Maranti said. She trickled oil from the ewer onto the join between two floor stones; it flowed along the crack like a tiny river.

"The ground will have all of it, when we're finished," Iakinthu said. She took ewer and sponge and bathed Maranti as the Eldest Daughter had bathed her, paying particular attention to the taut muscles across her shoulders. The marks of adulthood had begun to touch the younger woman's body, maturing it from green youth. Maranti had looked like a boy till she was fifteen. She could have been a dancer, but she was more interested in politics. When she had borne a child, she would come into her beauty. She had plenty of time for that.

Iakinthu scraped the excess oil from Maranti's skin with a polished ivory bathing stick.

"Has anyone chosen Rhenthizu?" Maranti asked abruptly.

"Chosen him!" Iakinthu exclaimed, shocked. "Chosen him, before last night?"

"Thought of choosing him," Maranti said. "Spoken to you about him." She glanced at Iakinthu, sidelong, fresh-faced and bright-eyed despite having been up all night.

"He's too young to be chosen," Iakinthu said. "Who would choose a man so young?"

"I might," Maranti said.

"You're too young to be choosing anyone!" Iakinthu spoke, for once, without considering her words.

"I'm too young to be Eldest Daughter," Maranti said. "According to many, when you proposed my name."

Iakinthu loved her given child and she loved her young friend Maranti. She considered an alliance between them.

It's the best match any young man could hope for, Idaean or Islander, Iakinthu thought. But he's so young. Still, and yet, he's young to be Gephyra as well. Are my plans for him more important than to be chosen by the Eldest Daughter?

Iakinthu startled herself, as she seriously considered changing the pattern of the fabric she had been weaving for so many years.

"He's a given child," she said. "He must go back to his mother."

"Did his mother give him to you?"

"I saved his life for her," Iakinthu said. "It amounts to the same thing."

"Did she look for him?"

"How would she know where to look?"

"How do you know where to look for her?"

"My friends the Maisusutha have a long reach. Do you remember Uinthi?"

"I followed Uinthi around like a puppy, when I was little."

"Rhenthizu said the same."

"That was true. I cried when you took Uinthi back to Thamenthu."

"Uinthi will find where to look for Rhenthizu's mother."

Maranti rubbed Iakinthu's belly with the warm, fragrant oil. Iakinthu's eyelids drooped.

"Rhenthizu's mother must think him long dead."

Iakinthu brought herself abruptly back to wakefulness. She put her hand on Maranti's.

"My dear, all the more reason to take him back to her. To give her joy instead of grief."

"What if he decided to come back to Fair Island? What about her grief then?"

"My happiness would balance her grief, if he decided to return with me. And perhaps she'll come with him." She rubbed oil gently into Maranti's fingers. "Perhaps his grandmother will say, 'Go, have adventures!' Perhaps they'll all come back with us."

Maranti blew out her breath, exasperated, then laughed.

"And perhaps you'll find new trading partners, to add to your family's wealth."

"Of course," Iakinthu said. "Why else am I Gephyra?" She laughed in turn, then sobered. "Perhaps I'll find new trading partners for all Idaea," she said, "as I did with the Maisusutha and their neighbors. New friends, new allies to stand with us against the northerners."

"Bandits and pirates!" Maranti exclaimed. "When did any Idaean fear bandits and pirates?"

"Who spoke of fear?" Iakinthu exclaimed, stung.

"I meant—"

Iakinthu tightened her hand around Maranti's, and Maranti fell silent.

"I must take Rhenthizu home, Maranti, Eldest Daughter, if I can. I'm Iakinthu Gephyra, bridge-between-people. I want to take him across the Sunset Sea, across the Sunset Land, across the world to the place of his birth. I want him to be Gephyra to the most distant people. I want to take him home to his mother."

Maranti gazed at her, thoughtful and sad.

"Should I think of Idaea, and Rhenthizu?" she said. "Or should I think of myself...and Rhenthizu?"

"Did he please you?" Iakinthu asked.

"Oh, yes," Maranti said. She raised Iakinthu's hand to her breasts, to her lips, and kissed her henna-stained palm.

Iakinthu considered Maranti's desire for Rhenthizu.

She could withhold her approval. Maranti held her in high esteem of friendship, and they held each other in mutual regard. The Eldest Daughter owed her position to Iakinthu.

In turn, Iakinthu thought, I invested my influence to Maranti's benefit. I have considerable reason to support her now. Her judgment's good. I wanted the Eldest Daughter of Kunusu to possess wisdom leavened with audacity. Can I refuse the first thing she asks of me?

Maranti would like her desires to be the warp, and my preferences to be the weft, Iakinthu thought. As I would like her desires to be the weft to my warp. We've seldom disagreed, and I'm glad of it. Would she oppose me, if I oppose her choice?

How easy it would be, Iakinthu thought, to unweave my plans and string the loom in a different pattern, to encourage Maranti and Rhenthizu, to retire to Fair Island to raise bulls and train dancers.

If Rhenthizu's childhood memories were true—Iakinthu doubted but honored them—he came from a land of mountains ten times higher and rivers a hundred times wider than any Idaean had ever seen. He came from a land of strange magical animals. Perhaps it was true, for she had heard many stories of the Sunset Land: that it cradled civilizations whose buildings rivaled those of the Egyptians and people crueler than the pirates and wilder than the People, to whom Kilinkizu would return. Iakinthu had looked forward to visiting the Maisusutha again and to seeing the storied marvels of the Sunset Land.

Now, she questioned her own plans.

I am Gephyra to Egypt, she said to herself. To the Maisusutha. To the People. I've traveled in the southlands. I've crossed the greatest desert, and I've crossed the Sunset Sea.

But I do believe Rhenthizu's first home lies at a farther, longer distance than I've ever been. Is crossing the Sunset Sea enough for one lifetime, or must I cross the Sunset Land as well?

Instead of taking him home, I could accept Maranti's honor to him and to our family, and retire to Fair Island.

I've danced, Iakinthu thought, and trained dancers. I've destroyed pirates, and I've suffered living in Egypt, wretched hot place oppressed by gods and their afterlife. If I lived my last years in peace, others would honor me for it.

She chuckled softly.

"Why are you laughing, Iakinthu?"

"Because I'm nearly fifty. People must think it's about time for Iakinthu to stay home and settle down, a proper grandmother negotiating for the well-being of her given children and her daughter's born child."

Maranti raised a skeptical eyebrow. "If they say that, will you believe it?"

"Am I finished with adventures?" Iakinthu said. "Even Egypt has much to recommend it, though its history outshines its present. Issiia thrived there. She liked the luxury and the ceremony. It spoiled her a little, but every girl deserves a little spoiling. Perhaps she'll become Gephyra to Egypt."

"Or to the People."

"That would be an adventure, indeed."

Maranti picked up the bathing stick and stroked it down Iakinthu's back, smoothing away the excess oil.

"Tell me about Egypt," she said.

"We hunted gazelles with cheetahs, and we drove chariots, and we presented gifts to Pharaoh."

"She received them well, I'm sure."

"With fulsome praise. And then she put them away for her tomb, for her afterlife."

Maranti laughed. "Even your good wine? What a waste!"

"Have I met anyone," Iakinthu said, "have I heard of anyone, even north on the mainland among the pirates and the barbarians, who can spend and waste more of other people's time, than the royalty and the priests of Egypt?"

Maranti took a deep breath and returned to the subject of Rhenthizu. "Tell me what you'll do."

"Can I say for certain?" Iakinthu said. "Rhenthizu must tell me what he wants." His uncertainty this morning now made more sense, though Maranti's sudden choice surprised her. Perhaps Rhenthizu's enthusiasm made up for experience.

"Why must he cross the wild sea?" Maranti exclaimed. "What drives you to sail over the curve of the world?"

"You should understand. I chose you, to look ahead."

"That's what I'm doing, Iakinthu Gephyra, my dearest friend. But I see a different pattern. Has anyone, any adventurer, any diplomat, any trader ever gone as far as you? Are you allowed to rest?"

"Do you think I'm tired?" Iakinthu said. "How can I rest, when I should take my given child to his mother?"

"Does he ever speak of his mother?" Maranti said. "He speaks of his—" Her voice dropped. "His father."

"So shocking, my dear," Iakinthu said, "that he believes he knows his father."

Having failed to shock Iakinthu, Maranti scowled and folded her arms and changed her tack. "So dangerous. All those wild people—"

Iakinthu made a sound of derision. "You know better. Did we attack the Maisusutha? Did they retaliate? We approached as friends and parted as allies. To our mutual benefit."

"But—" Maranti stopped.

"You and I may argue. I may squabble with the family on the next farm. The mainlanders plot to raid our villages or plunder our ships. But the Maisusutha, or Rhenthizu's people? Why would they go so far to attack us, or we go such a distance to attack them? What a waste."

"You're right." Maranti dropped her belligerent stance, and her gaze. "It's so far. It is dangerous. The Maisusutha are your friends, but the weather? The monsters? The Sunset Sea? Iakinthu, are you afraid of anything?"

She picked up a glass bottle, poured light oil into her hand, rubbed her hands together to warm the oil, and stroked it into Iakinthu's long silvering hair.

"I'm frightened of any long voyage," Iakinthu said. "Will I come home again? Will my companions? Only youths are immortal."

"Are we?" Maranti said, her expression somber. "That must be why I'll think it's forever, when you take Rhenthizu away, until he comes back."

She arranged the curled lovelocks of Iakinthu's hair.

Iakinthu in her turn dressed Maranti's hair, arranging it in thick sleek coils. They ascended the steps, brushing the sand from their feet. In the anteroom, Maranti toweled Iakinthu with Egyptian linen, and Iakinthu did the same service for the Eldest Daughter.

"He would come back!" Maranti said. "Fair Island is his home, and he belongs to your family."

"If he came back," Iakinthu said, "I'd be most pleased of all."

Maranti's household fed Iakinthu an excellent lunch—how could a morning of bathing make me so hungry? she wondered—of pit-baked lamb, and hearth bread, and wine from their own vineyards.

Complimenting the food and the wine, Iakinthu thought, Fair Island wine is better. Can anything compare with the family's vintages? Yet Maranti's wine is perfectly acceptable...for Idaean wine.

She and Maranti took their leave, embracing, acknowledging that more remained to be settled.

Returning to her family's apartment, Iakinthu felt comfortable, well-fed, and sleek. Her hair hung heavy on her shoulders, combed into coils and gleaming with oil. She walked in a faint fragrant cloud of Maranti's perfume.

She walked in the cool shadow of the eastern side of the harbor-on-land. Gathering the afternoon's heat, the flat roofs and smooth ashlar walls blazed white in sunshine.

In the sleeping room, she sat on the pallet beside Rhenthizu and drew the bedclothes from his face.

"Wake up, sleepy bones," she said, "or you'll turn into a mountain for children to make stories of."

"I'm awake!" he said, his eyes still closed. "I've hardly slept."

Smiling, she patted his shoulder. "Can anyone sleep," she said with understanding, "the day after coming out of the fire?"

He sat up abruptly, wide awake, looked around, then sank back, puzzled, resting on his elbows.

"I thought... I thought Maranti—Eldest Daughter—"

"I bathed with her this morning. The scent is her perfume."

"Yes," he said, dreamily.

Rhenthizu sat up again, putting his hands to his head as if to push back sleep-tangled hair, encountering the shaven stubble just beginning to show. He rubbed his hands slowly over his scalp, then rubbed his scalp fast with his fingertips.

He grinned. "Itchy." He stretched, yawning loudly, throwing his arms wide. He took up more room than he had occupied the day before. Iakinthu smiled to herself. She enjoyed the way girls and boys, new-made into youths, gained more confidence.

"I will go," he said suddenly. "I'll honor your wishes. But will I stay, as Gephyra?" He frowned.

"Whether it's to stay with your born family, or your given family—both are my dearest wish," Iakinthu said. "Could I decide between them, in your place? You'll choose when it's time. When we've found your..." She hesitated. Fair Island was his home; could she give that designation to any other place, to a place half the world away? "...when we've found the people of your birth."

He smiled at her. "It will amaze you, Iakinthu. The mountains are so huge, so mysterious, ten times higher than any mountains you've ever seen!"

She patted his hand, thinking, he was small, so the mountains appeared so large.

In the land of the Maisusutha, the sun rose from the sea and set over land. Rhenthizu had told her that where he was born, the sun rose from the mountains and set into the sea. He came from so far beyond the farthest place Iakinthu had ever visited that the land ended and the sun set into a different sea, the sea beyond the Silk Lands, that the Sheng called Untamable Ocean.

Can I go that far? she wondered, and then thought, Rhenthizu came that far to reach us. Passed from hand to hand, sold and exchanged like livestock. His journey was erratic. It was interrupted. It was terrible. Yet, here he is.

"I know what I'm asking of you," she said.

"And what you're offering me," Rhenthizu said in his first language. "You've given me everything. Have you ever asked anything of me? When I come back, I'll be a worthy member of your family."

"You are," she said in the same tongue, "and always have been."

He remembered the languages of his childhood. Iakinthu had learned them from him while she taught him Idaean, when she took him as her given child. They spoke the language of his childhood occasionally, so they would both remember it.

When he had wakened shaking from nightmares, he cried out in the language of the child-stealers. Only Iakinthu understood him. She wondered how anyone could communicate in a language of abuse, curse, and demand.

"I wish I could remember..." he said. "The name of the village, the people, my mother's name." He dropped his voice. "And my father's."

And your own, Iakinthu thought. The name your mother gave you, Rhenthizu, my brave given child.

Chapter Two

Iakinthu strode down the beach. Rounded pumice pebbles scattered softly beneath her boots. Small boats had been dragged above the tide mark; people traded for fish and squid; cooking fires in the sand and in braziers scented the air with wood smoke and grilling fish. From all around Idaea, people gathered for the spring celebration.

Iakinthu sat on a drift log. She scooped up a handful of sand and water-worn pebbles, letting the sand sift through her fingers. She arranged the pebbles on the log beside her, in the outline of a lily.

A beautiful ship crossed the harbor, easily maneuvering among anchored boats. Its bright new blue-striped sails fell. *Flying Fish* lost way, slowing fast; after a flurry of activity on deck, the ship rested at anchor. Newly painted flying fishes gleamed along its blue sides.

How changed it is, Iakinthu thought. As bright as new. It had looked so shabby after Egypt, the long voyage, the wind and sand fraying its sails. A good refit, as always under Aranthau's direction.

Aranthau himself stood on the rail at the high bow, gazing toward the beach. Iakinthu raised her hand to gesture to him. He raised his hand, matching her motion, and dove.

He cut through the water toward her with his strong smooth stroke. On *Flying Fish* behind him, the companions lowered the ship's boat to row to shore for the spring celebration.

Aranthau splashed to his feet in the shallows off the beach. In a moment he was embracing her. He bent to kiss away the salt water that dripped to her face from his long curling hair.

"Aranthau, welcome home. I missed you so." She kissed him, teased him a little with a touch of her fingertips to the curve of his buttock. His hand on her breast, warm through soft linen, pleased her.

"You make me randy as a goat," she murmured.

Aranthau chuckled. He smelled of lavender from the scented olive oil Iakinthu made for him to spread on his skin against the sun and wind and water.

Garlands of spring flowers draped trees and people; perfume and smoke scented the air. As Iakinthu and Aranthau made their way up the slope, friends greeted them; even strangers gave them flowers. Iakinthu twisted the flowers into Aranthau's hair, caressing his cheek. He plaited flowers into her heavy curls, so the blossoms trembled precariously and petals fluttered like butterflies.

They were both wearing wreaths by the time the harbor-on-land rose before them, vivid ochre, intense blue, brilliant white, its columns rising and spreading as if to support the sky.

They walked past the peaceful courtyard with its diagonal processional path and the three great covered granaries that reached even higher above the ground than they sank below its surface, stone and brick and plaster protecting the stores and the seed grain from weather and vermin.

Cool shade crept around them as they climbed to Iakinthu's apartment. Iakinthu stroked Aranthau's palm with her fingertips, eager to be alone with him.

She closed the door of her private room. Cool and bright, the room looked out onto the central lightwell, the ancient glass of its windows rippling like water.

Aranthau slipped his arms around her waist from behind. She leaned against him, pressing against his warm body and the comfortable prominence of his penis. He unfastened the lacings of her jacket and freed her breasts.

She turned toward him, untying the cincture of his loincloth and letting it fall. He twined his fingers in her curls, bending down to kiss her, enveloping her in the warmth of his hands and his body. He drew his fingers, rough despite her perfumed oil, gently down her side. Iakinthu rubbed his back; she stroked her fingertips over his hips, snatched up the front of her kilt so she could press her bare belly against Aranthau's sex, and hooked her leg around his thigh.

He pulled at the tie of her kilt. The bunched fabric fell away. Iakinthu led him to her bed; they tumbled into it, laughing as the old-fashioned leather webbing creaked and sagged and rolled them together. Aranthau lay on his back and slipped his hand between her thighs, caressing her.

Iakinthu took a vial of scented oil from her table and poured some into her hands. She warmed it in her palm and smoothed it down Aranthau's belly and over his penis. He responded to her, his breath quick and deep.

She straddled his hips and gave him her breasts to kiss and caress. Her nipples hardened and throbbed. He reached for her center, drawing pleasure against her skin. She rose up over him and took him. She swived him. She cried out, ecstatic, sacred, as bright and hot as the sunlight painting gold across the age-polished floor.

Petals from their wreaths scattered over the bed.

Iakinthu moved against Aranthau, holding him, seeking to touch his center to hers. He arched against her, and Iakinthu let out her breath in a shudder of pleasure. Aranthau sighed, fell back without any release, and relaxed. He slipped from her body, smiling and content.

"Someday you'll hurt yourself doing that," she said fondly, though she did worry when he deprived himself this way.

She lay beside him, catching her breath.

"This is my pleasure," he said. "Are you content?"

"I am," she said. "But you spent too much time in Hind!"

"No more than you."

"And you learned so many strange things."

She turned toward him, guiding his hand between her thighs and holding it there, curling her hand around his sex. They lay together in a quieter pleasure while their breathing eased and their heartbeats slowed.

He told her of the business of refitting her ship. She thanked him for his care of *Flying Fish* and told him of Rhenthizu's passage to youth and of the earthquake.

"He'll be a good man," she whispered sleepily. Aranthau stroked her hair. "His mother will be proud of him."

"*Flying Fish* is ready to take him home."

He knew her plans; he supported and prepared for them. Whenever she proposed a new voyage, he planned it with enthusiasm and anticipation.

"*Flying Fish* is ready to take you anywhere you want to go," Aranthau said.

"Thank you, my partner, my chosen one."

Iakinthu drowsed. Through her eyelashes, she watched the patch of sun move along the stone and fade from gold to pink.

Aranthau snored softly, his long hair curling across his shoulder, a few strands sticking to his skin with lavender oil and the heat of the day.

Iakinthu rose, threw on her clothes, and twisted the thick mass of her hair in a coil down her back. She rescued a few relatively uncrushed flowers from her wreath and tucked them into her hair, then bent down, kissed Aranthau's forehead, and touched his lips gently as they curved in a sleeping smile.

In the common room, Iakinthu's numerator Kilinkizu sat copying figures from wax tablets onto paper with a brush and ink, in the Sheng way. She used her reading stone to magnify the writing, holding the transparent hemisphere just above the tablet's surface to avoid damaging the script or smearing wax onto the flat side of the reading stone. Despite the reading stone, she squinted to see.

Iakinthu accepted that paper was easier to store and keep than clay and more permanent than wax, but she still worried at its delicacy. In a fire, clay tablets grew stronger. Paper disappeared in smoke.

As Iakinthu entered the room, Kilinkizu put down her brush and slipped the reading stone into its padded pouch. She rose, a little dazed with concentration, turned toward Iakinthu, and touched her forehead in salute.

My footsteps were silent, Iakinthu thought. Kilinkizu's task engrosses her. Yet she knows everything and everyone around her. When I danced, the sound of the crowd sometimes vanished. If my mind were filled with numbers, what else could I think of?

"Iakinthu Gephyra," Kilinkizu said.

Flowers slipped from Iakinthu's hair and fell softly onto her shoulder, her breast. She caught them and twined them into Kilinkizu's bright lovelocks.

"Stop, now," Iakinthu said, "and have a cup of wine. The light's fading, how can you see to work?"

"Could I work at all, without the reading stone?" She blinked, and her forehead's parallel lines of concentration eased.

They walked together to the balcony where yogurt and honey and a flask of Fair Island wine waited on a table. They sat, and before Kilinkizu could serve her, Iakinthu poured wine for her numerator. Kilinkizu accepted it and quickly took a sip. Iakinthu understood that she meant it as a courtesy, testing for poison, protecting Iakinthu.

Has anyone been poisoned at Kunusu, in generations? Iakinthu thought, pouring for herself, sipping the young wine, savoring its strength.

Chapter Three

The corridors and balconies lay silent and deserted. Mother Moon's light paved the harbor-on-land with silver. Horned shadows thrust across alabaster.

Movement and sound, soft as a breeze in the top of a tree, opened the silence. The Moon gilded black hair, flounced skirts, jewelry. Maranti's companions approached from distant places, met, and flowed together like a stream.

With the other companions of the Eldest Daughter, Iakinthu and Kilinkizu descended into the familiar darkness.

Maranti received them. Baskets of spring lilies lined the walls and intoxicating smoke rose from a brazier, while Bdarde the musician played her lyre, filling the chamber with wild and joyous music.

Iakinthu joined Maranti's sister Sitharante. They kissed Maranti; she returned the greeting, her lips warm and soft on Iakinthu's cheek. Iakinthu unfastened Maranti's vest, while Sitharante untied the belt of her skirt. Maranti stood naked before them. Iakinthu poured warm wine over her shoulders. Black and opaque between reflected moonlight and Maranti's goldstone complexion, the red wine coursed down her breasts and over the curve of her belly and down her thighs like blood. Sitharante poured scented oil to wash away the wine. It pooled at Maranti's feet, floating on the spilled wine, gold over red as dark as sea-purple. Wine and oil seeped between the floor's paving stones, feeding the earth. Iakinthu drew the pins from Maranti's hair. Her curls cascaded over her shoulders, down her back, falling past her waist.

Her eyes as dark and wild as a deer's, the Eldest Daughter stretched her hands toward the Earth and cried out, raised them to the sky, and joined her voice to the music of the lyre.

The other companions threw off their clothes, their jewelry, their hairpins. Iakinthu dropped her skirt and jacket and sealstones. She stretched out her arm. Kilinkizu anointed her; the wine flowed over her skin, over her hand, down her fingers, onto Kilinkizu's breasts. She shivered as the wine cooled her skin, lifted an ewer and poured oil over Kilinkizu's body. The younger woman laughed, excited, scared. She cupped her hands beneath the oil and shyly stroked it onto Iakinthu's skin.

They added their voices to the song. The Eldest Daughter led them across the slippery stones to the inner courtyard as Mother Moon reached her zenith. She floated round and full, golden, pausing above them for a moment before continuing on her journeys.

They danced.

The sky whirled as if stars and Moon and Earth spun and only Iakinthu remained still. The singing of the companions surrounded her, buoying her in the dance. Her hair spread behind her like a cape in the wind. Her feet warmed the stones, dancing them to life.

She bumped against another dancer and stumbled. Instead of moving past her, around her, with her, Kilinkizu stood rigid in the moonlight, her fists clenched, squinting at the roof decorations, the stone horns.

"What do I see?"

Shocked to awareness, Iakinthu took her hands, slick with perfumed oil.

"Shadows. Only shadows."

Wondering that Kilinkizu had seen anything at that distance, Iakinthu drew her back among the others, into the circle whose center was Eldest Daughter. Touching, twirling, spinning past and around each other, they danced.

A great deep howling filled the courtyard.

The men ran toward them, covered with the raw hides of slaughtered beasts, their voices discordant against the song. The women danced, as calm as the men were wild, circling them, pulling away the bloody hides. They danced, they spun, they sang, taking the men's wildness, celebrating it. One by one, the men ceased their angry howls and joined the adults, singing, dancing, learning the joy of human people. The scent of women and men, of desire and sex, of lavender and rose-essence, mixed in the sweet smoky air.

The young Idaeans, Rhenthizu among them, joined the group, appearing from their secret shadows, smiling and laughing to think they had gotten away with watching the adults dance.

Iakinthu danced a circle around Rhenthizu, merged her circle with the Eldest Daughter's, and gave Rhenthizu to her. The Eldest Daughter touched him, stroking him, sleeking his body with oil.

The circles shifted, moving apart, centers changing. Kilinkizu, putting aside her anger and outrage, gazed into a great distance, danced naked in the moonlight with her bright hair whipping around her.

Giving birth, reborn, Mother Moon slipped between the carved stone horns of the western roof, sliding along the curve to nestle for a moment in the representation of the mountain's womb. The dance slowed and the song fell to a whisper, to silence, to stillness. The last notes of Bdarde's lyre flowed away. The courtyard lay sanctified.

The Eldest Daughter led her companions into her receiving chamber, and the men vanished into the false dawn.

The flickering of lamplight made the gryphons stretch and purr, the dolphins leap through their painted waves. Iakinthu stepped gratefully into the perfumed warmth. Sweat ran down her sides and between her breasts; she breathed heavily. The night air had chilled her in the few paces from courtyard to apartment. When she was younger, the heat of the dance would have sustained her for hours.

The Eldest Daughter glowed. Her eyes shone obsidian green with her exultation. She breathed easily.

Iakinthu and Sitharante rubbed her to sleekness. They dressed her hair with pearls and jade beads and arranged her lovelocks. They fastened the long flounced skirt around her small waist and the bodice beneath her breasts. Iakinthu rouged the Daughter's nipples and her lips and the palms of her hands and the shells of her ears. Sitharante arrayed her with gold flower earrings and a necklace of shimmering golden dragonflies.

Iakinthu and Sitharante conducted the Eldest Daughter to her chair between the flanking gryphons. She sat, smoothed her skirts, and accepted a cup of wine. Holding it in both hands, she drank.

Iakinthu and Kilinkizu dressed each other in their ceremonial clothes. Iakinthu gathered an armful of spring lilies. A tendril of their cool fragrance twined through the heavier scents of perfume, oil, and poppy smoke. The Eldest Daughter kissed each of her companions.

At dawn, she led them to the outer courtyard.

A great cry of welcome rose from the crowd. People had gathered around the courtyard and on the hillside, waiting all night, sleeping there to be ready at dawn. The Eldest Daughter descended the stairs; she led her companions along the processional path.

The people fell silent. The lyre whispered.

Barefoot on the cool, polished stone slabs, Iakinthu followed the Eldest Daughter. Moving in single file along the narrow processional, the companions reached the platform and climbed the wide stairs. Behind them they left a path of bright lilies, gold and green in the early light. Before them stood a bronze tripod decorated with gold, flanked by a smoking brazier and a nippled ewer painted with octopuses and starfish.

The savory smoke of the meat cooking on the brazier overwhelmed the green scent of crushed lilies. Iakinthu's mouth watered and her stomach growled. She chided herself: All your attention should be on the celebration. And then she thought, What mother would reprove a child who said she was hungry?

The Eldest Daughter stood on the platform behind the tripod, her companions flanking her. Only one of her companions had been moved to carry the double axe instead of lilies: Kilinkizu bore a tall shaft topped with the double leaves of gold.

Did the People teach her to carry a weapon? Iakinthu thought, sighing. She wishes she were a weapon, herself.

The double axe caught the morning sunlight where it slanted past the roof of the harbor-on-land.

Aranthau and Nendi, a given child to Kunusu from Idaea's eastern shore, grown up and returned for the spring festival, carried the new offering disk to the Eldest Daughter and placed it on the tripod before her. The disk, overwhelming and magnificent, represented rejoicing and appreciation for the abundance of the past year's crops, the hopes and expectations for this summer's bounty of field, forest, and sea. The disk of sky-iron was the width of Maranti's armspan.

Aranthau and Nendi settled and steadied the offering platter. Pinpoints of gold in an intricate design of leaves and grain, olives, agrimi, and bulls danced around the tripod.

The Eldest Daughter stepped to the disk. Smiling, she raised her hands, arms outstretched, to the crowd.

Encouraged by their grandmothers, urged on by sisters and brothers who had preceded them in earlier years, children climbed the stairs to receive the Eldest Daughter's kiss. Some shy, some bold, all joyful, one by one they filled the disk's depressions with the wealth, native and foreign, of Idaea: a handful of wheat grains, a wedge of cheese, a splash of red wine, dried sweet grapes, a handful of tiny fried fish. A sizzling bit of lamb plucked from the brazier and juggled quickly to its place on the offering disk. A sealstone of precious amber, intricately, delicately carved. Beads of copper, of glossy hematite, of goldstone dark and gleaming. Needles of southern earth-iron, held to the disk by an invisible hand. A puff of cloud-white lambswool. Honey, milk, water, a miniature nippled ewer, painted as a bird-woman. A spray of lavender, a fragrant splash of rose-oil, a fragment of myrrh. A tiny bronze bull, a nugget of river-gold, a bangle of silver. A polished carven gryphon of jade from the land of the Sheng, a lapis lazuli pendant from Egypt, and a strange and beautiful veined stone as blue-green as shallow sea. The blue stone was said to come from the most distant land beyond the curve of the world.

Like Rhenthizu, Iakinthu thought.

Phialta climbed the steps with uncharacteristic restraint, cupping a lacy murex shell in both hands. He set it down, careful of the Idaean purple dye that filled it. A few flecks of the valuable dye flew out and spotted his fingers with color. Maranti smiled, bent down, and kissed him.

When the thirty-two receptacles around the rim of the disk had been filled and all the children had run back to their grandmothers, the Eldest Daughter unknotted a pouch from her apron. The sky-blue silk gleamed and shimmered. She opened it, reached into it, and drew out a handful of saffron. She placed the powdery threads, a deeper gold than the sun, into the central depression.

A dove flew over the courtyard. It circled, fluttered, hesitated, and landed on the head of Kilinkizu's double axe. Iakinthu caught her breath. The shaft dipped, then Kilinkizu steadied it, her cheeks flushing in amazement. The dove gave a soft sweet moan, like a lover's cry. Even the smallest children watched in silence.

Moving carefully, slowly, with a glance at the dove, Iakinthu lifted the ewer of perfumed oil. The Eldest Daughter received it, raised it, and poured the oil over the disk. Iakinthu pulled a burning brand from the fire. The Eldest Daughter received it, drew it across the pooled oil, and stepped back.

Transparent in the sunlight, flames played across the disk. The offerings caught and flared and smoked.

"May our gifts find our Mother Moon," the Eldest Daughter said, "to tell her of our prosperity and our love."

With a twittering cry, the dove launched itself into the air and flew up, up, through the smoke, around the plume, and away to disappear against the bright morning blue of the sky.

The flames died; the smoke tendrilled away. Heat rose in ripples from the disk. A drift of ashes, bones, and shell remained. A soft buzz of anticipation and curiosity rose from the crowd.

The Eldest Daughter bent down and blew upon the disk. The ashes rose in a cloud and fell to the ground, leaving a bare space on the disk, between the central depression and the thirty-two representations of the mother's other aspects. She picked up a long wooden skewer of roasting lamb and placed it across the disk, a gesture of forgiveness to the mother's condemned lover.

The buzz of anticipation rose into a cry of approval. Iakinthu nodded. She picked up a lily from the platform and flung it onto the disk. It wilted from the heat, its sap sizzling. All the other companions followed the Eldest Daughter's lead, except Kilinkizu. She held the double axe. Everyone pretended she held it steady.

Her life had been too hard for her to learn magnanimity.

The Eldest Daughter led her companions down the stairs and along the processional, taking the fork of the diagonal path to circle the granaries. Finally, they returned to the cool pillared sanctuary.

The spring feast lasted all day. Iakinthu joined Maranti by the granaries; they sat in the shade of a tasseled wool awning to measure out the seed grain. It had come through the winter dry and clean of mold and mildew, barely nibbled by vermin that the guard snakes kept at bay.

Kilinkizu sat nearby, bending close to her work, recording each distribution to each farm, each family. Her brush flew across the paper, writing much faster than she could have done with a wax tablet and stylus.

A grandmother, from a farm a day's journey west along the coast road, raised her eyebrow. "Too weak," she said to Maranti as she pinched the paper's corner between thumb and forefinger. Kilinkizu glanced up, squinting, then bent back to her writing.

"It's stronger than it looks, Grandmother," Maranti said. "In the east, the Sheng have used it—oh—forever. It's easier to store. We can keep the records year to year."

"Why would you?"

"So you know what happened. How well things worked. So you can compare."

"I remember all that, Granddaughter." She added fondly, "But you have more, I suppose, to remember. Me, I remember how the plantings did from before you were born, and the plantings of the farms around ours, too. Could I remember all the farms who store their seed grain at Kunusu?" She nodded toward the paper. "I might put one harvest into my memory… And another might fall right out." She chuckled. "But I want a proper seal to take home with me, mind."

"Of course, Grandmother."

Iakinthu counted out the tokens that represented the grain the grandmother had stored in the fall to plant in the spring, dropped them into a small clay jar, and plugged it with wet clay. She pressed the pattern of spring into the stopper, and Maranti added the impression of Mother Moon holding a sheaf of wheat, attended by a gryphon. The grandmother wrapped the little jar in a bit of leather and slid it into her apron pocket. Patting the awkward bulge, she smiled and nodded to Maranti.

"It will be a good year," she said. She jerked her head toward the platform where the disk of sky-iron stood. She kept her gaze away from it, and Iakinthu and Maranti did the same. "You were kind, my dear, to give him a bit of meat."

"Thank you, Grandmother."

The elder nodded and walked away, leaning on her staff. She joined her handsome grandchildren, some grown, who were attending the line of her family's donkeys, small matched grays with delicate hooves and white pasterns, long ears swiveling, each one loaded with jars of seed grain.

On the platform, the offering disk stood cold and grimy with soot and grease. Aranthau led a group of men up the stairs. Rhenthizu was among them for the first time, easy to pick out, his remaining hair straight, his complexion a shade darker than that of the Idaean men, even after winter. Everyone in the plaza, everyone on the nearby hillsides, even the children, looked everywhere else. The men lifted the heavy disk from the tripod without ceremony, carried it down the stairs and across the plaza, and vanished.

Aranthau had gathered a large group of more than a dozen men this year to attend the sky-iron disk. In past years, before Maranti, they had less hope of the Eldest Daughter's approval and attention. During the last years of Maranti's predecessor, the men had begun to feel ill-used. They would carry the disk into the mountains to a pillared cave high on the slope. They would place the evidence of the Eldest Daughter's generosity on a polished stone pillar. They would present the mother's exiled lover his bit of meat, the first in years. They would try again to show him that he could give up his anger and his banishment. He could learn the ways of civilized adults.

But the men had been trying to teach him this for many years, hundreds of years, thousands of years.

Maybe since the beginning of time, Iakinthu thought. And all he does is offer them his fury. Still, the earth trembled and shook with his violence. Until he calmed, their mother would never return and never release him.

If the men succeeded in resisting him, they would rub the sky-iron with oil, and wrap it in oiled leather to protect it from rust, and leave it hidden until they came to fetch it and polish it and bring it to the Eldest Daughter again next spring.

If they failed to resist him, if they joined him in his exile, who knew what would happen?

Should I know all this? Iakinthu thought. All the men's secrets? She smiled to herself and thought, And should Aranthau know any of the women's secrets? We pretend, but we know.

Chapter Four

Rhenthizu stood at the edge of the plaza, crushed herbs cool and fragrant beneath his bare feet. He was excited by the festival, proud of his new place in the world, gloriously exhausted. Light sparkled around the edges of his vision.

His family's passage gifts to him, the new linen loincloth with the edging of sea-purple, the sealstone at his wrist, gave him every reason to be proud. All his friends, everyone at the festival, wore their best clothes and jewelry. His finery was the match of theirs.

He strolled toward a group of young women and men, a year older than he. Sidiinzu grinned at him and beckoned him nearer.

"Welcome," he said. "I looked for you, but I heard you were occupied."

They had been friends when they were children, but after Sidiinzu went through the fire last summer, he had avoided Rhenthizu, leaving him puzzled and hurt.

"Sidiinzu, have you spoken to me more than a word at a time for the past year? Why would you look for me?"

Sidiinzu gave a startled laugh. "My friend, did you realize—? How could I talk to you when you were still a boy and I'd gone through the fire and I wished to yearn for you?"

Rhenthizu understood.

I should have understood long before, he thought. Do I love him? Do I yearn for him?

Rhenthizu esteemed Sidiinzu. He handled a small boat better than anyone; he always knew where to find the fish.

I missed his friendship, Rhenthizu thought. "Will we be brothers again?" he asked.

"Yes," Sidiinzu said, resigned. "We'll be brothers."

They embraced.

Gilimbiia broke the awkward moment by bending over the nearby brazier to slide sizzling chunks of lamb onto torn bits of bread. She was from an ancient and prosperous Idaean farm, and she looked favorably on Rhenthizu.

She gave Sidiinzu a bit of bread and meat, ate one of the morsels herself, savoring it, then picked up another and offered it to Rhenthizu. Her straightforward gaze made his heart pound. He accepted the bite of meat and ate it, unsure whether to hold Gilimbiia's gaze or to look away modestly. He kept looking into her beautiful brown eyes. She glowed with strength. Henna tinged the shells of her ears, her fingertips, her nails.

Rhenthizu picked up another bit of lamb with a torn bit of hearth bread, to offer to Gilimbiia. She waited, smiling. He wondered if she felt as aroused as he did. He felt a little envious of women's secrets and glad of the fashionable extra fold of fabric wrapping his penis. But even that fashion would soon fail to conceal his eagerness. Were Gilimbiia's cheeks flushed, and if they were, was it because of rouge, or sun, or excitement?

"Rhenthizu!"

He stopped with the morsel nearly at Gilimbiia's lips.

To his astonishment, Kilinkizu strode across the plaza toward him. She usually ignored men and boys; he tried to recall the last time she had spoken to him.

Why is she angry at me? he wondered.

"Come speak with me," she said.

"He's speaking with me," Gilimbiia said quite reasonably.

Ignoring her, Kilinkizu squinted at Rhenthizu.

"Last night—"

Sidiinzu stilled them all with a gesture.

"We're all lost, friends," he said, resigned.

Maranti, with Iakinthu at her side, crossed the plaza toward them. Iakinthu smiled, at Sidiinzu, at Kilinkizu, finally at Rhenthizu. Her smile was luminous. Rhenthizu soaked it in, like sunlight, grateful for her pride in him, her generosity and kindness.

Rhenthizu and his friends all greeted Iakinthu and Maranti, welcoming, deliberately casual. Awe would insult Maranti. Now, this evening, she was Maranti. But they all remembered that at dawn she had been Eldest Daughter.

"Rhenthizu," Maranti said, "will you walk with me?"

Gilimbiia and Kilinkizu, at the same time, said, "Rhenthizu—"

They stopped; they glanced at each other; they glanced at Maranti.

Maranti smiled. "Rhenthizu must decide."

After a moment, Kilinkizu stopped scowling and touched her fist to her forehead. Surrendering gracefully, Gilimbiia grinned, plucked the savory bit of lamb from Rhenthizu's fingers, and popped it into her mouth. She made a gesture toward Rhenthizu as if bestowing him on Maranti."Are we needed here?" she asked lightly. She led the others away; they were as bright and elegant as a flock of birds. She glanced over her shoulder, wistful but resigned.

Rhenthizu smiled after them, then turned, flattered and apprehensive, to Maranti.

"Will you walk with me?"

"Gladly."

As Rhenthizu and Maranti strolled away, Iakinthu flipped Kilinkizu's hand into the crook of her arm. Her numerator's muscles were clenched so tight that her fingers trembled.

"My dear, what's the matter?"

"Why did you say I saw only shadows?"

"Why are you so angry?" Iakinthu asked mildly.

"He spied on us—sneaked to the roof, hid among the horns, watched while we danced, while we danced naked—"

"You've seen each other naked since you came to us."

"That was different. He was a boy. Now he's a young man. He was spying, we were dancing."

Iakinthu restrained most of her amusement. "Was he alone?"

"He—what?"

"Seven new-made youths, young women and young men, hid among the horns to watch us." She considered. "Perhaps six. One might have been a shadow. My eyes are less sharp at night than they used to be."

Kilinkizu looked away. "I saw...only the shadows."

"You were dancing."

"You saw them."

"I know where to look."

"Do they spy every year?"

"Oh, yes."

"I wish someone had told me."

"Did you come to us as a child? You were already a woman. Why would they bother you? Children and new-made youths like to fool the grown-ups when they can."

"But why? Why did they do it, when they were supposed to be safe inside, why did they spy on our secrets—?"

Iakinthu chuckled. "How else will they know what to do, when it's their turn?"

"Initiation. Teaching. Fasting and study and ecstasy—"

"They'll do all that, when the time comes." Iakinthu smiled. "But sneaking a look is so much fun."

Kilinkizu stared at her, astonished. "Did you—?"

"Of course I did. When I was Rhenthizu's age, I did exactly as he and the others did last night. I climbed to the roof and watched from the largest set of mountain horns."

Kilinkizu whispered, horrified, "You climbed the horns? Were you afraid?"

"Afraid? Of what? I was safe, protected in Mother Moon's womb. She allowed me, I thought. Her light shone through dappled clouds, and disguised me."

"You were lucky. She might have blasted you down with a thunderbolt."

"Is Mother Moon known for blasting thunderbolts?" Iakinthu said. "The clouds held no thunder." Iakinthu laughed again. "One year, I followed the men and watched their ceremony."

"The men! They might have…" Kilinkizu stopped. "How can you laugh at this?"

"I thought I was so clever, I thought I was the first to say, 'Let's sneak up on the roof and watch.' But everyone does it, and everyone knows."

"If I had ever done such a thing…"

Iakinthu sighed. "You spent too much time among people whose gods are of an angry and unpleasant nature."

"Did I have a choice? That was all I knew, until I met the People and until I became your given child."

"You had everything forced upon you by people who chose to worship cruel beings. How foolish."

"They're afraid."

"Of thunderbolts?"

"Yes."

"If you stand on top of a hill and wave your arms around during a thunderstorm, to dare a thunderbolt to blast you—"

"If a god wants you—"

"Am I telling you the truth? Have you ever seen anyone blasted, unless they were acting like a fool?"

Kilinkizu shrugged.

"Must you fear the gods you fled? Must you accept them, even now?"

"Can you understand?" Kilinkizu said.

"Tell me, and we'll see."

"Their gods are with them," Kilinkizu said. "Yours sail away to explore other worlds and leave the angry ones imprisoned."

"I prefer our choice," Iakinthu said. "After all, I sail away to explore." Iakinthu stepped off the pathway, stooped, and patted the ground. "Do we have gods? We have Grandmother Earth." She rose and gestured to the sky, toward the western horizon, brilliant with gold clouds. "Sister Sun and Mother Moon. Everchanging. They're like us. They prefer peace to war, affection to fear."

"Should I be angry at Rhenthizu, or any of the young people?" Kilinkizu sighed.

"In a few years he'll join the men, they'll join the dance, and he'll have to know the pattern."

"Before the People, before Idaea, I had to dance naked for too many men."

"Ah," Iakinthu said. She squeezed Kilinkizu's hand. They had walked all the way around the plaza.

The sun's rim touched the top of the forested hill.

"Goodnight, Sister Sun," Kilinkizu whispered.

Iakinthu slept deeply, hardly stirring when Aranthau returned from the mountain. He smelled of cedar branches. His hair was damp from a mountain stream. She woke long enough to welcome him into bed beside her, and fell asleep again.

In the morning sunlight, they sat together on the balcony and ate bread and honey. Along the Kunusu road, one group of pack-donkeys followed the next as the people who had come to celebrate spring, to flirt and court and make alliances, to receive their share of the community's seed grain, set off toward their homes.

"Remember the year it rained and rained?"

"All too well. The hillside turned into a river. I felt like a drowned rat."

"A drowned mole," Iakinthu said. "Covered with mud."

He laughed. "Did I believe you'd ever invite me into your bed?" he said. "I'd come all that way, I hoped..."

"I thought it was my bathtub you lusted after."

"That, too."

He stroked her arm; she licked the honey from her fingers and took his hand and kissed his knuckles, one by one.

"And then we danced," she said. "All night long."

"With Mother Moon gazing through the clouds, gilding the puddles, gilding your skin..."

He rubbed the back of his hand over her cheek, across a lock of her long silvered hair.

"And my gaze on you, where it will always stay."

"I love you," she said. "You're my dearest companion. Shall *Flying Fish* take us home to Fair Island?"

"*Flying Fish* is always ready to do your bidding," he said. "As am I."

Dozing on the shaded balcony, tired after two late nights, Iakinthu woke when Maranti whispered her name.

"Iakinthu Gephyra?"

"Yes, my dear?" She rubbed the sleep from her eyes; she gestured to a chair. "Will you have wine?"

In response to Iakinthu's welcome, Maranti joined her.

She comes to me as Maranti, Iakinthu thought, regarding her young friend's plain kilt and vest, her skin bare of rouge, her large dark eyes bare of kohl.

"A cup of wine would please me."

Iakinthu served them both. They sipped, and nodded in appreciation of the strong red wine. Iakinthu waited for Maranti to say why she was visiting. Does a friend need a reason to visit? Iakinthu asked herself.

Maranti broke the silence.

"Soon you will take Kilinkizu home," she said. "May I go with you?"

A thin haze of clouds softened the sky, leaving the sea a thousand shades of blue and green and purple, from faint to intense. *Flying Fish* coursed toward Fair Island. The island's cliffs plunged steep and stark into the water, layered with the shores of past worlds. Iakinthu stood at the prow; striped porpoises played in the bow wave, riding it as birds ride the wind, hardly moving but for a flick of fin or fluke.

Flying Fish passed over a patch of deep wine-purple sea. The stories said the sea people kept their wine in these spots. If a land person dove in and tried to drink it, it would change to sea water. The land person would change to a sea person and swim away forever.

His voice attenuated by the whisper of wind and spray, Aranthau controlled the steering oar and directed the ship. When she was a girl, Iakinthu crewed along with everyone else, pulling lines or climbing the mast, clothed in a loincloth, riding *Flying Fish* as if it were a dancing bull. Sometimes, now, she thought she might climb the mast again, but when she asked herself why, the answer escaped her.

Could I still do it? she asked herself. Is that what I want to know? Perhaps, but will I ever try? As easily expect Terebinthu and me to appear at the bull dance.

The island's high, strata-striped cliffs gleamed in the afternoon sun.

Maranti joined her at the prow. She glanced back and up, seeking out Rhenthizu, high above in the rigging. The companions of *Flying Fish* shouted to each other, laughed, arranged the sails in response to Aranthau's calm commands.

"I remember when you first brought me here," Maranti said. "I thought the ship would sail straight into the cliff."

"I remember, too," Iakinthu said, putting her arm around Maranti's waist. "I told you to watch."

They stood together, as in the past, watching the cliffs come closer.

Under Aranthau's hand, *Flying Fish* slipped around the headland and between the lips of the harbor, the most perfect harbor of the most beautiful island.

The wind died to nearly nothing. *Flying Fish*'s speed diminished until the ship barely moved through the limpid blue water. To either side, the harbor's cliffs plunged into the water.

Before them, Central Island swept to the water, its gentle slopes covered with tame and wild shades of green, new with spring: pale early sprouts of wheat, dusty olive and almond leaves, dark stands of cedar. The intense green of spring pastures crowned the island.

The small town stretched along the shore, each house a different color, blue and red and yellow, black-glazed hot water tanks crouching protectively on each flat roof.

The companions of *Flying Fish* drew down the sails and disappeared belowdecks. A moment later the rowing ports opened, the long sweeps thrust out, and the rowers stroked the ship toward its mooring.

Home, Iakinthu thought.

Rhenthizu slapped the tight-folded sail in satisfaction, followed the other companions belowdecks, and took a place on the rowing bench.

Whenever he took up his sweep, he spent a moment reminding himself that he was rowing, rowing the ship of his given family. Still, it reminded him of paddling his little canoe in the cold surf of his childhood home. He had been playing in his canoe the day the enemy came. He had struggled to outdistance them. They chased him down until his hands blistered, until the paddle slipped from his bleeding hands. He stood precariously in his canoe, nocked an arrow, and shot it at the enemy leader.

The next few days blurred with pain and confusion. He remembered a voice calling him from the waves, calling him to leap into the water, to leap to escape and safety. He remembered the frigid water closing over his head. He remembered the enemy's great canoe speeding past, hands and nets grabbing at him, pulling him from the hands of the sea.

They took him. A long time later he understood that they could have taken him at any time, that they had followed him, laughing, letting him think he might escape them, until they grew bored with the game.

Did they think it was a game when I pierced their leader's chest with my arrow? he thought.

Soaked with sweat, pulling the sweep violently, Rhenthizu lost the rhythm of the rowing.

"Easy, easy," said Bdarde, behind him, her voice calm but firm.

Coming back to himself, Rhenthizu flung away the memories and settled into rowing. He was here with his given family, rowing through a sea warmer, saltier, bluer, quieter, than the sea of his born family. Here, no enemy existed worthy of the name.

But soon I'll return to the green land I remember, he thought. To my born family, if they still live.

He wanted to return, yet he wanted to stay. He wanted to see the cold gray sea and the mysterious dark forests and the enormous distant mountains again. He wanted to show it all to Iakinthu.

He wanted to show his father that he was free and respected. But he also wanted to stay with Maranti. Whenever he thought of her, of her delighted laugh, her sweet voice, the warmth of her body, he forgot everything around him. She had sought him out on the night of his coming of age.

She found him after the spring ceremony. She made love to him in her forest pavilion, with the sides rolled up so the cedar-scented breeze cooled their sweat. They bathed each other, in water, in steam, in oil. His scalp, with its dark stubble, gleamed with the rose perfume she had given him.

Here on board *Flying Fish* they shared a hammock that pressed them together.

She took him to her bed and to her heart.

"Rhenthizu!" said Bdarde, even her endless patience tinged with annoyance.

Rhenthizu settled himself again so his sweep stroked with the others, so the back of his head stayed a safe distance from Bdarde's chin.

Flying Fish rode its sweeps toward the docks below town. The ship dropped its anchors in the narrow band of shallower water near the shore, where the deep blue of the perfect harbor shoaled to green.

Pulling in the sweeps with a clatter, everyone leaped up and climbed to the deck. Small boats put out from the docks to meet them; *Flying Fish*'s boat dropped, splashing pearls of water into the slanting sunlight.

Aware of Maranti watching him from the bow, Rhenthizu leaped onto the rail, stood easily balanced on it, and dove into the sea. The warm water closed around him, cleansing him of sweat. It buoyed him up, pressing him to the surface. He shook his head, a habit of his past boyhood to fling the water from his child-locks. His near-naked scalp felt strange.

Maranti tossed him a line. He climbed up the side of the ship and joined the other companions of *Flying Fish* as they prepared themselves for home. Maranti received him and kissed him and ladled fresh water over him to wash away the salt.

She shook out his new loincloth; the linen was stiff and fine. She arranged it for him and tied his belt. He admired himself in the fashionable folds and knots she created.

She giggled. "Later," she said. "Soon."

Iakinthu watched the companions of *Flying Fish* bathe and dress and primp before going ashore.

"Sit down now," Maranti said to Rhenthizu. "Hold still."

She swirled a brush in a small pot of kohl, bringing the fine bristles to a point. She stroked dark lines around his eyes, extending the corners in the Egyptian fashion, then sat back to admire her artistry.

The old-fashioned style suited Rhenthizu. The kohl intensified his good looks and his dark eyes.

Iakinthu wondered, Will a few weeks, a visit to Fair Island, then on to the land of the People, give Maranti what she wants? Does she want more than a few days' pleasure with a new lover?

She wondered if the Eldest Daughter already had from him what she wanted, the beginning of her first child. If that were true, the Eldest Daughter honored their family immensely. Everyone would know Maranti had chosen Rhenthizu. Everyone in Iakinthu's family would watch the child in proud silence. Everyone would recognize a child Rhenthizu had helped begin. Silent honor would accrue to his given family.

She is so very young, Iakinthu thought.

The overcast broke. Burning away, it left the sky a gleaming lapis blue and washed the sea's color to luminous gray.

A ladder clattered against *Flying Fish*'s side. Aranthau handed her down; Kilinkizu reached up from the boat to steady her. She could still climb in and out of a ship's boat by herself, but she appreciated their solicitude, their respect. Maranti followed her, giving precedence to Iakinthu. Fair Island was Iakinthu's home, and today Maranti was only Maranti.

The beach crunched under the ship's boat as they dragged it from the water. Iakinthu let Kilinkizu hand her out. The shore was quiet in the noon heat. Small fishing boats lay still, their bright sails limp, on the far side of the harbor.

Iakinthu breathed in the beauty of Central Island. The air was as soft as Sheng silk. Patches of brilliant color stood out against the tapestry of green: drifts of gold lilies, wildflowers of intense orange, blue, scarlet. At rare intervals, spring water traced a bright line down a hillside.

Iakinthu picked up a handful of the gray pebbles, warm from the sun, surfaces smooth with wear, rough with the myriad of open spaces that broke through their skin. She let them cascade into the water, but they were all too soaked to float. "I love this place," she said to Rhenthizu. "Whenever I come home, I want to stay forever."

"Until you grow tired of the quiet," he said.

"Yes." She smiled. "Will I have time to weary of the quiet, this trip?"

A donkey tap-tap-tapped along the road from town, moving in and out of sun and shadow as it passed the trees shading the route.

Issiia urged her mount on. She wished she could have kept her Egyptian horse. Instead, she had brought from Egypt the elaborate bridle and Egyptian linen she tied to the donkey's back like a saddle.

Issiia wrapped her legs tight around the donkey's narrow barrel. The linen saddlecloth would slip before it gave her any purchase. If the donkey stopped or shied, he had no withers to steady her and very little mane to grab. His ears swiveled intelligently when Issiia spoke, but his eye held a sly look.

They approached the group on the beach. "Iakinthu Gephyra—" The donkey's rough gait jolted Issiia's voice. She brought him to a halt before she spoke again. "Iakinthu Gephyra, Grandmama."

Issiia dismounted as gracefully as possible under the circumstances and approached her grandmother.

"I'm so glad to see you." Iakinthu swept Issiia up in a hug. For a moment Issiia embraced her fiercely, then wriggled to get down. Being held in her grandmother's arms in public contradicted the formality of the courtly manners she had learned in Egypt.

"I'm too big to pick up."

Iakinthu set her down.

"It's true you're growing. At least a handsbreadth since we parted!"

Issiia frowned, taking the joke literally. "You've been away less than one Moon's cycle," she said.

A Moon's cycle, from cradled infant, to mother, to age-bent grandmother, through darkness to the newborn Moon again, was as long as they had ever been parted.

"Maybe a finger's width," Issiia said, considering carefully.

"Perhaps that," Iakinthu said with a smile.

"Kilinkizu, sister—Rhenthizu, brother." Issiia greeted them with equal formality.

"Little sister," Kilinkizu said, touching her fist to her forehead.

Kilinkizu knelt down to hug her. Issiia kissed her cheek. Issiia always lightened Kilinkizu's somber moods.

Kilinkizu pulled a leather thong over her head and handed it to Issiia. A triangular gray stone, fitted with a gold bail to create a pendant, dangled from the leather.

"I brought you a present."

"Is it a tooth?"

"A stone tooth, from past times, when the animals and the people all were made of stone."

Issiia inspected it with wonder. "How could they move, if they were made of stone?"

"They moved like avalanches," Kilinkizu said. "Like rockslides."

Issiia laughed, delighted, and put the thong around her neck. She hugged Kilinkizu again, then remembered her manners and pressed her fist to her forehead.

"Maranti, Eldest Daughter, welcome to Fair Island."

"Thank you, Issiia," Maranti said.

"Little sister," Rhenthizu said, "do I get an embrace?"

"You look so different," she said, suddenly shy.

Rhenthizu drew his hands over his shaven head. He lifted Issiia and swung her around. Her child-locks fanned out, dark and shining. She shrieked in pleasure, remembered her status, and cried, "Put me down!"

He obeyed her, laughing.

"And you do, too, so grown up since your visit to Pharaoh."

Issiia took the compliment as her due.

"I'm almost the same," Rhenthizu said. "A handsbreadth taller, that's all."

She laughed, for he was the same height he had been when she left for Egypt. "Maybe a finger's width."

Two boats were brought crunching onto the beach, having fetched the companions of *Flying Fish*. The passengers leaped out, laughing, their finery soaked from a contest of oar-splashing.

More members of Iakinthu's household came to greet her, smiling, waving, calling. Several children ran to her and danced around her; she always brought trinkets and toys from Idaea for them. Rhenthizu's younger friends greeted him with awe, or feigned indifference to his new status; his older friends welcomed him with kisses and rough-housing, which he returned in kind.

A thread of sadness marred the fabric of Iakinthu's joy. Even now, five years after her mother's death, she expected the donkey-cart to roll creaking down the road, bringing her mother to meet her. Her eyes filled with tears. She missed the grand old lady, who had honored her with love and confidence.

Theirs was a short-lived family. Iakinthu's mother had died before the age of seventy. Aranthau's seafaring family, on the other hand, had five generations still living, from his ancient great-grandmother who watched everything with bright eyes like a bird-woman, his dour and practical grandmother, his cheerful mother, and his sister, to her newborn daughter. He sometimes joked about too much loving family, too many obligations, too many opinions about his life. Iakinthu envied him a little, even the opinions.

Iakinthu's daughter Omempau strode toward her, reserved as always, elegant even in her homespun kilt and short-sleeved jacket, her hair tied back for daily work.

"My dear," Iakinthu said.

They embraced, they kissed. Omempau was taller than Iakinthu, like Aranthau and his sister, though few had the bad manners to comment on the resemblance between Iakinthu's daughter and Iakinthu's chosen companion.

The other members of the household gathered round, welcoming Iakinthu and her companions home, picking up baggage from the boats and flinging it over the donkeys' pack saddles. Iakinthu sank happily into the bright cacophony.

"Will you ride, Mother?" Omempau asked. "You must be tired."

Omempau seldom traveled farther than the family's summerhouse, for she managed their farms, the house in town, the production, the trading. She was convinced that any travel must be exhausting.

"I'm well rested, my dear. Aranthau sails *Flying Fish* so smoothly, and the winds have been so obedient—I hardly know we're moving, I hardly lose my land legs."

"Is Aranthau visiting?"

"Yes." She nodded toward *Flying Fish*, lying gentle at anchor, surrounded by smaller boats. "He's supervising the cargo."

They strolled up the road from the beach till the town of bright-painted houses enclosed them. Two- and three-story buildings lined the narrow cobbled streets of the old quarter. The outer walls gleamed with whitewash and fresh paint, applied after winter rains, and any number of houses showed new cracks in their walls, in various stages of repair. Omempau followed Iakinthu's gaze.

"Our houses endured well," she said. "But it was a powerful tantrum. I think he's getting stronger."

Omempau was far more devout than Iakinthu, taking the old stories literally. In that, of course, she most resembled Iakinthu's mother. Iakinthu kept her opinion to herself.

An old lover, Nessu, called to Iakinthu from atop a ladder.

"Are you back for long, my friend?" he asked, pausing in his application of plaster to a deep diagonal crack between the windows of the second floor.

"Only a short time," she called back cheerfully. "Long enough for you to come to dinner. Are you staying with Geathotu?"

"These many years."

"He must come too."

Iakinthu knew perfectly well that Nessu and Geathotu were long-time lovers; it was Geathotu's house he was repairing. But where other people might expect things to stay the same, Iakinthu expected things to change.

Cedar House stood near the top of the first slope, facing the sea. Despite its name, it resembled all the other houses, built mostly of stone and plaster. Rebuilt within the last generation, it had more beams, more wooden braces and lintels, than older houses. Because of them, as Omempau said, it stood up well to earthquakes. The beams' scent faintly perfumed the whole house.

"In the east," Iakinthu said, "at the end of the Silk Road, the Sheng make houses so cleverly that earthquakes never break them. The joints fit together so cunningly that they do without nails."

"With floors and walls of beaten gold, no doubt," Omempau said drily. "And ceilings dyed sea-purple. What extravagance!"

"It's because you're so practical," Iakinthu said, "that we can afford Cedar House."

Omempau laid her head briefly, fondly, on Iakinthu's shoulder.

Hot and sweaty from the climb, they entered Cedar House. Cool air, refreshing after the heat, enveloped them. The central lightwell illuminated the surrounding rooms without baking them in direct sunlight. Omempau took charge. When Issiia came back from the donkey pen carrying the Egyptian bridle and the saddle cloth, now a little grimy, Omempau insisted that Issiia must have a nap as soon as she finished some bread and honey— "But I'm too old to take a nap!" Issiia cried, afraid to miss anything— "Maybe you are," her mother said, "but you hardly slept last night, from excitement."

Issiia looked to Iakinthu in supplication.

"Your mother's right," Iakinthu said with sympathy. "Have a rest before dinner. After you clean the bridle."

"In Egypt—"

In Egypt, slaves did the work of grooming animals and cleaning bridles. Iakinthu thought, Can I let Issiia think I approve of that? "Egypt is Egypt," she said, "and home is home."

Stamping her feet just enough to communicate annoyance without earning herself a scolding, Issiia climbed the stairs and disappeared around the corner to the third floor.

Iakinthu chuckled.

"She missed you so," Omempau said. "This next year..." She cut off what she had been about to say. "Come upstairs, Mother, please, and drink some wine with me."

They sat on the roof, shaded by a black woolen awning, its fringe swaying gently in a faint breeze. Omempau poured wine from a bird ewer. Its neck formed the head, its beak the spout, with painted spirals for the wings. They drank from fine Egyptian glass, chosen by Issiia for Omempau, because Pharaoh drank from similar goblets. Iakinthu liked the way the red wine turned inky purple against the deep blue glass.

"Mother, will our next given child be your daughter, or your granddaughter?" Omempau asked.

"If she wants to dance, she must be my granddaughter."

"Will I ever have a given sister?"

Iakinthu raised an eyebrow in surprise.

"Someone like Kilinkizu," Omempau said. "I'd like to know how to enumerate as she does. It would be useful in running the household."

Kilinkizu is unique, Iakinthu thought. I wish we could keep her, too. I always wish I could keep my given children.

"She's on her way home," Iakinthu said. "Can we keep a given child past her time with us?"

"She's a woman grown. She can decide for herself."

"And she will, when I take her home to the People, to her mother."

"Which mother?" Omempau said, challenging her. "Which home?"

Iakinthu acknowledged that Kilinkizu's path was different from that of the usual given child.

"Would I send her back to the village that surrendered her? To the bandits who took her? She'll go back to Celestial Wind, to the People who rescued her and adopted her."

"Her knowledge is wasted there," Omempau said. "What do the People need with enumerating?"

"For trade. For managing their horses. For keeping track of their treasure caches," Iakinthu replied. "But what does that matter? What's important is taking her home."

"She might decide to come back."

"If she does, that would please me. I have to take her home before she decides."

Omempau laughed ruefully. "And people say you're such a radical."

"I have some radical ideas, but we should preserve our customs for given children. Otherwise, what would they be but hostages? How could we expect our own children to come back to us?"

"Issiia will come back to us," Omempau said. "Can you imagine my daughter choosing to stay with the People?"

"I can imagine her choosing to stay in Egypt."

Omempau gazed at her wine glass, drank the last swallow, and poured more wine for her and for Iakinthu.

"I can, too." She sighed. "I wish the next given child would be more interested in farming than in diplomacy or dancing."

"My dear, do I know if a given child will want to dance? If she wants to dance, I should teach her, until I retire."

"I wonder if you ever will retire."

"Yes," Iakinthu said. "I will. Soon. After I take Kilinkizu home. After I take Rhenthizu home."

"You can change your mind," Omempau said. "Why risk *Flying Fish* for such a distance? Who knows where you'll end up? You could sail to Alashya—"

"Alashya? I might as well send a trained messenger to the next room with a message for Cook."

"You could go to Hind."

"I've been to Hind."

"Profitably."

They had traded wine and olive oil, fine pots and delicate gold jewelry, sea-purple and Egyptian linen, for spices and silk and pearls. Because of Hind, her family and all its companions lived comfortably.

"A voyage to Hind has its own dangers," Iakinthu said. "Pharaoh cares very little about the canal anymore." The sands of the desert spilled down the sides of Pharaoh's Canal. It was dangerously shallow. Pharaoh lacked will or attention or resources to maintain it.

"Will it be lost?"

"It could be."

Maintaining the canal was beyond Iakinthu's reach, beyond the reach or the ability of anyone on Fair Island, any community of Idaea, all of Idaea combined.

Hind could maintain it, Iakinthu thought, despite the distance. She put the idea away for another time.

Omempau glared in frustration. "Mother, I'm only saying that *Flying Fish*—and you—could do other things than sailing off to chase Mother Moon."

"I'm sailing off to return our given children to their mothers." Iakinthu spoke a little sharply, annoyed at Omempau's use of a metaphor for impossibility.

"Is Rhenthizu a real given child? Did his mother give him to us?" Omempau asked belligerently. "Does she have a child of ours to return, to ally our families?"

"She must long to see him again."

"Who knows?" Omempau said. "Who knows if she's alive? Enemies attacked Rhenthizu's people. They could all be dead. And who knows what lies at the other side of the Sunset Sea? Giants, monsters, wild people who howl, and grunt—"

"Our friends the Maisusutha live on the other side of the Sunset Sea. Did Uinthi howl or grunt? Did Uinthi's mother?"

"Have I ever met Uinthi's mother? How should I know the way she speaks? Uinthi grew up here, and speaks as I do."

"Uinthi's mother is a civilized person, a peace chief, a prosperous farmer." Iakinthu paused, surprised. "Did you ever say a word to me about visiting the Maisusutha? Did you want to visit them?"

She tried, and failed, to imagine Omempau thriving at Pharaoh's decadent, fading court, or in the elaborate, complicated maze surrounding the Sheng emperor, or in the palaces of Hind. Yet she could imagine Omempau visiting happily with Uinthi's mother among the Maisusutha.

"I'm your daughter. It's my place to manage the farm and the household. I like my place. When I think of your voyages, I think of discomfort and danger, and I fear for you."

"Ah, my dear," Iakinthu said. "I'm sorry you are afraid for me, but the place of Gephyra is to talk to other people. To talk to them I have to go to them." She paused, to bring the subject back to Rhenthizu. "Rhenthizu came to us speaking his own language. Two languages. Did he howl or grunt?" She repeated herself, using the language Rhenthizu spoke best when he first came to them.

"He was always remarkably silent," Omempau said in the same tongue, her words awkward from lack of use.

Omempau was older than Rhenthizu, almost old enough to be his mother. She had already gone through the fire when he came to them; she already enjoyed the confidence of her grandmother, Iakinthu's mother, in learning to manage the family's holdings. Despite her obligations, she had learned a few words of Rhenthizu's language so she could speak to him and treat him like a little brother.

"Does he pine to return to his birthplace?"

"He's young, does he pine for anything? He yearns — for Maranti."

"I wondered, when I saw them..." She considered the honor, taking it in. "Did she choose him?"

"They enjoy each other," Iakinthu said, avoiding a direct answer. "After he came through the fire, she honored him with her company."

"Do you know —"

"If she plans a child? Am I a midwife?"

Omempau shrugged. "Should I have asked? Could the most experienced midwife tell so soon?"

"We'll know, next winter, if Rhenthizu —"

Omempau blushed at Iakinthu's bluntness about knowledge seldom admitted or discussed. Iakinthu fell silent, sorry to have embarrassed her daughter.

"If he stays," Omempau said, "Maranti might choose him."

"If he returns."

"Out of respect to you, Mother, and out of respect for tradition, she'll let him go. She knows you want to find his mother, to forge another alliance on the other side of the Sunset Sea."

"Yes," Iakinthu said.

Omempau gazed out at the harbor. Iakinthu sipped her wine, a fine old year from the upper vineyard. The sun sank toward the striped cliffs of Fair Island's western edge.

"Mother, please stay," Omempau whispered. "Please stay home."

Astonished, Iakinthu said, "Why do you ask me that?"

"I'm alone," Omempau said. "Do I have a sister to help me, or even a brother? An aunt or an uncle? And Grandmama, I miss her so..."

"I do, too, my dear."

"Oh — you argued all the time."

"She was my mother, and I miss her." Iakinthu thought, It would be too easy to say I was meant to have only one child. It would be too easy to say our line has always been narrow. The truth is, I took time for only one child. I had so many other things to do. I still have so many other things to do.

She kept her silence about Issiia, who was nine years old, an only child.

Did Omempau ever choose a companion? Iakinthu thought. Have I seen her with anyone in recent years? Besides, a sister of Issiia would follow in Iakinthu's footsteps rather than learning the ways of managing the farm and the household. Omempau would have to wait for her grandchildren, Issiia's children, after Issiia came through the fire, years from now.

It saddened Iakinthu that Omempau chose to live without a chosen companion, woman or man, someone with a stake in her happiness. Now was a poor time to express such regrets.

"If I stayed here," Iakinthu said, "you and I would argue all the time. I'd trespass on your authority —"

Omempau raised her head abruptly and raked her hands through her long loose hair, as if Iakinthu had challenged her.

"You manage the stud," she said. "Have I ever argued with you about that? You negotiate the contracts. Have I interfered with a single term? If you took over the farm —"

Iakinthu burst into unrestrained laughter. Offended, Omempau fell silent.

"My dear daughter—" Iakinthu stopped to catch her breath. "I'm laughing at the idea of managing the farm, about which I know only enough to be dangerous. How could I take over a task that gives you so much pleasure, and that you do so well?"

"Of course I do it well," Omempau said with poor grace. "But I do it all alone."

"Why did you wait until now to say so? How can I do anything to help you so soon before I leave?"

"You always say, so calmly, that you might never come back," Omempau whispered. "I'd grieve, you know. Would I know what happened to you? If you died so far from home?" Her dark eyes gleamed; tears spilled down her cheeks. Iakinthu went to her, took her in her arms, and stroked her hair. Omempau sobbed against her breast.

"I expect to die at Old Farm. I expect my bones to turn to stone in the earth of Fair Island. After I get back from my last voyage."

"Long after," Omempau said.

"Long after," Iakinthu agreed, amazed to be reassuring her daughter, who had so seldom needed any reassurances, who always faced the world with confidence.

Omempau sniffled and felt in her apron for a handkerchief, wiped her eyes, and blew her nose.

"I'm bare-faced," she said, gesturing to her eyes, her cheeks, which were bare of kohl or henna or rouge. "It's a good thing, or my face would be all streaks and stripes."

"You're beautiful bare-faced, or painted, or all streaks and stripes," Iakinthu said. "Issiia and I are going to Old Farm in the morning. Can you come with us? Can you come away from town?"

Omempau hesitated. "I have so much to do—"

"It will all be here when we come back."

"So it will, though some of it may wonder where I've gone." Omempau smiled at her. "I'd like to go home with you, Mother. Yes, I will."

Chapter Five

"Iakinthu!" Kilinkizu called softly. She hurried to Iakinthu's side, clutching her writing box as if it would shield her.

"What's the matter? Why are you whispering?"

"Your visitor…"

"…is Tuola. An old acquaintance. A long-time trading partner."

"…is armed."

"Of course she is. Would you walk around unarmed with a pocketful of diamonds?"

"I'd walk around with a bodyguard."

"Then, my dear, the bodyguard would be armed." Iakinthu chuckled. "Her reputation—and her dagger—protect her."

"Does she need protection in your house?"

"Does she mean to offend me? I understand her habits." She arranged a tendril of Kilinkizu's bright hair in a proper curled lock in front of her ear. "Come meet her. Help me welcome our guest." She took Kilinkizu's hands. "I might talk about private business."

"Would I ever repeat your confidences?"

"Only on your paper." They smiled. In complete trust, Iakinthu led Kilinkizu into the visiting room.

A new fresco extended across the long wall. *Flying Fish* sailed upon the fresh plaster, its blue-striped sails and sides brighter than the sea, its painted flying fishes leaping. Dolphins cavorted in its bow wave.

Leaning on a wooden staff ringed with gold, the trader Tuola stood on the other side of the room gazing at an older fresco. A great spotted bull plunged across the wall, leaping and tossing its horns with joy.

"Tuola!"

The trader turned, smiling, instantly recognizable despite many years' absence, welcoming Iakinthu with open arms.

"Iakinthu Gephyra!" She spoke the language of Idaea as if she were singing. A leather bag, bulging with erratic shapes, lay on the floor by her feet.

They embraced. As always, Tuola wore garments mixed from all her travels: pleated white trousers of Egyptian linen with fine gold threads woven in, a black overskirt of fine Idaean wool with three bands of fringe, a tunic of heavy gold Sheng silk. And, of course, the iron dagger on her silver belt. Across her shoulders she wore a shawl of mountain wool so fine the fabric was nearly transparent. She rearranged it to cover her throat.

"Are you cold?" Iakinthu asked.

"I'm always cold when I travel," Tuola said.

"You always travel."

"And I'm always cold, in these places where the sun slants all the time, as if it were evening."

Iakinthu nodded. She had the same experience when visiting the Maisusutha, whose land lay in northern regions.

"But I came to see you! And your friend?"

"Kilinkizu, a given child to my family, who holds the place of granddaughter."

"Welcome," Kilinkizu said.

"Come sit in the sun," Iakinthu said. "Shall I get you a blanket?" She saw Tuola and Kilinkizu to chairs by the wide window over the street, making sure Tuola sat in the patch of bright sun. Tuola hefted her carry-bag and set it beside her.

"The sun will warm me," she said.

"How is your family? How is Oladele?"

"He has his own ship now."

"I'm pleased to hear it." Tuola's son had been a given child. Aranthau taught him how to sail.

"He accompanies me on this voyage, while his ship is refitted."

"Will we see him?"

"He visits Maranti's family."

Iakinthu smiled. Oladele was a companion, of many years, of Maranti's mother Gientiia, staying at her house in town or her farm whenever he visited. Iakinthu liked to see them together, all three dark-haired, Gientiia's complexion of pale amber, Oladele's obsidian, Maranti's shining goldstone.

"Gientiia must be very proud," Tuola said, "that Maranti is Eldest Daughter."

They left unsaid what Oladele might think about Maranti's high position.

The door creaked; one of the children peeked in, waited for Iakinthu's nod, lugged a heavy basket to Iakinthu, and gazed curiously at the stranger. Iakinthu took the basket and kissed the child on the top of her head.

"Thank you, my dear. That's all we want for now."

Iakinthu opened the basket. Beside the water and wine on the painted clay table, she set out bread and cheese, olives and dates, and the honeycakes Tuola liked particularly.

"You remembered," Tuola said, pleased.

Iakinthu smiled and poured wine for them all. She offered water to Tuola, who declined, and cooled her own wine with a splash of water.

Kilinkizu opened her writing box and prepared her ink.

"I wondered when you'd give up wax and clay," Tuola said with approval.

"It's very convenient. Kilinkizu is a skilled numerator."

Iakinthu sat between Kilinkizu and Tuola, so their small half-circle faced the window, the sloping town, the harbor.

"To your fortune," Iakinthu said.

"And to your own."

Tuola the traveler came from the distant south, from a people as adept at trading as any Idaean. Her people carried earth-iron, ivory, strange pelts, precious stones. They dug the iron from the ground as the Alashians dug copper, and melted it from rock, and forged it into the best nails in the world and excellent ship fittings and tools.

They also dealt in slaves, but they left their slaves behind when they came to Idaea or Fair Island. Iakinthu knew of only one Idaean who had ever bought a slave: she herself had bought Rhenthizu from Tuola when they met in Alashya. Tuola had rescued him from his long line of captors; nevertheless, he had been her slave.

Iakinthu and Tuola maintained the polite fiction that Iakinthu gave Tuola gifts, and Tuola gave Rhenthizu to Iakinthu.

I gave him his freedom, Iakinthu thought, but, still, I trafficked in slaves.

Have I ever spoken of it? she thought. Has Rhenthizu? It embarrasses me. I hope he was too young to understand his status when he came to us.

"Where have your travels taken you?" Iakinthu asked.

"Back and forth across the world," said Tuola. She stroked her fingertips over the sleeve of her gold shirt. "South from home, then to the east, all the way to the Untamable Ocean. Then I circled back toward Hind, from island to island, each stranger than the next. Around the tip of Hind, and past great deserts, and north and west, and so through Pharaoh's canal, where sand nearly swamped us. And the price, and the bribes!"

Iakinthu nodded in sympathy.

"Someone should fix that canal," Tuola said.

"So I've been told."

"Someone from a great seafaring family."

"Someone from a larger, richer seafaring family than my own. From a larger, richer seafaring land."

Tuola put a slab of cheese on a slice of bread and munched it.

"Have you crossed the Untamable Ocean?"

"I circled the eastern world," Tuola said. "That's enough for me. I like to stay in sight of the coast. Do you think a ship can go all the way around the world, Gephyra? Does a way exist? The people who sail the Untamable Ocean, days and days out of sight of land—in canoes, can you credit it? With reed mats for sails—" She shuddered theatrically with horror. "They say too much land lies in the way. You have to go north or south into angry seas and desperate cold."

Kilinkizu's brush shusshed softly as she noted the conversation.

"Tuola, my friend, you think Fair Island is cold."

"And so it is, and they would agree with me—they're tropical people, turned golden by the sun. My people are burnished black, and we are even more sensitive." Tuola's skin was as sleek as ebony, her palms a soft light brown. She nibbled a honeycake and brushed the crumbs carefully from her bright shirt. "The sailing people would say Fair Island is cold, but would they say the water around the island turns to ice? That is what they say about the north and the south. The water turns to ice. Great floating mountains of ice."

Water froze in winter in the land of the Maisusutha, but did Iakinthu believe in great floating mountains of ice?

"I heard that you sailed west," Tuola said. "You said you might, when last we met."

"I did," Iakinthu said. "Through the gates of the sea and west, far west."

"Out of sight of land?"

"A long way from the sight of land."

"Who did you trade with, in the sea? The sea people, who own nothing and want nothing and use pearls and sunken treasure as playthings?" She laughed. "The sea people could bring me pearls, but why would they? What would they ask of me?"

"I visited the Maisusutha. I sailed west until I met them, in their own land."

"Was it cold?"

"Yes." Iakinthu remembered the winter.

"Did the sea turn to ice?"

"The sea remained very wet."

"I've sailed a whole day out of sight of land," Tuola said. "But as seldom as possible." She leaned down and rummaged in her bag. "You may sail west, Iakinthu Gephyra. I'll happily listen to your stories."

"I'll happily tell you my adventures. They were profitable journeys, in trade and friendship, and in a dearest given child, Uinthi. I took Uinthi back to Thamenthu, to the Maisusutha, and I hope to see them both soon."

"I'd ask them to come to me."

"Uinthi's mother prefers their home."

"Uinthi's mother is a wise woman."

"What have you brought to show me?" Iakinthu said. "I think of the nails made by my friend Tuola's people, and iron rings, and ship fittings."

"Oh, all the captains are down on the beach doing iron business," Tuola said.

Iakinthu imagined the conversation, where Aranthau would be trading wine and provisions for ship fittings: He would say: Iron is so very expensive. He would warn that the ships must re-use what they had until the fittings rusted and all were lost; the harvest had been poor (Iakinthu smiled: exaggeration was an important stock, when trading) so the grain was as expensive as iron. Last year's wine was the best in memory, worth its weight in iron.

Tuola laid out packages from her carry-bag, packages of leather, oiled silk, and paper covered with beeswax. Iakinthu refilled Tuola's wine cup and her own and, for formality's sake, poured a few drops into Kilinkizu's cup, which was still full. She might drink it after she finished recording their meeting and their agreements.

"A few trifles," Tuola said. "And some better things." She drained her cup, sat back on the low couch and said, "To business!"

"To business," Iakinthu said.

Kilinkizu took up a fresh piece of paper and touched the tip of her brush to the ink.

They began the pleasant work of haggling over the usual things Idaeans and Tuola's people always traded. Their offers began far apart, but quickly converged. The elephants ran away as fast as cheetahs, so ivory demanded a great price. Iakinthu replied that olives and grapes were very difficult to capture and squealed loudly when pressed. Tuola laughed and countered: the Sheng barter so hard for their silk that hardly any profit remains.

Iakinthu enjoyed spinning flights of fancy as much as Tuola did, and they came to agreements each knew the other thought to her own advantage.

After they finished with the basics, they moved on to the interesting things.

Crossly, Tuola said, "What I had that you would have liked best, I never brought you."

"Why?"

"He died," she said. "I kept him for you particularly, I thought you would want him."

A flush sprang to Iakinthu's face. Ashamed to look at Kilinkizu, who sat in silence, she held herself very still.

"I regret your friend's death."

"Friend? Make a friend of a slave?" Tuola snorted. "I thought you might like him, he reminded me of that boy you got from me."

"Rhenthizu came through the fire. He's a young man now."

"Ah. I'm glad he lived."

"He stands in the place of a grandchild to me, a beloved given child. The Eldest Daughter favors him. He's a fine young man. He is free."

"There, you see, I thought you might like another of the same breed. This one was older."

Iakinthu remained silent. She would have bought the slave, hoping he would know more about Rhenthizu's people—and she would have freed him, but would that balance the shame of buying a slave? If her dealings became known, more slavers would come to Fair Island and to Idaea; they would take more people from their homes; they would make more slaves.

"His breed is rare," Tuola said. "They come from so very far."

"What did he tell you about his home?"

"They brought him all the way across the Untamable Ocean," Tuola said, "where his people live on its wild shore."

"Who went so far?" Iakinthu asked.

"I bought him from the Sheng. Their ships can go anywhere—but the emperor forbids more voyages and plans to close their borders."

"Even the silk road?" Iakinthu had heard these rumors. How could they be true? The Sheng profited greatly from the silk trade.

"He wants all the silk for himself, I suppose," Tuola said.

"What did he tell you about his home?"

"The emperor?" Tuola said, with mischief.

Iakinthu raised an eyebrow.

"Could the stranger know what direction it lay in, after so long a voyage? He spoke of giant mountains and mysterious forests."

"How did you speak to him?"

"In Sheng. We each spoke it so badly, we understood each other."

"What happened?" Iakinthu asked, disappointed by the lack of information. "Did he contract cold fever?"

Iakinthu often grew briefly ill when she visited a new place; so did all travelers. Usually the illnesses were uncomfortable but brief, nasty head-clogging afflictions of sneezing and dripping snot. But on her very first trip to Pharaoh's land, when she was barely past girlhood, she had contracted cold fever and nearly died. It still sometimes plagued her. She wondered why the dripping snot and cold fever illnesses each returned again and again.

"He grieved to death."

"I'm very sorry," Iakinthu said.

"It happens." Indifferent to the odd scruples of Idaeans, Tuola shrugged. "If he'd been taken younger, like your Rhenthizu, who knows? I knew the risk when I bought him, but I thought... It's past. So. Perhaps you'll like this."

Tuola broke the wax on a parcel, peeled away the coating, and unfolded the paper wrapper. Inside lay a battered, wrinkled length of cloth. Iakinthu plucked it carefully from the parcel, holding its ragged corners in her fingertips. It folded open, nearly as thin and fine as Sheng silk. It was firmer and more opaque than silk, smoother than wool, lighter than linen. The even threads and the fine, tight weaving impressed her. Fuzzy streaks and stains of paint or ink marred it.

"What is it?" She turned it over.

Symbols and drawings covered its other side. Iakinthu tried to make them out, but the script was unfamiliar to her. The drawings mystified her: overlapping lines, circular patterns with rippled boundaries, a long irregular streak against the raveled edge. Could it be more than decoration, this collection of interacting designs?

"It's writing," Tuola said. "It's how they write in the Sunset Land."

"How do you know?"

"The man I bought for you tied it around his head. He pretended it was nothing, to hide it from the pirates." She hesitated. "To hide it from me."

A thrill of wonder tingled along Iakinthu's spine. She showed the cloth to Kilinkizu, who bent close over it, squinting, then passed the reading stone over it to see it more clearly.

"It's scribbles," Kilinkizu said. "The mother of the child who made those marks grew very angry."

Iakinthu carelessly folded the fabric.

"I like it for the weaving," she said. "I'll buy it for my curiosities."

They haggled again. Iakinthu drove a harder bargain than usual so Tuola might believe she gave the scrap little value. Yet Tuola drove the price up to a full storage jar of wine.

"Because, scribbles or script, I've never seen its like," she said. "Is Iakinthu Gephyra the only person who has curiosities?"

Iakinthu laughed, agreed to the price, and made sure Tuola paid well for several dragonfly necklaces.

"Perhaps this will please you," Tuola said. From a bag of thick silk, she drew out a long curved shape, heavy, the color of ivory, similar to a tusk, but far too short, far too thick. She handed it to Iakinthu, using both hands. From point to end, it was the length of her forearm.

Iakinthu turned the ivory over in her hands, stroking the polished tip, the complicated curve of the sides, the flat end, ringed like a cut tree. The flat end was as wide as her two hands together.

"It is ivory," she said. "But from what creature?"

Pharaoh's elephants, lamenting in their captivity, had much thinner tusks. The sealstone carvers at Milatusu, who imported the finest, largest tusks for their work, would be amazed by this one.

"From the giant elephants of the Sunset Land," Tuola said. "That's the tip of its tusk. The giant elephants have tusks the size of trees, and they're covered with fur."

"Their tusks?"

"Their skins." Tuola grinned.

"So they can live on the ice mountains," Iakinthu said, doubting every word. "And do they breathe fire, to melt caves for themselves?"

Tuola snorted, well aware she was being made sport of.

"I'm surprised you never saw them," she said, adding quickly, "all the creatures there are giants, and the men, too."

"Rhenthizu is the size of any other young man," Iakinthu said.

Tuola shrugged. "He grew up on your small island, so he'd be small, like the rest of you. If he'd grown up in the Sunset Land, which is too big to imagine, he would have grown large."

"Tuola, friend, the Maisusutha are the same size as everybody else." Iakinthu believed in giant people even less than she believed in furry giant elephants. "And they never mentioned giant elephants." But how to explain the tusk? she wondered.

Her sealstone artists would make something wonderful of this ivory, something to make even Milatusu's artisans envious.

Iakinthu knew what she would trade Tuola for the ivory.

"Kilinkizu, would you fetch me a bundle from the cedar chest? The one wrapped in white silk?"

Kilinkizu touched her fist to her forehead, set aside her writing desk, and rose. When she opened the chest, the scent of lavender and cedar flowed around them.

"Ah," Tuola said. "That scent always makes me think of Iakinthu's wonderful gifts."

Iakinthu raised her eyebrow. Gifts? Tuola, the savvy trader, might have it in her mind that Iakinthu would make good Tuola's loss in the matter of the man from the Sunset Land.

I'd compensate his family, she thought, if he died in my care, as if he were a given child. But fond as I am of Tuola, she may wait forever for that event.

Kilinkizu brought the white silk package and helped her unwrap it, revealing a long cloak of silky pelts, brown with golden highlights. Kilinkizu stroked it, her hand lingering on the soft fur.

"What is that?" Tuola asked, reaching for the cloak.

"It's from the Maisusutha," Iakinthu said. "I thought of you when I saw it." In truth, she had wrapped it around herself and been warm for the first time since she landed on the Maisusutha beach. "I thought, 'This will help Tuola be warm.'"

Tuola stroked the fur with a delicate touch. It was irresistible. Iakinthu remembered the first time she had touched it. No pharaoh's cat was as soft and plush, no house snake as smooth.

"What creature is it?" Tuola asked.

Iakinthu had seen some unworked pelts: the sharp claws remained, and the small round ears, and a tail half the length of the body, and a snout with small sharp teeth.

Shall I tell Tuola that the creature looks like a weasel in a fur coat? she wondered. She decided the nature of the creature was best left to her friend's imagination.

"I thought of you when I saw it," Iakinthu said again. She handed it to Kilinkizu. Tuola, who usually feigned indifference to the items she most coveted, followed it with her gaze.

Iakinthu settled back to haggle again, looking forward to driving a good bargain. She wondered if Tuola had more than one piece of giant ivory among her packages.

Kilinkizu stroked the fur, gently set it aside, and took up her writing box again.

"How could I ever afford something so fine?" Tuola said. "You should take it to the Sheng. They'd like it, in the east—fur like silk. You can take it to them in your great strong ship. They'd make you rich forever."

"Such a long trip!" Iakinthu said. "If I had a whole shipload of furs—the Sheng might even open their borders to me. But I have only the one cloak. The creatures are very rare, you know."

"The northerners would like it."

"The pirates?" Iakinthu laughed. "Yes, they'd wrap themselves in fine fur, surely, if they had a chance, or spill grease on it, or tear it into bits between them, out of envy. But what would they give me in return? Do they have anything I want? They'd do better if I took them perfume as a gift of charity."

"They could afford to pay you—they steal all their gold, so how would they know its value? It would warm me, and my poor cold hands and feet, but could I afford to eat after buying it?"

Iakinthu tsked in sympathy. "Perhaps I should keep it, for my trip back to the Maisusutha, in case we stay the winter." She had, indeed, planned to do so, but Tuola's unexpected visit changed that plan.

In the end, they agreed to trade the tusk for the cloak, as they had known all along they would. They drank a last glass of wine, embraced, and bid each other farewell. Tuola left most of her new possessions for her crew members to come and carry away for her, but she flung the cloak around herself and sighed in pleasure.

"I'll be warm now," she said. "Thank you, Iakinthu Gephyra, and may your long voyage be smooth and profitable."

After Tuola left, Iakinthu sat gazing at the ragged bit of cloth. The tusk interested her, but the scrap was far more intriguing.

Kilinkizu dropped her brush and cried out when it spattered ink on the fresh white plaster. She moaned in despair.

She burst into tears.

Startled, Iakinthu jumped up. The frayed cloth and the tusk tip fell from her lap, the tusk rolling in an uneven circle.

"Forgive me, Iakinthu." She spoke between desperate wails, fighting to stop. The sound keened, unbearable.

"My dear, what's wrong, it's only a few drops of ink—"

Iakinthu held her, hugged her, stroked her hair. Kilinkizu sobbed, wailing aloud. She struggled in Iakinthu's embrace, her gentleness possessed by the strength of panic.

"It's all right, it's all right." The floor hard against her knees, Iakinthu held Kilinkizu, trying to ease the fear and the pain from her.

Collapsing against Iakinthu's breast, Kilinkizu cried to exhaustion, her wails turning to sobs, sobs to whimpers.

"Tell me."

"How can I?" Kilinkizu asked. "You'll despise me…"

"I stand in the place of your grandmother," Iakinthu said, "and I know you're good and courageous and honorable. Would a secret change my mind in an instant? Did my secret change your mind?"

"What secret?" Kilinkizu asked, puzzled.

Amazed that Kilinkizu gave little thought to Rhenthizu's past as a slave—and Iakinthu's moment as a slave buyer—Iakinthu said, "Is it important? What's important is what grieves you so."

She dipped her handkerchief into the water ewer and stroked the damp cloth across Kilinkizu's face, wiping away smudges of kohl.

"The northerners," Kilinkizu said. "The pirates, the bandits. When you and Tuola spoke of them, when I carried the furs…" She drew in a long breath. "The northerners have furs and gold and perfume. They owned the village where I was born.

"When he took me," Kilinkizu said softly. She stopped and began again. "They lined up all the young girls, and we stood blushing and giggling, waiting to be taken. Their leader, their king, walked up and down and drew a girl forward, and placed her hand in the hand of one of his men. He did that again and again. I was ashamed when he passed me by.

"But he took my hand and he kept me instead of passing me along, and I walked away with him, and I was so proud.

"Then I found out what it meant to belong to him. I thought I would die. I thought I should die. He kept me. He made his men and his slaves and his other women watch me. When I ran, he caught me. Once I got all the way home." She drew in a shuddering breath and sighed it out again. "And my village gave me back to him. And then…

"After a while, I even lost the wish to die."

Tears spilled down her cheeks. Iakinthu wiped them away.

"When I bore him a son—" she raised her head, defending herself. "They wrapped him in the finest fur, like Tuola's cloak, and allowed me to nurse him. He was ferocious, and he suckled me dry.

"They believe they know who fathers every child. They believe they can watch women so closely that only one man will ever take her." She smiled ruefully. "Every time he slept, or turned around, or closed his eyes when he sneezed—his women deceived him."

Kilinkizu spoke Idaean well, and seldom misused a word or debased the language. Her mistake was deliberate, applying the word for ownership of property, instead of the word for relationship or kinship or friendship, to women.

"It's what they think!" Kilinkizu said. "How else can I say it? They believe women exist to be owned, that we must be owned. The women believe it. I believed it."

"I understand how it is, my dear." The Sheng among others believed the same thing. Iakinthu had been many places where it was the custom for the man to choose the woman, for the woman's family to choose a man for her without her consent. "But it grieves me that you were subjected to such indignity."

Kilinkizu closed her eyes; she bent forward, her bright hair tumbled in tangles around her face. "He thinks of himself as a shepherd, but he lacked the kindness of a shepherd. He acted like a herd stallion who screams and charges and bites and kicks if anyone opposes his will or challenges his desires. Does he have a lead mare to guide him? He carries all the power. His people share some of it. He chose when, he chose whether, he chose who. He chose to possess me," Kilinkizu said, using the word for ownership again. "He chose to possess my son. His son."

Iakinthu flushed, both embarrassed and angry for her given child.

"Tell me about him," she said. "Your son."

"I could rejoice, or I could despair, because he was a boy." Her voice caught. "He lived, knowing who his father is, learning to kill, learning hatred, hating all women, hating his mother, wanting to possess the world. After a few weeks, they took him away to be raised by the men, to be suckled by a wet nurse. It was the beginning of spring. At the end of winter, I bore another child, a daughter."

"Two babies, in a year?" Iakinthu exclaimed, shocked. Inconceivably dangerous, stupid, damaging. "I knew you were strong, my dear," she said, her words inadequate. "Now I understand how strong."

Kilinkizu's laugh was high, tight, like a spark of pain.

"The king lusts after one woman he gave to his first subordinate, because she's borne his man twenty children, most of them boys. They even let her keep some of her daughters, to serve the boys, to give to his favorite men. The king thinks of taking her back, but his subordinate might challenge him."

Indifferent to the quarrels of northerners, Iakinthu exclaimed, "Twenty children! Does a woman of the north have litters? What does she do with them all?"

"She has one every year, one every three seasons if she can. If one dies in her womb she must try to have another. What does she do with them? Can she say? The man who owns her—"

"Please, my dear, I understand you. Can I bear to hear obscenities from your lips?"

"They are an obscenity." Kilinkizu looked away. "Did I ever mean to tell you this?" She looked Iakinthu in the eyes, searching. "Shall I stop speaking, Iakinthu Gephyra? I will, if you wish it."

"Finish your story, Kilinkizu, my given child."

"They take their boys to learn to steal and to kill or be killed. If the boys displease the men, the men kill them."

Iakinthu poured strong wine into Kilinkizu's goblet. Kilinkizu gulped it so fast it made her cough.

"They sound crazy," Iakinthu said. "If they kill their children, where do they get their adults?"

"They get plenty of sons," Kilinkizu said. "Villages give young women like me as tribute. If a village resists, the northerners raid and plunder and kill the men and the boys and the mothers and grandmothers, and take the daughters away."

"How did you escape?"

"The People," Kilinkizu said. "The northern men made the mistake of abducting one of them. They came to save their sister and to teach the northern men a lesson. I was lucky. I was in the same camp. They took me with them. I was drinking at the sea of grief. They brought me back from its edge."

"What of your daughter?" Iakinthu imagined that the People might have kept her, a given child from their adopted sister Kilinkizu. She imagined a daughter of Kilinkizu's line...

Has she loved either woman or man, Iakinthu thought, since I knew her? I wondered if she would ever give her mother a grandchild. But perhaps she already has.

"My daughter?" Kilinkizu said, her voice flat with grief and fury.

Iakinthu understood, suddenly, what bearing a daughter to a northern man meant.

"Iakinthu, they dashed her brains out before me, to punish her for being a girl, to punish me for wasting king's seed—they believed—on a girl." She closed her eyes. Iakinthu could only imagine what Kilinkizu saw in her memory. Tears caught on Kilinkizu's eyelashes and spilled down her cheeks. Iakinthu wiped her face again with the cool cloth.

"After they murdered my daughter, I fell into a fever," Kilinkizu said. "The northerners are cruel, and obscene, and they're filthy. They make each other sick. I'm lucky..."

She shuddered.

"I heard the People attack. I smelled the fire, and the blood, I heard the screams... I thought it was a dream—"

"A nightmare," Iakinthu said, in sympathy. She admired the People, but their ferocity awed her.

"A wish dream!" Kilinkizu exclaimed. "I thought I would die, and I was happy, because I was surrounded by death and they'd all die too.

"When I woke, the People had carried me away, and given me medicine to heal me, and wrapped me in fur by the fire until I came to myself." She let Iakinthu refill her cup and drank. She put down the cup and pushed back her hair in an angry gesture. "Will I ever come back to myself?" she asked.

The sun had set, and the light grown dim, without their noticing.

"You're here now. You're safe."

"Is anyone always safe?" Kilinkizu asked. "With the northerners sniffing at our shores like hungry dogs?"

"They've sniffed at our shores before, and you know what that got them."

Kilinkizu smiled, straightened up, and patted Iakinthu's hand as if she were the one in need of comfort.

"The northerners may try to take me again," she said. "They will fail."

Chapter Six

On this fine warm night, everyone in the household slept on the roof, carrying the sleeping pallets up the stairs, lying beneath coverlets woven from fine-spun lambswool. When Kilinkizu snarled in her dreams, Iakinthu left Aranthau gently snoring and held Kilinkizu's hand. She stroked her hair while the stars streamed through the black sky. When Kilinkizu finally slept deeper than her dreams, Iakinthu dozed.

The earthquake moaned its quiet warning, waking Iakinthu a moment before the ground, the house, the air around her trembled and groaned. Beams creaked against stone and plaster. Sleep still froze her, and by the time it released her, the temblor had ceased. Beside her, Kilinkizu gasped awake.

Iakinthu rose, naked and stolid in the faint false dawn. Mother Moon Everchanging, a morning crescent supported by Grandmother Sun, held up the sky in her curving arms.

Kilinkizu sat up, gazing around, blinking, then squinting to see. Her nightmares must have been even worse while she lived with the People, so much nearer the time of her captivity. Were the People ever caught asleep by weather or earthquake or northerners? Even friendly neighbors claimed the People lived without sleep.

Iakinthu gathered the children, some frightened, some excited by the tantrum beneath the earth. "Only an earthquake," Iakinthu said. "A small earthquake."

"I'm used to them, Grandmama," Issiia said. "Am I ever afraid of earthquakes?"

She drew Issiia close.

Iakinthu scanned the rooflines all around for smoke, for fire going wild. Aranthau and Rhenthizu, Omempau and Kilinkizu and Maranti disappeared down the stairs, to be certain the kitchen fires remained banked and contained, to check the lamps. Even a small earthquake could cause great damage if it freed the fires.

Neighbors opened their front doors and called to each other, to Iakinthu on the roof, to family members, reassuring themselves that the fires remained tame.

"Your household?" Iakinthu called to Sitharante on the roof of the house next door. Hers was an old house, built mostly of stone, lacking extra beams to spread the shaking.

Sitharante leaned over the edge of the roof; her daughter's young lover called up from the street. "All's well."

"We're well, we're well," Sitharante said to Iakinthu, who waved an acknowledgement.

Iakinthu's companions gathered on the roof again. Iakinthu missed Aranthau, but knew he would go along the street to smell smoke and down to the beach to speak to the sea, to listen for great waves. In the harbor the central island lay protected, but the outer coast of Fair Island was vulnerable.

Iakinthu tucked a coverlet around Issiia, planning to sit by her to ease her fears.

"Shall we leave some flowers in the niche tomorrow?" Issiia said. "For Mother Moon?"

And she fell asleep.

Iakinthu greeted friends and acquaintances as she and Kilinkizu, Omempau and Issiia, Bdarde the musician, and half a dozen other members of her household walked toward the uphill edge of town a little after dawn. Issiia's donkey, pack saddle contrasting with his bright Egyptian bridle, contentedly carried their belongings.

A few new cracks marred facades. Plaster buckets and paint pots already stood on the cobbles or balanced on scaffolding. Householders waved as the little caravan passed, and went back to considering whether to change the color of the house or paint the wall niche a contrasting hue.

Omempau gave Issiia a honey-cake from her parcel and nodded with approval when Issiia broke off corners of it, between nibbles, to put in wall niches for the Mother. She was less approving when Issiia slipped a bit of honey-cake to her donkey, but allowed it.

"Another earthquake for your list," Iakinthu said to Omempau, who had kept track of the small earthquakes for years; they came at any season, as frequently in summer or winter as in spring, though everyone thought of spring as earthquake season.

"They're coming more often," Omempau said.

"Hope they continue," Iakinthu said. "They saved us once."

"Yes," Omempau said. "Sometimes he directs his anger for our benefit. If we pay his price."

The town gave way to countryside. They walked along the well-kept road, passed sometimes by fleet messengers, sometimes passing donkey caravans bringing wine and oil, spring greens, or lambswool in round bundles to the market or the harbor. Now and then a shepherd drove shorn sheep or lambs along the road. Iakinthu and her group moved aside, nodding to the shepherd as the bleating naked creatures tumbled past them. The donkey snorted.

Gazing at the ground, lost in thought, Kilinkizu strode ahead, outdistancing the rest of the party. Issiia kept up with her for a while, then turned from the path to pick wildflowers.

Iakinthu, too, did her best to keep up, but the pace was too fast for the littlest ones and, she admitted, for her. She slowed to a more comfortable walk.

When Kilinkizu had outdistanced the group by fifty strides, she turned and called to Iakinthu, walking backwards, peering shortsightedly down the path.

"Are you all right?"

"Perfectly," Iakinthu said, and added, "Are we racing?"

Kilinkizu stopped, nonplussed, then laughed. She returned to Iakinthu's side, passing Issiia, accepting a flower from her bouquet.

"I was thinking of the People," she said. "They like to race. Being in the countryside brought me back to them."

She walked at a more reasonable speed.

"Your stride is half again the length of mine," Iakinthu said.

Kilinkizu gazed down at her; Iakinthu was a head shorter.

"If you want to stretch your legs, my dear, you might wait for us at the spring."

"Perhaps later," Kilinkizu said.

The silence stretched on.

Iakinthu waited.

"Iakinthu Gephyra…"

"Kilinkizu, my given child."

"I am a numerator."

"Yes."

"The People think of enumeration as men's work."

"Do they? Do they think of you as a man?"

"They think of me as...different. Do they think of me as Kilinkizu? They thought of me as Fire-from-Cold-Ashes. They will think of me as One Hundred Four."

"Ah."

"They would have me spend my time in the men's hut, keeping their records and writing their exploits."

"Writing their exploits would be interesting," Iakinthu said.

"They like to exaggerate."

"Why else have exploits?"

Kilinkizu quirked her lips sadly. "There'll come a time," she said, "when I'll be too shortsighted to keep records, even with the reading stone."

"Oh, my dear..."

"My sight is getting worse. Will the People need a blind numerator? Will the Idaeans? Will you?"

"Can I speak for the People? I can speak only for myself, and I'll always welcome you."

Kilinkizu gazed up the path, squinting to find Issiia on the hillside.

"And Issiia?"

"She'll miss you," Iakinthu said, "if you stay with me instead of going with her to the People. She loves you. But when she agreed to be a given child to the People, she expected to be the only Idaean among them."

"Now she thinks I'll be with the People too."

"Yes."

"Will she be angry?"

Iakinthu hesitated. "She'll be sad."

The wind picked up, as it always did in the middle of the day. It swooped along the distant cliffs and over the edges of outer and inner islands and across the hillsides. It sculpted trees into windswept shapes. It ruffled the distant harbor from glassy smooth to ripples to small whitecaps breaking on the farther shore.

Iakinthu paused at the view-spot, letting the rest of her companions continue along the road. She sat on a flat-topped stone, oblivious to the wind, and let the afternoon's beauty sink into her. She faced the valley of Old Farm.

Olive trees grew on the slopes to either side of the valley. Lower on the hillsides, grape vines huddled out of the wind, each in a protective circle of brambles. A field left fallow rioted with wildflowers, and a new-planted patch turned green, then silver, then back to green, as the wind riffled its delicate shoots.

The house lay brilliant white against the hillside, its flat roof topped by the lightwell, the staircase and, like a small black hat, the hot water tank. Other, smaller houses lay scattered across the hillside, the houses of other families connected to the farm. Many had new rooms, new stories in the midst of being built, new paint, and each had its own hot water tank.

Farther up the valley, red and black mothers of bulls dotted the new green of pastures, and the practice ground lay clear and smooth.

Iakinthu smiled with pride.

She rose and walked along the common road, down the hill from the view-spot, until she reached the turnoff to the farm. In the turnoff, pebbles filled the winter ruts made by donkey carts, and a footpath meandered alongside. Path and cart-track separated, the track leading behind the house and on to the barn, the path leading her and her companions, including Issiia's donkey, to the front door.

The breeze fell. At the house, the shutters banged open to the light and the air, and the front door swung wide. A huge white-and-black dog loped out and gallumped toward Issiia.

Woof stopped a pace before Issiia, sat, and offered her paw. Issiia took it like a diplomat, then dispensed with formality, fell on her knees, and wrapped her arms around Woof's neck. The dog's black muzzle showed silver, but she retained her dignity and her attention.

Issiia brought her to Iakinthu, one hand twined in the dog's mane. Woof sniffed politely at Kilinkizu's outstretched hand and leaned contentedly against Iakinthu's leg as Iakinthu scratched behind her ears.

They were expected. Iakinthu's cousin Psarau — a distant, beloved cousin — and the other members of the household, connected families, ran out to greet them and to ask for all the latest news. Omempau, you're back from town, finally! How did the negotiations go? Iakinthu, did Rhenthizu walk through the fire? Was *Flying Fish* refitted? Will Aranthau and Rhenthizu come to the farm, or must they stay with *Flying Fish* on the shore? Did you see the new hot water tank? Such luxury! Was the spring festival successful and a joy? Issiia, you are so grown up since your trip to Egypt! Kilinkizu, we are glad to see you again before you return to your mother!

How does Maranti fare as Eldest Daughter?

The answer to that took a few moments and resulted in questions Iakinthu did her best to answer: I hope she'll visit Old Farm. For now she is visiting Rhenthizu.

That brought on a whole different set of questions, comments, speculation.

"We will have to see what happens," Iakinthu said.

In the cheerful chaos of welcome and greeting, cousin Psarau led them through the cool, bright house to the gathering room and food.

They ate; they complimented Psarau for the cooking and Omempau for her management of the farm and the gardens. Bdarde took up her lute and played soft music.

Iakinthu felt full and content, and ready for a nap, but Psarau brought around a plate of the honey-cakes she was so proud of, and Iakinthu found room for honey-cakes.

"Yours are the very best," she said, savoring the almonds, the delicate sweetness dissolving on her tongue.

Psarau offered the plate to Kilinkizu, who chose a small square.

"You're so polite," said Psarau fondly.

"Polite?" Kilinkizu asked, puzzled. "While I gobble up your honey-cakes like a little boy?"

Psarau sat beside her, keeping the plate within her reach. "I think you like some other sweet better—you must tell me what, so I can make it for you. I think you eat this only to please me."

"I like these more than anything," Kilinkizu said.

"Then why," Psarau asked, genuinely curious, "do you always take the smallest piece?"

Kilinkizu squinted at the plate, licked the honey from her fingertips and considered.

"Do I?"

"Always."

"Psarau is right," Iakinthu said. "Ever since the first day we welcomed you."

"I..." She hesitated. "I suppose I want to be sure there's enough for everybody."

"Would I bring less than enough?" Psarau exclaimed. "There's enough! There's more than enough. You may have all you like!"

"I do like them," Kilinkizu said, smiling into the elder woman's eyes. "I will have another honey-cake, if I may."

"You may have all you like," Psarau said again. "All you like."

The prettiest pasture on Old Farm possessed lush grass, meandering stone walls dry-laid, a grove of gnarled oak trees, a thatched stone shelter, and a pottery trough supplied with water from the hillside spring.

Iakinthu climbed the stile beside the heavy gate and stepped alone into the pasture.

She wished Issiia had shown an inclination to play here. Will any of my family ever dance with the bulls? she wondered.

She stepped away from the stone wall into grass as high as her boots.

"Terebinthu!"

She had been away from the farm for a year and more. She wondered if he would remember her voice. She called out again and drew a stem of dried grapes from her pocket.

A reply as loud and low as storm wind over a horned mountain rolled from the oak grove.

The great, red-spotted bull strolled out of the shade, lowing, snorting. The shadows of leaves and the golden sunlight dappled his hide, turning him all shades of henna, copper, bronze, and gold.

He no longer galloped across his pasture, hooves thundering. He was ancient for a bull, his hips bony, his eyes clouded. But his coat was sleek as a cat's, his parts still swung heavy and low, and his horns swept forward in long unbroken curves.

He walked proudly to Iakinthu, lowered his head, and slid the left horn past her side. He came to rest with the horn pressing sideways against her breast and his forehead leaning against her upper arm, against the deep scar. She patted his wide chest; she stroked his powerful shoulders, his side. He sniffed and snorted, smelling the grapes. She fed them to him, and he munched them with contentment.

"What a civilized creature you are," she said.

If she asked him, he would lumber toward her, arthritic joints groaning. He would toss his head as she grasped his horns, lift her in a long wide leap over his head, onto his back. But her joints would protest as painfully as his.

Her team had disbanded to Alashya, to Idaea, to the outer ring of Fair Island, all to teach the dancing art.

Iakinthu thought the best dancing bulls came from Old Farm's line. Terebinthu had enriched the farm and its families ever since he went to stud. The mothers of bulls, who lived in the farm's largest pasture, had done the same for generations.

She raised her arm from Terebinthu's horn and scratched the whorl on his forehead. He leaned against her hand and snorted grassy breath tinged with the sweetness of grapes.

Her team danced at the harvest festival at Kunusu, with Terebinthu's sire, then with Terebinthu, from her tenth year till the year she turned twenty, till the dance of her accident.

I should have stopped the year before, she thought. I should have known better. Am I making the same mistake with the coming voyage?

"Shall I retire, my old friend?" With one hand on his muzzle and the other on the back of his neck, she guided him toward the stile. She climbed the steps, clambered onto the wall, and eased herself onto Terebinthu's back. He raised his head and snorted. His days of training new dancers were over, but he remembered. He was ready to run. He looked around.

"Only me," she said, sitting deep to keep him calm and slow. He walked around the pasture, stopped, lowered his head when he found a particularly succulent patch of grass.

Iakinthu slid from Terebinthu's back. He continued to graze.

"Will they ever see our like again?" Iakinthu said.

The Mothers of Bulls never could be mistaken for ordinary cows. Massive and as long-horned as Terebinthu, they cropped the grass and chewed their cuds with regal disdain for the antics of their calves. Even Iakinthu hesitated to climb into the pasture with the Mothers of Bulls. Terebinthu was tame, a dancer. The Mothers were wild. They lived to protect their calves.

She stood in the shade of an almond tree and let herself imagine, let her mind wander.

If I were to train a dancer, which of the calves would I choose? For next year's calves, which of the Mothers would I introduce to Terebinthu?

She kept careful records so as to avoid too much inbreeding and back-crossing.

Would I want a strange bull? Or one as stupid and foolish as the pharaohs who only marry their sisters have been?

As Pharaoh now is a woman who lacks a brother to marry, she might choose someone who could give new life to her line, Iakinthu thought. Iakinthu hoped this would happen. She had her eye on one of Pharaoh's scribes, a young man of good family and good intelligence whose beautiful dark gaze darted away from Pharaoh's whenever he noticed someone looking. What Iakinthu expected, though, was that Pharaoh would allow her advisers to persuade her to marry her first cousin, a man for whom Iakinthu had a particular disregard. Pharaoh might already have chosen him. The potential husband was as inbred as Pharaoh, for his family followed royal customs to which they were less than entitled. He was a big, strong, nearly handsome man, his looks marred by the eyes of a weasel and his character marred by secret episodes of terror and suspicion.

One of the Mothers of Bulls strode out of the herd. The others gave way to her. She was large and ferocious. She stood out among her red-spotted companions. Black from her eyes to her tail, from her back to her shoulders and flanks, she was splashed with white on her muzzle and belly and legs and the tip of her tail. Her horns glowed gold. She bossed the herd.

A young bull calf followed her. He was brown and white, but his mother always bred true to her coloring, so Iakinthu expected him to be black and white after his first shedding.

And what will your temperament be, young bull? Iakinthu wondered. So far his mother also bred true to her ferocious temper. What Iakinthu wanted was a bull with the dramatic black and white coat and the civilized temper of Terebinthu.

Will I give you a name, young bull? Iakinthu wondered. The Mothers of Bulls went nameless, because how could one name a wild thing? The wild sons had to be culled because they were useless.

Iakinthu watched the calf frolic with its age-mates and hoped it could be tamed.

II
Coastal Waters

Chapter Seven

Iakinthu looked fondly at the score of companions of *Flying Fish* who would accompany her on the voyage to Kilinkizu's home and to Rhenthizu's.

"It's time," she said, "to take our given children, Kilinkizu and Rhenthizu, back to their mothers, and for Issiia to become given child to the People."

Kilinkizu and Issiia stood among the companions; Rhenthizu and Maranti stood together. Maranti was only Maranti today; she had left off the finery of Eldest Daughter and looked like any ordinary companion.

An ordinary companion whose heart I may break, Iakinthu thought sadly.

"Kilinkizu's mother lives a few days' sail distant," Iakinthu said. "We'll go to the land of the People first."

Her companions murmured their agreement.

"Rhenthizu is different," she said. "We've welcomed given children who were southern people and taken them home through Pharaoh's canal," she said. "But is Rhenthizu a southern man?"

Her companions chuckled, for he bore less resemblance to the southern people than did the people of Fair Island. Sometimes southern people, like Tuola's son, came as given children. Sometimes they stayed to be people of Fair Island. Iakinthu often wished one of her great-grandmothers had been a southern woman, for then Iakinthu might be related to Tuola and might be less susceptible to the cold fever.

"We've visited the Sheng." She wished the Sheng would allow given children, but they always refused, and everyone knew it. "But is he Sheng?"

Her friends laughed and murmured. Rhenthizu was a little like the Sheng, but everyone knew he came from some other land.

"Rhenthizu, my given child, came from across the Sunset Sea," she said. "He's very like our friends the Maisusutha."

Aranthau had accompanied her to the Maisusutha. Most of the other companions were young; her companions of earlier voyages had retired from the sea, to farms or towns. A few had died.

"But he's from beyond the Maisusutha," she said. "Did Uinthi know of Rhenthizu?"

Maranti slipped her fingers beneath the edge of Rhenthizu's fashionably tight belt, keeping her gaze on Iakinthu. Rhenthizu stood straighter. Maranti smiled.

"The voyage will be long, but it's my task to take him to his mother, to show her that we love him and honor him. He may remain with his given family. He may return to his born family. We must take him to his mother, so he has a proper choice."

The companions replied with agreement and approval. Maranti and Rhenthizu glanced quickly at each other, and away, Rhenthizu distressed and Maranti with a stubborn set to her jaw.

"*Flying Fish* is sound, and Aranthau dances with the Sunset Sea," Iakinthu said. "But the voyage will be dangerous and long, and it will reach new places."

A few of the experienced companions nodded in agreement. Voyages, even to the most well-known places, always carried risks. Iakinthu herself had contracted the cold fever in that most civilized of countries, Egypt. Sometimes the cold fever took her with little warning, shaking her like a dog shakes its prey.

When they visited the People, some of the companions and some of the People would come down with sniffling and sneezing, red eyes and stuffed noses.

At least the People seldom give anyone the drip, Iakinthu thought. Sniffles and sneezes go away by themselves, but the drip requires treatment, caution, isolation.

"When we return from the People's gathering, you may decide to stay on Fair Island, or accompany Maranti when she comes home to Kunusu."

Maranti glanced up, surprised and pleased that Iakinthu had decided to accept her as a companion of *Flying Fish*, even for a short time. Rhenthizu, too, looked happy, and the two stood with their arms around each other's waists.

Will it be more difficult for them to part when we come back from the People's gathering? Iakinthu wondered. Will I regret this decision?

Flying Fish approached the mainland shore, a gathering place of the People. The sails fell; the oars thrust through the ports and dipped into the water. The ship hesitated, then plunged ahead, lunging with each stroke.

Dressed in ceremonial jacket and tiered skirt and dragonfly necklace, her hair dressed with lavender oil, Iakinthu joined Aranthau at the bow. Low on the horizon, the sun stretched their shadows across the deck.

"Come close," Aranthau said. Iakinthu slipped beneath his arm and held his waist, keeping her head down. Aranthau swayed, swinging the weighted measuring line till it hummed through the air. He released it. Its song ended with the plash of carved jade into the sea.

Aranthau drew the line taut. When it hung straight, he took note of the color of the bright bit of silk sewn through the twist of the line. He pulled it up. Droplets of sea water spattered onto the deck. Every few armspans, different colored silk passed through his fingers.

He threw the line again, again, to measure the sea bottom, while *Flying Fish* approached the shore. As the sea bottom shoaled, the color of the silk changed, moving from deep rare sea-purple, through the colors of the rainbow, to the dark red of henna.

Great tall headlands, each crowned with a wall of stones, thrust out to embrace a crescent of beach.

"Slow," Aranthau said, and the rowers' whispered song quivered, then steadied at a slower tempo. *Flying Fish* moved softly into the shelter of the headlands.

"Stop."

The rowers backed their oars and pulled them in; the anchors splashed onto the surface and sank. The ship settled like a living thing, nearly quiet, resting.

"I give you your ship, Iakinthu Gephyra," Aranthau said formally, "safe returned to land."

"Thank you, my love," she said, with equal formality.

Two of the young rowers, sleek with sweat, brought a cold brazier and set it near the bow. The sharp scent of rock oil rose from the kindling.

Kilinkizu and Issiia joined them. Maranti and Rhenthizu followed, one with a lamp, the other with a long match.

"Is this your will?" Iakinthu asked.

"Yes," Kilinkizu said.

"Yes," Issiia said.

Iakinthu lit the match from the lamp and plunged it into the brazier. The oil-soaked kindling and bits of rag burst into flame. Dark, oily smoke rose in a thin plume, straight till it crested the shield of the headland. The wind touched it, bending it like a stroke of ink above the shore.

The beach remained deserted.

Sunset gilded the puffy clouds, turning their white messages orange, purple, gold, silver-gray. The light turned hazy.

Kilinkizu stood in the bow, squinting into the distance, into the forest. The headland fell steep to the beach, and the beach rose gently to a hill dark with trees. This was a good harbor, though all harbors suffered when compared to the perfection of Fair Island's.

"Are they there?" Kilinkizu whispered.

"I see only beach and trees," Iakinthu said.

Darkness completed itself.

Suddenly a torch blazed among the trees. A fire burst into flame on shore, then another, and another, till a curved line of flaring light welcomed them.

Kilinkizu unfastened her short jacket and her kilt, folded them carefully, and laid them on the deck. Naked, pale in the brazier's flickering light, she climbed the bow, balanced, and dove. She stayed underwater so long that several of the companions murmured with concern. She surfaced a good distance from *Flying Fish*. She swam toward shore, the eerie light of the sea trailing in her wake, flowing from her body, flying from her hands like sparks.

Issiia glanced at Iakinthu, questioning, and Iakinthu drew her close. "Stay with me," she said. "We'll go ashore in the boat."

The companions of *Flying Fish* filled the ship's boat with bundles and jars and lowered it to the water. Rhenthizu climbed lithely down, balanced standing, and gave his hand to Maranti as she descended. Issiia managed the rope ladder, as composed as any adult.

Iakinthu carried three lily staves to the gunwale. One by one, she handed down the long shafts with their flaring gold blades. Maranti accepted them and fitted them into their steps. The lilies stood upright in the boat, three abreast, gold edges gleaming.

Iakinthu threw her boat cloak back over her shoulders and climbed down the side, accepting the assistance of Aranthau at the top, of her companions at the bottom. The rowers set out, following Kilikinzu, the boat riding low, heavy-laden.

Kilinkizu rose, covered in sea light. A gentle swell caressed her. Her unbound hair spread in tendrils across her shoulders, her back, her buttocks, its ends lifted and twisted by the sea.

She waded to the beach and stood alone and naked, facing the line of fires.

The boat hovered just offshore, oars dipping and pulling to hold it steady.

"I am Kilinkizu, who was Fire-from-Cold-Ashes."

Shadows passed between the fires, the light sparking from jewelry, gleaming on their faces, haloing their forms.

The People faced Kilinkizu: women with white hair, women with black hair, short, strong women, an old woman leaning heavily on a crutch, women with babies in slings at their breasts, and little girls, golden-skinned and dark-eyed.

"Fire-from-Cold-Ashes, who is now Kilinkizu, my daughter." The ancient woman hobbled forward, her feet and her crutch scuffling on the beach pebbles like the quiet shushh of the small waves. Firelight made a nimbus of her wild white hair. Kilinkizu hurried forward and embraced her.

The companions freed the boat from the restraint of its oars and let the water push it, scraping, onto the beach. They sprang out and pulled it higher. Beside Iakinthu, Issiia sat demure, her hands in her lap, even more dignified than Iakinthu.

Rhenthizu handed Maranti from the boat, and Issiia, and finally, honored even above Maranti, Iakinthu. Aranthau handed her the lily staves, and she gave them, one by one, to Maranti, to Issiia, to Rhenthizu. They preceded her up the beach.

Iakinthu walked between her companions, climbed the gradual slope, and stopped behind Kilinkizu. Bringing the parcels from the boat, her companions flanked her.

Thrust into the sand, the lily staves consecrated the beach.

"Mother," Kilinkizu said to the ancient one of the People, "here is my grandmother, Iakinthu Gephyra. Iakinthu, here is my mother, Celestial Wind." Iakinthu and Celestial Wind smiled at each other through the ceremonial introduction; they had known each other since Celestial Wind was young, and Iakinthu a girl.

Iakinthu came to Kilinkizu's side and gave Celestial Wind a phial of Egyptian glass. Celestial Wind sniffed the stopper, chuckled, and thrust the gift into her vest. She beckoned, and two young People came forward carrying a large irregular shape wrapped in leather. They placed it at Iakinthu's feet and unwrapped it.

Iakinthu caught her breath. Her companions gazed at it in wonder.

The skull caught the firelight in all shades of red and gold. Everyone knew gryphons had bones of agate. This was the first gryphon skull Iakinthu had ever seen. Like the gryphons on the frescoes at Kunusu, this one possessed a massive beak and a frilled agate ruff, and eyeholes for two huge eyes and two of a more normal size. Iakinthu bent to stroke its smooth curves.

"You told stories of gryphons," Celestial Wind said. "This came from the east, where it guards the gold mines beyond the land of the Sheng. I thought you would like it."

"I'm overwhelmed by your gift."

"Would you dance with this creature?" Celestial Wind asked curiously.

"I would try," Iakinthu said. She estimated its size: taller at the shoulder than Terebinthu, if they were of the same proportions. She wondered if its ruff would give any purchase for leaping. "Has anyone ever seen one alive?"

"Perhaps," Celestial Wind said, "but the gryphons eat anyone who approaches. Those stories are lost."

The younger People carried the skull to a driftwood log and set it there for everyone to see.

Celestial Wind, ancient of the People, Kilinkizu's mother, tucked her crutch under one arm and held out her hands to Iakinthu, the younger woman, Kilinkizu's grandmother.

Iakinthu smiled. "I'm honored to see you again, Celestial Wind, daughter, mother of my given child." And she was glad to see her. She was so old, Iakinthu had feared she might have gone.

"Welcome, again, Iakinthu Gephyra," Celestial Wind said. "So now you are my mother." She laughed.

"You gave me..."

Iakinthu hesitated, for the ritual saying described the usual pattern. Kilinkizu's path was far different. She continued: the ritual held its own truth.

"You put a girl, Fire-from-Cold-Ashes, in my trust. I return with Kilinkizu, a grown woman, an Idaean, and one of the People."

Celestial Wind clutched Iakinthu's hands awkwardly, still leaning heavily on her crutch.

"We welcome her with pride."

The fires flared and sparked. The trees loomed dark above the shore, and in the distance horses snorted and stamped.

Iakinthu and Celestial Wind stood eye to eye. Celestial Wind chuckled again. "Have you grown, Iakinthu? Or have I shrunk to your size? I was taller than you, when we first met."

"That happens frequently, Celestial daughter," Iakinthu said. "Everyone is taller than I."

She beckoned to her companions, Kilinkizu's friends. One by one they came forward and presented their parcels, laying out the gifts they had brought so Kilinkizu would return to her mother honored and rich. They dressed her in shirt and loincloth of fine Egyptian linen, patterned trousers like those she had worn when she came to them, fine wool dyed with saffron, an overshirt of heavy silk, sea-purple, and boots of soft leather. Among the gifts were a pot of henna for her hair and palms and the soles of her feet; a bronze sword in a sheath tipped with silver; a pile of copper ingots, flattened blobs with a leg at each corner for handles, each ingot longer than an armspan; sealed jars of wine in their loading nets; olive oil; and baskets of dried grapes on their stems.

Rhenthizu brought her a thick wool cloak, heavier than any ordinary Idaean garment, and slung it around her shoulders.

Bdarde the musician offered Kilinkizu a little silver flute. Kilinkizu accepted it, smiling.

"Thank you, my friends."

Issiia took her gift to Kilinkizu, offered it up, and pulled it partway from its sheath.

Kilinkizu accepted it and pulled free the dagger of sky-iron, revealing the complex pattern of the blade's forging. She tested the edge against the fine hairs on her arm, blew away the shorn hairs, sheathed it, and pushed the sheath beneath her belt.

"Thank you, Issiia, my sister."

Uncharacteristically shy, Issiia backed away to Iakinthu's side.

Last, Iakinthu unclasped the necklace from around her own throat. The chain of tiny gold dragonflies, their wings cut delicately of lapis lazuli by the finest craftswoman of Kunusu, trembled as Iakinthu reached up to fasten the necklace around Kilinkizu's throat.

"Thank you, Iakinthu Gephyra, grandmother."

Iakinthu brushed away tears and stepped one pace back.

Kilinkizu looked entirely different now that she had returned to Celestial Wind.

Is she one of the People? Iakinthu thought, gazing at Kilinkizu. Or an Idaean? What has she decided? I would like for her to stay with me. I would like for her to stay with Issiia.

Celestial Wind nodded her approval of the gifts.

"How can we match such wealth, the wealth of the sea queens?" Kilinkizu's mother said. "We're poor nomads. We make do with what we can carry in our saddlebags."

"I've heard of your saddlebags," Iakinthu said, smiling.

The People brought gifts of their own to their returned adopted sister, their rescued child. One by one they came to her, kissed her, and gave her the belongings that would establish her in their community–a saddle, much lighter and finer and more intricate than the thick woolen pads of donkey-saddles on Idaea, a bridle of gilded leather.

"Dragon Claws!" Kilinkizu said.

Dragon Claws, stocky and middle-aged, kissed her and unrolled a hide tanned a shiny black.

"Northern ox," she said. "The best for body armor. I'll fit it for you myself."

Two young People, their wrists heavy with gold bracelets, carried out a thick roll of woven wool and flung it open on the beach. The tent was big enough for two, if they were lovers.

Hoofbeats pounded the wet sand of the lower beach. The companions stepped closer to Iakinthu, circling her for protection. But the People remained at ease, and, when the spotted pony galloped into the firelight and circled them, kicking up sand, they laughed and cheered.

A little girl stood on the horse's croup, balancing as easily as if she were riding astride. She guided the pony with a leather thong in its mouth, waving with her free hand. She circled three times, then brought her mount to a stop, and leaped to the ground.

A second horse, a red-gold mare with black mane and tail, followed the spotted pony, as horses will, and stopped nearby, snorting.

The little girl took the reins from where they were tied at the horse's poll, untied them, and handed the reins to Kilinkizu. Kilinkizu bent forward and blew softly into the horse's nostrils. The horse, calming, returned the greeting.

"Minnow!" Kilinkizu said to the young rider. "You've grown so!"

"I was Minnow," the girl said. Her grin showed a half-grown-in front tooth. "Soon I'll have a new name."

Kilinkizu's elderly mother of the People came to her last of all. Celestial Wind lifted a pair of saddlebags, the People's saddlebags of fabled capacity, and dragged them along the sand. Dragon Claws moved to help her, but stopped at Celestial Wind's glare. She let the bags fall at Kilinkizu's feet. She gestured, now, for her companions to help her. The People opened the saddlebags and drew jewelry of heavy worked gold from its pockets; they presented each piece to Celestial Wind, who adorned Kilinkizu with bracelets, earrings, a headdress of hundreds of strings of tiny gold beads that dangled over her forehead and down the sides of her face.

"You honor my given child," Iakinthu said.

"We honor her as you honored my daughter," said Celestial Wind. "Now, sit, eat with us."

The ceremonial gathering broke apart as Kilinkizu's sisters and companions from each of her families embraced her and admired her finery. The People brought out haunches of venison and boar and pulled strings of new-caught fishes from the cold water. Fires blazed with dry driftwood and dripping fat. The scent of roasting meat hung thick over the encampment, while the music of drum and lyre and flute ran fleet-footed through the night.

The venison tasted as strong and wild as the music. The People breached a jug of good Fair Island wine, and another. Firelight gleamed on their jewelry, on the hilts of their knives, on the blades of the lily staves thrust into the sand.

Sitting on a camp stool in the firelight, Iakinthu felt as if she had returned to an earlier time, when she first heard of the People and brought together an expedition to meet them. The People had traveled from the north and east until they reached the sea, then, lacking knowledge of ships, having little fondness for water—as their pungent scents of sweat and fur and perfume proved—they stopped. They ranged the forests and the hills as lions ranged the plains. They hunted, they traded, they raided the camps of bandits who dared to challenge them. Iakinthu had had hopes that Idaean ships could end the piracy of the sea and the People could end the piracy on land.

Now they danced in celebration, the People and the companions of *Flying Fish*. The People even welcomed the Idaean men, flirting, offering tender looks. Sweaty, bright-eyed, the gold headdress shining even more brilliantly than her hair, boar grease on her lips, Kilinkizu danced with them.

Nearby, Issiia sat on a driftwood log, daintily nibbling a chunk of venison. Minnow walked over to her, sat down beside her, and offered her a handful of nuts. Ever the diplomat, Issiia accepted the offering despite Minnow's grubby fingers.

"Do you dance with the bulls?" Minnow said.

"I attend my grandmama at the court of Pharaoh," Issiia said.

"Is that fun?"

"It was…instructive," Issiia said.

Iakinthu beckoned them to her.

"Do you want to dance with the bulls, little Minnow?" Iakinthu asked.

"Did you see me ride Surefoot, standing on her back?"

"I did."

"It's very hard."

"You do it very well."

Celestial Wind hobbled over and lowered herself stiffly to a camp stool.

"Tonight is your sister's celebration," she said to Minnow. "Tomorrow is time enough to talk about dancing with bulls. Girls, would you get your grannies a cup of wine?"

"I'll show you how to attend," Issiia said, leading Minnow away.

Iakinthu gazed into the dance circle, where Celestial Wind's People and Iakinthu's companions danced or slipped off together beyond the firelight, hand in hand. A few of the People gave their hands to men of the companions.

"Some for joy, some for sport," said Celestial Wind. "And some perhaps are thinking to the end of next winter. A new child or two—we may be grandmothers all over again."

The comment, from an Idaean, would have been insultingly coarse. Iakinthu granted Celestial Wind the freedom of her own customs.

"I'm grandmother only to my daughter's daughter and to a few given children," Iakinthu said without offense.

Celestial Wind laughed. Iakinthu thought drily that she was giving the old woman more than her share of amusement this evening.

"Even we, who the bandits call wild and ignorant, less than animals, know a man's necessary for a child," Celestial Wind said. "Why do you pretend such ignorance?"

"We know a man is necessary," Iakinthu said. "What we ask is, which man? Who can pretend to know?"

Celestial Wind snorted. "You have too many men, and you let them run around however they like. Keep them properly shut up, and you'll be sure of them."

Iakinthu started to speak, to object to the sense of this, then thought better of it. The approach worked for the People. How many men do they keep? she wondered. She had only ever heard of Kilinkizu's teacher, One Hundred Three, the numerator, and his apprentice, a boy. She doubted he liked being shut up any more than Kilinkizu had. Iakinthu had visited lands where the women liked their place even less, and she had remained diplomatically silent.

She put it in her mind, to send only girls to the People as given children. Though it might be amusing for a moment, to see the look on Celestial Wind's face if she were presented with a boy.

"What do you do with your boys?" Iakinthu asked, trusting that Celestial Wind would answer her question in return, rude though it might be.

"Our enemies say—"

"Your enemies are foolish," Iakinthu said. She had heard stories of cannibalism and human sacrifice among the People, and discounted every word. She wondered if Celestial Wind discounted similar stories about the Idaeans.

Celestial Wind laughed again. "That's true—the pirates would rather make up stories than know what really happens. We give boys to the farm-holders in the hills. They're glad to have them, more boys, stronger for the fields. It frees more girls to go hunting and snaring and herbing. Boys are no good for that, clumsy and noisy."

"They must frighten the herbs," Iakinthu said.

Celestial Wind laughed. "The boys step on them, which is frightening enough. A few extra boys at each farm—the young women thank us. When the boys are grown men, each woman has a better choice. Or she can have two if she likes."

"That's a sensible solution," Iakinthu said. More than one of her companions took more than one lover. She had done the same herself, in younger times. Nowadays, she preferred sharing her bed with Aranthau alone.

Issiia and Minnow returned, each carrying a wine cup carefully in both hands.

"Don't look at it," Issiia said. "It will spill."

To spare the children a lewd conversation about the place of men, Iakinthu fell silent. Celestial Wind's ancient eyes gleamed at her, but the leader of the People allowed the subject to fade away.

Issiia formally presented the cup of wine to Celestial Wind. Minnow, carefully mimicking her, offered Iakinthu her cup.

"Thank you," Iakinthu said. She drank; Celestial Wind eyed Issiia's Egyptian finery with a doubtful eye, for it would hardly stand up to a year with the People. Celestial Wind gulped her wine greedily. If Issiia held an opinion of Celestial Wind's manners, she was disciplined enough to keep it to herself.

"Come and have a rest," Iakinthu said to Issiia and Minnow, whose eyelids were drooping with exhaustion. She spread her boat cloak for them and wrapped them in it as they curled up at her feet like kittens.

Iakinthu and Celestial Wind sat talking by the fire until dawn. A few of the People remained by the campfires, tending the flames, watching the other children, nursing the babies, among the soft night sounds of the waves, of branches crackling in the heat, of a distant burst of laughter or cry of ecstasy.

The sun brightened the sky above the eastern headland. Celestial Wind's chin dropped and she dozed, snoring softly. Iakinthu's eyes felt gritty with wood smoke and lack of sleep.

The celebrants came trailing back to camp, exhausted and happy and scented with leaf-mold and sex. On the shore, Rhenthizu and Maranti left separate small groups of People and came together again, kissing, their passion increased by the night. The People laughed and teased them, Rhenthizu especially.

Aranthau flung himself onto the sand beside Iakinthu, leaning back, resting his elbows on the driftwood.

"Why, I wonder, am I more tired than the last time we celebrated with the People?"

"Because you're even more attractive than last time we visited," Iakinthu said fondly. "Why else?" She looked for Rhenthizu and Maranti, but they had disappeared. Her bittersweet smile reflected her pleasure in their passion for each other, her sadness that they must separate, her happiness that Rhenthizu surely would leave a part of himself with his given family, never acknowledged, but known to everyone.

Dragon Claws and Kilinkizu appeared, carrying several pheasants. Soon the savor of roasting meat tinged the air.

Issiia peeked out of the nest of Iakinthu's boat cloak, where Minnow still slept. She gazed at Kilinkizu.

"Grandmama, will I ever see her again?" Her voice quivered. Iakinthu tried to recall another time when Issiia had been in danger of losing her poise. She stroked Issiia's dark tousled hair. She had left it loose, unplaited, the night before. Now it hung tangled around Issiia's shoulders, like Kilinkizu's.

"I spoke to her." Issiia said carefully. "She wants to belong to Fair Island."

"I know about her sight, my dear."

"I'm glad she told you. Would I ever break her confidence?"

"You're discreet. An excellent quality for a diplomat."

"If she stayed with the People she'd have to be their numerator's boy. His other boy. He already has one."

Issiia scrambled into Iakinthu's lap, hugging her, hiding her face against her breasts like a much younger child, hiding her tears, which fell warm against Iakinthu's jacket.

"She'll be with me when I come to fetch you next spring," Iakinthu said.

Issiia shivered.

"Do you want to stay with the People?" Iakinthu asked. "It's your choice, as it's Kilinkizu's."

Issiia pulled out her scented handkerchief and wiped her eyes before looking up at Iakinthu.

"The People want a given child. An Idaean given child."

"Yes," Iakinthu said, stroking Issiia's hair.

"And, Grandmama, you want another companion like Kilinkizu, who knows the People well. You want agreements between the People and Idaeans."

"Yes, my dear."

"I'll be that companion. I'll stay with them."

"You're very brave. I'm proud of you."

"*And* I shall teach them to bathe," Issiia said.

Iakinthu smiled, thinking, When I return, the People will bathe like Idaeans and wear henna on their hands and dress their hair in Idaean curls. And Issiia will draw a bow and wear trousers and ride down the shore standing on her pony's back.

Dawn spread pink light across the beach and the sea as if Sister Sun had plunged the tips of her rays into rouge. Kilinkizu brought bread and wine and roasted pheasant to Iakinthu. Minnow led Issiia away to show her how to bake hearth bread.

"Dragon Claws hunted the pheasants," Kilinkizu said. "She had them in her bag before I ever saw them."

"I'll thank her," Iakinthu said. "I value hunters, but I value my numerator even more." Kilinkizu rewarded her with a smile.

The morning sentinels left to take their posts, to worry themselves with staying awake until the sun's zenith. The night sentinels returned, yawning, reporting only quiet. Iakinthu had a high regard for the vigilance of the People; she trusted that any bandit lurking to take Kilinkizu or any of her sisters would think better of it.

Or his thoughts would pour away forever as he died.

Several of the People accompanied a donkey from the forest and down the beach. A boy led the beast, and the others walked guard. An elderly man rode the donkey side-saddle, to protect his vulnerable parts. Kilinkizu went to meet him, helped him from the saddle, embraced him, touched her fist to her forehead in salute. She led him to Iakinthu and Celestial Wind. He saluted in his turn.

His boy held the donkey's lead, scowled at Iakinthu, at Issiia and even at Minnow and especially at Kilinkizu. He turned away, refusing any refreshment.

"Welcome home, student," the old man said to Kilinkizu. "What knowledge have you brought to me from Hind?"

Kilinkizu smiled fondly and a little sadly. "Too much to relate quickly, teacher," she said. "Iakinthu Gephyra, this is One Hundred Three, the

People's numerator. My teacher, this is Iakinthu Gephyra of Fair Island, who brings the People her granddaughter as given child." She gestured to Issiia, who touched her fist to her forehead. The old man blinked.

"Iakinthu welcomes my sister Minnow as her own given child."

"Minnow wishes to dance with the bulls," said One Hundred Three.

Does he remember me? Iakinthu wondered. He's very old; does his mind wander?

"That is a different subject," Iakinthu said, thinking, Will I come out of retirement to form a new dancing team? Or will I find Minnow a younger teacher?

"Yes. We must negotiate," One Hundred Three said.

He was the one hundred third numerator of the People. By their reckoning, that made their civilization more than four thousand years old, as old as Egypt, Iakinthu thought, and older than the oldest place on Fair Island.

The gifts of Issiia and the gifts of Kilinkizu were accepted as equal. The training of a bull dancer, on the other hand, required negotiation.

Iakinthu wished the night before had included more sleep and less wine. She held her own with One Hundred Three, though. His sharp edge had dulled a little over the years, so she let him argue for three more jars of wine, and the exchange was fair.

"Now you may have an Idaean name, a name from my family, if you wish," Iakinthu said.

Minnow nodded once, sharply, in the way of the People.

"Will you be Paissu? He was the brother of my grandmother."

Celestial Wind cocked her head. "He?"

"He was a renowned bull dancer. We've saved his name for a worthy recipient."

Celestial Wind chuckled. "Idaeans!" she said. "You have such odd customs."

Minnow, now Paissu, nodded once. "I will be Paissu," she said. "I will surpass his achievements."

"Welcome, Paissu," Iakinthu said, smiling.

"There is the matter of the gryphon," said One Hundred Three.

Iakinthu arched her eyebrow. "The gryphon is a gift from Celestial Wind," she said. "Outside the scope of our negotiations."

"It's very rare—"

"It's unique," Iakinthu said, willingly handing him a point. "I treasure it. I would be in Celestial Wind's debt—except that she gave me the gryphon."

"One Hundred Three," Celestial Wind said, yawning. "The night was long. You've done well, and it's time for you to go home and have your breakfast. Minnow-now-Paissu will honor us all, and Iakinthu will bring me something wonderful from the other side of the world." She smiled. "As wonderful as my gryphon."

"I will indeed," Iakinthu said.

One Hundred Three sighed. He must have looked forward to our arrival, Iakinthu thought. A moment of excitement in his constrained life.

One Hundred Three's boy helped him to his feet. His guards lifted him onto his donkey, and the boy led him away at a dignified walk. They vanished into the forest.

Iakinthu stroked her fingers across the gryphon's great frilled skull. It lay on red deerskin, its four empty eye sockets staring over the water, looking toward some ancient time. The gryphon skull glowed in shades of red and brown and yellow, purest agate. Iakinthu wondered if Mother Moon had turned the skull to precious stone as a memorial to her gryphon companion or if jewels formed the bones of all the creatures who guarded the distant gold mines.

She wrapped the deerskin around the skull, tied it with a braided leather rope, and saw Aranthau and Rhenthizu pack it safely into the boat.

The People saddled their riding horses and loaded their pack animals and filled their drinking skins with the last of the night's wine. Iakinthu's companions stowed their own gear into the boat.

The People and the companions of Iakinthu faced each other to bid each other good-bye. Issiia stood with Celestial Wind, and Minnow-now-Paissu stood with Iakinthu. Paissu wore a new Idaean kilt, with a stripe of sea-purple, while Issiia stood arrayed in the dress of the People: trousers and dark tunic, her hair unbound and undressed.

Kilinkizu crossed the sand, every bit one of the People in her riding trousers. Her bright hair tangled loose down her back. She was taller than all the others. She glowed. She glittered with the gold of her jewelry. The beads of the headdress touched with a sound like spring rain, and the bracelets rang together like finger cymbals.

She stopped before Dragon Claws, who turned away, her face hard.

Ah, Iakinthu thought. She's told her friend of her decision.

Kilinkizu turned to Issiia, bent down, and kissed her forehead.

"I recognize you now," Celestial Wind said to Kilinkizu and, to Issiia and Paissu, "I would hardly recognize either of you!"

She opened a small pouch, stuck her finger in it, and brought out a blob of blue paint. She traced wavering blue lines across Issiia's forehead and patterns of chevrons on her cheeks.

"Now, you're one of us." Without a mirror, she striped her own face with strong certain lines.

She turned to Kilinkizu.

Kilinkizu bent her head, but instead of letting Celestial Wind paint her, she pulled off the gold headdress. She went down on one knee and arranged it on Issiia's dark curls.

"I belong to Fair Island now," Kilinkizu said.

A murmur of shock and surprise and disbelief passed through the People. Dragon Claws, who already knew Kilinkizu's decision, glowered at her. Issiia gazed at Kilinkizu with only the barest tremble of her lower lip. The little girl kissed Kilinkizu on the forehead.

You are glorious, my granddaughter, Iakinthu thought. Glorious, and brave.

"Will you see me next spring?" Issiia said.

"I'll come back with the companions of *Flying Fish* to fetch you," Kilinkizu said.

"Did I believe you'd prefer a rich, soft life?" Dragon Claws said to Kilinkizu, her voice tight with anger.

"Hush." Celestial Wind stopped the show of bad manners.

Kilinkizu took off the gold earrings and fastened them in Issiia's ears. She drew the gold bangles over her hands and slipped them onto Issiia's wrists, pushing them to her upper arms. She gave her the dagger of sky-iron.

She took off the clothes of the People and folded them on the sand, keeping only a sash. She tucked Bdarde's flute beneath it. She faced the People.

"I give all my wealth to Issiia, my sister," she said, "and I give her the name the People gave me, if she wishes it, Fire-from-Cold-Ashes, until she finds her own."

"Bring the horses," Celestial Wind said.

As the People strode up the beach toward the saddled horses, Paissu-who-was-Minnow moved from Iakinthu's side and took Issiia's hand. She pulled off her necklace, the leather thong strung through the ancient sealstone.

"Will you keep this for me?"

"Until next spring," Issiia said.

Paissu looped the thong around her neck.

The beach stones clattered as the People mounted their horses and herded up the pack ponies. Dragon Claws cantered down the beach leading three horses: a black, Minnow's gray Surefoot, and Kilinkizu's fine red horse. She handed the reins of the black to Celestial Wind. She scooped Issiia up roughly and set her astride Surefoot, who swiveled her ears. Insulted by the affront to her dignity, Issiia sat up straight. She had only ever ridden her donkey, but the donkey was notoriously difficult and sly. Surefoot struck Iakinthu as an honest steed.

Kilinkizu reached for the red horse's reins, to give the horse to Issiia. Dragon Claws snatched them back.

"The horse is yours!" she cried. "Only yours! I chose it for you. I bred it for you. I know its dam and—yes!—listen!—I know its sire. Only you may ever ride it."

She drew her knife and cut the red horse's throat.

Blood sprayed out, splashing Dragon Claws' hands and clothes, spattering Kilinkizu's bare skin, gushing full against Paissu's face. Paissu cried out, shocked despite herself, and stumbled back against Iakinthu.

The People's horses, used to the smell of blood in hunting and in raids, stood as still as Kilinkizu, who never moved when the red horse fell soundless at her feet. Its legs flailed, pumping in futile flight as its blood ran out and it died.

Celestial Wind climbed stiffly onto her horse and galloped up the beach without a backwards look. Dragon Claws flung a final ferocious glare at Kilinkizu, pivoted her horse roughly on its hind legs, and followed. Issiia's Surefoot took a step after its fellows, pulling at its reins. Issiia glanced back for a moment, then thumped her heels against the pony's sides. It sprang after Dragon Claws and Celestial Wind.

The People disappeared into the forest.

Even the sea fell silent. The gentle tide turned.

Kilinkizu sank to the ground beside the red horse, stroking its sleek shoulder.

"Iakinthu, Iakinthu," Paissu cried.

Iakinthu knelt beside her and held her, careless of the blood.

"I'm blind, my eyes—"

"It's the blood," Kilinkizu whispered.

"It's all right," Iakinthu said. "Cry, Paissu, your tears will wash the blood from your eyes."

Rhenthizu ran to the boat and grabbed up a sealed jug of water.

Iakinthu glanced at Aranthau. He nodded. Though he was as shocked and pale as everyone else, gray beneath his tanned skin, he set the companions to putting out the fires, gathering the last of their gear, pulling the boat down the wet sand to catch the retreating water. Steam and smoke swirled across the beach.

Iakinthu pulled the wax from the jug's stopper and poured water into her hand, wiping Paissu's face, splashing clean water into her eyes. She covered the spray of blood on Paissu's tunic with her cloak. She hugged the child, scooped her up gently, and set her in the boat among her companions. She gave Maranti a glance, silently requesting her help. Maranti nodded, pulled off her boat cloak, and handed it to Iakinthu.

Maranti and Rhenthizu stepped into the boat. Maranti sat beside Paissu, putting her arm around the little girl till her shocked stiffness dissolved and she leaned against Maranti. Rhenthizu sat facing them, chafing Paissu's fingers between his warm hard palms.

"Wait here in the sun," Iakinthu said. "We'll go to *Flying Fish* soon."

Iakinthu retraced her steps.

Alone on the shore, Kilinkizu crouched by the little red horse, silent and stoic, her face set. Iakinthu used the rest of the water in the jug to wipe blood from her face, from her breasts. She wrapped her in Maranti's boat cloak.

"Come with me, my dear."

"Such a waste," Kilinkizu said. "She was a sweet-natured creature. She would have carried Issiia well."

"Could you know this would happen?" Iakinthu said, meaning to comfort her friend.

"Do I know the People?" Kilinkizu said. With an edge of anger, she said, "Do I know Dragon Claws?" She sighed. "I told her—I thought she understood, as Issiia understood—about my sight..."

Iakinthu drew her to her feet. "It's time to go," she said.

"She died nameless. Must I leave her unburied?"

The red horse's blood lay dark and clotting on the sand. Kilinkizu slipped the bridle from the red horse's head and unfastened the cinch of its saddle, to leave its spirit free. Iakinthu strode to the edge of the forest and scooped up two handfuls of dark earth.

Together, she and Kilinkizu scattered the rich dirt across the red horse's cheek, its neck, its flanks.

"Let's leave this mainland shore."

Comforted by the ritual, however modest, Kilinkizu allowed Iakinthu to lead her to the boat. When she climbed in, Maranti touched her shoulder gently. Kilinkizu sat with her head bent, her bright hair knotted with blood, as the dark wool of the cloak soaked up the warmth of spring sunshine.

Aranthau handed Iakinthu into the boat, looked into her face, touched his fingertip to his tongue, and then to her cheek, brushing away a spot of blood. Leaving Paissu and Kilinkizu under Maranti's sympathetic gaze, Rhenthizu jumped out of the boat. He and Aranthau and Bdarde pushed the boat into the waves, splashed alongside, and jumped in. The companions rowed the boat toward *Flying Fish*.

"She was magnificent," Kilinkizu said. "Issiia is magnificent."

"She is," Iakinthu said. "But Dragon Claws is very angry."

"She has a great temper," Kilinkizu said. "Her anger rides on me."

"In the spring," Iakinthu said, "Issiia will ride to us as one of the People, in her golden headdress… And she will have taught them all how best to bathe."

Iakinthu sat on her camp stool in the airy stern shelter. Aranthau stood nearby, his hand on the steering oar, his gaze moving from sea to sail as *Flying Fish* moved along the water. Paissu sat on the deck near Iakinthu.

Kilinkizu finished writing the list of Paissu's gifts from the People. She laid it in the sunshine. When the ink had dried, she folded it, wrapped it in a piece of oiled silk, and tied it with a silk cord. Iakinthu lit a candle, sheltering the flame, dripped wax onto the knot, and impressed the seal of her gryphon on it.

She handed the list to Paissu. "This represents your belongings. Keep it safe."

"I would remember," Paissu said.

"I know," Iakinthu said. "The list is proof."

"Would anyone doubt my word?" Paissu asked. "I'd have to challenge her."

"With a list, would you have to offer a challenge? A list is easier."

Paissu doubtfully took the sealed list and tucked it into the pocket of her kilt.

Iakinthu dictated to Kilinkizu. "To my given child, Kilinkizu, who has the place of granddaughter: Welcome to my family. You will always have a place at Old Farm, at Olive Farm, on *Flying Fish*. This is the promise of Iakinthu Gephyra, of Fair Island."

Kilinkizu set the page aside to dry.

"Should anything happen," Iakinthu said, "if I'm gone—"

"Must I think about a time when you're gone?"

Iakinthu acceded to Kilinkizu's wish, tied the parcel up, and sealed it.

"Thank you," Kilinkizu said.

"Thank you," Paissu said, properly, if a few minutes late.

"You're welcome," Iakinthu said to them both. "And you are welcome among the companions of *Flying Fish*." She smiled at Paissu. "Little Paissu, would you ask the companions to gather here with me?"

"Yes, Gephyra." Paissu ran off to do her bidding.

When she had gone, Iakinthu regarded Kilinkizu fondly.

"I'm glad you stayed."

"They have One Hundred Three. He'll teach his boy well, and the boy, who can stop fearing me, will be One Hundred Four. Do I have any more to learn from them? Do they have anything to learn from me?"

"Perhaps the knowledge of Hind," Iakinthu said.

"One Hundred Three would like it, but does he need it? He counts things. That's what the People need." She shrugged. "Iakinthu, I honor your knowledge, I have knowledge the Idaeans need. From Hind. And..."

Sunlight, glinting from the water, painted her face.

"About the northerners," Iakinthu said. "About the pirates." I'll listen to her, Iakinthu said to herself, but she wishes to persuade me that I have more to fear from them than they have to fear from me. Can I ever believe that?

"Yes."

"You may always tell me anything you think I should know," Iakinthu said.

Kilinkizu took her hand, squeezed it, and held it to her breast. *Flying Fish* pressed on through the gentle sea, its sails set. Iakinthu laid her hand on Kilinkizu's cheek.

She put aside her concern for her friend, her worry for her fear. The sea always held pirates; Idaea held them in check. The foolish men—they were always men, as Kilinkizu said—ventured unready into the sea and burned their quartz-colored northern skin to an ugly shiny pink. They worked harder and put themselves in more danger and received less in return for their efforts than if they had presented themselves at any town, on Idaea or Fair Island, and asked for work, at any farm and asked for help and food and occupation. They lived without homes. She pitied them.

Chapter Eight

High on the mast, standing on the yardarm, Aranthau whistled shrilly. Iakinthu responded to the signal, leaving the stern shelter and shading her eyes to look up.

"A ship," he said. He gazed out at the horizon. Suddenly Paissu was beside him. Iakinthu took a moment to be pleased by Paissu's audacity and balance.

She'll learn to ride *Flying Fish*, Iakinthu thought, and then she'll learn to dance with bulls.

"I see *Dolphin*," Aranthau said. "Who could mistake it?"

Siurthi, *Dolphin*'s owner and captain, painted the sides of her ship with striped dolphins, their eyes an unnatural blue, an evil eye to drive away witches. As Iakinthu saw no evidence of witches, she found the choice of blue dolphin eyes unappealing. But she could look the painted dolphins in the eye, while other people looked away, as they looked away from Kilinkizu's lapis-lazuli eyes.

"We'll greet our friends," Iakinthu said. "Perhaps we'll sail in company."

Aranthau called out a few words; in a moment, the companions heeled *Flying Fish* around to glide toward the friendly ship. They looked forward to seeing old acquaintances, to exchanging news, to hearing of the profits of *Dolphin*'s voyage.

Dolphin might take Maranti home, Iakinthu thought, while *Flying Fish* sails on to the Sunset Sea. We would have the gift of extra days of sailing, of crossing the Sunset Sea before its great storms begin.

She moved to the bow and soon saw *Dolphin* rise up from the horizon. She watched for Siurthi, who might climb the mast like Aranthau. Spray touched her face and misted in her long black curls. *Flying Fish* twisted its bow wave into a skein of spume.

Above, Aranthau gazed steadily toward the approaching ship. A small shadow without a thought to her precarious position, Paissu mimicked him.

"Someone strange has the handling of *Dolphin*," Aranthau called.

Iakinthu drenched a flare of concern. "*Dolphin*'s companions would call Siurthi when they saw us."

"They would."

Iakinthu alerted the companions of *Flying Fish*. Everyone free of handling the ship gathered near her, carrying their spears, their bows, their shields and swords. Bdarde the musician, carrying two spears, offered one to Iakinthu. Iakinthu accepted it and wished Bdarde held only her lute.

"Arrows, be ready to climb the mast," Iakinthu said. "Spears, stay in the bow. Swords, below the gunnel. We want surprise."

The companions dispersed. The spear-carriers clustered in the bow, their weapons out of sight, so *Flying Fish* looked like any ship about to meet an old friend, ready to welcome its companions and break open jugs of wine.

Iakinthu gestured for Paissu to return to the deck. Paissu complied. Aranthau followed, crossed the deck to the steering oar, and heeled *Flying Fish* toward *Dolphin*.

Iakinthu gathered Paissu to her side and led her to Maranti.

"Paissu, take Eldest Daughter below and watch out for her."

"I will, Iakinthu Gephyra," Paissu said, folding her hand around the hilt of her sky-iron knife.

"The companions of *Dolphin* are valiant," Maranti said. "Could they ever fall to pirates? This must have another explanation."

"I hope so," Iakinthu said. "Maranti — Eldest Daughter — please go below."

Instead of claiming a right to fight alongside her friends as Maranti would have done, the Eldest Daughter gathered her pride around her and allowed Paissu to lead her away.

The pirates seldom attacked Idaean ships, preferring the easier targets of coastal boats. But *Dolphin* would be a rich prize, a temptation that might overcome the pirates' fear.

Flying Fish, the faster craft, approached. Iakinthu had a clear view of *Dolphin*; her aging sight revealed details that she would have missed as a younger woman. She saw what Aranthau had seen: *Dolphin* swam clumsily. Its companions, standing along its side rail, remained eerily still, moving only to sway with the motion of the ship.

As *Flying Fish* approached, *Dolphin* abruptly raised every sail. Its speed increased and it jibed awkwardly from the convergent course.

Pale northern men came out of hiding.

"Is it the pirates?" Kilinkizu squinted toward the fleeing ship. She clutched at Iakinthu's spear-hand. Wincing, Iakinthu placed her free hand over Kilinkizu's fingers, soothing her, causing her to ease the pressure.

"They've taken our friends," Iakinthu said, her voice dull with grief. "They hoped to surprise us, too. They lost their surprise thanks to Aranthau. Their only chance is to flee."

The pirates had made a poor choice. *Flying Fish* gave chase. Before Sister Sun had traveled a handsbreadth farther across the sky, *Flying Fish* plunged within arrow-shot of *Dolphin*. The companions mirrored the dread and anger Iakinthu felt. They lined the railing; they climbed the rigging for a better vantage point. They nocked their arrows.

"Arrows, hold," Iakinthu said. "Until we're certain..."

Kilinkizu leaned over the rail, peering shortsightedly, her gaze intense, her cheeks smudged with the blurred blue chevrons of the People.

"They're dead," she said, her voice harsh. "The northerners use the bodies of their victims as shields, as concealment. Iakinthu Gephyra, I'm sorry, they're gone."

"Can you see—?"

"I know the northerners."

"Then they must follow the companions of *Dolphin*."

Flying Fish closed the distance. Rhenthizu rode the bow like a bull dancer, swinging a grappling hook. It bit into *Dolphin*'s sail, ripped through it, and caught in the rigging. Rhenthizu flung another, and a third.

Aranthau maneuvered *Flying Fish* to pull *Dolphin* off its course. The ripped sails flapped in the wind. The grappling lines sprang taut with a twang like a great untuned musical instrument.

"Arrows in flight," Iakinthu said.

The companions loosed their arrows across the deck of *Dolphin*, finding their marks, ignoring the arrows the pirates sent back.

Flying Fish possessed the advantage, kept it, and used it. Its bow touched the flank of *Dolphin* with a rumbling thud like the beginning of an earthquake, then the grinding cry of planks shrieking past each other. The mast of *Dolphin* swayed and shuddered and whipped, flinging men screaming into the sea.

The skein of the wakes combined, roiled, diminished to threads.

The companions of *Flying Fish* leaped over the rails with swords and spears, shouting, overwhelming the smaller ship and the pirates who had taken it.

Her spear poised, Iakinthu joined them.

Dolphin, nearly as familiar to Iakinthu as *Flying Fish*, had become foreign and eerie with a grotesque ritual of death. The dead companions of

Dolphin stood braced and tied against the rail, stripped of any adornment except necklaces of blood. The pirates had cut their throats.

Iakinthu clenched her jaw against the reek.

I've smelled death before, she thought. But so *much* death...

Death surrounded her: the deaths of her friends on *Dolphin* and the deaths of the pirates. The companions of *Flying Fish* sat on the deck, exhausted and bloody from the frenzy of their attack.

The companions of *Dolphin* had died by cruelty, while the pirates died by just dispatch. The companions of *Dolphin*, her friends, had died by murder, more horrible even than war. The companions of *Dolphin* stood limp, braced, tied to the railing, forced upright with staves and crosspieces and their own broken spears. The horror on their faces blurred through her tears. Their blood ran down their breasts. Her old friend Siurthi hung limp, her head held up by her hair, tangled and knotted around a spear-shaft. When the ship rolled, the terrible wound in her throat opened.

Iakinthu moaned. Aranthau put his arm around her. She leaned against him, glad to borrow his strength. She put her hands on her head, grieving.

The two ships, bound together, rode quietly on the gentle sea.

Iakinthu gripped Aranthau's hand, then collected herself.

Together, they moved cautiously among the bodies of the pirates, tumbled broken on the deck. The pirates had wasted the lives of Iakinthu's colleagues at the cost of their own. The companions of *Flying Fish*, in a fury, had killed them all. The stench of their deaths filled the air. They were pirates, uncivilized murderers. They had abandoned the responsibility of being human, if they had ever had it.

Her companions, silent, drained by the killing madness, wrestled the bodies of the pirates over the side, sending them to be food for sharks.

Buckets of sea water sluiced the deck clean. Iakinthu and Aranthau unbound Siurthi and laid her body in the shade of the stern shelter. Iakinthu, too, had let herself be possessed, and now paid a price of grief and exhaustion. She plunged her hands into a bucket of sea water to wash away the pirates' blood.

Tears blurred her vision. Such a waste, she thought. We must bury the companions of *Dolphin* properly and come back for their bones.

"An island?" she asked Aranthau.

"Nearby," he said, understanding her question.

They put Siurthi in the proper position, arms against her body, knees pulled up. Aranthau stroked her hair clumsily, blinded by tears.

"Ah, Siurthi," he whispered. "Ah, Siurthi," over and over again.

"Iakinthu!" Rhenthizu's voice held distress, urgency.

She hurried forward beyond the mast, to the bow.

Rhenthizu crouched, chest and arms brown with drying blood, the blood of pirates. Tears cut streaks through the blood on his face, and fresh blood surrounded him. For a moment she feared he was wounded.

"Iakinthu—"

Bdarde the musician lay with her life spreading out around her from the stab to her belly. Rhenthizu tried to stop the bleeding, his hands red.

Iakinthu thought, She's gone, my sweet lute player.

Bdarde opened her eyes. She gazed at Rhenthizu.

"Everything will be all right," he said. "Iakinthu knows what to do."

Bdarde searched Iakinthu out. "Iakinthu, please, cure me with your lavender salve." She closed her eyes again.

Iakinthu knelt beside her. "I will, my dear."

But she feared she had heard Bdarde's final words.

"Will you ask Kilinkizu—" Iakinthu looked up, looked around, searching for her friend. "Where is she? Where is Kilinkizu?"

"To me," Aranthau said, gathering several of the companions. They disappeared belowdecks to search the ship.

"Stay with Bdarde." Iakinthu said to Rhenthizu. She gestured to another of her companions. "Send for my lavender and poppy." She hurried after Aranthau into the dim interior of *Dolphin*.

Shadows moved around her. Aranthau raised his hand and everyone stopped, listening.

A whimper, quickly silenced. Iakinthu tried to make herself believe it was the boat snake catching a rat.

Aranthau stopped short. Iakinthu pushed her way through the companions.

In the hold, one of the pirate men pressed himself against bolts of white linen. Trapped, he held a dagger in one hand and rested the other on the shoulder of a boy.

Kilinkizu stood before them, her spear ready. But the man held the boy in the path of the spear.

"Come forward," Kilinkizu said, "and your death is quick." She spoke the trade language, the common language of all the coastal people and all the traders who visited them.

The pirate understood. He laughed at her. He was a northerner, his skin and hair and eyes very pale, shades of gray in the dim light. He wore a stained leather tunic that concealed his body instead of celebrating it.

Iakinthu looked at the boy, expecting him to be one of Siurthi's, surprised to find that he was a northerner, dressed up in child's armor, a barrier between the pirate and the spear of Kilinkizu. The boy held his head high and thrust out his skinny chest, presenting himself as shield and protector.

Kilinkizu spoke again, using the harsh northern language.

The pirate laughed again. "He's mine," he said in the trade language, using the word an Idaean would use for ownership instead of affinity or kinship. "His father has others. He gets more every year. Can this one go home before he's distinguished himself in my eyes? It's his pride and his duty to serve me." The northerner stroked Kilinkizu's body with his gaze, as boldly as a lover. "As it should be yours." He stared at her in the dimness. "I know you," he said.

A blush rose from Kilinkizu's breasts, climbing toward her face.

The northerner laughed at her a third time.

Kilinkizu cried out in anguish. Gracelessly, she thrust the spear.

The northern man's shocked scream collapsed into wet gagging as the spear fell away and his blood sprayed from his neck. The boy turned toward him in horror. The pirate collapsed to his knees. The motion of his body pushed the boy away. Kilinkizu pulled the boy to her, ignoring the blood that splashed his face, his shoulder, his back. The pirate collapsed onto the deck, gurgling his last few breaths.

Kilinkizu bent down to look the boy in the eyes.

"Do *you* know me?" she asked.

He tried to draw away, but she held him, ignoring the blood that smeared her hands.

"I am your mother," she said.

"I belong to my father!" he shouted.

"You belong to me," Kilinkizu said. "I won you, and I've taken you."

The boy shouted at her.

"What did he say?" Iakinthu asked.

"He said, 'Am I afraid to die?'"

"Better if he were," Iakinthu said. She nodded at the pirate's body and said to her companions, "Over the side with him, and mop up his blood before it stains Siurthi's cargo."

She left the scene of death behind, hurrying to attend to Bdarde.

A swift could circle Kunusu in the time Iakinthu had left Bdarde, but even in that short time the lutenist had faded. Iakinthu's basket of medicines hunkered on the deck beside her. Iakinthu knelt and drew out a pot of lavender salve. Rhenthizu held a vial of poppy extract to Bdarde's lips. The tincture dribbled from the corner of her mouth.

The extract would be wasted. Can she swallow? Iakinthu said to herself. Does she still breathe?

She did; she shivered, she moaned, and the wound continued its slow bleed.

"Rhenthizu, find me a burning brand or a coal."

He set down the vial, leaped up, took two running steps, and jumped from *Dolphin* to *Flying Fish,* where he could find a banked fire without a search.

The salve would sting viciously before giving relief. Instead of applying it, Iakinthu found her pipe, its bowl shaped like a poppy seed-head, and a package of dried poppy sap. By the time she had arranged the sticky ball in the bowl of the pipe, Rhenthizu returned with a smoking coal in fire-tongs. He lit her pipe as she inhaled deeply. The sap melted and smoked. When the smoke reached its potency, Iakinthu breathed it into Bdarde's nose and mouth.

She does breathe, Iakinthu thought, as Bdarde's shivering eased. Iakinthu sucked on the pipe again, growing dizzy, and kissed her young musician with smoke to give her more relief. Bdarde's eyelids flickered.

Can there be hope? Iakinthu asked herself; but she smelled the stink of a wound that would fester, a wound puncturing the victim's bowels. Even the Sheng, who claimed medical ability approaching the magical, shrugged at such wounds, gave the victims to their apprentices, and left the apprentices to watch the victims die.

Iakinthu took apprentices only as dancers.

Iakinthu gave the poppy to Rhenthizu, too dizzy to continue the treatment herself. He hesitated a moment, then sucked at the pipestem. He coughed violently.

"Keep the smoke in your mouth," Iakinthu said.

He tried again; he breathed smoke from his mouth into Bdarde's.

Knowing her work to be futile, Iakinthu gently spread lavender salve across the wound, pushing it open so the medicine would penetrate. Bdarde lay still, her breath and pulse shallow.

"Will we take her back to *Flying Fish?*" Rhenthizu asked.

"She might wake if we move her. Would you fetch her bedroll?"

Rhenthizu touched his fist to his forehead. This time when he returned to *Flying Fish* to do Iakinthu's bidding, he moved slowly, carefully, dreamily.

He passed Kilinkizu, who dipped and poured bucket after bucket of sea water over herself and the boy. Blue paint and blood mixed and ran down her breasts, down her legs, along the seams of the planks. The boy crouched, hiding his face, flinching as the water soaked him.

His mother? Iakinthu thought. Could it be? Or did Kilinkizu mean she claimed a boy from the northerners to replace the boy—or the girl—they had taken from her?

Rhenthizu returned with blanket and sheepskin. Iakinthu turned her attention from her numerator to her lutenist.

In the night's deepest darkness, Bdarde burned with fever. Lantern glow bathed her sweating face as Iakinthu bathed her with fresh water, stroking back her hair.

Bdarde moaned. She gazed wide-eyed around her, watching phantoms. Iakinthu drew the poppy back to light and bent to kiss the smoke into Bdarde's mouth. As they touched, Bdarde flailed and shuddered and cried out and vomited. The sour vomit splashed her face, her blanket, Iakinthu's hands and lips and kilt. Iakinthu gagged and spat and turned Bdarde on her side so the vomit flowed from her mouth instead of into her lungs.

Bdarde moaned when Iakinthu moved her. She tried to speak, she failed, she shuddered and vomited again.

Iakinthu wiped the vomit from Bdarde's skin and from her own. Tears blurred her sight.

Rhenthizu brought a bucket of salt water to wash the deck, Maranti brought a clean blanket, and Paissu brought a bowl to catch the vomit. The girl stood nearby, waiting, watching, sad.

She's seen her People die this way, Iakinthu thought as she rinsed the cloth and wrung it out and poured on it a few drops of lavender oil. The People must fight to keep their wild places, to maintain their ferocious reputation. Iakinthu thought of gentle Issiia, riding bravely alone among them as their given child. She felt a moment's spark of anger at Kilinkizu for leaving her behind, among strangers, and then she thought: But here is my dear Bdarde, dying, and any of us might have died at the hands of the northerners, like all the companions of *Dolphin*. Even Issiia, if she were with us.

She wiped Bdarde's face again, glad of the lavender scent that cut through the rising stench of death.

As the night passed, Bdarde's friends came to kneel beside her, to whisper to her, to leave beloved trinkets tied in scraps of cloth, to part from her, crying.

Iakinthu sat with Bdarde all the night. The lavender salve failed to cure her wound; the poppy brought on racking bouts of vomiting instead of easing her pain. The lavender oil wafted through the air, and vanished.

At dawn, Bdarde opened her eyes to the first light of Sister Sun. In a moment of clarity, she grasped Iakinthu's hand.

"Will Sister Sun want another musician?" she whispered. "Will Mother Moon, in the next life?"

"They'll argue over you, my dear," Iakinthu said.

Bdarde tried to smile. Her lips were cracked, her face flushed with fever. "But I like this life," she cried.

This life flowed from her; her hand slipped from Iakinthu's; she died.

The companions keened and cried for Bdarde. Iakinthu's sorrow blended with the other voices, high-pitched, wordless.

When the keening diminished, dispersed, and faded, only the sea broke the silence. Sister Sun broke over the horizon, her scarlet light covering the world as if with blood.

Iakinthu rose, stiff from her long vigil. Rhenthizu offered her his hand. She took it gratefully and let him help her to her feet. She resisted the urge to pat him as if he were still a boy. He was a young man now, graced with a certain reserve.

"I thought she'd be all right," he whispered, his voice hoarse. "I thought—the blood stopped, so I thought—"

The blood stopped, but the wound remained, penetrating Bdarde's body, beyond the reach of Iakinthu's salve.

Grief made Iakinthu weary.

"She died bravely," Kilinkizu said, her voice as rough as Rhenthizu's. "Her death had meaning."

"Oh, foolishness!" Iakinthu cried. "Is that what the People believe? Is that what the pirates believe? The pirates wasted her life. She should have died an old woman, at home, in her bed. She should have died singing in an old woman's voice. She should have died teaching her grandchildren her poems and her songs."

Too angry to say more, she strode away.

Rhenthizu remained beside Bdarde's body.

Bdarde, he thought, how is this possible, that you were alive and smiling and singing when the sun rose yesterday, but now, at today's sunrise, you're gone?

Rhenthizu closed Bdarde's eyes. He washed her body; he smoothed her hair as best he could, for it was still short and rough, growing out from the shaving of her child-locks a year ago. He nestled her arms against her belly and drew her knees against her chest.

He stood abruptly. His knees trembled. He stumbled. Blood streaked his loincloth. He unwrapped it and pulled it off. Like the other companions, he worked naked until he had time to wash.

Iakinthu descended into the eerie silence of *Dolphin*'s lower decks and thence to the hold, looking for oil and herbs and cloth for shrouds.

Unlike the Egyptians, who would beggar their families and their companions for their own afterlives, Idaeans wished for only a few possessions to take with them into the next life. They took pride in setting off to make their own way. They left the wealth of their first lives behind them.

Would I send my friends off in rags or naked? Iakinthu thought.

Bolts of Egyptian linen, flat ingots of Kyprian copper, and jars of rock oil filled the holds. Most of the Idaean wool from Siurthi's family's farm had gone in trade for the Egyptian and Kyprian goods. But finally, in a single compartment, Iakinthu found what little remained of *Dolphin*'s original cargo: a few jars of wine and olive oil, flagons of herbed oil and perfume, bolts of finely woven white Idaean wool.

What would the pirates have done with white linen or white wool? Iakinthu thought angrily.

She tried to pick up a bolt of woolen cloth and found herself unable to lift it. When she had been a dancer she could have carried it, thrown it, juggled it. Frustration and anger combined with her grief, and she burst into tears again, holding her hands to her head and wailing.

"Iakinthu," Aranthau said softly. He appeared beside her in the gloom and put his arms around her. "My dear Iakinthu." They stood together, her tears falling onto his chest, his dampening her hair.

Together, they carried the bolt of cloth to the deck, where the companions of *Flying Fish* attended the bodies of the companions of *Dolphin*, preparing them for burial.

The ships lay in peace, sails lowered in the light air, motionless on the quiet sea. Iakinthu raised her head, turning her face toward Sister Sun, who sank toward the horizon through the clear sky. She was intensely weary, as if the marrow had been sucked from her bones by invisible creatures. She had never believed in such demons, but she understood why people might think they existed.

How else could one become so tired in so short a time? she thought.

Sister Sun passed below the horizon without Iakinthu's taking note of her setting. Mother Moon, on her journey from fullness to wisdom, still lay beneath the sea.

It's always this way, Iakinthu thought. Such a short time. A few spans of the sun across the sky, and Siurthi-who-was-here is gone. Bdarde-who-was is gone.

She sat crosslegged on the deck. The reek of tar mixed with the soothing salt tang of the sea breeze and with the soft scent of lavender oil. The odor of death had been washed away. A few hours remained before corruption's odor became noticeable. The bodies must have a proper first burial. Iakinthu drew a deep breath, seeking balance, seeking her center. And when she released her breath, she burst into tears.

Her grief for Bdarde and Siurthi and the companions of *Dolphin* flowed out of her in a keening wail.

"Iakinthu, Iakinthu," Paissu whispered. The child crouched beside her, embracing her, patting her hair, her shoulders, with small warm hands.

Maranti appeared as silently, as unexpectedly, as Paissu, and knelt beside her, in her fine linen, on the damp deck. "Sister."

Aranthau hurried to her side. The child and the Eldest Daughter and her lover held her, honoring her grief, tears flowing with hers. Maranti's rose perfume enveloped them all. Maranti opened a vial of Egyptian glass and poured its whole contents of rose and myrrh onto Bdarde's shroud. Iakinthu laid her face against Maranti's shoulder and cried.

Chapter Nine

Iakinthu crewed *Dolphin* with companions of *Flying Fish* who had planned to travel only to and from the gathering with the People. They would return *Dolphin* to Siurthi's family on Idaea, and her family would grieve, and honor them with gifts from *Dolphin*'s trading venture, and divide the cargo among the families of the ship's companions.

Dolphin sailed around the burial island into the day, its decks washed clean. The ship skimmed the sea as its companions, dressed in loincloths or kilts soaked free of blood, tested its mettle.

Iakinthu watched as it gathered itself, as its sails filled, as it made way with increasing steadiness.

She wished Maranti were on board *Dolphin*; she wished it were already on its way home to Idaea. But she had been too exhausted to insist that the Eldest Daughter give up her last little time with Rhenthizu before the ships parted for months, for a year. *Dolphin* would return to *Flying Fish* and the companions of both ships would say their farewells; *Flying Fish* would pay its respects to Eldest Daughter and *Dolphin* would receive her.

Iakinthu dozed.

A shadow passed over Iakinthu's face. She kept her eyes closed, wishing it would go away and let her sleep in the sun. It remained, and she slitted her eyelids. Kilinkizu stood before her, holding the hand of the boy she had saved. Kilinkizu had washed his face and replaced his bloodstained toy armor with a clean Idaean kilt. He stood with his head down and his shoulders hunched.

Kilinkizu brushed her fist against her forehead.

"Please forgive me," she said.

"I will," Iakinthu said. "Tell me about this one."

"He's my son," Kilinkizu said.

"I'm the son of my father," the boy said.

Kilinkizu had used the word for kinship, Iakinthu realized with surprise. "Your born son."

"Yes. My born son."

"How did you recognize him?"

"I knew…his trainer. The man I killed. From before. Iakinthu, look at him. He's mine."

Iakinthu looked the boy up and down. The boy's hair had an auburn cast. The hold had been too dim for her to see the color of his eyes or the shape of his face.

"Look at me," she said, using the trade language.

He continued to glare at the deck, and his hunched shoulders tightened.

"Does he understand?"

"He does," Kilinkizu said. She spoke to him sharply. He snarled a reply, his young voice made ugly by the tone.

"He left his manners behind in the hold," Rhenthizu said, from the shade of the stern shelter. "Or his bravery."

The taunt made the boy look up angrily. He did have lapis lazuli eyes like Kilinkizu's, but what did that mean for a northern boy? The northerners tended to have blue eyes, along with skin the color of red chalcedony.

He understands enough to know an insult, Iakinthu thought.

Then he squinted at her, shortsighted, and she saw Kilinkizu's face reflected in the boy's.

"Is he brave enough to approach me?" Iakinthu said, following Rhenthizu's lead.

The boy stood still.

Kilinkizu wishes to give him a chance to behave in a civilized fashion, Iakinthu thought. Will he make her proud, or will he embarrass her?

Kilinkizu's consideration for the boy stretched on far too long. Rhenthizu rose easily from the deck, took the boy by the scruff of the neck, and guided him forward. He tried to keep a straight face when the boy resisted.

Iakinthu remembered Rhenthizu when first she met him. He had been a beaten, frightened, starved little boy, and though Iakinthu had been barely a head taller than he before he got his growth, he had been terrified of her. Even terrified, he had been more civilized than Kilinkizu's son.

"She'll show you kindness," Rhenthizu said softly.

"I want—" The boy stopped, struggling to say what he wished in the trade language. "What do I need with kindness?" His voice was shrill. "How will I be a man, with kindness?"

"I see you've had a bath, with good soap and fresh water," Iakinthu said. "On a sailing ship, that's a considerable kindness. Man or boy, would you rather be dirty and uncomfortable?"

"What do I need with comfort? Do you want me to smell like—" His last few words, in his own language, were incomprehensible.

Only Kilinkizu understood what he said. She spoke sharply again, and again received only a snarl. When Iakinthu glanced at her expectantly, she looked away.

"He's my son, but he speaks obscenities, ignorantly copying the northern men. Must I translate?"

"I hope you will."

She blushed, hesitated, and spoke. "He said, 'Do you want me to smell like a perfumed whore?'"

"You're too young," Iakinthu said to the boy. "Too young for perfume and too young to choose to be a courtesan."

She gazed at him; she glanced up at Kilinkizu.

"What do we call him?"

"They named him after they took him from me," Kilinkizu said.

"Would I tell my name to a stranger? To a *woman?*" the boy said.

"Do I care what your name was?" Iakinthu replied. "Among us, you're Bdarde-who-is."

Startled, Rhenthizu said, "Why? Bdarde-who-was lies unburied—"

"You've lived with us in times of peace," Iakinthu said to Rhenthizu. "This is a custom of war. To carry on her name."

"Her name?" the boy shouted. "Are you giving me a woman's name? Are you sending me back to the women? You should have killed me with the warriors!"

"Hush," Kilinkizu whispered. "Hush."

"We honor you," Iakinthu said. "It's up to you whether you deserve the honor." She sighed, intensely weary. "He must stay out from underfoot," she said to Kilinkizu. "But if you want him, you may keep him."

In a cleft of a tiny waterless island's steep cliffside, the companions of *Flying Fish* performed the first burial for Bdarde-who-was and for the companions of *Dolphin*. The cleft hid the bodies from pirates, from the northerners.

And what would they steal? Iakinthu thought, as she nestled the small offerings from the friends of Bdarde-who-was into her shroud. I suppose they might defile the bodies.

She assured herself that they would miss this islet; it lacked water, game, shoals for fish or shore for shellfish, or any harbor better than the island's lee side.

When *Flying Fish* returned from its voyage, it would stop here again and retrieve the bare bones. Iakinthu would return the bones to their families for a proper final burial. She sighed. She had done it before; she could do it again.

Goodbye, my friends, she thought.

Rhenthizu rowed the ship's boat to *Flying Fish* from the deserted burial island. Dust covered him; bird droppings smeared his bare feet. His passengers were equally dusty and dirty, but they had done their duty to their friend and to the companions of *Dolphin*.

Rhenthizu threw a line from the ship's boat to the deck of *Flying Fish*, then let himself fall backward into the deep clear water. The dust and dirt and guano flowed from his body. The others climbed up the side of *Flying Fish*, leaving one person to row back to the island for the last few companions.

Few Idaeans swam. Rhenthizu had taught Bdarde-who-was to swim, when they were children. Until the last year when she, a young woman, avoided him, still a boy, they had often swum together, wading out from shore or diving from her little fishing boat.

He rose to take a breath. His tears were warmer than the sea water and less salty. He submerged again to wash them away, then kicked to the surface and floated. The gentle swells lifted him, lowered him. When he was a child, on the shore below his village, he swam in frigid water, rougher waves. Everyone swam. If his little canoe capsized, he splashed into the sea and swam after it, pulled it to land, emptied it, and launched it again into the surf.

Fair Island drew him one direction, the shore of his village the other. Iakinthu's wishes claimed his loyalty, and Maranti's wishes claimed his desire.

What if I change my mind? he asked himself. I could go back to Idaea with *Dolphin*. With Maranti. Siurthi's family will share *Dolphin*'s cargo with those of us who retrieved it. I could take my place in Kunusu with my own wealth, a member of Iakinthu's family. I could go home to Fair Island.

What if I change my mind? he wondered again. Would Iakinthu be relieved, or disappointed?

What if Iakinthu changes her mind, after what's happened? Would I be disappointed?

She would answer him, if he asked.

He wondered, Do I want to know her answer?

Rhenthizu swam back to *Flying Fish* and clambered up the side. The others stood beneath the bathing spout, taking turns to wash, to pump clean sea water up on deck.

Maranti was among them.

Joy flashed through his grief and exhaustion and confusion. He climbed over the rail, took a step toward Maranti, then sat abruptly, embarrassed.

"May I have my loincloth?" he asked one of the companions, nodding toward the white linen hanging on the rail to dry.

"It's still wet," she said.

"And will be again."

She tossed it to him. He wrapped it around his hips, leaving aside the complicated folds and knots, and stood up again, covered, less embarrassed.

Maranti raised her arms above her head and lifted her face to the water. Her hair, unbound, tumbled in wet waves down the sleek curve of her back and buttocks.

He strode across the deck, swaggering a little, proud. He stepped into the cool salt stream of the pump and stopped behind Maranti, sliding his hands up her arms. She leaned against him, knowing his touch. Their bodies fitted together, warm within the splashing salt water. Rhenthizu entwined his left hand with hers and took the soap from her other hand. He rubbed it down her arm, across her shoulder and collarbone, over her breasts, raising little lather in the cold salt water. Wild rose scented her soap, like her perfume, wrapping her in a delicate fragrance that opened to include Rhenthizu and left all the other companions in the ordinary spray.

They walked hand in hand to the stern cabin. With a scrap of linen, he dried Maranti's back.

"The sun and the breeze are pleasant," she said. "I'll be dry soon."

"And itchy, if you leave the salt on your skin." He grinned at her. "Is this your first sea voyage?"

"I've been to Fair Island!"

"This *is* your first sea voyage."

He fetched an ewer of olive oil and an oil scraper. He warmed a palmful of oil between his hands and smoothed the warmed oil across her skin. Touching her aroused him. Speaking with her aroused him. Looking at her aroused him.

She smoothed oil onto his skin in turn, and he could hardly bear it.

She put on her kilt and vest; he arranged his damp loincloth.

"What are we going to do?" he said.

If she had an answer, Kilinkizu's filthy little boy interrupted her. Kilinkizu herded him on deck. She had insisted that he attend the burial.

"My father will catch you!" he shouted. "He'll catch you and kill you, kill you, kill you! The whole fleet is coming to enslave you, to—" he searched for a word and failed to find it "—defile you all, to kill you!"

Kilinkizu dropped to her knees beside him and embraced him, holding him firmly, gently, pinioning his flailing arms, ignoring his shrieks and his bare, kicking feet.

"I— I—" he shouted. He struggled for the words he wanted. Perhaps they existed only in his birth language, for he broke into ugly, incomprehensible gibberish and unraveled into rage.

Maranti hurried to Kilinkizu. Startled, Rhenthizu ran after her. Others of the companions had moved to help; Maranti could keep a proper distance from such uncivilized behavior.

He touched her arm to stop her, but she kept going. The other companions made way for her.

"It's easier with two," she said, shrugging him off. She knelt beside Kilinkizu and the boy. She put her arms around them both, stroking the boy's hair, whispering.

"Kill you!" Bdarde-who-is screamed. "Kill you and destroy your villages and, and, and, you'll serve him like you used to, like you should do!"

Maranti ignored this foolishness, but Kilinkizu shook with distress. Together, they soothed the boy to gasping cries. When he had exhausted himself and merely sobbed and sniveled, Kilinkizu gathered him into her arms, nodded gratefully to Maranti, and carried him to the bathing spout.

"My little cousin had tantrums at that age," Maranti said. She rubbed her ear. "How they can scream."

"You must go with them," Rhenthizu said, nodding after Kilinkizu.

Maranti raised an eyebrow, for few people gave orders to the Eldest Daughter, even during ordinary times when she was only Maranti. Rhenthizu looked at her and spread his hands in demonstration, explanation. She glanced down at her kilt, her hands and arms. She was smeared with dirt and snot.

"Back to the bathing spout," he said.

"Kilinkizu may want a little more help," she said. "Do children ever like baths?" She followed Kilinkizu to the pump, where the wild boy stared apprehensively at the dripping water—the pump had yet to begin spouting—and tried to twist from Kilinkizu's hands.

Maranti and Rhenthizu and Kilinkizu bathed him and themselves, and Maranti rubbed her clothes clean again. After a struggle when the water first gushed down on his head, the boy stood stiff and proud as if he were untouchable, even when his bathing ended and Kilinkizu shaved his tangled, unkempt hair with her sky-iron knife. She left the locks in the pattern of a much younger child. Everyone would know to expect very little of him. He began to look like a civilized person, and he cried tears of despair rather than fury.

Maranti returned to the stern shelter, wringing the water from her hair, clean again, unperturbed.

"Before I came to Fair Island," Rhenthizu said, "before I came to Iakinthu..." He fell silent as he rubbed her dry.

"Tell me, my dear."

He smoothed olive oil onto her skin again, to take away the salt.

"Would my owner caress me if I screamed?" Rhenthizu said. "He'd beat me."

"So you came to Iakinthu, and she took you to the Fair Island, where people are civilized," she said. "And know how to treat children."

Iakinthu stood in the bow. The day was so beautiful it cut through grief. *Flying Fish* waited for *Dolphin* to return through a calm sea with a light wind. The ships would meet; *Dolphin* would return Maranti to Kunusu, the harbor-on-land, to her proper place as Eldest Daughter.

Iakinthu would take Rhenthizu home.

"Will you walk with me?" Maranti said, coming up beside her.

"Of course." They walked together, hand in hand.

"When you asked if I would be Eldest Daughter," Maranti said, "you promised me an adventure."

"This trip should be enough adventure for anyone," Iakinthu said. "Did I promise to take you beyond the curve of the world?"

"That's something I'd like to see."

"We chose you to be Eldest Daughter at Kunusu."

"Kunusu can do without me until autumn."

"Will *Flying Fish* be back by harvest time?" Iakinthu said. "I've told you—!"

"I know," Maranti said. "But things have changed."

"Things change all the time."

"I want him, Iakinthu," Maranti said. "More than I've ever wanted anything in my life."

"More than being Eldest Daughter?"

"What's the point of being Eldest Daughter if I have to give up my dearest wish?"

"Oh, my dear," Iakinthu said. "That's exactly the point of being Eldest Daughter."

Iakinthu wondered if Maranti would stomp off along the deck, alone, like a fractious child, like Kilinkizu's Bdarde.

Instead, Maranti laughed. "You're right," she said. "I value your counsel. I have to honor my promises and my vows and my position and my predecessors."

She kissed Iakinthu lightly on the cheek.

"You are tickling my whiskers," Iakinthu said. "And my whiskers are tickling me back."

"Iakinthu! Would I behave like one of Pharaoh's advisers, saying one thing out of one side of my mouth and something entirely different out of the other? I've said I'll keep my promises, and I mean to do so."

From above, at her lookout post atop the mast, Paissu whistled.

"Aranthau! A ship, a ship!"

He strode back from the bow and climbed the mast, shading his eyes to follow her direction. Iakinthu wondered which Idaean ships had come out in this direction; Kilinkizu would know. She wondered where Kilinkizu was; most likely her numerator would be somewhere with her unpleasant little boy, no doubt trying to persuade him to eat some Idaean food to which he objected, or wear some clean Idaean clothing which he considered less than properly manly. She sighed.

Aranthau returned to the deck and joined Iakinthu.

"A black-sail ship," he said quietly. "The northerners."

Chapter Ten

Paissu remained at her lookout, gazing toward the black-sail ship. The northerners behaved in a sneaky way.

Can anyone ever trust them? she wondered and received her answer a moment later.

"Aranthau," she called.

He, and Iakinthu, looked up at her.

"Two more black-sail ships."

Aranthau climbed up beside her again. They stared toward the approaching vessels.

"Good work, little Paissu," Aranthau said. "No wonder they were able to overwhelm the companions of *Dolphin*."

~

From the deck of *Flying Fish*, the black-sail ships lay below the horizon. Iakinthu considered Aranthau's report.

"Will they follow us? Or *Dolphin*? Will they separate?"

"They believe *Dolphin* is under their control. They think it's returning to the mainland with a cargo of new wealth. *Flying Fish* is their quarry. Their plan is to cut us off from home."

"Can they catch *Flying Fish*?"

"The ships could, if they were well-handled. Their men are inexperienced."

To hear a ship's companions described as men struck Iakinthu as odd, but surely it was true of the northerners.

Aranthau paused, frowning. "If we turn back, they could capture us."

"Then we must forge ahead. Outsail them. By the time they give up, *Dolphin* will be safely distant."

And Eldest Daughter will be safely ahead of them, Iakinthu thought, with us, with Rhenthizu.

She sighed.

~

Far behind *Flying Fish*, the top of *Dolphin*'s sail had disappeared beneath the curve of the world. The black-sail ships ploughed ahead, dots on the horizon, falling behind. By morning, they would have lost *Flying Fish*.

Far ahead, the sun sank toward the sea. The blue of the sea darkened with the sky. The clouds turned white and gray and gleaming silver, then blazed briefly with the colors of fire. Sister Sun drew the curve over her face, and the sky changed color to deep sea-purple, studded with points of gold and silver, carnelian and lapis lazuli, while the sea turned deep blue, iron gray, the deep black of good red wine at night.

The companions separated into several groups, collecting in slightly different patterns now that their comrades had gone back to Idaea. Aranthau brought out a brazier and set it on deck near the stern cabin. He kindled a fire from last night's banked embers and settled down to wait for the firewood to burn to coals. The smoke perfumed the soft evening air. Along the deck, the three other braziers cupped fires that snapped and sparked against the darkness. The light of the flames gleamed on bare arms, bare legs, slow movements, quick movements to catch and crush a flying ember. They had time to cook a hot meal, but when night fell all the lights must be extinguished.

Grief penetrated her moment of peace. Iakinthu went to Aranthau and sat beside him, leaning against him, seeking his solid strength. He slipped his arm around her. They came together in an embrace and comforted each other in silence.

Rhenthizu went below, anxious to attend Maranti to her sleep. He wished she were safe back at Kunusu; he anticipated her touch. *Flying Fish* would surely evade the black-sail ships, but what other dangers were the companions sailing toward?

As he descended, his shaven hair prickled at his neck. He stopped at the bottom of the ladder, gazing into dimness. Faint shrouded light from the sleeping cabin's lantern wavered across the planks. He hesitated, reluctant to go deeper into the ship.

What do I fear? Rhenthizu asked himself. I should anticipate the comfort of sleeping with my companions, as I've always done.

Overcoming his unease, though still puzzled by it, he proceeded.

The sleeping cabin was clean and pleasant, inviting, with the pallets laid out on a low platform. Among her companions, Iakinthu sat in a nest of white linen and thick black woven wool. Aranthau combed her long hair, coiling it around his fingers. Aranthau seldom slept the night through when the ship was at sea, but he would nap beside her. Maranti whispered with Paissu, head to head, as if they both were children.

Rhenthizu threw himself on the pallet and lay sprawled next to his lover. He gave her a quick, uncertain smile. Maranti bent to kiss him and offered him her wine goblet. She smiled, and he thought, she has no fear, only anticipation.

He rose on his elbow, drank, and filled the goblet again. They shared it and gave Paissu a drinking bowl of water made safe with a few drops of the good wine.

Maranti raised a corner of the blanket for him to come in beside her. He moved nearer, if just for a moment, to kiss her again.

"It's my turn at steering soon," he said, and added softly, "but I'll come back to you when I can."

The peace of the sleeping deck ruptured. Kilinkizu strode in, ducking her head to avoid the lintel. The wild boy-child followed reluctantly, pulling back at her hand. He cried something in the unpleasant foreign language.

"Keep a civilized tongue," Kilinkizu said.

"I want my father!" the boy-child screamed.

No one knew what to do. A foreigner's rudeness could be ignored, but the child was Kilinkizu's, now an Idaean, and so they all had some responsibility for his upbringing.

"Where did a boy-child learn so many obscenities?" Iakinthu said without rancor. "The poor thing has been badly taught and led astray."

"I know it, Iakinthu Gephyra," Kilinkizu said, "and I hope you and all my other companions will help me teach him well, and kindly. He fears we'll beat him."

The idea was nearly as shocking as his obscenities.

"I—I—" The boy had such trouble with the language. "Do I fear beatings? Do I fear beatings by men? You are only a woman!"

Kilinkizu inclined her head. "I beg your pardon," she said. "He *thinks* we might beat him, men and women."

"Do Idaeans beat their children?" Iakinthu said. "Man or woman? You've heard untruths about us, I fear."

"My father said—"

"Hush, now, hush," Kilinkizu said, embarrassed, holding the boy-child close to muffle his foul language. He struggled against her, but she held him calmly, rocking back and forth, humming.

Rhenthizu understood his own reluctance to come below, to endure the misbegotten boy-child. He took Maranti's hand, putting the distant pirates out of his mind, ignoring the tangles of the boy-child, which had nearly unknotted.

"I should go back on deck." He almost said, Even the Eldest Daughter's chosen one must take his place at the steering oar. "Will you come with me?" he asked instead.

"Another night," she said. "I'm undressed already; I'm far too lazy to put my clothes back on."

She could wrap herself in her blanket or in her boat cloak; but she had declined his invitation.

Should I argue with the Eldest Daughter? he thought.

She kissed him and let him go so easily that he wondered if she had changed her mind. He bid goodnight to his companions and paused beside Iakinthu for an embrace.

"Goodnight, my dear given mother," he said.

"Goodnight, my dear given child."

Outside, the cool night air anointed him with the smell of salt. He stretched his arms and strode down the deck to take his place at the steering oar.

Rhenthizu enjoyed sailing at night, with the world so wide around him. The clear sky glowed with the Mother's Path of stars. He looked after her in the sky. He held the oar, watching the sails, keeping them full of wind as *Flying Fish* glided through the sea. A path of phosphorescence shone in the ship's wake.

They were long out of sight of land. The world curved before him, behind him, beneath him. Some of his companions had laid their bedding on the deck farther forward to sleep in the cool night air, but he was quite alone.

Iakinthu lay beneath her covers on the sleeping platform, the cool linen warming against her body, the thick woolen blanket a welcome soft weight. Most of her companions already lay snuggled together in the dry comfort of a calm voyage. Later on, in the rough wild Sunset Sea, or if bad weather caught them, they would be lucky to sleep at all, in damp bedding on sodden planks, drenched through working seams at every squall of rain or plunge of the ship into the waves.

Aranthau lay wide awake beside her, staring at the deck above. Ordinarily he slept easily and soundly and woke every little while to modify the course. Sometimes, in unfamiliar waters, near dangerous shoals or unknown islands, he would ask for the ship to stop; he would dive in and listen to the music of the sea.

Nearby, Paissu lay with the covers pulled halfway over her face, but she peered over the edge of the blanket, her dark eyes wide. The boy-child slept, inert with exhaustion. Kilinkizu lay with her arms around him, her eyes closed. Iakinthu doubted that she slept.

Everyone is too full of exhaustion, and grief, and horror, and anticipation, and even excitement, Iakinthu thought. Surely it would have been worse had we anchored overnight by the burial island. She dismissed the idea of ghosts and spirits, but many Idaeans of a more traditional outlook believed they hovered until their bones received a proper burial.

She glanced at Paissu and patted the blanket beside her. Paissu scrambled to huddle next to her.

"Idaeans can fight like People," Paissu whispered.

"We can if we must." She stroked the child's sleek dark hair. "You are valiant, I am so proud of you. Dragon Claws would be proud of you."

"I'm one of the People," Paissu said in a matter-of-fact way. "Would the pirates dare to attack the Eldest Daughter and Iakinthu Gephyra?"

They would indeed, Iakinthu thought. They would like nothing better. And I've brought Maranti into peril.

But in response to Paissu's assertion, Iakinthu kept her silence. Should I frighten children without reason? she thought. Could I make her safe by doing so? Besides, the size of *Flying Fish* and the reputation of my companions will give us all some protection.

"They would surely think again about it," Iakinthu said. "Can you sleep?"

Paissu cuddled against her. "Do you think Issiia is warm enough? She's used to being inside."

"I think she is," Iakinthu said. "We left her with the best Idaean cloak."

"Dragon Claws will give her furs from the giant northern creatures. They're so warm!"

"That's good." Iakinthu sighed. Tears caught in her throat.

Paissu patted her shoulder, then tried to stifle a yawn. Iakinthu managed to smile.

"Sleep now."

They dozed together until Aranthau threw off his covers and sighed. Iakinthu woke sleepily.

"Must you go?" she asked. "Rhenthizu knows *Flying Fish*. He can keep the course true."

"Of course he can." Aranthau's somber expression brightened with his smile. "Where will I be, when he knows everything?"

"You'll be my ship's dear captain," she said. "Could anyone else guide it as well as you?"

She gave him a quick kiss before he slipped away into the darkness, wrapping his loincloth as he went. She understood his moment of uneasiness; she shared it for herself at the same time that she felt it unworthy of either of them.

III
The Sunset Sea

Chapter Eleven

The Horns of the Ocean framed the portal to the Sunset Sea. *Flying Fish* eased toward the wide passage, riding the tide, steadied on wind and steering oar. To the north, the great rock loomed in dawn fog; the Southland, gleaming like gold, bounded the southern horizon.

The black-sail ships had fallen behind days ago, suspended between one lost quarry and another. Aranthau predicted fair weather; Rhenthizu trusted his storm sense but hoped a squall might drive the pirate ships onto a rocky shore.

Rhenthizu joined Aranthau in the stern, watching the older man intently.

"Rhenthizu," Aranthau said, "listen to the sea. Steer the ship."

Rhenthizu gripped the smooth wood of the steering oar. The sea pressed it, resisting. *Flying Fish* continued its certain path. Rhenthizu tested his strength, knowing the ocean could destroy him without a moment's warning. And yet he felt joy rather than fear, and the certainty that the sea would take him safely and surely where he wished to go. He guided the ship to keep the sail bellied out, to spin *Flying Fish* along the swell. The edge of the sail snapped in the wind, beating a rhythmic accompaniment.

In the bow, the companions of *Flying Fish* gazed with wonder at the looming cliff, the golden land. Rhenthizu felt dizzy. He released his breath in a rush and gasped in a new breath.

The coast opened on either side, stretching away north and south, leaving before them the open Sunset Sea. The ship flew beyond the Horns of the Ocean, free and light as a dancer.

The companions cheered, hugged each other, stretched down over the bow rails to catch the spray in their hands. Of the companions, only Iakinthu and Aranthau, and Rhenthizu when he was a child all unwilling, had sailed the Sunset Sea.

Iakinthu and Maranti sat together in the stern cabin, in the shade of the canopy, three sides rolled open, the fourth stopping the wind and spray. Iakinthu smiled softly at Aranthau and nodded with approval to

Rhenthizu. Maranti turned her dark, brilliant gaze on him. He grinned at her, proud and happy.

Maranti left the shelter of the cabin. She wore a kilt and short jacket, but had left her cloak behind. The wind gave a bright flush to her cheeks and whipped her hair from its simple arrangement. She was a companion of *Flying Fish* now, as well as Eldest Daughter. She ducked beneath his arm and hugged him around the waist.

"You've been here before," she said.

"I sailed from it," he said. "Across it, from it, to Idaea. Did I have any knowledge of where I was or what I was doing? I was too hungry and too frightened." He remembered the fear and the hunger, if not the Sunset Sea, and he shivered, thinking, Did I believe I'd survive that journey? Did I know what death is? Or life?

He pulled himself from his reverie and grinned at Maranti again. "This is better."

Aranthau stood nearby, his hands flat on the railings as if the ship's vibration spoke to him. Perhaps it did, mused Rhenthizu.

"Can you feel the difference?" Aranthau asked Rhenthizu.

Rhenthizu felt the power of water and wind as they connected through the steering oar. It felt exactly the same as before.

"What difference should I feel?" he asked.

"The size of the swells, the color of the water. How the ship floats, and the wind's knowledge that nothing will slow it for a quarter of the world."

Aranthau was transformed. Iakinthu's quiet lover took a deep breath of the sharp sea air and released it, laughing out loud. His hair curled wild around his face and shoulders. His power and joy wove together like a whirlwind.

Rhenthizu listened and watched in vain for the changes Aranthau described. Aranthau waited, his gaze quizzical.

"It's the same," Rhenthizu said reluctantly, sadly.

"Never mind," Aranthau said. "It takes time. You'll learn."

"Am I descended from a sea god?" Rhenthizu said, thinking, Did I believe it of Aranthau before? I believe it of him now.

"Have I ever claimed sea gods?" Aranthau said. He smiled, the lines at the corners of his eyes making deep crinkles. "Only sea people."

Aranthau left the steering oar in Rhenthizu's hands and called the others to him. Soon the companions of *Flying Fish* set to work. The sail furled. The ship slowed abruptly and lay adrift, pitching easily in the gray waves. With the help of two rowers, Rhenthizu kept *Flying Fish* heading into the swells. The companions replaced the lateen sail with a square rig, for the first time this voyage. The square sail would carry the ship before the wind.

"Maranti, my dear," Iakinthu said, "come sit by me, if you will." I'm glad, she thought, that Maranti's regard for Rhenthizu is more than infatuation. But someone must explain that she must let him fulfill his other responsibilities, his responsibilities to the ship.

Maranti returned to Iakinthu's side, staggering a little as *Flying Fish* pitched.

"When will the sea calm?" she asked.

"The new sail will steady the course," Iakinthu said. "But we have to prepare for rougher seas. Look—" She gestured toward Rhenthizu. His shoulders gleamed with sweat even in the breeze. "He needs the strength of his whole body to hold the ship."

"And I distract him?" Maranti said. She twined her fingers with Iakinthu's. "I understand. But Iakinthu, I should use my strength for the ship, too. Will Aranthau teach me the secrets of the ocean?"

Iakinthu found, to her astonishment, that Maranti's question made her deeply uneasy. The Eldest Daughter learn the craft of sailing and the art of reading the ocean that Aranthau practiced? Her responsibilities were to the earth, rather than to the sea.

"You must have something to do during the voyage," Iakinthu said reasonably, putting aside her qualms. She smiled. "Otherwise, you'll be dreadfully bored."

Aranthau climbed to the top of the mast and gazed into the distance, into the west.

"He loves the sea as he loves me," Iakinthu said. "He understands it as he understands my body."

The yard for the square rig rose; the companions sang a rhythmic song to aid their pulling.

"Can he rouse the wind and calm the waves, like a lover?" Maranti asked.

The yard was secure, the new sail ready. Aranthau called for a moment's rest.

"Sailing would be easier, if he could," Iakinthu said. "But I wonder if even the sea people can do that."

Aranthau unwound his loincloth and let the linen strip fall fluttering to the deck. His body, his motion, gave Iakinthu a twinge of pleasure, anticipation, desire. Naked, Aranthau walked to the end of the yard, barely touching the stays, as secure as if he were walking a mountain path back on the island. The yard projected well over the beam of the ship, out over the water. At the end, Aranthau paused.

He dove.

Maranti's fingers tightened around Iakinthu's hand. Her whole body tensed, but she remained silent and still. Aranthau arrowed into the water and disappeared. All conversation ceased, and the ship lay in stillness. Iakinthu laid the back of her hand across her lips to signify silence, then patted Maranti's hand to reassure her.

The silence stretched on, broken by the creak of timber and lines, the splash of water against the sides. Even the rowers raised their oars, and only the pressure of the steering oar steadied the ship.

A splash, a sputter, the long gasp of an indrawn breath: Iakinthu jumped up and ran to the stern. Maranti followed. The silence ended; the rowers plunged their oars downward, freeing Rhenthizu from his solitary struggle with the sea. The companions ran to unfurl the new sail.

Iakinthu leaned over the rail and flung down a line. Aranthau climbed up the stern. At the top, he grabbed her hand and vaulted to the deck, dripping, shining, his hair curling down his back. He breathed hard.

A less showy leap than a bull dancer's, Iakinthu thought, but elegant in its simplicity.

"Come and tell me what you found," she said, "and I'll dry your back."

Overhead, the sail snapped in the wind. As it billowed and filled and rose to the yardarm, *Flying Fish* steadied, gathered itself, and plunged forward with the waves.

One of the companions brought a rough wool towel, an ewer of olive oil, and Aranthau's loincloth. Iakinthu was glad the loincloth had fallen to the deck instead of into the water, for it was fine linen with a broad sea-purple stripe. She rubbed Aranthau dry, blotting the salt water from his skin and hair and the dark curls around his sex.

"What did the sea tell you?" she asked.

"That the wind is steady and the sea is calm from here to the Stepping Stone," he said, moving his shoulders like a cat stretching beneath her hands.

"These waves will stop!" Maranti exclaimed with relief.

"The waves?" Aranthau said. "They'll continue. This is the Sunset Sea."

"You said it would be calm."

Aranthau chuckled. "This is calm," he said, "for the Sunset Sea."

Iakinthu rubbed oil into Aranthau's hair, over his shoulders, down his back. She kissed his shoulder blade, salt tangy on her lips, dribbled oil on his skin and rubbed it in, and kissed him again. The oil tasted like thick summer sunlight.

"Ask Rhenthizu about the storm he survived," Iakinthu said. "Before he came to Idaea."

Maranti glanced from Iakinthu to Aranthau and back, grinned, and took the hint. She circled the stern cabin on her way out, drawing the linen curtains back into place without a word, pulling the front curtain to as she disappeared.

The white linen walls shone with the reflected light of the sea; the painted swallows flew with the touch of the breeze. The tiny gold leaves fluttered against each other with soft faint music. Iakinthu rubbed oil over Aranthau's chest and his belly and his thighs. He wrapped his fingers around her wrist, guiding her. As she roused him, she opened her short jacket. Aranthau buried his face against her breasts, kissing her and teasing her with the warmth of his breath. She unfastened her kilt and drew Aranthau down beside her on the cushions. The slick oil warmed between them. Iakinthu twined her hands in Aranthau's thick black hair. She held him to her, feeling through his body a connection to the Sunset Sea, its ebb and flow against the land, a mystery she could know only through him. She cried out in pleasure, in wonder. He shivered and gasped against her.

They lay together in the stillness of the stern cabin. The groan of planking, the creak of rigging, the billow of the sail had all receded to a great distance. Even the voices of their companions might have come from a different ship, brought faintly to them on the wind.

"Calm weather, steady winds, and a clear path," he said again. "But beyond that, only the wall of the Sunset Land. Can I find a passage to the Untamable Ocean? If it exists, it hides itself well."

"Its own people call the Sunset Land an island," Iakinthu said reasonably. "So the sea must surround it."

"Perhaps the passage lies far north, or far south," Aranthau said. "Can my sight reach such a distance?" He shrugged. "If I could only ask the sea to tell me..."

He sighed and closed his eyes, his dark lashes long on his cheeks. Water and oil and Iakinthu's towel had smeared the kohl. The history of his family celebrated their connection with the sea people, the man of the sea taken into Aranthau's many-times-great-grandmother's bed. The people of the sea could speak to each other and to other sea denizens, at great distances. Ever since that liaison, some of Aranthau's family had possessed the ability to listen to those conversations. Aranthau heard them, understood them, and mapped the sea in his mind.

"If only I could reply," he whispered.

Paissu swung down from the rigging as fast as she could, landing on the deck and running a few steps to stop. She spun around in the sunlight for the joy of it. She loved the ocean and the ship. Sailing was like riding Surefoot at a dead run across the surface of the water. She liked it best when the waves rose and the ship bucked in crossing them; but she had always liked riding spirited horses as well and had tamed Surefoot from her mother's herd as soon as she could scramble onto her back.

Nearby, Rhenthizu sat plaiting a net. Paissu approached him warily. The Idaeans moved so casually among men—the men are Idaeans, she reminded herself, just like the women—and she must learn to do the same, though she found it strange.

"Hello, little Paissu," he said. "What did you see, from the top of the mast?"

"Waves like running horses," she said. "I wonder if any horses live in the sea?"

"I think the dolphins are the sea's horses," Rhenthizu said.

"Can you ride them?" Paissu asked, entranced by the idea of racing through the sea on a dolphin's back, even faster than *Flying Fish* could sail.

"Would they like that?" he said. "They prefer to be free—and how would you saddle one?"

She laughed. "Too many straps!" she said, imagining a harness that would keep a saddle from slipping off over a dolphin's tail.

"Sometimes the dolphins save drowning people," he said, "and carry them to land."

She cocked her head, wondering if he were telling her a tall tale.

He smiled at her doubt. "Truly," he said.

"What are you doing?"

"Fixing my net," he said, "though I wonder when we'll stop in a bay where I might catch a fish."

"Catch some here!" she said. The People ate fish seldom, the Idaeans often, and Paissu liked fish, especially when it was fresh.

"It takes a bigger net than this one to catch fish out in the ocean," he said. "A longer one, to go deep, a stronger one. Why, I might catch a seahorse."

"Or a sea person," she said.

"Would I do that?" he exclaimed. "That would make the sea people angry."

"What could they do? We're safe in *Flying Fish*."

"They have the wind and the waves and all the other inhabitants of the sea at their service," Rhenthizu said.

His solemnity scared her. She glanced around quickly, at blue sky and gray sea.

"Should you be frightened?" Rhenthizu asked gently. "We're at peace with the sea people. My net is too small to threaten them. We honor them, as they honor us."

"Have you seen them?" Paissu whispered.

"I wish I had," Rhenthizu replied. "Aranthau listens to them when he dives into the sea."

"I want to dive in and listen to them, too."

"Maybe you can," he said. "But you have to learn to dive."

Paissu imagined being surrounded completely by the ocean, water so deep that it might take a thousand paces to reach the sea-floor, water so wide that all land disappeared. She wondered if it would be like floating in the sky, surrounded by luminous water like the path of stars.

"Then I'll learn to dive," she said. "Will you teach me?"

"If you like," he said. "When we reach a bay shallow enough for me to catch a fish."

"Until then, I'll learn to read," she said, "and write and figure," and she marched off to find Kilinkizu, who had promised to teach her.

Thick pyramids of glass, projecting through the deck, carried sunlight down into the forward cabin where Kilinkizu kept the records. She nodded to Paissu. Her sullen little boy crouched on the corner of the bench, as far away from his mother as he could be. He glared at Paissu. She thought, if we were home, we could send him away to a farm and be rid of him.

But he was just a little boy, practically a baby, and she ignored him most of the time. She would learn to read and write and figure and dive and sail and finally dance with the bulls; but who knew what might happen to Bdarde; and in the meantime she had the world to explore.

She sat on the bench facing Kilinkizu and waited expectantly. Kilinkizu handed her a scrap of paper, already written on one side, and a brush. A cake of ink sat in the middle of the table.

"Did you know how to write when you came to us?" Paissu asked.

"Yes, enough to keep the tallies in the village where I was born," Kilinkizu said. "One Hundred Three taught me to be a numerator, and I went to Hind to learn more, to be more useful to Iakinthu."

She offered paper and brush to Bdarde. He glared, said nothing, and kept his hands clasped around his knees. His nose ran and grime blackened his fingernails. Paissu wondered how he got so dirty on *Flying Fish* where no dirt existed, and where everyone bathed every day, if only in cold salt water and a handful of olive oil.

The little boy shouted words in an unpleasant language.

"Keep a civil tongue," Kilinkizu said.

"I—" He stumbled, unable to find the words for what he wanted to say. "Is this my language?"

"Is it Paissu's? Is it mine? But we speak it out of courtesy to our friends so they'll understand us."

"I hate them! I hate you." He grabbed the paper and crumpled it. Kilinkizu took it from him and smoothed it out on the table.

"It's harder to write on wrinkled paper," she said.

She put the brush down within his reach and turned to Paissu, who had begun to wonder if Kilinkizu would spend all her time with the nasty little boy. She wondered if Bdarde-who-was would like to have had her name given to someone so different from her.

"Shall I show you your name?" Kilinkizu asked.

Paissu nodded eagerly and watched while Kilinkizu drew three symbols. "Pa-is-su." She drew them a second time, slowly, so Paissu could see how she made the strokes. She dipped Paissu's brush in water, rubbed it on the cake of ink, and rolled it into a point.

"Will you practice drawing them?"

Paissu took the brush and stared at the mysterious drawings that signified her name. They looked like decorations. She tried copying the first one. Her attempt looked a little like Kilinkizu's. She tried again. After several drawings, the brush-stroke turned to fine dry lines. Paissu dunked it in the water and rolled it on the ink. The ink turned watery gray and soaked into her paper. She glanced up to ask Kilinkizu's advice, but she was trying to coax Bdarde into writing. Paissu rolled the wet brush on the dry ink again. Better: the ink turned black. But now her brushstrokes were too thick.

Iakinthu hurried into the forward cabin, her cheeks flushed and her hair tied on top of her head.

"Have I missed my lesson?" she asked.

"You're welcome, always," Kilinkizu said. "Look how well Paissu is doing."

Iakinthu bent over Paissu's shoulder and admired her work. "It looks very like writing," she said.

"It's my name," Paissu said.

"If I do even a little as well, I'll be pleased with myself," Iakinthu said.

Paissu gazed in astonishment at Iakinthu, wondering why the Gephyra had any need to learn to write or figure.

Iakinthu turned her attention to Bdarde's blotches. "Is this northern writing?" she asked.

"Bdarde wished to play before he worked, but he's a boy-child, so we must be patient."

Bdarde shook his clenched fist. The inky brush spattered black droplets across Iakinthu's jacket. Before Kilinkizu could react, Iakinthu took Bdarde's hand and gently restrained him.

"This is women's work!" the boy cried, struggling to free himself.

More ink flew across the table and the paper. Kilinkizu snatched away the brush. Paissu snatched away her paper, outraged that he had marred it.

"I—" Bdarde stumbled with his words, as he did so often. "Should I do women's work?"

"It's women's work indeed," Iakinthu said, "young women's work! Kilinkizu and Paissu are patient and kind, to let a boy-child and an old woman slow them down." She nodded to the younger women. "I'm grateful to you both."

Paissu stared at Iakinthu, almost as startled as Bdarde, but Iakinthu smiled at her, perfectly serious.

"The brush is too difficult for you yet," Kilinkizu said to Bdarde. "You'll do better with charcoal." She gave the boy a stick of charcoal and glanced ruefully at Iakinthu's spattered jacket. "I'm so sorry."

"Never mind, it's old and threadbare," Iakinthu said. "I fear I might spill ink on it myself."

"Maybe she should use charcoal," Bdarde said in a tone that would have got him a sharp smack if he were living with the People. But the People would have given him away long since. Paissu wished the pirates had taken him away. She wondered if they had left him behind on purpose, but decided that saying so would be too mean.

And Iakinthu laughed. "Maybe I should!" she exclaimed.

"Try the brush first," Kilinkizu said, her fair cheeks flaming with embarrassment at her boy-child's manners. She spun the brush on the ink, drew it back to point it, and handed it to Iakinthu.

Iakinthu's first rough attempts straggled all over the page. The lines jittered and ended in blotches.

"Easy," Kilinkizu said. "Be easy."

She took the brush gently from Iakinthu's hand and rubbed her fingers. "It's the cold and the damp," Kilinkizu said.

"Do I feel it more than you do? More than the children?" Iakinthu shrugged. "But it's true, my dear, I'm usually cold during these long sailings." She laughed. "Or sometimes too hot!"

Kilinkizu's lips quirked with curiosity. "But you chose Aranthau."

"How could I resist him?" Iakinthu asked. "He pleases me, and the men of his family—sometimes the women," she said with an uncomprehending shake of her head, "but usually the men—are the best ship managers of all Idaea."

"He's always away."

"Must we be together all the time?" Iakinthu said. "He's away perhaps half the year. But now, he'll be with me for a year at least. Our longest time together." She drew her hands from Kilinkizu's massage. "Thank you. Now I'll practice, so Paissu and Bdarde will know I want to learn to write as much as they do. And the learning will pass the time."

Bdarde gave her an angry, stubborn glare.

They practiced until the light faded from the deck prisms. The world grew gray, and the syllables blurred.

"Can you see?" she asked the others. She laughed at their uncomprehending reaction, then sighed. "I saw like a cat, too, years past."

She still could see well enough to notice that Paissu's writing nearly matched Kilinkizu's graceful brushstrokes. Her own had grown better, then worse. Bdarde had smeared his paper black with charcoal.

"I'll get a lantern," Kilinkizu said.

"Enough for one day," Iakinthu said. "I smell the cookfires. Will you eat with us, you and your boy-child? Though we're only having lentil stew."

"Yes, thank you."

"Lentils, pew, pig-food! You eat pig-food, and it makes you fart!" Bdarde shouted at his mother.

Kilinkizu turned to him with an expression of such anger and despair that Iakinthu feared she would lose her temper.

"Bdarde," Iakinthu said sharply, drawing his attention and Kilinkizu's. "Do you wish to eat with us or to sit with the copper ingots while we eat?"

Stubbornly, the boy glared at the floor and kept his silence. Iakinthu deplored his manners.

"I see you're too polite to admit your scorn for our food and our farts." She smiled at him. "We come from a small island—how can we avoid offending you?" She frowned to keep from laughing at him. "Would we offend our guest? Perhaps tomorrow we'll have something to eat that you approve of."

She rose from the bench, stretching her back. She took Bdarde's filthy hand. Ink stained her own fingers. The boy-child hung back, but he was too young to resist her.

The copper ingots, piled high and lashed down with strong leather ropes, loomed like cliffs in the dim hold. Stray light caught a spark of copper where the dark patina had been scratched. Iakinthu led Bdarde in and looked down at him.

"You may stay here," she said, "since the sight of us eating troubles you so."

"What will I eat?" he asked belligerently.

"You're our guest," Iakinthu said, "and we offer you the best we have, to eat with us. It offends you." She said, again, "Would we offend a guest?"

Poor Kilinkizu, she thought. How could they make her boy-child so angry? How can we civilize him?

She wondered if perhaps she should have laughed at him.

She left the boy in the hold, latching the door behind her, sorry to leave him in the dark but afraid of what he might do with an open flame. Instead of screaming at her, as she expected, he stood rigid and silent, glaring after her.

Chapter Twelve

Climbing back to the forward cabin, Iakinthu looked for Kilinkizu, but her numerator had disappeared into the darkness.

She may want a moment to compose herself, Iakinthu thought. As do I. She gazed for a moment at Kilinkizu's elegant writing, at Paissu's sample, improving with each line, at her own awkward attempts, and at Bdarde's smeared blotches.

He is very young, she said to herself.

Climbing to the open deck, Iakinthu joined her companions around a cookfire. She slipped beneath Aranthau's arm and leaned against him for comfort. Neither spoke; he held her close, and his warmth soaked into her. She loved the smell of him, sweat and plain oil and the salt of the sea. He wore perfume only when he returned to land.

Stars gleamed brighter than sparks. *Flying Fish* sailed on into the purple night, its passage nearly silent, the hull pushing through the gentle swell, the sail beating a soft rhythm.

Rhenthizu stirred the lentils. Maranti poked at the cookfire, less than careful of the sparks. The two young people touched each other at every chance, Rhenthizu stroking his fingertips across Maranti's hair when she bent to feed the fire a bit of wood, Maranti rising gracefully, brushing him with her hip. Her bread was less accomplished. She patted it into irregular blobs and laid it on the grate. Nearby, Paissu watched with an expression of disbelief that anyone could be so clumsy with the camp-bread. But Rhenthizu only grinned at Maranti and showed her how to shape the dough.

Such bad timing, Iakinthu thought. What if he prefers to stay with his born family? Can Maranti choose to stay with him? It's against custom, for if she chooses him he should return with her. Even if she wishes to break custom, she must return to Kunusu.

A few weeks ago, Iakinthu would have been certain of Maranti's return. But now?

The yeasty smell of the grilling camp-bread and the savory scent of the lentils made Iakinthu's mouth water.

"It's done," Rhenthizu said. "I'm starving."

Iakinthu smiled fondly. He was still growing; he complained of hunger however much he ate. He had made enough lentils for everyone to eat twice. He ladled the stew into painted bowls, filling them so full that the lentils slopped over the edges when he stuck in a wedge of bread. He served Iakinthu first, then Aranthau, then Maranti. On board *Flying Fish*, that was proper. Iakinthu used her bread to scoop up a mouthful of lentils, and the other members of her fire circle ate, too.

I'm hungry, too, she thought, almost as hungry as a growing youth.

Rhenthizu hesitated with a full bowl in his hands, glancing across the deck.

In the shadows, Kilinkizu sat with her legs beneath the railing, her feet dangling over the side, her arms folded on top of the rail to pillow her chin. Her stillness and the night had made her invisible to Iakinthu, though light from the stars, from the campfire, glinted from her bright hair.

Am I blind? Iakinthu wondered, distressed. In her youth, she would have seen Kilinkizu as soon as she came on deck.

She put her unfinished bowl of stew on the deck and went to Rhenthizu. "I'll take it to her," she said.

Gratefully, he gave her the bowl and returned to his own dinner, and Maranti.

The warmth pressed through the sides of the bowl and into Iakinthu's hands, and the thyme-scented steam provoked her hunger. She crouched beside Kilinkizu. Her knees cracked, and she grimaced.

"The stew is ready, my dear," she said.

Kilinkizu continued to gaze into the distant sea. She bent her head, wiped her eyes against her bare arm, and drew her legs from beneath the rail. The starlight caught on a streak of tears down her cheek.

"All I do is cry," she said.

Iakinthu put the bowl down beside them and took Kilinkizu's hands. "It's difficult," she said.

"I nearly struck him," Kilinkizu whispered. "How could I do that?"

"Did you touch him?" Iakinthu exclaimed in protest.

"I might have, but you spoke, you took him aside, you protected him—and me." She grasped Iakinthu's hand and held it to her heart in gratitude. "How can I be his mother, if—"

"Are you his grandmother?" Iakinthu said. "Have you raised a child, my dear? Yourself?"

Kilinkizu gazed at her, uncomprehending. "They took him from me," she said, "when he was a day old. My little girl..." Her voice failed her.

"And you were, I remember, the youngest of your family."

"Of my brothers and sisters and all my cousins."

"Then who would you learn with? Your doll, or your puppy? Should any young woman raise a child? Should a grandmother raise one alone? Your mother gave you to me, so I'll stand in her place, as grandmother to Bdarde-who-is." It would be more proper for Omempau to have the charge of Kilinkizu's child. But when have I, when has my family, done everything in the most proper way? She smiled, thinking how her stubborn daughter and Kilinkizu's obstinate Bdarde might get on.

A great thundering clang rose through the ship. Kilinkizu gasped. Iakinthu jumped to her feet. So did Aranthau, so startled he dropped his bowl. It cracked on the deck, and the lentil stew splashed across the planks.

Another clang broke the silence. Shocked and confused, Aranthau clapped his hands to his ears. He searched the dark sea all around the ship, seeking the rocks and waves that might make such a dreadful and dangerous noise. Others of the companions snatched up their knives or hurried toward the hatchway to fetch spears and bows.

Clang.

"It's the boy," Iakinthu said. "Only the boy."

The fear lifted as everyone recognized the sound of a blow against a flat copper ingot.

The pounding and clanging continued. The whole ship reverberated like a gong.

Did I think he'd be safe from trouble in the hold? Iakinthu said to herself. She smiled wryly at Kilinkizu. "You've brought forth a smart one."

"What use is mischief?" Kilinkizu cried. "Mischief, and anger, and malice? How could they bring him up this way?"

"Make him stop," Aranthau said, his voice full of pain. "He'll attract the thunder — or the monsters."

With anyone else, Iakinthu would have laughed, but she trusted Aranthau's knowledge of the sea even when it sounded entirely fanciful.

"He'll tire soon."

"That will be too late!"

Kilinkizu strode toward the hatch. This time she would strike the boy, and his anger would win. Iakinthu ran after her, descending into the heart of the ship as if into a drum. The clanging beat at her hearing.

They reached the barred door together. Iakinthu stopped Kilinkizu's hand.

"Let me," she said, in the midst of a violent clang. "Let me," she said again, into the brief silence.

Kilinkizu withdrew reluctantly, her expression hard with fury and despair.

Iakinthu flung open the door and rushed into the hold.

"Bdarde! Bdarde, dear child, are you hurt?" She clambered to the top of the pile of ingots, completely ignoring the fact that the boy lay on top of them, perfectly uninjured, kicking his feet and slamming his fists against the metal, making the whole pile ring like thunderclaps.

She scooped him up out of his tantrum and held him close, as if he lay still instead of kicking and squirming.

"You must have tripped, to make such a noise! Oh, we feared the ingots had crushed you, but you've only fallen down!"

The boy continued to struggle, but Iakinthu held him and, after a moment's confused hesitation, Kilinkizu knelt beside her and embraced him as well. Iakinthu held his head firmly against her shoulder, to prevent his biting.

"I'm—" He struggled with his words as he struggled with his body.

"Poor child, he's too distressed to remember how to speak like a civilized person."

"I remember!" Bdarde cried, but then he shouted something in his own language that caused Kilinkizu to flinch. She gazed at him in despair.

"I...tripped?" he shouted. "Could I trip? I'm my father's son, as graceful as a stag!"

Iakinthu rose, carrying Bdarde, aware of his weight. I'm out of practice, she thought. In times past I could carry a five-year-old without a second thought. He thrashed in her arms when she lifted him, kicking his bare feet against her. Suddenly he whimpered. She set him down again, afraid for a moment that her story of his falling was true. He collapsed on the deck, crying and grabbing his feet. In his tantrum, he had bruised his hands and heels on the copper. Iakinthu kept herself from laughing.

Would laughter help him now? she thought. Instead, he should have a soothing tea. And lentil stew, if he would deign to eat it.

"There," she said. "You hurt yourself. This happens sometimes. Your mama and I can carry you, and we can make the aching stop."

Whether from exhaustion or pain, or from confusion, he lay quiet in her arms when she picked him up again. She carried him toward the ladder, Kilinkizu trailing behind. The ship rolled, and Iakinthu staggered. Kilinkizu caught and steadied her. The ship pitched forward, then back, and rolled again.

"The wind must be changing," Iakinthu said. "Or the waves."

They lifted Bdarde up through the hatch, taking care against the uncomfortable rolling. Rhenthizu and Maranti carried him to the main deck; Iakinthu and Kilinkizu climbed up after him.

Flying Fish's sails lay crumpled beneath the lowered yard. The uncomfortable pitch and roll gave the ship its only movement. Iakinthu wondered uneasily if Aranthau had stopped the ship to dive and listen to the sea again. When he dove at night, she always worried.

Iakinthu pulled her attention back to Bdarde. She wrapped him in a boat cloak, making sure of several layers of wool beneath his heels. She asked Maranti to heat water for tea, thinking, She'll do better with the water than with the camp-bread.

"Bdarde fell," she said to her companions. "The poor boy fell and bruised his feet."

"I— Did I fall?" the boy cried angrily.

"Of course you did," Iakinthu said. "What else could have happened?"

"I kicked!" the boy exclaimed. "I kicked and pounded and shouted and kicked!"

"You did?" Iakinthu asked, feigning surprise and confusion. "You hurt yourself? But why would you hurt yourself?"

"To make noise!" Bdarde shouted.

"Be quiet!" Aranthau's voice, hoarse and urgent, startled the child to silence. "Be quiet, and be still!"

Kilinkizu wrapped her arms around the boy in his boat-cloak cocoon.

Aranthau climbed the mast. Paissu, ever curious, followed. Iakinthu hoped Bdarde would try to join them—she would allow it—but he lay stiff and angry in Kilinkizu's arms.

Instead of diving, Aranthau searched the sea from above. The tip of the mast wrote irregular spirals against the night sky's constellations, pointing at the Ceremonial Boat, at the Tree, at the Wine Jar. Aranthau rode the motion as easily as Iakinthu once had ridden Terebinthu.

Below him, Paissu clutched the mast and gazed in the same direction. Aranthau pointed; the starlight glinted along his arm.

"I—" Bdarde said loudly.

Kilinkizu gasped and clapped her hand over Bdarde's mouth. She jumped to her feet, carrying him, so he, too, could see where Aranthau pointed.

A slick, shining shape curved over the surface of the sea. The back of a whale, Iakinthu thought with relief, for whales often swam beneath ships, and if their shadows beneath the keel terrified inexperienced seafarers, their bodies and flukes and huge powerful tails slipped past without a touch. Whales meant safety, not danger. Even sharks kept their distance when the whales swam nearby.

Iakinthu waited for the creature to blow and breathe, to release a great cloud of warm steam, to flex its graceful bulk and swim, to arch its back, to flip its tail and slap it upon the water, to sound and disappear. But the shape moved unlike any whale. It lay still upon the surface, breathless, motionless. It tilted its body. Its huge glowing eyes rose from the sea. A massive flower of tentacles opened between them. A sharp beak shone in its center, opened, and closed with a rasping click. When *Flying Fish* tipped toward it, its long glittering back rose higher than the deck. Kilinkizu gasped and squinted, trying to see more clearly. The boy whimpered. Everyone else stared, silent with awe. Iakinthu, for a moment, regretted the recent loss of her longsight.

The giant squid fluttered its fins. Luminescence played along its sides like sparks of green fire. It moved closer, waves rising and falling beneath it. A pair of tentacles, immensely long, twisted from the flower of shorter arms, probing toward *Flying Fish*, stretching out and up into the darkness.

All the people froze. Even Bdarde lay silent in his nest of wool, in the restraint of his mother's arms.

The squid bumped against *Flying Fish*. The ship shuddered. The squid's body stretched the length of the hull; the long tentacles extended twice again as far. The beak clicked, opening, closing, splashing and spitting water. The tentacles slithered up along the rolling side of the ship and along the rail. They touched the deck, their tips as delicate as feathers. Rhenthizu clutched the handle of his sheathed knife. Iakinthu took one quick glance at Kilinkizu's belt where the knife of sky-iron hung in its sheath. Above, Aranthau cut the air with the edge of his hand, a silent warning. Iakinthu steeled herself to do as he asked, however difficult his request. The squid's enormous eyes glowed, reflecting light like a cat's. She thought of speaking to it, of telling it she knew her ship was an interloper in its domain and that she was conscious of its power. She held her words, as Aranthau wished.

The long slender tentacles waved upward, touching the fallen sail, reaching the mast. They crept along the polished wood, exploring its smooth surface. They touched the ropes that raised the sail, twined around them, unwrapped themselves, returned to the mast.

High above the deck of *Flying Fish,* Paissu held as perfectly still as the rocking and pitching of the mast allowed. Other times, the motion exhilarated her. Now it made her feel sick.

The monster's tentacles twined toward her. She clutched the mast. She trembled, biting her lip to keep from crying out. How could the monster even notice a stab from her knife? She was more frightened even than when she was little and saw the lions. When she had seen the lions, Dragon Claws had been nearby and chased them off with a whoop of challenge.

The lions would have laughed at a whoop of challenge if they had been hungry. Paissu feared that the monster would laugh at a whoop of challenge even if it had recently fed.

She stared down, frozen. The tentacle's flattened tip flicked against the mast, climbing, climbing, to a handsbreadth from her bare foot.

Aranthau wrapped his fingers around her wrist. She flinched, startled by a touch from an unexpected direction. He leaned far down, holding on with one hand and his legs. He drew her upward. She loosed her grip with her hands, with her feet. She dangled free, now bumping against the mast, now swinging far from it as it tilted. When it rocked back, Aranthau raised her as high as he could. She grabbed the mast again and scrambled to its top, past Aranthau, above him.

She watched, terrified, as the monster's tentacle reached up to the place she had been, touching each spot she had pressed against: her feet, her knees, her belly, her hands, reaching toward Aranthau. The tentacle's underside bore suckers and claws.

Iakinthu's chosen companion gazed downward, his expression calm, sweat streaking his face, shoulders, and arms with a bitter reek. He sang softly, a melody that mimicked the sounds of the sea.

The tentacles hesitated an armspan beneath Aranthau. They stopped. They writhed, searching and seeking, dipping and turning. The wet sheen of the skin had begun to dull in the wind, and the sparks to fade. Paissu wished for the monster to seek some other prey, to sink back into the comfortable sea-depths and leave the dry air and the wind above it. She shivered again, as much from cold as from fear.

The tentacle shot upward.

Aranthau snatched it. It twisted in his hand, its claws flexing inward. Blood flowed down Aranthau's wrist, down the tentacle.

He bent his head and touched his sweat-slick forehead to the flattened leaf of the tentacle's tip.

The monster flinched at his supplication. The tentacle flexed and tensed and whipped from Aranthau's hand. The monster jerked its arm away, twisted and untwined it from the mast, slithered it across the deck, and pulled itself back into the sea. It thumped against the side of *Flying Fish*, and the ship shuddered and rolled. The monster clenched its whole body. Water spurted from it, splashing onto the deck, and the creature sped away, down, its tentacles streaming behind it. Its glowing eyes vanished like shooting stars; its lights trailed behind it like sparks.

Paissu gasped. She had been holding her breath so hard she felt dizzy. Below her, Aranthau held tight to the mast, his eyes closed, gray and pale. She clambered down, trying to figure out how to help him as he had helped her. His body blocked her descent.

"Aranthau, Aranthau," she whispered.

He raised his head, his dark eyes dull with pain. He gripped the mast with both hands. Blood seeped from his palm, and he trembled.

"It's gone," she said, "you sent the monster away. Can you climb down? Can I help you?"

On deck, the companions clustered around the base of the mast. Rhenthizu shinnied toward them.

"Hold my hand, little Paissu," Aranthau said.

She gripped his wrist; he wrapped his fingers around her arm so his wounded palm pressed against her skin. The heat of his blood scared her. She supported hardly any of his weight—if he fell, so would she—but his hand stopped trembling.

Rhenthizu reached them.

"Aranthau, Aranthau, Rhenthizu's here to help us."

Aranthau nodded, his eyes closed with weariness. Rhenthizu climbed to just below Aranthau, where he could brace him if he slipped.

Could either of us stop him if he fell? Paissu thought. It was more likely that they all would lose their grip.

"Aranthau, follow me." Rhenthizu steadied Aranthau's legs and moved down the mast.

Aranthau followed slowly, painfully, still gripping Paissu's wrist. His hand trembled, and his grip weakened. Paissu came with him, whispering as if to a sister, awkwardly leaning to hold his wrist, keeping her grasp as the mast tipped back and forth, first lying solidly under her, then tilting her backwards till she hung precariously by one hand and her legs.

Rhenthizu jumped to the deck and helped Aranthau down. Paissu scrambled after them, still gripping Aranthau's wrist as he gripped hers. The rolling deck felt very solid after the whipping of the mast. Iakinthu took Aranthau in her arms and held him close and gathered Paissu and Rhenthizu into her embrace as well.

"Is it safe to sail?" Rhenthizu asked.

"Sail," Aranthau said. "Her memory is short."

Rhenthizu gathered the companions with a gesture.

Paissu kept hold of Aranthau's hand as Iakinthu helped him cross the deck. The lines and blocks creaked; the sail rumbled up the mast. The canvas flapped wildly, caught the wind, billowed and spread taut above them. *Flying Fish* stopped its rolling, cut into the sea, and plunged through the waves. The speed of the ship made Paissu feel easier, though the monster could surely catch them if it cared to.

In the stern cabin, Iakinthu eased Aranthau into her chair. Maranti fetched cloth and soap and water and lavender salve. Kilinkizu brought a lantern and a jar of wine. Bdarde stood nearby, wrapped and shadowed in the boat cloak, his bruised feet forgotten by everyone.

Paissu freed her hand from the sticky blood on Aranthau's wrist, leaving the prints of her fingers in blood. Aranthau loosened his grip, but flinched and caught his breath when he tried to lift his hand.

"Hold still," Iakinthu said. She soaked and washed his hand, easing him free of the clotting blood. The giant squid's claw had gashed his palm deeply. The wound bled fresh from his swelling hand. Iakinthu spread lavender salve across the gash.

Is it infected? Paissu thought. It's too soon to be infected. Did the creature sting him? Is he poisoned?

Kilinkizu held a cup of wine for Aranthau. He drank thirstily. He had stopped sweating; he was flushed and dry. His gaze drifted, fixing on vague spots where nothing stood. Paissu was scared and cold. Kilinkizu offered the cup to Paissu, as well, without even watering the wine.

"Only a little," she said. "It will make you feel warmer."

She drank, coughed at the sharp taste, and sipped again.

"I want some!" Bdarde said.

"Be quiet," Kilinkizu said. "Give me the cloak for Aranthau."

The tone of her voice silenced the boy. Paissu tried to remember hearing Kilinkizu speak in an angry tone, back with the People, when Paissu had been Minnow and Kilinkizu had been Fire-from-Cold-Ashes.

Bdarde let the cloak drop from around his shoulders, gathered it up in his arms, and held it out to his mother.

For days, Aranthau lay ill in a hammock, muttering incomprehensibly about things that only he could see. Iakinthu tended his hand with lavender salve and kept him covered and warm, even when he tried to throw off the blankets. She knew how he felt, for the cold fever had the same effect on her, waves of heat and cold and discomfort; she feared he would catch a chill and grow even sicker. She bathed his face and his body and combed his hair and rubbed oil onto his dry lips, so desperately worried that sometimes her tears flowed even when he slept calmly.

Paissu hovered nearby, fetching everything Iakinthu asked for and anything Paissu thought might be of use as well.

"Did it sting him?" she asked one morning, as Iakinthu put a poultice of dried lavender flowers soaked in oil onto the cut. The swelling in Aranthau's hand held the cut open and kept it from healing. "The monster?"

"He told me once its claws are poison," Iakinthu said. "I thought he was telling stories. Exaggerating, as sailors always do. Did I believe in a squid bigger than my ship?" She sighed. "But he told me the men of his family, and some of the women, are safe from the creatures." She smiled sadly. "Exaggerating, as sailors always do."

"He made it go away!" Paissu said. "He saluted it, and it swam away."

"He said he could sing to its breed," Iakinthu said. "I wish it had recognized him. I wish it had listened to him before it stung him."

"It will listen next time," Aranthau whispered, "and all its breed too. If I speak to them more often, they'll remember me."

Relief swept over Iakinthu, and she found herself crying again.

"I hope they'll stay away, love," she said, "no matter what you say to them, or they to you. Have you come back to me?"

Aranthau glanced around the cabin. "The purple squidlets have left off climbing down the walls," he said. He smiled. "I've come back to you. As I always will."

She took his uninjured hand, kissed it, held it to her heart.

"Help me go on deck?"

It broke her heart to see him so shaky and pale, but she admired his determination, and she was grateful for it. *Flying Fish* had been sailing blind, for only Aranthau had navigated these waters. He had described their course and the look of the sea and the currents and the waves to Rhenthizu, who had hardly slept as he kept the ship sailing west.

Is a description as good as Aranthau's sailing? Iakinthu thought. Rhenthizu, and *Flying Fish*, must have Aranthau's guidance.

When they came out on deck, Rhenthizu greeted Aranthau with a smile of relief and joy. He embraced the older man.

"Now you'll find us," he said.

"Are we lost?" Aranthau asked.

"And have been, since you vanquished the monster."

"It vanquished me," Aranthau said, "and I asked it to leave us in peace, and it deigned to agree."

He gazed over the bowsprit, past the bright-painted eyes of *Flying Fish*.

"Are we lost?" he asked again. "How long have we been sailing?"

"A long time."

Iakinthu followed his gaze.

A drift of layered white clouds lay just above the horizon, directly before them, the clouds Grandmother Earth collected to clothe her mountain peaks.

A gull flew overhead, looking for food scraps.

"Rhenthizu, you've done well." Aranthau said. "We're found."

Chapter Thirteen

Iakinthu walked along the rocks above the shore of the Sunset Land, hand in hand with Thamenthu, her Maisusutha friend of many years, and still a friend, despite their separation of long distances and long times.

The tide crept out, leaving the beach golden and glittering, speckled with sea-foam and striped with strands of seaweed. Offshore, *Flying Fish* rode at anchor. Its small boat lay high on the beach. Groups of people, Idaean and Maisusutha both, dug together for clams along the shining sand bars.

"Did I ever think to see you again?" Thamenthu said, speaking Idaean. "It's been so long, I despaired."

"The years pass so quickly now," Iakinthu said with a sigh. She spoke Maisusutha, aware that her accent had suffered from lack of practice. She smiled at her friend. "Will we speak our language again?"

She and Thamenthu, as youths, had spoken in a mix of the two languages that only they understood.

Thamenthu laughed. "If I can remember it!"

Thamenthu had grown more beautiful with age. Her life showed in her face, with lines of laughter and of pain. Beneath her leather shirt, her breasts hung heavy from the touch of her several children. She was respected and prosperous; broad, rich strips of purple and white shell beads decorated her leather shirt and skirt; an intricate pattern of dyed porcupine spines covered her moccasins.

"I'm so glad to see you," Iakinthu said.

"You're lucky I'm here!" Thamenthu said. "We came home to the longhouses at the last full moon. We're planting, but we came to the shore today because of the tide. Oh, I've missed you."

"I always asked after you—"

"Your sailors brought your messages," Thamenthu said. "But I wished they would bring you."

"And here I am, dear Thamenthu."

Thamenthu chuckled. "With the same accent, charming as always." She had teased Iakinthu forever about her accent when speaking Maisusutha.

"Whatever language you speak, it sounds like Idaean." She said her own name, and Iakinthu repeated it; Thamenthu said it again, laughing. To Iakinthu, it sounded like "Thamenthu."

"Never mind," said Thamenthu. "It will be easier for the children."

"Tell me everything," Iakinthu said. "In Idaean or Maisusutha, or our own language. Everything that's happened to you since we parted. I'm sorry about your father."

"He was very old," Thamenthu said sadly. "I miss him, but he died at the end of his life's most splendid autumn, before the snow set in."

"Your little daughter is beautiful! So energetic, and so smart! Your father must have been so proud."

Thamenthu glanced away. In the time Iakinthu had lived with the Maisusutha, she had decided to be charmed rather than offended when they stepped aside from a compliment. She still was mystified that they did it.

"It will take all summer to tell you everything," Thamenthu said. "You'll stay the summer? Till the maize harvest? And then the sea will be too rough to sail back until spring. You can stay the year."

Iakinthu loved the Maisusutha, different as they were from Idaeans; she loved the Maisusutha land, even the rocks sticking out of the soil. Here near the shore, rough stone caught the soil in its cracks and supported waves of short, springy blueberry bushes. Iakinthu's mouth watered at the memory of fresh blueberries bursting on her tongue as she bit through their dark skins, the tiny seeds crunching between her teeth. She loved the spring and the summer and even the autumn, gloriously red and gold and orange, despite its threat of bitter cold. The winter oppressed her; whether she wore Idaean wool, or Maisusutha furs, or both, whether she stayed inside the lodge near the fire or went outside to warm herself by moving, she always felt the winter's cold.

Thamenthu responded to her hesitation. "Or is this only a trading trip, a few weeks here and then back across the sea to Fair Island?"

"I'm taking my given child to his home," Iakinthu said. "I hope Uinthi will tell me where that is."

"I hope Uinthi will come home soon," Thamenthu said.

"I do, too," Iakinthu said, aware that her own wishes had sent Uinthi away, as given child and as explorer.

"Rhenthizu's a given child," Thamenthu said, "but did his mother ever give him?"

"She gave him unwillingly, and I took him gladly," Iakinthu said. "So I must take him back to his mother."

"You could keep him," Thamenthu said. "That's what we'd do. Is he valiant? We would adopt him."

"I hope he'll choose to stay with us," Iakinthu said. "But he has to decide."

They stood on the low rocky promontory watching their companions dig clams, swim, chase each other, splash through the pools. Paissu ran fleet-footed across the smooth hard beach with Thamenthu's daughter Thukui and a group of other children her own age.

Paissu must be so lonely, Iakinthu thought, the only young girl on *Flying Fish*. She wondered if Thamenthu might agree to sending Thukui with the Idaeans.

Do I have a given child to leave with her? Iakinthu thought. Then she realized she had forgotten completely about Bdarde, which embarrassed her a little, but a boy-child of five was more responsibility than playmate for a child of ten. Besides, the boy-child was so uncivilized that Iakinthu only counted him because he was Kilinkizu's. She thought Kilinkizu would object to leaving Bdarde as a given child. Besides, how could Idaeans offer an uncivilized boy?

She looked around for the boy-child and found him perched on a huge beach rock, staring across the water, his arms wrapped around his knees.

"Have other ships visited you? Black-sail ships?" Iakinthu asked Thamenthu suddenly. "Strangers' ships?"

"Stranger than Idaean?" Thamenthu asked dryly.

Iakinthu chuckled. "Are we so strange?"

"You're my sister, but I had to get to know you, and even a sister can be strange." She shrugged. "Idaean ships visit. We hear of Sheng ships, but so distant, who would ever see them? They sail across a different sea and visit the land beyond the rivers and the endless expanse and the mountains."

Hearing that Sheng ships had crossed the Untamable Ocean interested Iakinthu, but she was more concerned with Kilinkizu's warnings.

"I mean pirates. People who come for war instead of peace and trade."

Thamenthu frowned. "Who would come so far for war? How could they bring enough warriors?" She patted Iakinthu's hand. "Who fights people so far away? What if you had come as warriors? Your companions are as valiant as mine, and your arrows are sharper. But if you'd come to make war on us, we have other villages to help us. What village would you call on to help you?"

"Would we be so foolish as to fight you?" Iakinthu said.

"If you were, you'd all be dead."

"We prefer you as our friends."

"I'm glad you came in peace. My father was peace chief. I'm peace chief. Would I want to be war chief, like my grandfather?"

"We prefer you as friends," Iakinthu said again, "but the pirates prefer enemies." Iakinthu pointed to Bdarde. "That child. Let me tell you about that child. My numerator Kilinkizu tells a story..."

"When the People rescued me," Kilinkizu had said, "I was starving, put aside and punished for wasting my master's seed on a daughter.

"As if he had too little seed to spare! If you said so, he would fly into a rage. If you questioned his contradictions, he would fly into a rage. He took any opportunity to fly into a rage. He would fly into a rage if you asked if he could rage. Or if he could fly!"

Kilinkizu had grinned, and they both laughed.

"Why did the People rescue me?" Kilinkizu said. "Will I ever know? When I asked them, they said, 'Oh, we liked your hair,' or other silly things. I was starving, I was ill. They fed me venison broth. They stole a goat and milked it dry for me every day, till I crept back toward life." She looked away, embarrassed. "When I bled again, I waited to be clean, in despair. They would give me to a man—"

"The People! Give you to a man!"

"Did I know any better? I thought a man would come and force me to his will, until he planted a son or I took his gift and perverted it with secret women's evil." She touched her cheek. "The People's hands were rough, but they were women's hands. They blessed me with sage smoke. They gave me wine until I came back to the world."

She curled her lovelock around her finger. "Had I bathed, had I combed my hair, had I anointed myself with perfume? I must have been a sight. When I first saw Dragon Claws, I thought she was a man. Then I begged her for perfume, so I'd please the man she would give me to. We were both very confused."

"I imagine you were," Iakinthu said.

"I knew so little, and everything wrong. In stories the People steal children, even little boys, who they bewitch into girls. Could they have their own children? They unman men with a touch, and they have teeth where teeth should never grow."

Iakinthu laughed. "I've heard all that."

"When Dragon Claws took off her cape, I saw her flat breast. I was afraid she'd cut off one of mine!"

"Her cuirass is very cleverly made," Iakinthu said.

"I covered my breasts, as if I could stop whatever she wanted to do to me, and she laughed and asked if I believed everything the bandits said about the People. She took off her cuirass and revealed her breasts. Both breasts! The leather held her right breast close against her body, out of the way of her bowstring."

"They made one for me," Iakinthu said, "when I was a girl. Very practical for archery. Before I had it, every time I shot an arrow, I had a terrible bruise."

"They made one for me, too. I wore it, but could I see to shoot accurately? They sent me to learn numeration before I shot a person instead of a deer."

Iakinthu patted her hand sympathetically.

"Dragon Claws gave me perfume, because I asked it of her. I told her my name, because she asked it of me. 'A name of the People will suit you better,' she said, and gave me a new one."

Iakinthu had leaned forward and wiped away Kilinkizu's tears.

It felt good to run as far as she wanted without a railing or a line or a brazier or another person in her way. Paissu raced along the hard wet beach sand, her kilt hiked up and her hair flying. The other girls ran with her, some faster, some slower. She liked them, though they spoke a different language and she had to talk to them with signals. Rhenthizu's language received giggles in reply, it sounded so different from their language.

They reminded her of her friends back home, sturdy and strong, so different from Issiia, delicate but determined as she rode away with the People. Paissu wondered if Idaean children were all like Issiia, indulged and comfortable. Maybe the People would do Issiia some good. But Iakinthu must have been different all along, because she had been a bull dancer. And the companions of *Flying Fish,* men and women, were strong enough. She decided to figure it all out another day. Today she would take pleasure in the running.

She ran with the others to the far side of the harbor, where a jumble of rocks spilled down to stop the beach and protect it from the wind and sea. She clambered up the rocks, thinking to go farther inland and explore the edge of the forest.

One of the other girls climbed after her, caught up to her, and from below her pulled at the edge of her kilt. Thukui—her name sounded like Thukui to Paissu—shouted something at her. The rest of the girls clustered together on the beach, waving her back down.

"What's the matter?" Paissu said. She climbed to the top of the rocks.

Thukui followed, peering around, looking across the rise of stone and the clumps of bushes, gesturing with one hand and twining the other in one long black braid.

"I only want to see the forest," Paissu said, pointing.

Thukui spoke. Neither understood the other. Thukui raised her hands above her head, curving her fingers into claws, and roared. She roared at the other girls, and they ran away a few steps, shrieking, then turned back unafraid and gestured to Paissu and Thukui to come back to the beach.

Thukui roared again and pointed to the forest.

Paissu roared back at her, startling her, for she roared like a lion.

"We have lions," Paissu said. "I know to stay away from lions." Then she howled like a wolf. "The wolves will tell you where the lions are!"

Delighted, Thukui howled, and the other girls joined her. All together, they howled.

"Do you have wolves?" Paissu asked. "I saw them running, just before I came to stay with Iakinthu, the night before, they were running, and one turned and I saw her yellow eyes in the moonlight. Wolves!" She howled again.

But do I know how the wolves here speak? she thought, any more than I know what Thukui means when she speaks to me? Would I understand, if a wolf of the Maisusutha warned me of lions?

She climbed back down the rocks with Thukui, and together with the other girls they ran back down the beach, jumping to make the clams squirt, yipping and howling like a pack of little wolves.

Iakinthu opened a clam with the point of her knife. It offered little resistance, having been steamed in a pit of coals and seaweed. Thamenthu had already opened one and given it to Thukui to eat. They had a good system, Thukui pulling clams from the seaweed with a wooden rake, Thamenthu opening them with the knife of sky-iron that had been one of Iakinthu's parting gifts.

"Like this," Iakinthu said to her companions. She juggled the hot shell, blew on the clam until it stopped steaming, and poured it, juice and all, into her mouth. She swallowed the clam and its sweet, salty juice. In the circle around the clambake pit, Iakinthu matched Thamenthu clam for clam. Paissu watched Iakinthu's demonstration with interest, Kilinkizu with doubt, while Rhenthizu opened a clam and offered it to Maranti.

"What does it taste like?" she asked, eyeing it, and her lover, askance.

"Nectar," he said. "Try it! You come from a long line of mariners — surely you'll like clams!"

Iakinthu smiled and opened another clam and offered it to Paissu. Maranti came from a long line of farmers. She preferred meat to fish.

Paissu gulped down the clam, closing her eyes and wrinkling her nose.

"Oh! It's good!"

Maranti swallowed, coughed, nearly choked.

"Nectar! Is that your idea of nectar?"

Rhenthizu shrugged and grinned. "Sea nectar!"

"I'd rather eat seaweed," Maranti said. She picked up a strand from the pit and nibbled it. "Tasty."

Rhenthizu fetched her some corn mush from a nearby cookpot. She tried that, and it was more to her taste.

"Later in the year we'll have fresh corn to add to the pit," Thamenthu said. She pulled a fish from the steaming seaweed and put it on a curved dish of tree bark for Maranti. Nearby, where a stream cut the beach and flowed into the sea, her companions had tied a basket net to catch fish as the tide went out. Flapping silver creatures filled the nets. Tomorrow Thamenthu and her people would carry them back to their longhouses and their fields and use them to fertilize new hills of corn and beans and squash.

"My sister Iakinthu liked fresh corn more than anything," Thamenthu said. "But the corn is all dry now, and little enough left of it to eat, only to plant."

"It tastes better than anything, right off the stalk," Iakinthu agreed, "better even than milk and honey."

"So you see — you must stay till the end of summer, till the first harvest."

Iakinthu imagined a quiet summer in the Maisusutha country, hearing everything that had happened to Thamenthu over the years, telling Thamenthu about her life. She could visit the other villages and renew other old friendships. She could talk to the traders who ranged long distances and collect information about Rhenthizu's origins. She could play with the children of Thamenthu's family.

If the pirates appeared, as Kilinkizu feared, Iakinthu would have allies against them. Since the destruction of Siurthi and the companions of *Dolphin*, Iakinthu felt less inclined to dismiss her numerator's fears.

If we have to defend ourselves against the pirates, Iakinthu said to herself, could we find better allies than the warriors of Maisusutha?

"We'll talk," she said, tempted. "We'll visit. Then we'll decide."

She gazed down the beach, where several other cooking pits sent tendrils of steam into the violet dusk. Fires snapped and sparked. The young men of both groups lay on the sand, satiated with clams and fish and corn mush and Idaean wine, while the young women compared finery and conversed with gestures.

She thought of dancing, but decided it was too soon, for the Maisusutha followed more reticent customs than the Idaeans. She hoped some of her companions would choose Maisusutha during the visit, for they were strong and handsome and they stepped easily within the world. She doubted the Maisusutha would choose any men from among her companions, for they married and kept the men in their villages.

Would any of the men among my companions stay here forever? she wondered.

An itching sting touched Iakinthu's arm. She slapped at it, crushing a mosquito. It left a small dark smudge and a blot of her blood.

"I forgot about the mosquitoes," she said ruefully to Thamenthu.

"Will you let them drive you away from me?" Thamenthu exclaimed. She gestured to a nearby group of young men. "Boys! The mosquitoes!"

The young men got up, brushing the sand off their bare skin, their long legs. The Maisusutha men wore as little as the young men of *Flying Fish,* though their leather breechcloths concealed rather than celebrated their sex. They sauntered off to a patch of beach grass, gesturing for the companions of *Flying Fish* to help. They returned with armsful of the rough green blades. On the fire, the grass smoked copiously and drove the mosquitoes away. The smoke made Iakinthu's eyes water, but she preferred that to the mosquitoes and the welts they raised.

"Thank you," Iakinthu said to the young men, then, to Thamenthu, "What wonderful children you have."

Nearby, Paissu and Thukui played in the sand, digging ditches around a sand house. The last light of sunset painted red highlights over Thukui's dark braids and gleamed along her delicate cheekbones. A scattering of small scars touched her skin.

"The sores will never take her away from you," Iakinthu said, with joy. "How lucky she is!"

"It very nearly did take her," Thamenthu said. "As it took..." She hesitated, speaking of a subject both difficult and dangerous. "It took my son."

"I'm so sorry," Iakinthu whispered. Thamenthu would talk about her dead son only to a true friend.

"How old was he? What was he like?"

"Like a deer, like an eagle, like a young tree," Thamenthu said softly, so only Iakinthu would hear. "He died the winter before the spring of his quest. He left me as a child. Thukui nearly died that winter, too. I nursed them both. Why did the sores take him? Did I fail, did I neglect him?"

"Oh, my friend," Iakinthu said. Her sight sparked with tears. Thamenthu's eyes glistened. "The sores take people from us, our children, our lovers, our friends — can we control it, can we predict it? I think it's a mystery even to Grandmother Earth."

Thamenthu gripped her hand.

"Uinthi escaped the sores, and now I always fear they'll come back and take another child of mine." She sighed. "I've tried poultices against fever, against swelling. I've danced, I've fasted." She spread her hands in distress and surrender.

"I've heard…" Iakinthu hesitated to tell Thamenthu the strange operation traders from the east had reported to her. She hardly believed it herself, though the Sheng had such a reputation for healing. "The Sheng touch a knife to the sores of a cow — cows are like deer, only —"

"You had a cow with you, do you remember?" Thamenthu said. "A wild thing! Such horns. You took her back with you. Did she have sores?"

"I forgot about her," Iakinthu admitted, surprised at herself. "The Sheng choose cows with sores, I'm told, and touch a knife to the wound, and then cut themselves with the same blade."

"Why?"

"To make themselves ill."

Thamenthu made a sound of incredulity. "Why?"

"Because the illness is mild, and afterwards, they're immune to the sores — the sores that afflict people."

"You've seen this?"

"I've heard of it. I sent to buy one of the cows. I must have one of theirs — I invited a Sheng physician to Fair Island. I offered an immense gift with the invitation." She shrugged. "When I get home… I'll see how she answered."

"If it's a true cure…"

"I'll tell you what I discover."

Thamenthu nodded her thanks. "Will you smoke with me, and sleep on the beach tonight?" she asked. "And come home with us tomorrow?"

Iakinthu weighed returning to *Flying Fish* against sleeping on dry land again; she weighed sleeping in her hammock and blankets against smoking with Thamenthu.

"The sand is soft," Thamenthu said. "Even for our old bones."

"I'll stay," Iakinthu said.

The fires burned to bright embers on the beach. The young women and young men of the Maisusutha sat by separate fires, and though Iakinthu had grown used to the custom, and though it was a common custom among other people she had built bridges to, nevertheless she still thought it strange. Even Rhenthizu and Maranti had separated for the evening.

Iakinthu and Thamenthu had their own fire, one set between two huge drift-logs. Iakinthu sat on one of the logs, leaning comfortably against its spread of bare roots. The sea had ripped the bark from the trunk and polished the wood to silver silk. The salt breeze blew a flare of sparks from the fire; they flew into the darkness and burned out. Iakinthu reached for her boat cloak, then changed her mind and poked the branches of the fire. The blaze rose, warming her.

Kilinkizu stood uncertainly outside the firelight of the young men's circle. Bdarde ran in and out of the shadows, carrying cups, struggling with an ewer half his size, to serve the young men, disappointed when the Maisusutha tasted the wine and spat it out, laughing that anyone would drink such stuff.

He preened if they spoke to him. For once he did as he was bid, eagerly, and if they stopped paying attention to him for a moment, he ran around more furiously and wrestled the ewer from one to another, until they noticed him again.

"Kilinkizu," Iakinthu called.

Her numerator glanced toward her, glanced uncertainly toward her son, and followed Iakinthu's beckoning gesture.

"Yes, Iakinthu?"

"Sit with us," Iakinthu said. "Your place is with the grown-ups. The young men will watch Bdarde for you."

"He'll anger them," Kilinkizu said. "They'll beat him —"

"He delights them," Thamenthu said.

"The young men of the Maisusutha are as gentle as Idaeans with children," Iakinthu said. "My dear, do you think they're pirates? They are civilized."

Chastened, Kilinkizu sat on the silken wood of the drift-log and accepted a cup of wine. Even Thamenthu drank with them, though she only sipped. She had always found the taste of wine bitter and the effects unsettling. Iakinthu smiled when she noticed Thamenthu adding water till her cup must hold only a few drops of wine.

"Last time I was here, we both sat with the youths," Iakinthu said to Thamenthu.

Her friend chuckled. "And a few of us drank too much. Only once! My father was so angry."

"And I tasted tobacco for the first time."

"We'll smoke together now," Thamenthu said. "To renew the ties of our families."

Thamenthu picked up a leather bag, beautifully decorated with quills. Tiny shells tied into its fringe rattled with soft music. She drew out a smaller sack and a bundle, and unwrapped a carved soapstone pipe. The intoxicating scent of dried tobacco leaves drifted into the air when she stuffed the bowl with the long golden-brown shreds.

A coal glowed; blue curls of fragrant tobacco smoke swirled up, tangling into the fire's woodsmoke. Thamenthu drew a long breath through the pipe. She handed the pipe to Iakinthu.

Iakinthu pulled smoke into her body for the first time in many years. Its rough heat scraped her throat; she struggled to keep from coughing. The smoke rushed and twisted through her mind, turning the world sharp-edged and mysterious.

She handed the pipe to Kilinkizu. As Iakinthu exhaled, she coughed violently, smoke spilling from her nose and mouth.

Kilinkizu held the pipe, her expression doubtful.

"Just a little puff," Iakinthu said, still coughing. "For ceremony's sake."

Kilinkizu obeyed, as aware as any born Idaean of the importance of ceremony. She breathed gently from the pipe and handed it back to Thamenthu, who watched her exhale without coughing, and nodded in approval.

She and Iakinthu shared the tobacco while Kilinkizu watched, bemused. The smoke made Iakinthu giddy. Wine calmed her and made her sleep, but tobacco gave her the sharp, bright energy of a youth. She jumped up, grabbing Kilinkizu's spear.

"We should hunt," she said to Thamenthu. "As we did when we were youths."

"If we hunt tonight," Thamenthu said, "the forest people will smell the tobacco. They'll know hunters are coming—foolish hunters, and they'll laugh and run away. Tomorrow, we'll bathe, and then maybe we'll hunt."

Iakinthu sat down again, reluctantly acceding to Thamenthu's wishes. She shivered. They would bathe in the stream, and the stream was cold. She thought wistfully of her Kunusu apartment, of the bath house at the farm, of warm water soaking into her.

"We should have a sweat," she said. "I sent to you — did I? — that I built a sweat-house when I went home."

"Yes," Thamenthu said, passing back the pipe. "It pleased me. It helped to strengthen your young men, I'm sure."

Iakinthu chuckled. After a sweat, strength was the last thing the young men thought of. They wiggled like octopus tentacles.

"You know what I mean," Thamenthu said sternly. Iakinthu smiled fondly at her and drew in another breath of smoke. She gazed into the sky, rising toward it.

I could read the patterns the stars make, she thought, if I studied harder. Kilinkizu could read them already, if she would take a little more smoke. But her numerator had fulfilled the demands of ceremony.

Iakinthu turned the pipe around and looked it in the face.

"What face is this?" she asked. "Is it a bear? Have I seen this face before?"

"Only if you're a thousand years old," Thamenthu said. "It's the face of a creature that roamed the forest with our many-times-great grandfa — grandparents. The wildest creature who ever lived."

Gazing into the smooth cold eyes of the snarling creature, baring her teeth to inadequately match the long sharp fangs, Iakinthu could well believe it.

"Where did it go?" she asked.

"Some say they were all killed," Thamenthu said, "but some say, the lion people and the human people met in council and smoked together and agreed to separate one group from the other. Otherwise, it meant war."

"You've gone to war," Iakinthu said.

"They would have killed us, and we would have killed them," Thamenthu said. "Then who'd be here to thank the land and the spirits? They journeyed to the other side of the hills, and we came to live here, between the hills and the shore."

Iakinthu imagined great striped lions with long massive fangs, surging through the woods as smooth as water. She opened her bag and rummaged among gifts, cosmetics, a change of clothing that she hoped to wash in fresh water before she had to wear it again. She found the pouch that cushioned her ceramic poppy box, drew out the box and untied the leather string, and chose a bitterly fragrant bead of hardened poppy sap.

"I shall smoke poppies in honor of the lions," she said. "Will you join me?"

They passed the pipe back and forth; even Kilinkizu joined in the poppy smoking. The world grew bright and dark around Iakinthu, and she saw ghosts of old friends, ghosts of lions, in the shadows. She imagined, or saw, the shade of Bdarde-who-was, standing alone at the edge of the firelight, a young woman gone too soon. The dead young woman gazed toward the group of young men, where Kilinkizu's son, Bdarde-who-is, fell suddenly silent.

"We gave him your name," Iakinthu whispered, "to keep your memory. I hope he'll live up to you."

Bdarde-who-was walked past her, through the wavelets chasing each other along the beach, and into the surf, but instead of diving through the waves, she turned to water and splashed into the sea, a momentary waterfall.

Over in the group of young men, Bdarde-who-is uttered a high-pitched shriek of excitement or fear, the child-sound that made the hair stand up on any mother's neck. All three women turned to look, and Kilinkizu jumped to her feet.

"He's all right," Iakinthu said. "Only excited."

"He should be asleep," Kilinkizu said, but sat down again on the drift-log, knowing Bdarde would stay awake until the young men slept, whatever she said or wished.

Thamenthu gazed with intense fascination at the poppy smoke curling up from the bowl of her lion pipe. The smoke drifted toward Iakinthu, who waved it toward her, cupping it in her hands like flowing wine, pouring it over her face and her breasts.

"This is easier than a long fast," Thamenthu said. "I wonder if it's too easy?"

"If it were too easy, would the ghosts speak to us?"

That struck them both as very funny. Iakinthu laughed until her sight sparkled with tears. She blinked; she caught her breath. She glanced at Thamenthu and they both dissolved into laughter again. The second time they recovered themselves, they heard the young men trying to talk together, speaking louder with each phrase as if it would help the others understand.

Iakinthu laughed till her stomach hurt. "Stop," she said to Thamenthu, "oh, my dear, stop laughing!"

"You first!"

Kilinkizu's silence stopped Iakinthu's laughter: her silence, her sad smile. As soon as Iakinthu stopped laughing, Thamenthu too managed to control herself.

"You looked so unhappy," Iakinthu said to Kilinkizu. "Can poppies lighten your spirits?"

Kilinkizu smiled, fond but far away. "Poppies take away my ghosts," she said, "and then I'm…content."

A burst of laughter from the young women drew their attention for a moment, and even the young men fell silent to watch them. Maranti stood in the midst of the group, her back to Iakinthu, firelight silhouetting her and glowing through the pleated linen of her skirt.

She must be cold, Iakinthu thought, shivering in sympathy herself, at the same time admiring Maranti's grace. Her body swayed and her hands moved in the air as she told a story. Both Idaeans and Maisusutha watched entranced, though Maranti knew little more than how to say "hello" in the Maisusutha language.

She could tell a story in silence, Iakinthu thought, and everyone would understand it. Everyone might understand a different story, but everyone would understand.

Kilinkizu's little boy's high voice crossed the sand, bright and hard in the chill spring evening.

"I'll give you some more wine, Rhenthizu, I want to give you more wine. I want to give Aranthau wine. Where is he?"

"He prefers to be on *Flying Fish*."

"Why?"

"Ask him," Rhenthizu said, though he knew it was because the people on this side of the Sunset Sea believed men descended from the sea people sometimes visited them with disease. "Such a foolish story!" Rhenthizu said.

Bdarde scowled. "Question the captain? I would be whipped."

"Shh, shh," Rhenthizu said, and took the ewer from him and put it on the ground and tried to turn the little boy to watch Maranti and listen to her. She was so beautiful she brought tears to Rhenthizu's eyes. She spoke so softly only her own circle could hear, but he saw in her motion a story of love and passion and pleasure, and he blushed a little and felt proud of himself and proud of her, because the young Maisusutha men stared at her with wonder and awe.

"Rhenthizu!" Bdarde said.

Rhenthizu smoothed Bdarde's hair but kept his gaze on Maranti, entranced. "Maranti is Eldest Daughter," he said in the trade language he had learned as a child, though in truth it was unknown in this country. "The Eldest Daughter of Mother Moon, the eldest granddaughter of Grandmother Earth, the elder sister of Sister Sun." In a whisper, he added, "And she chose me."

Bdarde pulled at his hand. "Rhenthizu! Rhenthizu! I'm thirsty!"

"The wine is here, the stream is there," Rhenthizu said, annoyed. "Are you a baby, or can you get your own drink? Perhaps you should go to your mother."

"I've been with the men all winter!" Bdarde cried. "I hate you!" And he stomped away, though the sand soaked up the sound of his angry footsteps.

Rhenthizu let him go. The beach, full of fires and people, was perfectly safe. Perhaps Bdarde's temper would improve after a walk to the stream. He rather wished the boy would take a drink of wine and fall asleep.

He returned his attention to Maranti.

Has my attention ever left her? he thought. Has it left her since the first moment she touched me and spoke to me?

She stopped speaking, stopped gesturing, and sat down. The others laughed and giggled and exclaimed with approval over her story. She became one among the circle, her sun-lightened hair highlighted ruby by the fire, and perhaps, to Rhenthizu, brighter than the others.

Chapter Fourteen

A canoe rode the blue waves, a fragile shell skimming parallel to shore. A single person paddled it, expertly balancing it against the swell of the sea. The canoe turned toward shore; it rode the precarious surf over the sand bars, rushing in, skewing, straightening. The paddler leaped out, splashing into shallow water as the wave receded. Maisusutha and Idaean alike watched for a moment, astonished by the newcomer, who wore greasy, torn and mended, ill-tanned shirt and leggings.

"Uinthi!" Thamenthu and Iakinthu exclaimed.

Everyone ran down the beach, shouting welcome, surrounding the canoe, helping pull it above the high-tide line. It was as worn and patched as Uinthi's clothes.

Uinthi is all grown up, Iakinthu thought. And how handsome, how strong. But so thin!

Uinthi embraced Thamenthu amidst the raucous greetings of the young Maisusutha men, the quieter welcome of the young women. When mother and child had made their greetings, Iakinthu joined them, smiling, holding out her hands to her grown-up given child.

"Uinthi, my dear."

"Iakinthu Gephyra," Uinthi said. "I hoped you'd visit us this spring—Did I believe you'd be on the beach waiting for me when I returned?"

Uinthi knew more of Iakinthu's plans than anyone but Aranthau. Iakinthu beckoned to Rhenthizu.

"Uinthi has returned," she said when Rhenthizu joined them.

Uinthi greeted Rhenthizu, first in the language of Idaea, then in the language of his childhood.

Rhenthizu gazed at Uinthi. "It's been so long..." He said, in his own language, "Do I know if I would have recognized you?"

"We all change," Uinthi said, and laughed. "I've grown up, and you, too. Would I have recognized you?"

"I remember your voice," Rhenthizu said, "speaking my own language."

"You taught it to me," Uinthi said.

"Come and sit," Thamenthu said, "come and eat, you're so thin, there's plenty of time to talk."

Thamenthu shepherded Uinthi to the drift-log near the fire and brought a bowl of maize porridge and some steamed fish wrapped in seaweed. Uinthi ate hungrily.

"I missed home. I longed for my own town, my family's house, my own bed." Uinthi scooped up another mouthful of porridge. "And my mother's food. And when I saw my given mother's fine ship—what a distance I could see it at!" Uinthi gestured at patched and unadorned clothes, worn moccasins. "Though I wish I were more presentable!"

The Maisusutha dragged Uinthi's canoe all the way up the beach, then unloaded leather-wrapped parcels and brought them to the fireside, everyone clustering around, curious. But Uinthi left the bundles in a pile.

Iakinthu waited impatiently while Uinthi ate, as hungry for Uinthi's story as Uinthi was for Thamenthu's food. She tried to wait as calmly as Rhenthizu.

Uinthi put aside the bowl and sighed.

"Thank you, Mother."

"You're so thin!" Thamenthu said again. "Did anyone feed you, along your way? I expected better hospitality—!"

"I was well received," Uinthi said, then grinned and nodded toward the parcels, "and generously welcomed. Even when I journeyed between towns whose people viewed each other with enmity. But since the snow began to melt, I've traveled." With a nod to Rhenthizu, he continued, "Iakinthu planned to bring you here, the spring of your ceremony. Could I greet her without the answer she asked of me?"

"And you brought the answer." The words burst from Rhenthizu. "Did you visit my home, did you talk to my people?"

Uinthi gazed at him for a moment, then continued the story as if Rhenthizu had remained silent. Rhenthizu flushed.

"When I came home, when Iakinthu brought me, a given child, back to my mother, for a year I spoke to every trader, every visitor," Uinthi said. "I told them of Rhenthizu— 'What name is that?' they asked. 'Whoever heard of such a name?' It's an Idaean name—who has heard it on this side of the Sunset Sea? I spoke to everyone I met in the language of Rhenthizu's people, and in the trade language. Did I ever hear a reply? The stories I heard grew more fantastic: stories of old forest people who live in cities on the tops of huge trees, the beaver women who live in the streams and late at night venture out to steal human children to raise." Uinthi snorted in disbelief. "When spring came again, I said to my mother, 'Can I discover what Iakinthu wants to know by talking? I must find out for myself.'"

Thamenthu touched Uinthi's arm, as if to reassure herself that her child had returned safely.

"I set out to the south, for I had to find a land where it snows only once in the wintertime. I left the land of our neighbors, and I visited the lands of distant people."

Uinthi opened one of the parcels and brought out a wide leather belt covered with the finest shell beads, purple and white, a peace belt. Uinthi handed it, ceremoniously, to Thamenthu. She accepted it, laid it across her knees, stroked its surface.

"It introduced me, announced me, protected me," Uinthi said, and smiled. "It's the only thing I have left that I started out with."

Uinthi gazed into the coals of the fire.

"The weather grew warmer—the warmth of the south combined with the warmth of summer. I traveled to places where it snows once each winter, if at all, but the sun rose over the ocean and set over the land. When I reached a place, finally, where the sun set into the ocean, had the people ever heard of snow? Have I ever been in a place so hot, with so many mosquitoes? When I described snow, had anyone ever heard of it? I reached a town so big that I saw in a moment more people than if I walked through our town each day for ten days."

A sigh of amazement, even disbelief, rose from the listeners. Rhenthizu sat leaning forward, his elbows on his knees, intent.

"I thought, If I can ever find someone who understands Rhenthizu's language, surely I'll find someone here."

Uinthi paused. Iakinthu admired the performance, but she was as anxious as Rhenthizu to hear the end of the story.

"I did find someone."

"What was he called? Who were his people? Why did you leave him behind?" Rhenthizu's questions burst out.

"He spoke the trade language—a little. You and I speak it better. He traded with people who traded with the people of the Salish Sea."

"The Salish Sea," Rhenthizu whispered, trying the words, testing them. "The Salish Sea."

"I believe I can find it," Uinthi said, gravely, "but it's a far, long way. Distant by land, and over mountains—"

"Do we fear mountains?" Rhenthizu said, laughing.

"These mountains stop the clouds," Uinthi said, "leaving forests on one side, where it always rains, and desert on the other. Ice covers them all year long, and when you climb one range and expect to see the lowlands—you see another range of mountains."

"How far away is the Salish Sea?" Iakinthu asked.

"Three seasons, by canoe and on foot— Spring is gone already, and who can travel in the winter? Who would think of it? Perhaps two, if one traveled fast and light." Uinthi's gaze traveled fast and light over the companions of Iakinthu, children and youths and elders.

"Do Idaeans travel light?" Iakinthu said. "Can we return Rhenthizu to his mother without his gifts? Who would think of it?"

Uinthi scowled. Rhenthizu leaped to defend the discoveries.

"Uinthi discovered what I forgot," he said. "How else would we ever find the Salish Sea?"

"Your discoveries awe me," Iakinthu said sincerely to Uinthi. "But if Rhenthizu's mother lives on the shore of the Salish Sea, we can sail to it. All the seas are connected."

"So they say," Uinthi said. "But they also say one passage leads through ice, and the other leads through fire. Better to walk on solid ground."

"Perhaps in my youth, I might have walked from one sea to the next," Iakinthu said. "I want to hear about every day of your journey, for I'm too old to follow your footsteps across plains and deserts and mountains."

"We could send for horses," Paissu said shyly.

"Dear Paissu," Iakinthu said, stroking the child's hair. "The People could ride cross-country, but could I?" She shuddered. "I rode a horse once, and the next day I never felt such pain! I sent Aranthau from my bed for days, poor man, and poor me."

"It takes practice," Paissu said, "and then it's fun."

"What's a horse?" Thamenthu asked.

"It's like a deer," Uinthi said, "only big enough to carry a person on its back. And calmer—tame, like a dog."

"If we sent for horses," Iakinthu said, "they'd arrive in deep summer, or autumn. We'd have to feed them and shelter them all through the winter. Could a horse survive your winter?" She spread her hands, having just enough acquaintance with horses to understand how little she knew. She glanced at Paissu.

"Our horses live through the winter," Paissu said. "But in the spring they want sunshine and young grass and time to play with their foals." She spread her hands as Iakinthu did, agreeing with her. "If we sent for horses, we might as well go back home to get them, and come again next spring."

"We have our own seahorse," Rhenthizu said. "*Flying Fish,* which will carry us on its back to whatever shore we choose."

"Through fire?" Uinthi asked. "Through ice?"

"Do the companions of *Flying Fish* fear ice?" Rhenthizu said, swaggering a little. "Do we fear fire?"

"Have you seen ice?" Uinthi said. "In the winter, when the river freezes, you have to pull your canoe from the water or the ice crushes it. Can you pull *Flying Fish* from the sea?"

"*Flying Fish* is stronger than any canoe," Rhenthizu said.

"Even an Idaean ship is weaker than the ice."

"Aranthau will tell us," Iakinthu said, "whether *Flying Fish* would prefer ice or fire."

If Iakinthu had forgotten that she brought a cow to the Maisusutha country on her first trip, she had also forgotten what it was like to camp on the beach. As she woke, she tried to remember the last time she had slept outside, on the ground, under the stars and the dew and the cold. Her bones ached. Her head pounded, the result of the tobacco. She wished Aranthau were beside her.

But the smell of tobacco would trouble him, she thought.

She poked her nose from beneath the warmth of her boat cloak, into the cold, wet, salty air. She expected dawn. But the sky had only begun to lighten. Loud splashing from the stream nearby had awakened her.

Who's bathing so early, so loud, so close to camp? Iakinthu thought, hoping her own companions had better manners. She squinted into the crepuscular light.

The shadow in the stream loomed larger than any Idaean, any Maisusutha. It grumbled and splashed and lumbered through the stream to the basket net that filled with fish as the tide went out. The wicker snapped and sprang apart at the touch of the creature's enormous paws. It plunged its snout into the water and rose with a fish. A smaller shadow yowled and splashed beside it, begging.

The enormous mother grizzly, thin from winter hibernation, yielded her fish. The cub growled and shook it and dragged it to the edge of the stream and settled to eat it. Before the mother grizzly could catch herself more than two fish, the cub returned, splashing into her fishing hole, crying for another.

Iakinthu glanced around, thinking Paissu or Rhenthizu might be in reach of a warning touch. Paissu curled next to her, wrapped in a cloak in a nest of sand; Rhenthizu and Maranti lay together on a soft fragrant bed of evergreen fronds, and Kilinkizu lay with her arms wrapped protectively around Bdarde. All her companions, like all of Thamenthu's, lay awake in their beds, watching the mother grizzly and lying still as stones. Nearby, Thamenthu herself lay wrapped in a fur blanket, as silent and still as the young ones. She left her knife of sky-iron in its sheath, though it was in easy reach.

Who could fight a mother grizzly with a knife? Iakinthu thought. Better to behave like a friend and hope the mother agreed.

One of the young Maisusutha reached for a bow. Rhenthizu reached for his spear. Iakinthu raised her hand to stop him, and Thamenthu hissed a warning. Everyone in camp obeyed her command.

As they watched, the grizzly demolished the weir, eating fish, releasing fish, driving some up the creek toward her cub, who leaped at them and missed them all. Mother Grizzly snatched a fish between her sharp teeth and batted showers of fish to the shore with powerful paws. The cub galloped up the bank and jumped on the flapping fish.

When the sun's edge rose above the sea's surface, brightening the indigo sky to azure and gold, the grizzly sighed like any exasperated mother and waded up the creekbed, her cub tumbling and splashing behind.

When even the sound of wading had vanished into the forest, Thamenthu sat up and wrapped the bear-pelt from her bed around her shoulders.

"A good sight in the morning," she said.

"A certain way to come out of sleep," Iakinthu said, using the language of the Maisusutha. Her ear for the language was returning, though understanding still took effort. She stayed where she was, wrapped in heavy wool, both hoping the sun would soon warm the air and drive away the dew, and dreading bright light's effect on her headache.

"We men could have killed her!" said Bdarde.

"Perhaps," said Thamenthu.

"You should have let us!"

"We came to the shore to get fish for the maize, not to kill a mother bear. She was hungry—"

"And she ate your fish!"

"—and thin." Thamenthu continued as if Bdarde had remained silent. "And feeding her child."

The Idaeans watched the argument with fascination, while the Maisusutha pretended it was occurring out of their sight. "Did she offer you her life? If you kill her, you kill the cub as well, and soon the world would have no more mother grizzlies."

"The forest is full of bears."

"She might give herself to you in the fall, when she's fat for winter, or next summer, when she's sweet with berries and her cub might live on her own."

For a moment Bdarde glared at Thamenthu. Thamenthu gazed back quite calmly.

Kilinkizu jumped up, left Bdarde behind, and knelt before Thamenthu. "I beg your pardon, sister of Iakinthu. My son will understand that you're right about Mother Grizzly."

Thamenthu stretched her hand from beneath her fur robes and touched Kilinkizu's cheek. "Later, some other time, he can go on a proper hunt."

Iakinthu lay back in her warm cloak, just for a moment. Around her the camp came to life, everyone rising, bathing, dressing. Smoke from the cookfires tinged the air.

"Iakinthu Gephyra, would you like breakfast?"

Paissu sat on her heels beside her, peering at her with concern. The sun had traveled well into morning, warming the world and chasing away the dew.

Iakinthu blinked. Her bones still ached from the cold, from the night on the beach, and pain streaked from her right eye to the back of her head.

"Did I sleep again?" Surprised by the angle of the light, she rose. She pulled up the hood of her boat cloak to shade her eyes. As an afterthought, as a concession to the modesty of the Maisusutha, she pulled the cloak across her breasts.

I thought it was the cold that made me weary, she said to herself. But it's warm, and still I ache.

"We let you sleep," Paissu said. "In case you felt ill."

Iakinthu wished her susceptibility to the cold fever were less well-known, less likely to cause her companions to coddle her. Still, she appreciated Paissu's concern. She patted Paissu's cheek.

"I'm well, little Paissu," she said. "But I had better bathe before I eat. Have you bathed? Have you cleaned your teeth?"

"Yes, Iakinthu."

Iakinthu rose from her bed, wrapped the cloak close around her, and set off barefoot along the beach to the stream. The younger people worked at rebuilding the weir, to set it at the next high tide and hope Mother Grizzly came fishing only in the morning.

She walked along the bank of the stream, past the dunes and over the rocks and into the forest. The shade eased her headache, though her vision still sparkled. She let the hood fall back.

She remembered a glade, a grotto, that she had enjoyed. But the stream had wandered, over the years, or the grotto lay deeper in the forest than she recalled, and she stopped when she reached a pool beyond sight and sound of the others. A wide flat rock projected out into the stream, catching dark coarse sand in its eddy, warming in the late morning sun. She dropped the cloak and sat naked in the sunshine, unplaited her hair, and let it tumble over her shoulders.

Though she looked forward to bathing in fresh water, she hesitated on the bank. The warm stone and the sunlight had eased the aches from her bones. The cold water might bring them back. She would prefer a hot bath, but the custom of the Maisusutha was to bathe in cold water. Uinthi had thought the Idaeans remarkably delicate when introduced to their bathing customs.

But after a month or two, Iakinthu recalled, even Uinthi condescended to taking a warm bath in a tub instead of a cold plunge into a stream.

"Iakinthu…?"

She had been enjoying this time alone, after so many days aboard *Flying Fish*, but she was glad to hear the voice of her old friend.

"Here, Thamenthu."

Thamenthu strode over the rocks, put down a bundle of Iakinthu's clothes and boots, two bows and two quivers, and her ever-present carry-bag, and sat on the warm stone beside her.

"Are we going on an expedition?"

"I worried," Thamenthu said. "Mother Bear…"

"Mother Bear is napping," Iakinthu said, "if she's like every other mother bear of the Maisusutha."

"I admit it," Thamenthu said, smiling. "Like Paissu, I worried about you."

Iakinthu shrugged. "It's a long voyage across the Sunset Sea. And a longer voyage to come."

"At our age, perhaps it's better to stay home. Or to come only this far, and stay long enough for a visit."

"Age!" Iakinthu exclaimed. "Did I ever love long sea trips when I was young? I liked being in new places. I loved my time with the Maisusutha. But getting to new places bores me. Aranthau sees the ocean new every day. Every change delights him."

"What do you see?"

"Water. Water that sometimes rises into waves higher than my ship is tall. Waves that could crush *Flying Fish,* and drown my companions." She shivered.

"Waves saved you."

"A thousand years ago. At a great price."

The headache pounded again. Iakinthu pulled the hood of the cloak over her eyes, but a flush of heat rose up her body, across her breasts and shoulders and over her face. Her skin prickled. She flung the cloak onto the rock and splashed forward into the pool without another word. The cold shocked the heat right out of her. She floated in the clear cold water, kicking gently to hold herself against the current. The water moved more slowly here, where the banks widened to embrace the pool. Downstream, the water rushed and sang against the rocks.

Thamenthu took off her moccasins and dangled her bare feet in the stream.

"Join me," Iakinthu said.

"I bathed this morning," Thamenthu said. "Iakinthu, are you changing?"

"Yes, finally!" Iakinthu said. "Did I have to wait till I was fifty?"

Thamenthu chuckled. "We all change sooner or later."

"I'd rather it had been sooner. I wish it were finished! I get so snappy. I cry without reason."

Thamenthu raised one eyebrow. "How does that make you different from any other Idaean?"

She made Iakinthu laugh. The Maisusutha seldom cried, seldom lost their tempers, and thought the Idaeans charming but too undisciplined in their character to be considered entirely civilized.

"Will I miss the bleeding?" Iakinthu said with satisfaction. "Messy and inconvenient— I'll be glad to be rid of it."

Thamenthu smiled again. "I always enjoyed those days, by myself or with my friends—with you. In the quiet and the peace, giving my blood back to the earth."

"I liked the time we had to talk," Iakinthu said. "But spending every full moon that way— I think we'd soon tell each other everything there is to know about each other."

"Must we have talked all that time? There's something to be said for silence."

"I like to dance in the full moon," Iakinthu said. "Dance, and take my lover to my bed, and exhaust him."

Thamenthu glanced away; Iakinthu fell silent, sorry to have embarrassed her friend, yet amused by the delicacy of the Maisusutha in intimate matters.

Thamenthu picked up her bow. "Are you finished boiling the water in my fish pool, old friend? Come out before you make soup of them all. I brought your clothes. Let's go hunting."

"For Mother Bear?"

"Mother Bear is promised to Kilinkizu's son," Thamenthu said. "If she ever chooses to give herself instead of eating him."

"What of breakfast?"

"The rest of us breakfasted at daybreak. Now we'll find something for supper."

Iakinthu stood up. The water reached only to her breasts, hardening her nipples with gooseflesh when the cool air touched her wet skin. She waded to the shore, water rushing down her sides and dripping from her long hair.

"The scar is new," Thamenthu said.

"Old," Iakinthu said, "but, yes, I acquired it after I left the Maisusutha. It told me I should retire from bull dancing, and retire Terebinthu, too."

She wrapped herself in the cloak to dry, the wool prickling against her skin.

Thamenthu drew out a handful of small red berries from her leather carry-bag.

"Strawberries!" Iakinthu exclaimed, delighted.

"Early ones, of an early year."

The berries, only the size of Iakinthu's little fingernail, burst in her mouth, sweet and fragrant. The tiny seeds popped between her teeth as the flesh of the berries melted on her tongue.

The forest cast dappled shade over Iakinthu, letting sunlight pass between new leaves. Violets spread patches of deep green and purple on the forest floor. In deeper shade, trillium glowed white against its pale green foliage. Here and there a charred branch lay decaying into the loam, but most of the marks of recent fire had already vanished. Iakinthu brushed one end of her bow along a burned branch, scattering bits of damp charred wood.

"Autumn before last?"

"Yes. The underbrush was about to take over, so we burned it."

Thamenthu bent and plucked a few leaves from a solitary plant, twisted them into a bundle, and put them in her carry-bag.

"I'll make a tea for you, when we get back. It will ease your changing."

Iakinthu sighed. "Granny tea."

"You are, after all, a grandmother. Will you bring Issiia to visit us?"

"She might come herself, when she comes home from the People. Soon, I'll give *Flying Fish* to her."

"What about Aranthau?"

"He'll sail it as long as he wishes, if Issiia has any sense—and she does, for all that she's a little spoiled. I hope Aranthau will stay with me more often, when I'm done traveling. But he's happier with the sea."

"I can hardly imagine Iakinthu done traveling."

Iakinthu smiled sadly. "I can. The voyage hurts my bones, and I wish it were finished instead of barely begun."

"Uinthi saw great wonders," Thamenthu said.

"Will you come and see them, too?"

"Have you ever known me to travel far from our hills?" Thamenthu said. "Even when we both were young? Now I'm peace chief. You'll have to go without me. I'm sorry."

"I, too." Iakinthu had hoped, rather than expected, to persuade Thamenthu to accompany her.

She yearned to accept her friend's invitation and remain with the Maisusutha through the summer. She could beach *Flying Fish* during the season of summer storms, or sail it into the river, into safe harbor, and let the fresh water kill the barnacles and worms. If she stayed, Uinthi could have a proper visit at home, and act as guide afterwards.

Iakinthu feared to wait so long to set out toward the Salish Sea, to sail away in autumn, without assurance that they could reach their destination before winter. She wondered what sailing through fire would be like, if they reached it in the winter.

After a moment's hesitation, Iakinthu asked, "Will Uinthi guide us?"

Thamenthu flung out her arms in protest.

"Uinthi has only just come back to me. Will you take my child away again so soon? Uinthi is ragged through, and starving."

"We'll be on *Flying Fish*," Iakinthu said. "Safe, warm, well-provisioned, with every comfort—"

"Except running streams to bathe in, and land to walk on, and quiet places away from human people. And such hard work!"

"If the wind failed, would I ask my guide to row?"

"Would Uinthi sit idle while everyone else rowed?"

"Uinthi did everything I asked and more," Iakinthu said gratefully. She hesitated again. "Will Uinthi guide us to the Salish Sea?"

Thamenthu also hesitated. "Yes," she said, sadly, softly.

"The handsome child has grown to beautiful youth," Iakinthu said.

"Yes. Beautiful, and solitary." Thamenthu sighed. "I'd like to have grandchildren. Will Uinthi give them to me?" She shrugged.

"Thukui will."

"Thukui is young. Will I have grandchildren while I can still play with them?"

"Uinthi might choose to give them to you. Two-spirits sometimes do, after all."

"Two-spirit," Thamenthu said, and laughed. "Or three, or four—too many for the world to hold!"

Iakinthu took Thamenthu's hand and gripped it. "An exceptional child."

The trees opened out into a glade covered with wildflowers. Rabbits, drawn by the sweet flowers to graze during full daylight, hunched nibbling hungrily at the succulent growth.

Both women nocked their bows with rabbit arrows, drew, and shot. Iakinthu thought, when did I last shoot an arrow?

She missed.

Thamenthu's arrow hit its mark; her second arrow took another fat spring rabbit before the rest took fright and fled and disappeared.

"Enough meat to flavor the pot," Thamenthu said. She knelt by the rabbits and stroked their soft fur. "Thank you," she said to them. She gutted them on the spot. Both were males, Iakinthu noticed. Thamenthu might take female rabbits, but only in autumn or winter. How she could always be right about them mystified Iakinthu.

Thamenthu picked handfuls of the herbs the rabbits had grazed on. Their pungent and resiny scent mixed with the hot odor of rabbit blood. Iakinthu picked more and wrapped them into a bundle, pinching the leaves and flowers between her fingers. The fragrance, lingering on her hands, brought back memories of another spring, when she and Thamenthu both were young. Thamenthu took the bundle from her and laid it inside one of the rabbits, and put the rabbits in her carry-bag.

The prospect of fresh meat made Iakinthu's mouth water. She craved fresh food after the long voyage. She wished they could build a fire and roast the rabbits here and now, but all her companions craved fresh meat as much as she did.

On the way back to shore, Thamenthu and Iakinthu picked mushrooms till the carry-bag bulged, and Iakinthu carried some, awkwardly, in a fold of her kilt. They picked up a few acorns and some hickory nuts, but discarded them.

"I always hope to find a few before the worms get them," Thamenthu said. "But this time of year, it's a foolish hope." She smiled. "Unless a squirrel leads you to its cache."

The weir stood ready to drag into the stream when the tide reached its height. A few of the withes remained from the first fish-trap, but Mother Bear had broken most of them. Maranti and her companions, Idaean and Maisusutha, cut new branches and stripped bark for tying, while the young men took the branches and built the new trap.

Back on Fair Island, the two groups would have worked as one, men and women alike. The Maisusutha followed different customs. To Rhenthizu, the customs felt acceptable.

Perhaps this is the way of my own people, he thought. I wish I could remember.

Despite this, he longed to work beside Maranti, to be close enough to touch her and kiss her, to be within reach of her hands. Just thinking about her aroused him.

A touch to his elbow startled him.

"Come with me," Uinthi said in the language of Rhenthizu's childhood.

Uinthi walked down the beach, without explanation, leaving Rhenthizu to follow or stay behind.

Curious, Rhenthizu caught up his spear, followed Uinthi, and paced alongside. The sounds of camp, the smoke of the beach fires, fell behind and vanished.

In silence they walked around a headland. When the mouth of a small creek appeared, spreading a delta of sand and pebbles into the ocean, Uinthi angled up the beach, across hard sand to soft sand to a low bank of dunes. Rhenthizu climbed the slope, the harsh sea-grass rasping his bare legs.

No wonder the Maisusutha wear leggings, he thought.

The forest loomed ahead. The creek burst from it, a dark shadow turning silver when the water touched the sun.

"Where are we going?"

"To the sweat lodge."

Uinthi walked along the bank and between the trees. After a moment, Rhenthizu followed.

I'm on the shore of my own land, Rhenthizu thought. The opposite shore, to be sure, and how shall I reach the other side?

When he tried to remember his abduction from his home, his journey to Idaea and Fair Island, he remembered mostly endless days, and cold, and hunger, and misery. The men who took him had been well-clothed, and well-fed—he remembered the scent of meat, roasting for their dinner, and the scraps they sometimes threw him. So perhaps the land could be crossed in a state higher than despair. Uinthi, after all, had crossed much of it, and returned.

A deep narrow stream left tiny sharp cliffs of wet sand and rills of water. Uinthi followed it, and Rhenthizu followed Uinthi. The beach gave way to loam, slicked with dead leaves from the previous autumn as they turned back into earth. The shade of the spring forest lay over them, dappled with sunlight. The stream sang across its bed of stones.

The stream's song rose at a rockfall that narrowed the streambed, then quieted at the pool the gathering water formed. A low dome of branches and earth, the sweat lodge, rose from the bank.

Uinthi flung hot stones into the center of the small shelter, balancing them on a forked stick. Their heat wilted the leaves of branches covering a gap broken out by winter or rain or wind. The hot green scent mixed with a tendril of woodsmoke from the banked fire. Uinthi dipped water from the stream with an Idaean bowl and set it inside the entrance of the lodge, then stood to undress. Rhenthizu sat on the ground to pull off his boots. As Rhenthizu unknotted the wrap of his loincloth, Uinthi's shirt fell to the ground, followed by loincloth and leggings. Rhenthizu glanced up, startled, having believed the Maisusutha to be shy where the Idaeans were bold. But of course Uinthi was practically an Idaean.

Doubly startled, he looked at Uinthi as if for the first time, as if for the thousandth time. Uinthi gazed back at him, straightforward, amused, and ducked through the leather curtain into the sweat lodge.

Rhenthizu followed. The hot air shocked him, clamping around his chest. His skin prickled with sweat. A little light seeped in. Uinthi guided him to sit on the warm ground, dipped a leafy branch into the water, and sprinkled it over the stones. Thick hot clouds of steam rose around them. Sweat poured through Rhenthizu's short hair, dripped down his face, streamed down his sides and his chest and his belly and over his sex. His vision sparkled, and his eyes stung with salt.

Uinthi faced him in the sweat lodge, sitting on a section of log stripped of its bark, cracked and shiny from the heat and steam.

He remembered, now, more about Uinthi, the first given Maisusutha child, back on Fair Island.

How could I forget anything about Uinthi? he wondered. He felt foolish, though he was in good company with both the companions of *Flying Fish* and all the Maisusutha.

Did I forget everything I knew as a child? he wondered. He reached back into his memory, trying to remember what he had thought when he was very little. He did remember, better than he remembered others from that confused time when he was still returning to himself.

Did I only notice Uinthi as someone, like Iakinthu, who listened to me and learned what I meant when I spoke words only I could understand? Did I notice anything else?

Perhaps, he thought, Uinthi wondered too, still learning, still discovering both spirits.

He recalled so little of his first year at Old Farm. He had seldom felt safe; often he believed the raiders would come once more, despite the great distance, and steal him away. Then Iakinthu would hold him and comfort him and say, Would the raiders dare come here? How could they find you, if they did? Old Farm is far from the sea. Could they paddle their war ships along our tiny stream?

Sometimes when he slept, he dreamed that they did pass up the stream, ghostly and fierce, riding against the current. But when Iakinthu said it, he could laugh.

"You do remember me," Uinthi said.

"Yes," he said. "Everything."

"I'm glad."

Uinthi ducked out of the sweat lodge, beckoning to Rhenthizu. The cool spring air sent shivers over his skin. Uinthi dove into the clear water of the stream pool. Rhenthizu followed.

The water closed over him, so cold he gasped. Choking and coughing, he struggled to the surface and toward the bank. Frigid water burned in his throat. Uinthi swam up beside him, hair trailing long and loose. He scrabbled out, slipping on the rocks.

"What's the matter?"

"It's cold!"

"Of course it is," Uinthi said, matter-of-fact, and picked up a stone from a shaded spot beneath the surface of the stream. It sparkled. A thin coat of ice broke from it, shattering and melting and dripping down Uinthi's arm.

"The stream moves too fast to freeze on the surface, but the rocks grow cold and cover themselves with ice."

"Fair Island's water's warm," he said. "Ice comes from the tops of the mountains in winter, and we cover it with straw and sawdust to last into the summer."

"Yes," Uinthi said. "I remember. And I remember that Idaeans take hot baths." Uinthi climbed out of the stream, strode past him, and returned to the sweat lodge.

He followed, glad of the heat.

Am I too much an Idaean? he wondered. Too given to luxury and comfort?

Uinthi sprinkled more water on the stones, using the branch that was now sadly wilted. The steam closed in.

Three times Uinthi dove into the stream. The second time, Rhenthizu hesitated on the bank, reluctant to submit himself to the freezing shock of cold. He nearly sat on the bank; he nearly said, "I'll watch you swim…here where it's cool, instead of cold."

But instead, he dove again.

The third time he dove in without hesitation, as quickly as the first time, knowing the result, resigned to it, even feeling the pleasure of it.

Chapter Fifteen

Uinthi climbed out of the pool, pushing with both hands, one foot on the wide flat rock, hair dripping water to splash onto the stone. Treading water in the pool, Rhenthizu felt sorry for Uinthi's gauntness: bony hips and ribs, muscles taut against thighs and calves.

Uinthi undertook a long and dangerous journey for my sake, Rhenthizu thought. All alone. What courage.

Uinthi sat on the sun-warmed stone and drew an intricately carven comb from the pocket of the ragged shirt to smooth out the tangles, then sighed with contentment.

"Now I'm clean. It's hard to stay clean on a journey." Uinthi glanced at the travel-stained shirt and leggings with disgust. "Would my mother like it if I returned to camp unclothed?"

Rhenthizu thought to offer his loincloth, but it covered a person in less than the Maisusutha fashion. He climbed out of the pool and sat, dripping.

"If we stopped before the point," he said, recalling the path they had taken from camp to sweat lodge, along the beach and around a weathered headland, "I would get my boat cloak and bring it to you. Though," he admitted, "it's rather stiff and salty." If he were back at camp, he would be washing it.

"Then everyone would think..." Uinthi laughed. "They hardly know what to think of me, a given child of Fair Island, a traveler—what would it matter?"

"It does matter—what people think," Rhenthizu said.

"I suppose." Uinthi chuckled low. "They might think I had changed. That would surprise them."

"Why?"

"They want to marry me. They hope for me—because my mother is peace chief, and I'd be a good alliance. If they'd listen and pay attention..."

"What keeps them from listening?" Rhenthizu asked, puzzled.

"The men think of hunting, they think of war, they complain that peace gives them too little chance of proving their courage and their valor. Why should they concern themselves with anything else?"

Uinthi scooped up water in the Idaean bowl and poured it on the dying fire, stirred the ashes till the last tendrils of smoke and steam drifted away, looked askance at the worn, stained clothes, shrugged, and slipped into the shirt and often-mended moccasins. Taking up bow and quiver, Uinthi strode along the stream bank toward the forest path. Rhenthizu rose, wrapped himself in his loincloth, and picked up his boots and his spear.

"Wait, wait—my feet are used to the smooth deck." He balanced precariously on one foot, shoving his other foot into the boot, trying to hold his spear under his arm. Uinthi laughed and continued through the trees, nearly disappearing by the time he had pulled on his other boot.

Paissu saw the little boy sneak away to follow Rhenthizu. She held her silence. Better that he should pester Rhenthizu than task Kilinkizu any more today. She felt a little jealous of Bdarde. She had been glad when Kilinkizu chose to stay with the Idaeans, one familiar face among so many strangers. Of course the Idaeans had passed beyond being strangers now. Paissu held Iakinthu in awe and admiration; Rhenthizu was like a sister, and, to her surprise, Aranthau had earned her fondness. She still found men essentially mysterious. Boys, too. Was Kilinkizu a true member of the People? Would any of the People put up with Bdarde's behavior? Paissu laughed and said to herself, Would any of the People put up with a son at all?

When one of the People bore a son, she cried with the unending grief at the loss of a daughter, and sent the boy baby to be adopted and raised by villagers.

Paissu wandered off by herself, conscious of the warnings of the Maisusutha children but confident of her ability to watch out for herself. She strolled into the forest's edge, comfortable among the shadows and the trees. The People revered the forest and took refuge in it when confronted with overwhelming odds.

Paissu wished Surefoot was with her. She imagined riding the mare down the sandy beach at a dead run, splashing at the water's edge, hoofbeats pounding like drums against the low rolling chant of the breakers. She loved this ocean, as wild compared to the sea back home as People were wild compared to village girls.

If any danger threatened, she would urge Surefoot up the bank and between the low dunes and into the dim welcoming forest.

She saw berries that tempted her, but she knew better than to eat strange new fruit in a strange new land. She would ask Iakinthu, or Thamenthu, or, if she could make herself understood, Thukui. She picked a handful of violets and twisted their stems to put in her hair. She wished her hair were long enough to plait like the Maisusutha did. Her Idaean child-locks made scraggly braids.

She walked along in silence and pleasure.

At the first whisper of voices ahead, she slipped off the trail and vanished between trees. Iakinthu and Thamenthu walked past, side by side, talking softly. Thamenthu's carry-bag bulged. Paissu wished the elder women had asked her to come along on their foraging trip. The People always discovered, as soon as they could, what a new land held for them.

Paissu stepped from behind the trees to announce herself just as Thamenthu stopped and turned toward her.

"Paissu, are you by yourself?" Iakinthu asked.

"Is one of the People ever alone, when she walks in the forest?" Paissu said.

Iakinthu chuckled. "You're always in company. But would your mother like it if I returned to her and said, Paissu remained behind, in the forest of the Maisusutha, turned into a tree?"

"She would miss me," Paissu said. "But my sisters would tell stories about me, forever after."

"Come with me. Stay with us. They might tell stories about you if you stay in human guise."

Paissu took Iakinthu's outstretched hand.

"What did you find?"

"Lobsters," Thamenthu said. "Mussels."

"And rabbits," Iakinthu said. "Thamenthu hunted them. My aim is out of practice."

"Will you show me what's good to eat here?" Paissu asked, "and tell me how to find it? Otherwise, I'm a stranger in your forest and on your shore."

"That would please me," Thamenthu said. "If you stay long enough."

They strolled along the beach, their shadows reaching toward the salt pools and sand bars of low tide. Kilinkizu hurried toward them from the beach camp.

"Is Bdarde with you?" she asked.

Paissu blinked. Kilinkizu had said foolish things when she first came to the People, but once she learned new ways she had spoken and acted sensibly. When she first came to the People, she was odd and pitiable, but she had learned decent behavior as fast as her health improved.

But what member of the People would ask another where any man or boy might be?

"He followed Rhenthizu and Uinthi down the beach," Paissu said, pointing toward the headland.

"I thought he was with you."

"Why would he be with me?" Paissu said. "Is he a baby, that you would ask me to watch him?" She had cared for little sisters as long as she remembered, but what did she know of boys, except that this one always spoke rudely to her?

Paissu and the other children had watched out for Kilinkizu when she first came to the People, before she joined the Idaeans as a given child. Maybe she was remembering those times and expecting Paissu to teach Bdarde proper ways.

The sun fell toward the treetops in the west.

"He'll be all right with Rhenthizu and Uinthi," Iakinthu said.

"He has no cloak—it's getting dark, and cold."

"Cold!" Thamenthu laughed. "Come along. They'll all be back soon and warm by the fire, and we'll eat lobsters and rabbit stew."

Kilinkizu put her fist to her forehead in salute and respect, but instead of accompanying them to camp, she walked away toward the headland. The tide of the Sunset Sea, turning, ate up the sand, obliterating the traces she sought.

Rhenthizu caught up to Uinthi, who was walking along with bow and quiver over one shoulder, hair nearly plaited. He wished his hair was as long: it had grown out barely a finger's length. When he woke it stuck out in all directions instead of curling like an Idaean's.

Uinthi held up one hand, letting the plait fall and unbraid. The silent signal stopped him. Uinthi slid the bow free and nocked an arrow.

Rhenthizu flared his nostrils. An odor of rotting flesh and dying plants and dog turds, all mixed together, flowed along the path, like the outflow of the summer drains during the first strong winter storm. He gasped and nearly choked at the stench.

Uinthi moved toward bright sunlight that slanted through sparse trees. The trees gave way to a clearing. Rhenthizu followed as silently as he was able. On *Flying Fish* he could balance on the bowsprit, hands free, grasp the lines, and race to the top of the mast, sure of his balance. Here in the forest, he felt uncertain, shadowed by an unfamiliar fear.

The stench thickened. He stopped, then plunged forward, breathing through his mouth, when Uinthi beckoned to him without looking back.

A huge old tree-snag, charred and jagged and hollow, leaned out into the clearing. Uinthi edged around it and peered beyond it.

The scuff, scuff, scuff of an old man walking—a huge old man, an ancient giant—came closer, along with grumbling complaints and snuffles.

Rhenthizu stared out from behind the snag.

An enormous creature shambled across the clearing, its great claws tearing up moss and delicate spring flowers. It was twice the size of Mother Bear, with a longer neck; a drawn-out, foolish face; and a droopy, dragging tail. It paused to nibble a bite of the tender new growth, tearing at the flowers, breathing heavily.

"Is it the forest man?" Rhenthizu asked softly. Uinthi silenced him with a cut of one hand.

Did the forest man of childhood stories live so far from the mountains and moss-dripping forests of Rhenthizu's people's home?

If I can travel this far and farther, Rhenthizu thought, so can the forest man. But did I ever hear that the forest man smelled like this?

As the creature came closer, its odor intensified. Rhenthizu struggled to keep from gagging, and even Uinthi drew back, skin paling.

The beast lumbered along, walking on the edges of its paws, rolling from side to side. Its long curved claws projected inward, ripping up clods decorated with wildflowers. A gray-green cast dulled its ragged reddish fur.

In awe, Rhenthizu watched the great shambling creature. It was the largest being he had ever seen on land, bigger than Iakinthu's bulls, though its body was gaunt from winter. At the edge of the clearing it rose on its hind legs, twice the height of a human person, more, and hooked its great claws around branches to pull the tender new leaves in reach of its long tongue and nibbling lips.

It snorted and dropped to the ground, blinking its small bright eyes and snuffling into the breeze. Rhenthizu wondered how it could smell anything through the miasma of its own stench.

It lost interest in the breeze and sat back on its haunches and clawed at the branches above it. Bits of leaves and twigs showered around it. It munched steadily, eyes heavy-lidded.

Uinthi slipped the arrow back into its quiver. Together, hidden by the snag, they crept silently away.

Twenty paces down the trail, Rhenthizu took a deep breath, his first proper breath since encountering the forest man. Uinthi, too, breathed deep.

"His kind is rare, these days," Uinthi said. "My grandfather remembers when the forest people roamed in bands and ate all the leaves as high as they could reach. If the trees were young and small, you could follow the trail of the forest people by the sunlight shining through bare branches."

"So you put your arrow away—to let him live."

"I put my arrow away because the forest people have armored skin, and I'd only lose my arrow. He'd run right through your spear. But the arrow might have distracted him from us, if he decided we offended him."

Rhenthizu laughed. "He, offended? By our scent?"

Uinthi laughed in return.

A high-pitched shriek broke the silence. Rhenthizu thought it must be the cry of a huge bird, a predator. Who knew what size this land's eagles reached?

Uinthi spun and raced back toward the clearing without a word of explanation. Rhenthizu followed, reluctant as he was to approach the forest man again. The cry came again, piercing: a child's scream of terror.

Uinthi burst through the edge of the forest and into the clearing. The forest man was lumbering toward little Bdarde, a low rumble in its throat, small bright eyes squinty with suspicion.

"Take him down the path!" Uinthi said, and ran in front of Bdarde, cutting between the boy and the forest man like a sky-iron spear point.

The forest man reared back on its haunches in slow surprise. It rose, rose, rose, looming over Uinthi. It snorted a glob of green snot. Uinthi waved and shouted. Rhenthizu scooped Bdarde up and carried him out of the clearing and around the burned tree-snag. The boy struggled. Rhenthizu wondered where the sensible calm of Bdarde-that-was had gone, and whether this child would ever retrieve it. The boy squirmed like a lizard, so Rhenthizu let him go into the soft rotten wood of the floor of the snag's cavern.

"Stay here and be quiet!"

Rhenthizu turned toward the meadow, hesitating in the shadows.

Uinthi climbed to a sweeping branch above the reach of the forest man's claws, ripped off pale green new leaves, and dropped the tempting morsels around the forest man's long sad face. In a moment, temptation distracted it from annoyance, and the creature lunged at a falling cluster of leaves, snatched at another with slow tongue and heavy claws, and finally dropped to the ground with a long sigh, to lie amidst the rain of delicacies.

Uinthi moved quietly to the base of the branch. The forest man raised its head, seeking more of the new leaves growing out of its reach. It raised itself along the tree trunk with its great claws. It would be able to rake Uinthi's leg. Rhenthizu stepped into the clearing, readying his spear.

Uinthi made a sound of exasperation. A moment later the stained shirt fell over the forest man's head. It growled and pawed at the leather.

Uinthi ran out along another branch to a second tree, to a third, and finally, a sporting distance from the forest man, dropped to the ground and walked calmly through shadows and sun to rejoin Rhenthizu.

Rhenthizu unclenched his hand. It ached from gripping his useless spear. He and Uinthi returned to the snag, where Bdarde sat with an air of rebellion and anger fueled by fear. He shrugged off Rhenthizu's hand and came blinking out of the dark hollow into the sunlight. He bore scrapes and scratches from undergrowth and perhaps a fall or two.

"Were you lost?" Uinthi asked.

Bdarde stared at him.

"You're a girl!" he cried.

"Am I?" Uinthi's voice was unperturbed.

"I—I—" He scowled. "Cover yourself!"

"When did Idaeans grow so astonished at nakedness?" Uinthi said, amused.

"Is he an Idaean?" Rhenthizu said, astounded that Uinthi could mistake Bdarde for one of Maranti's people. "He's Kilinkizu's son by a northern barbarian, and bad-tempered. She only just recovered him, and he has yet to learn any manners."

"It's always that way with the ones who come from other bands," Uinthi said.

"Who needs manners to talk to a girl?" little Bdarde said, as arrogant as his dead master.

"You spoke to me in a well-mannered way this morning," Uinthi said. "Am I so different this afternoon?"

"Yes!" the boy shouted. "My people command women. And we would kill a woman who pretended to be a man."

"'Pretend'?" Uinthi's voice lost its amusement.

Rhenthizu felt a distressing and powerful desire to strike the boy. Instead, he tried to make a joke of what Bdarde had said.

"What woman will ever pay attention to you, unless you learn proper manners?"

"They all will," Bdarde said. "Or I'll beat them."

"Who needs manners," Rhenthizu said, at the end of his patience, "to talk to a rude little boy-child?"

And with that, he scooped Bdarde up and threw him over his shoulder and carried him down the trail to the beach, ignoring his outraged shrieks, holding his legs to stop his kicking, and putting up with the small fists pummeling his back.

"He's inexhaustible, I'm afraid," Rhenthizu said to Uinthi as they left the forest and scrambled down the bright sides of the dunes, Rhenthizu wary of falling and injuring the boy, whose writhing weight disturbed his balance. He slid once, on the dune's slope. Bdarde shrieked even louder. Rhenthizu's head hurt from the piercing noise.

He splashed into the sea and dropped Bdarde in waist-deep water.

"Be quiet!" he said, when the boy surfaced, sputtering. To his astonishment, Bdarde obeyed. Rhenthizu returned to Uinthi, at the water's edge.

"Did you strangle him?"

Shocked, he glanced quickly back at the boy, who struggled to his feet and waded toward shore, angling away from Rhenthizu and back toward camp.

"That was a joke, Rhenthizu," Uinthi said.

Rhenthizu tried to smile. "As funny as mine," he said drily.

Ankle-deep in the running waves, dripping, sullen, fists clenched, Bdarde glared at Rhenthizu.

"Go ahead and beat me!" he said. "Do I care what you do to me?"

"What a strange little boy you are," Rhenthizu said. "What does it benefit you, to prevent anyone from liking you?" The child had spoiled his enjoyable new day, his introduction to a new land. "Come along. Your mother will be worried."

Rhenthizu and Uinthi walked down the beach toward the headland. Despite himself, Rhenthizu glanced back to be sure Bdarde followed. The little boy stomped in the shallow surf of the incoming tide, glaring at sand and waves. Uinthi's shadow stretched out into the water, cast long by the falling sun, and Bdarde stamped upon that, too. Rhenthizu felt uneasy.

"Stop that," he said mildly. Bdarde looked up guiltily and tried to mask his guilt with anger. But he stopped stepping on Uinthi's shadow. Uinthi watched, with a quizzical expression, untroubled by Bdarde's anger and bad manners.

A breeze sprang up as the sun descended toward the vast forest beyond the beach. Rhenthizu shivered.

"Are you cold?"

Uinthi shrugged. "I've been much colder. When I returned from Idaea, I felt cold for a year, even in summer."

Another shadow appeared, dark within the shadow of the headland, and emerged from the shade: Kilinkizu, with her unmistakable bright hair. Uinthi hesitated, then shrugged again with a sigh and kept walking.

"Will you go in the woods till I fetch your clothes?" Rhenthizu asked.

"My modesty has been tried worse than this," Uinthi said dryly. "And what Idaean is troubled by a naked body?"

Kilinkizu strode toward them, boat cloak sweeping behind her. Rhenthizu waved at her, but dropped his hand when her only response was to keep walking.

A few paces from them, she stopped. She glanced at Bdarde. He looked away. She gazed in cold silence at Rhenthizu.

"Did we take him with us?" Rhenthizu exclaimed in self-defense. "We found him when we started home."

"He's wet, and cold—"

"He's lucky to be alive. He tried to get himself eaten by the forest man."

"This is difficult," Uinthi said, "as the forest man eats only leaves."

"Uinthi saved his life," Rhenthizu said. "At great risk and without thanks."

Though his explanation eased Kilinkizu's anger, it failed to ease her worry or her fear for Bdarde or her sadness. Kilinkizu gazed at Uinthi for a long moment, without surprise, ignoring nakedness.

"I thank you," she said.

"You're welcome."

Kilinkizu turned to Bdarde, who glared back with his customary resentful scowl.

"Do you have a story to tell?"

"Should she let me be killed?" he exclaimed. "What woman's life is worth more than a man's?"

"Does a man stand before me?" Kilinkizu said, her voice disappointed and her fair cheeks flashing scarlet with embarrassment or anger. The boy, still struggling with the Idaean language, puffed up for a moment, then realized what she had said, what it meant, and reverted to sullenness.

Kilinkizu held out the heavy boat cloak. Bdarde, shivering in the cool evening breeze, reached for it as if by right, but Kilinkizu handed it past him to Uinthi.

"Will my son someday understand what you risked?" she said. "I do understand, and I thank you for my son's life."

She took Bdarde's hand and led him down the beach toward the headland and camp, ignoring the boy's resistance when he hung back.

"What a strange little boy he is, yes," Uinthi said, agreeing with Rhenthizu.

Swinging into the boat cloak, Uinthi walked down the hard sand to the water's edge, letting the waves lap at the frayed moccasins, letting the breeze flutter the edge of the cloak, waiting for Kilinkizu and Bdarde to get far ahead.

"Now I'm too warm!" Uinthi exclaimed, letting the cloak droop. "I wish she'd given me her vest! How pretty, all the colors of summer flowers. I had one when I came home, but I wore it to pieces."

Rhenthizu glanced up and down the beach. Kilinkizu and Bdarde were crossing the narrow strip of bright beach sand and rocks at the point of the headland.

"The tide," Uinthi said. "Let's hurry before we have to climb the headland's neck. The rocks will come right through the holes in my moccasins."

The speed and force and distance of the incoming tide shocked Rhenthizu. The small tides of Idaea and of Fair Island rose and fell gently. He and Uinthi reached the headland as a glassy rush of water spread across the beach, pushing foam before it, and reached between the scattered rocks. Tide pools caught the wave. The wave receded, whispering. The sand gleamed dark and wet. As the next wave gathered to rush the beach, deeper and higher, Rhenthizu and Uinthi raced across the sand to the other side. Uinthi outdistanced him; instead of redoubling his efforts, he enjoyed the sight of long strong legs and the rippling cloak.

They stopped running, reluctantly, but unwilling to catch up to Kilinkizu, or, more to the point, to Bdarde. Rhenthizu felt sorry for the little boy, always behaving in a way to make people avoid him. He felt sorry for Kilinkizu, who must keep him.

Fire sparked and caught, and an enormous bonfire blazed high as they approached camp.

"What's the matter?" Rhenthizu asked.

"They should be preparing to go home. What's the fire for?"

Uinthi's worry passed to Rhenthizu. Together, they hurried toward the beach camp.

Iakinthu thought to follow Kilinkizu, to accompany her, but Kilinkizu knew more about the dangers of the forest, of any mainland, than Iakinthu did. If hungry Mother Bear came along looking for someone to eat, Iakinthu could only slow Kilinkizu down.

Iakinthu watched the young numerator till the encroaching tide snuck up on her and splashed her own feet. She danced away from the cold water. As it sucked back across the sand, leaving small bubbling holes to mark the burrows of clams, Iakinthu strolled back to camp with Thamenthu and

Paissu, admitting to herself that she was only making excuses, for she preferred to avoid Kilinkizu's unpleasant little son as long as possible.

The pirates have ruined him, she thought. Can we bring him back, or is he gone forever?

Rhenthizu and Uinthi hurried back to camp. Night closed in. The fires glowed and snapped. Uinthi smiled.

"I was wrong to worry. Another night on the beach, a feast. Tomorrow everyone will go home. Will the Idaeans stay?"

"Will you come with the Idaeans?"

Uinthi shrugged.

The scent of stew—fresh meat? Rhenthizu wondered, his mouth watering—hung in the salt air. He was ravenous; he had last eaten near dawn. He strolled toward the fire where the young women clustered. Uinthi elbowed him in the ribs and nodded toward the fire where the young men sat, laughing and talking, letting the firelight shine on their bared chests, pretending the young women were paying attention to something other than them.

Rhenthizu hesitated, but Maranti, a dark-haired woman among the other dark-haired women, stood out among them, goldstone complexion set off by Egyptian linen. He wanted to be near her even more than he wanted some of the savory stew. He continued toward the young women, with a thrill of happiness as Maranti turned toward him, crossed to him, embraced him.

Between the sweat bath, danger, hunger, the scent of Maranti's perfume, and the perfume of her touch, Rhenthizu's head spun. He swayed, leaning against her, bending down to bury his face against the curve of her neck and shoulder. She stood still, holding him, stroking the back of his neck, silent, till he steadied. Then she drew back and held out her hand to draw Uinthi, too, into their circle.

"My newest friend," she said, smiling. She took off her necklace of delicate gold spirals and put it around Uinthi's neck. Holding the rough boat cloak with one hand, Uinthi freed the other hand from the folds of wool and touched the necklace, surprised.

"Thank you," Uinthi said. "Do I have anything to trade? I gave all my things to my mother, I lost my old clothes, and the cloak belongs to Kilinkizu."

Maranti drew back the cloak to show Uinthi's throat and arranged the necklace. Its color, bright against Maranti's dark complexion, glowed brighter against Uinthi's skin.

"It's a gift," Maranti said. "Does an Idaean expect a gift in return?"

Rhenthizu knew what she believed, and so must Uinthi, after living with the Idaeans, but he remained silent. What would the Maisusutha think, if they believed he and Uinthi had made love? What would the Idaeans think, if they knew they had spent the day together, each aware of the other's attractions, but had remained apart?

Uinthi might rather have Maranti, Rhenthizu thought. Maranti might rather have us both.

Thamenthu and Iakinthu, Paissu and Thukui joined them and drew Uinthi and Rhenthizu farther into the firelight.

"A celebration!" Thamenthu exclaimed. "Of Uinthi's return."

Thamenthu whispered to Thukui, who listened gravely, jumped up, and beckoned to Paissu. The two children vanished beyond the fire's circle. A moment later they returned, burdened with parcels, dignified in their responsibility, about to break into giggles of anticipation. They carried the parcels to Thamenthu, who smiled her thanks and nodded toward Uinthi.

Paissu and Thukui placed the parcels at Uinthi's feet.

"Mother—?" Uinthi said.

"I wanted to see you in new clothes," Thamenthu said. "So I sent to our house."

She bent and opened the first parcel, drawing out a leather shirt with long fringe at arms and shoulders, very plain and simple and elegant. She held it against Uinthi, estimating the fit.

"Did I know you'd come home so thin, dear child? But from now on you'll have plenty to eat."

She handed the shirt to Rhenthizu to hold.

Thamenthu drew out leggings and breechcloth and moccasins, all in the same elegant and unadorned style. Those, too, she laid aside in Rhenthizu's keeping.

She brought out a second shirt, this one fringed and decorated with geometric patterns. Rhenthizu wondered what the decoration was made of. Firelight reflected from it, giving the muted colors a glowing sheen. Thamenthu gave the shirt, and the leggings and moccasins that matched it, to Maranti to hold.

Uinthi embraced Thamenthu, made awkward by the winglike folds of the boat cloak.

"Mother, thank you—"

"Am I finished?" Thamenthu said. She opened the last parcel. "You were gone a long time. Each time I completed something, I thought, this means my Uinthi will return tomorrow. Each of those tomorrows, I began something new."

The third shirt was made of white doeskin, so soft it flowed like Sheng silk. Long fringe adorned arms, shoulders, hem.

"I just finished this, so surely I was right." She smiled.

Beads covered the front of the shirt, ran down the sleeves, flowed along the shoulders: white and purple shell beads, turquoise and lapis lazuli and jade beads, Egyptian beads, and the golden glint of Fair Island work. Amazed, Uinthi stroked the exuberant stripes and curves of the elaborate design.

"My Idaean gifts," Uinthi said softly. The precious beads had been a gift from Pharaoh to Iakinthu, and Iakinthu's gift to Uinthi when Uinthi came home.

"You gave them to me when you returned," Thamenthu said, "and I waited for a proper time to give them back."

Iakinthu and Thamenthu and Maranti circled Uinthi. Rhenthizu found himself closed out of the circle; he stepped back, acquiescing, but thinking, I've seen Uinthi undressed—I can see others dress my new friend.

The circle opened again, displaying Uinthi like a flower's center, clad all in white doeskin adorned in gleaming shades of blue and gold, a young Maisusutha man, and Rhenthizu wondered if it would have been more proper for the young men, rather than the young women, to help Uinthi put on the new clothes.

Thamenthu watched, her eyes bright with unshed tears.

"I wanted to see you in it," she said. "At least once, and while it was new."

After a long hesitation, Uinthi said, "Then I'm to go with the Idaeans?"

Thamenthu remained silent, sad. "It is your choice."

"You're right," Uinthi said. "It is. I'll finish the journey. I'll go with Iakinthu."

Maisusutha and Idaeans feasted together that night on lobsters and clams and maize porridge, olives and bread and honey, olive oil and rabbit stew.

Uinthi sat beside Rhenthizu, eating slowly, savoring each mouthful, exhaustion overcome with joy, the colors of the fire playing against hair and face, white deerskin and golden spirals. To Rhenthizu's astonishment, Maranti sat on Uinthi's other side, putting Uinthi between them, in the place of honor that Maranti should have by right.

Perhaps Maranti does desire Uinthi, Rhenthizu thought, a little jealous despite himself.

Thamenthu brought Uinthi a lobster steamed under seaweed, and Iakinthu brought a bowl of warm olive oil and garlic. Thamenthu and Iakinthu dismembered the lobster into bits of red shell and morsels of succulent meat, juggling the steaming claws, blowing on their fingers against the heat. Rhenthizu dunked a cracked claw into the olive oil and sucked out the meat, savoring the taste of the sea, the spice of the earth.

The companions of *Flying Fish* stood ankle-deep in the surf, holding the ship's boat steady at the height of the tide. Iakinthu stood on the beach, just above the high-water mark. She took Thamenthu's hands in hers. Thamenthu leaned toward her, and Iakinthu kissed her cheek.

"I'll bring Uinthi back to you," Iakinthu said, "safe and wealthy."

"Can you know that for sure?" Thamenthu said. "I hope so, my dear friend."

"Come with us," Iakinthu said again.

Thamenthu laughed. "You Idaeans! You're relentless! Is it any wonder you make such good traders?"

"Aranthau's signaling," Rhenthizu said, from his place beside the boat.

"The captain of *Flying Fish* wants to leave with the tide," Iakinthu said, "and your cold sea is numbing the feet of my companions. I must go."

Bdarde, behind her, cried, "I want to push!" and shouted in anger when Rhenthizu, without a word of acknowledgment, picked him up and put him in the boat with the cargo.

"May we leave a given child for you?" Iakinthu said drily.

Thamenthu glanced over Iakinthu's shoulder at Bdarde. "He'll think you weak, till you treat him as he's accustomed to being treated."

Iakinthu sighed. "Then he must think we're weak."

With a final embrace, she turned away from her old friend, her given sister, waited a moment for the lull between two flocks of waves, and strode dry-footed down the beach, hand in hand with Paissu, to the boat. Rhenthizu and Maranti handed her in. Paissu scrambled in after, and they both turned toward shore to wave goodbye to Thamenthu, Thukui, and the other Maisusutha.

When the next flock of waves rushed in, their froth as white and woolly as sheep, the companions of *Flying Fish* pushed the boat off and jumped in, splashing and laughing, wet to the knees. They took up their oars and stroked hard toward the ship, aware of Aranthau's wish to sail on the turn of the tide. Uinthi rode a fragile canoe precariously over the swells, pacing the ship's boat easily in a craft more suited for slow rivers and still lakes.

Iakinthu clambered up the side of *Flying Fish*, torn between her wish to remain with Thamenthu and her other Maisusutha friends, and her desire to complete Rhenthizu's journey and weave alliances with his people. What I truly wish, she said to herself, is to go home. It is time for me to retire as Gephyra. I recognized the right time to stop dancing. Have I left my second retirement too late? If I still have time, it's time for me to be a proper grandmother.

It amused her a little, if sadly, that Maranti had known the right time, and Iakinthu had ignored her, and that Maranti was enjoying herself so completely.

She would have made an excellent Gephyra, Iakinthu thought, but she will make an even better Eldest Daughter. So I must get her home safely.

"Iakinthu Gephyra," Aranthau said as she climbed over the side rail. He spoke in a formal and distant voice; he stood back from helping her to board her ship, which was proper, but a change. He observed perfect propriety only when he felt annoyed.

I suppose I'll have to tease him back to me, she thought, before he'll forgive me the tobacco.

He overdid his asceticism, as far as she was concerned, and dearly as she loved him, as much as she admired his expertise in pleasing her and in pleasing her ship— I place the fortunes of my family in his hands, Iakinthu said to herself—she regretted all the pleasures he denied himself.

The companions of *Flying Fish* swarmed up the side as if it were a low rise. They pulled up nets of fresh food and dried maize and the bedrolls and awkward cooking utensils of their camp, and Uinthi's possessions and new clothes, tightly wrapped in deerskin. Iakinthu thought, I must find a good piece of oiled silk, against the salt water.

Finally the ship's boat came up the side, and Uinthi's canoe, a brand new one, a gift from the young Maisusutha men, and fur robes from the Maisusutha women.

The water jars stood in the hold, full, some still sweating from the cold of the spring. Iakinthu had left Thamenthu with gifts of linen and Egyptian beads and copper, and Thamenthu had sent her off with gifts of tobacco, carven soapstone pipes, beautiful clear sheets of mica, and food.

As soon as the companions hauled boat and canoe on deck, Aranthau called for the anchor to rise, for the sails to open and catch the wind, and for *Flying Fish* to head out to sea.

Chapter Sixteen

Iakinthu yearned for the touch of earth beneath her feet, for even so much as the sight of land. Her ship sailed smooth and steady—Aranthau's handling of it gave her pleasure and pride—and Sister Sun shone benevolently. Aranthau thought only of the safety of *Flying Fish* and its companions when he sailed so far from land, away from shoals and reefs, rocks and surf, unknown islands, lee shores.

Iakinthu knew all this. Yet she yearned for the sight of land.

Sister Sun rose higher and warmer with each day's southern sailing, till she crossed the sky in the same line she followed over Fair Island. Iakinthu glanced east, as if by wishing it she could see her home.

She sat on a camp stool in the shade of the stern cabin. Maranti and Uinthi sat nearby. Uinthi wore an Idaean kilt and vest, more utilitarian at sea than deerskin because they would dry more quickly. Maranti combed olive oil into Uinthi's hair with her mother-of-pearl comb, trying to arrange it in the Idaean style, curling the lovelocks around one finger. Maranti gave a final flip of her comb to Uinthi's hair, so it lay in beautiful glossy coils. She painted Uinthi's eyes with kohl.

"You are a perfect Idaean!" she said. "Will you make me a perfect Maisusutha?"

Uinthi combed and braided Maranti's hair in the Maisusutha style, fastening the braids with bright bits of silk, wiping away the kohl.

Several parcels thumped onto the deck from the hatchway. Rhenthizu followed, climbing up from the dimness. He brought the parcels to Iakinthu and set them at her feet: deerskin bundles, a length of oiled silk, sealing wax, a candle.

"Thank you, my dear," Iakinthu said. Rhenthizu brushed his fist to his forehead in acknowledgment and stretched out on his boat cloak to doze. He had spent half the night at the steering oar.

Maranti took his hand and inspected it, picking up her henna brush.

"The decoration will rub off if you paint my palms," he said, and closed his eyes.

She painted the back of his hand with henna while Iakinthu unfolded the oiled silk, to seal Uinthi's new clothes away from salt water.

Uinthi opened the deerskin parcel and touched the white doeskin, the elegant bright patterns.

"I remember when you brought the beads home. I remember when you gave them to me, a gift to a given child."

"And Thamenthu transformed them," Iakinthu said.

Uinthi smiled fondly.

"Will you wear this?" Uinthi said to Maranti. "To be a perfect Maisusutha?"

"I will," Maranti said. She protected the designs on Rhenthizu's hand with honey and a scrap of linen, then put on Uinthi's fringed and beaded leather shirt. Uinthi, in turn, slipped into Maranti's sea-purple jacket.

They stood together under the awning of the stern cabin.

Rhenthizu opened his eyes, gazed at them, smiled.

"Have I spent my whole childhood wishing for proper curls?" he said to Uinthi. He rubbed his hand over his growing hair. "It always stayed straight."

"A new Maisusutha and a new Idaean," Maranti said, laughing with delight. "Shall we be given children for each other?"

Gallant in Uinthi's leather shirt and fringed leggings, Maranti spun, stretching her arms to enjoy the play of the long fringe. She bent down till the fringe brushed against Rhenthizu's back, soft as Sheng silk. He shivered and opened his eyes.

Uinthi stepped forward, toes and palms and fingertips shining with a delicate tracery of dark red henna. Maranti and Uinthi spun and danced. Iakinthu and Rhenthizu watched them, entranced.

When finally they stopped and stood facing each other, out of breath, Uinthi's curls had unwound, lying thick and glossy and perfectly straight. Maranti's braids had come loose; her hair coiled in lovelocks before her ears and tumbled in curls down her back.

They laughed.

They changed to their shipboard clothes and became two young Idaeans again. Iakinthu wrapped Uinthi's deerskin parcel in oiled silk, sealing the seams with melted wax.

Maranti stretched, brushing her fingertips against the translucent linen top of the stern cabin.

"I'm so sleepy!" she exclaimed. "I want a nap."

"Are you ill?" Rhenthizu asked. "She was all right this morning," he said to Iakinthu.

Uinthi glanced at Maranti, blinked, and grasped her hand. "She's well."

Maranti smiled.

She had recently stopped insisting on doing a share of the hard labor of sailing. She had taken on lighter tasks instead. She tended the fire. She cooked—her camp-bread now excellent—and when she lost interest, her companions regretted it. She attended Kilinkizu when the latter taught writing and numeration to Iakinthu and Paissu and Bdarde, and Uinthi for a while, and she had begun to learn the characters despite Bdarde's loud resentful distractions.

"His whiny voice makes my ears ache," Uinthi said, and abandoned the lessons in disgust.

Now Uinthi said, "You're brave! And he—"

"Shh, shh," Maranti said.

"I only meant to say," Uinthi said, "that Rhenthizu is lucky to be chosen by such a brave woman."

Iakinthu gazed at them, understood, felt surprise at having missed the signs, and asked mildly, "When, my dear?"

"Do I know for certain?" Maranti said. "Halfway between home and the land of the Maisusutha? My child must be a Gephyra!"

"What better way to get a new Gephyra, Iakinthu?" Uinthi said. "I wonder if you planned it all."

"Am I an oracle?" Iakinthu said, and thought, Maranti is so young. But it is her choice, her decision.

Truth be told, the timing pleased her. Perhaps Maranti's child *would* be Gephyra. Better if the child were born in Idaea— Iakinthu had returned from Egypt so Omempau would be born on Fair Island, and of course Issiia had been born at Old Farm; did Omempau ever leave her home?

Iakinthu counted the months. A winter baby. Could they return home in time for the birth, home, where winter would be mild?

Surprised at herself, she thought, Maisusutha babies live through Maisusutha winters, and who knows what the winter would be like in Rhenthizu's home? He remembers rain rather than snow.

"Sit here a moment," Iakinthu said to Maranti, "while I ask Aranthau about a hammock, here on deck in the fresh air."

Maranti smiled and kissed her and did as Iakinthu asked.

Rhenthizu hurried to the stern of *Flying Fish,* a rolled-up hammock on his shoulder. In the stern cabin, Iakinthu settled Maranti in her own camp chair and bathed Maranti's face with lavender water. The sight astonished him so, he stopped for a moment. Iakinthu was kind, she was generous, but solicitous?

"Hang the hammock back here," Iakinthu said, nodding toward the sternmost pair of supports. "Where Maranti will have both air and shade."

He kept silent, but his heart pounded, and he straightened beneath the burden of the hammock — a trivial weight, he thought, proudly flinging the heavy wool open and tying one end to a support.

Uinthi tied the other end of the hammock. Rhenthizu felt a handspan taller. If Idaeans spoke only of mother and coming child, still they knew he was her chosen one. He knotted the hammock ties and pulled hard to test them. He even tested Uinthi's knots. Uinthi raised an eyebrow and said, softly, "Would I be careless? She's my friend, too."

Rhenthizu helped Maranti into the hammock, bent down to kiss her gently on the forehead, took the lavender water from Iakinthu, and bathed Maranti's face. She stroked his arm.

Aranthau strolled by as if to check the steering oar. "Ah," he said. "*Flying Fish* will be honored by its new companion."

Paissu stopped just outside the stern cabin, feeling unusually shy. The People bore babies. She had seen birth more often than death. Maranti drowsed in the hammock, sleeping through the heat of the afternoon as *Flying Fish* sailed slowly on flat water. Iakinthu bent over a spindle-whorl. The thread twisted and twisted as the whorl spun and slowed; the thread tangled and broke, and the spindle-whorl spun a few times like a top, then fell over and rolled away. Paissu snatched it before it could fall over the side. Iakinthu jerked awake.

Paissu handed the spindle to her. She took it with a smile.

"Thank you, my dear. I watched it turn, and it made me dizzy. How strange."

"I brought something for Maranti," Paissu said. "For her baby, I mean, when it's born. Will you give it to her?"

"You may give it to me yourself," Maranti said. "I was only resting. It will be a long time before my baby is born."

Paissu crept into the shadows of the stern cabin, blinking after the brightness of the open deck. The fringe and gold leaves fluttered and jingled, keeping a different tempo than the erratic flapping of the sail's edge. She held out her hand to Maranti.

Maranti touched the stiff brush mane of the little toy horse, made of bits of rope.

"I had one when I was little," Paissu said, "and one morning I woke up, and it was gone, and all that was left was the end of a rope, and I almost cried because I thought it had all unraveled, and I followed the rope, gathering it up — and there was Surefoot! My mother had seen me gentling her and gave her to me."

Maranti smiled and brushed Paissu's hair back from her forehead. Her fingers were soft and warm, her fingertips blushing with henna.

"Thank you, little Paissu. I know she'll like to play with it. And do you think a pony will appear in its place?"

Paissu considered, and decided she had better tell Maranti the truth.

"Do Idaeans ride?" she said. "The People ride, and it was time for me to stop riding behind my mother and start riding by myself. But if your baby needed a pony...maybe a rope would appear in place of her toy, but I think you would have to tie a pony to it yourself."

Maranti laughed.

"Are you happy with us?" she asked.

"I miss home a little. I think about my sisters, and I wonder if they're all all right." She whispered, so only Maranti could hear, "Dragon Claws is very old."

"Yes. But I'm sure she'll be there to welcome you home — a dancer!"

Paissu nodded.

"Do you miss your pony?"

Paissu nodded again, afraid to speak, afraid her voice would tremble. She swallowed hard.

"Surefoot will take good care of Issiia, and Issiia will take good care of her," she said, trying to convince herself.

Iakinthu stood leaning against the rail, gazing toward the haze that masked the distant mainland. *Flying Fish* sailed parallel to the coast, without any plan to stop. Iakinthu wondered about the people who lived there. Will I ever meet them? she thought. Will Idaeans ever visit them? Idaeans must meet them, someday soon, but Iakinthu thought this would be her last trip away from Fair Island.

Would I have set out, she wondered, had I known the voyage would take me to the other side of the world?

The sail's steady beat suddenly ceased, and the sail dropped abruptly. She looked up, surprised, and found Paissu and Aranthau at the top of the mast, gazing out to sea. She had heard Paissu calling to Aranthau, but had been too wrapped in her own thoughts to attend what she said.

Aranthau came hand over hand down the stays, as fast as a diving porpoise, and hurried to Iakinthu's side. Stripped of the steadying effect of the sail, of speed, *Flying Fish* rolled and wallowed in the slow seas.

"Ships," he said, his expression somber. "The black-sail ships. Paissu found them." He gestured toward the unmarred eastern horizon.

"Ships!" She squinted. Her sight had lengthened in recent years, making close work more difficult; but she saw only the perfect line of sea touching sky.

"I dropped the sail to conceal us," he said. "They're below our horizon, but Paissu can see their sails. They could have seen ours."

"The pirate ships."

"Yes. Iakinthu, they are badly handled, but they are Shipwright's design. Or the work of his apprentices."

"Shipwright is dead."

"So we believed."

"Do you believe..."

"That the northerners abducted him? Forced him to work for them?" Iakinthu shivered, thinking of the horrors the northerners were said to inflict on prisoners.

"Or...persuaded him."

She frowned. "To build ships willingly? For the northerners?"

He shrugged. "I'd wish to think better of him."

"What could they offer him that Fair Island lacked? He had the best house in town. Gifts. A share of every cargo..."

"And a wish for more," Aranthau said. "Did he ever dance in Mother Moon's celebration?"

Iakinthu sighed. "Can we know? How did they find us?"

"Even the northerners have sea people in their families."

She touched his arm and smiled. "Ours are more accomplished."

"I missed seeing them." He gazed in the direction of the invisible black-sail ships, the ships that were Idaean, yet alien. Paissu moved a few steps away, pretending her attention lay somewhere besides their conversation.

Iakinthu crossed the deck to the mast and climbed.

Paissu followed.

When is the last time I climbed the mast? she wondered. Have I climbed a mast since I retired from dancing?

The ship wallowed in the swells, sending the tip of the mast back and forth across the blue-white sky. Smooth wood and rough rope passed beneath Iakinthu's fingers and toes.

"Help me see the new ships, Paissu."

Paissu slipped up beside her, peered out to capture the ships again, and pointed. Iakinthu followed the line of her arm, glad for once of the changes to her sight that made distant objects clearer.

She found them, just on the horizon. Great shouting creatures stretched across their black sails.

"Idaean ships," she said. "But from a land other than Idaea."

"Arabia?" Paissu asked.

Iakinthu laughed, then thought, Could it be? The sailors of Arabia had always preferred the eastern routes, to Hind and the coastal provinces of Sheng, to contest with the pirates of the Great Archipelago. But they might have decided to venture west. So might Tuola's people. Could Shipwright have ventured to them, in search of more wealth, more influence?

"I wish they were," Iakinthu said. "But I would have heard..."

She perched on the swaying mast beside Paissu, sick, but with dread rather than seasickness.

She took a deep breath. "Let's go down, now, my dear. You've danced on top of this mast long enough for today. Thank you. I'm proud of you."

Paissu stared at her, pale beneath her tan, reacting to Iakinthu's distress.

"Are they the pirates?" she asked.

"I think they must be Bdarde's band."

"They're turning," Paissu said. "Aranthau, they're turning."

Paissu was correct. The strange ships changed their course, all together like a pack of hunting creatures, heading directly for *Flying Fish*.

Aranthau watched Iakinthu quizzically as she and Paissu descended.

"Idaean ships."

"Yes," Aranthau said.

Aranthau called the companions again, to raise the sail. The strange ships had seen *Flying Fish*; the strange ships sailed in pursuit. The wind filled the sail; *Flying Fish* pressed forward over the sea; the edge of the sail took up its rhythm.

"Where's Bdarde?" Iakinthu asked.

Kilinkizu brought the boy to her. Bdarde dragged back on her hand. Iakinthu regretted the distress on her numerator's face, regretted the care and worry that strained her.

She had been nearly ready to laugh again, Iakinthu thought, when this boy-child came along to remind her of bad times and distress and insult her.

"Your fleet has come," Iakinthu said to Bdarde.

Kilinkizu paled and gazed wildly around, searching the horizon for the pirate ships.

Bdarde puffed up his little chest and smiled.

"I told you," he said. "I told you, our fleet will find you, and catch you, and kill you!"

"Bdarde!" Kilinkizu exclaimed, but Iakinthu silenced her with one raised hand.

"Your brothers must have worked very hard on so many ships."

"Do my father's soldiers work?" Bdarde said proudly. "We fight. Others work for us. Even Idaeans work for us—or they die."

He jerked his hand from Kilinkizu's and ran away, leaping to the stern-post and clinging to the lines.

"Come and get me, father!" he shouted. "Father, I'm here, will you let them escape you?"

At the boy's torrent of obscenity, Kilinkizu collapsed onto the deck, letting her hair fall forward. Her shoulders shook.

"There, there," Iakinthu said, kneeling beside her. "Does he know any better? He's a baby, it will be all right."

Kilinkizu said something in the boy's language and something in the language of the People. Finally she raised her head to gaze at Iakinthu, her face wet with tears.

"Can I bear it?" she said. "Can I save him from them? Could I save his sister?"

Can I answer her without lying? Iakinthu said to herself. Instead of speaking, she stroked Kilinkizu's hair and held her until Aranthau lifted Bdarde down from the stern-post, and Kilinkizu stopped crying.

They had more to worry about than an ill-mannered boy-child.

Chapter Seventeen

Rhenthizu guided the ship through dark water. *Flying Fish* ghosted along in the shifting breeze, trailing phosphorescence. He wondered if the bright wake would lead the pirates to them.

"Still out of our sight," Aranthau said, gazing behind them.

"As we're out of theirs," Rhenthizu said. "Outdistancing them."

"Perhaps." Aranthau touched Rhenthizu's shoulder, a gesture of reassurance, and went forward, where he always returned when the ship sailed in strange waters. He barely slept.

The ship's companions slept on deck, the weather was so warm and pleasant. The night would be perfect but for the pursuers.

In the stern cabin, Maranti climbed out of the hammock, slipped silently past Iakinthu and Uinthi and Paissu, who dozed on pallets around her sleeping place, and joined Rhenthizu by the rail. He leaned against the steering oar to steady it, and took Maranti in his arms. She kissed him, pressing against him, letting her linen robe fall open so their bare skin touched. They held each other close.

"You should rest," he said softly.

"I'm tired of resting," she said. "You all pamper me too much. My sister was so sick, in the early days of her first child— I keep waiting for that. But so far, I'm only lazy. And you all indulge me."

"It's our pleasure," he said, thinking his words inadequate, wanting to do everything for her.

She stroked his back. He shivered beneath her touch. Reluctantly, he drew away. Maranti's eyes filled with sudden tears.

"I'm responsible for *Flying Fish*," he said. "Responsible for your safety, and everyone else's, whenever Aranthau sleeps. Can I neglect that, even for you?"

"Will you ever touch me again?" The tears spilled down her cheeks, smearing the kohl around her eyes.

"My love, my dear one—"

"I yearn for you. Your words, your touch, your body—"

"What about..."

She waited.

The excitement of their encounters aroused him. She smiled. He gasped when she touched him.

"What about the child?" he whispered.

"My child?" she said, frowning, stepping back from him. "What about it?"

"Might we hurt it?"

Her laughter wiped away her frown, her confused annoyance.

"Are you a brute, who'd injure us? A pirate, who'd ignore my wishes? You're gentle, my love, and we can make love as gently as *Flying Fish* makes love to the sea."

He gazed at her, aroused, uneasy, eager.

"You have such odd ideas, Rhenthizu," she said. "Sometimes I wonder how you could have lived with Idaeans so long and kept them. Why do you believe them, instead of me?"

"Before Iakinthu found me," Rhenthizu said, "I knew brutes. The way they spoke…the things they did…"

"Are they here now?" she said. "They're gone, and you're here, safe, one of the companions."

They are gone, he thought, but others are chasing us.

He embraced her again. He shivered. For all his joy at being near Maranti, he wished, desperately, that she had remained on Idaea, in Kunusu, the harbor-on-land. Even if it meant loneliness for him. Even if it meant they had been parted forever.

She kissed him quickly and returned to the stern cabin. Her perfume lingered. He shuddered with longing.

He thought a whole cycle of the moon must have passed before the eastern sky lightened. He thought his deprivation and dedication a secret pride.

A shadow approached him: Aranthau, coming aft from the bow, where he had dozed and listened to the sea at night. Rhenthizu wondered if Aranthau ever slept soundly when he was aboard *Flying Fish*.

Aranthau took the steering oar.

"Go to her," he said.

Rhenthizu hurried to Maranti's side. The first rays of the sun touched her face, reaching in through the open sides of the cabin. He kissed the smears of kohl on her eyelids. She opened her dark eyes. She slipped out of the hammock, leaving it to swing gently with the motion of the ship. Together they went belowdecks, to the deserted sleeping platform. In the dim warmth, with the water sleeking past on the other side of the heavy planks, with the sea stretching out behind, they made love as gently as *Flying Fish* caressed the ocean, as softly as the spring breeze flutters the new leaves of an awakening tree.

The black-sail ships appeared over the horizon. Iakinthu squinted toward them, searching for a distinctive style of eyes on their bows. Aranthau stood beside her. His uneasiness distressed her.

"Their sails are angry."

"Like Bdarde's band," Iakinthu said.

"Why are they chasing us?" he said, as much to himself as to her.

"Because they're pirates," Iakinthu said.

He laughed, short and sharp. "Why come so far," he said, "when they could wait and attack us when we return, carrying new cargo?"

Suddenly, Iakinthu understood. "Kilinkizu's son," she said.

He glanced at her, his expression quizzical.

She lowered her voice. "The pirate's son," she said.

Though she thought of the pirates every time Bdarde behaved in an uncivilized manner, she always thought of him as Kilinkizu's son, in the Idaean way.

She should have thought of this before.

"I'm becoming old and set in my ways," she said.

Aranthau gave her a look both amused and skeptical.

"How else to explain it?" she said. "I thought of Kilinkizu in the Idaean way. But—has Kilinkizu always been Idaean? Is her son in any way Idaean? Are the people who raised him? They think we've stolen him. Perhaps they'd want him back."

"Would we could oblige them," Aranthau muttered.

Iakinthu laughed despite herself, startled, for ordinarily Aranthau was tolerant to a fault.

Somber again, Iakinthu said, "Would they turn back if we gave them the boy-child? If Kilinkizu allowed it?" She shrugged. "They're better known for wreaking revenge."

"Even Bdarde deserves better than to be given back," Aranthau said.

The answer to her question was, to a seafaring man, absurdly simple. The sea would tell a seafaring man how to find *Flying Fish*, how to follow.

"Would the sea tell them Bdarde is with us?"

"When he screams," Aranthau said.

Iakinthu hoped and believed the black-sail ships followed *Flying Fish* without troubling the Maisusutha. If they had stopped to fight with Thamenthu's warriors, surely the Maisusutha would have bested them.

The companions of *Flying Fish* gathered at the stern, to catch a glimpse of the three pirate ships.

"We could fight them," Rhenthizu said.

"Three ships to one?" Iakinthu asked. "My dear," she said kindly, "even your valor might fail, faced with those odds."

He folded his arms, glaring belligerently toward the strangers. Iakinthu understood his anger, his uneasiness. She shared it.

"*Flying Fish* is swift and strong," she said. "We'll lead the strangers on until they separate and lose themselves, or until the sea takes them. If we must, we'll fight them, and defeat them. But the farther we lead them, the more likely we'll be to face them one at a time. And perhaps with your people as our allies."

That mollified him.

The companions watched the three ships on the distant horizon. The breeze freshened; *Flying Fish* soared across the sea. Soon the three pursuing ships disappeared again, falling beneath the curve of the world.

The sunset blazed like a wildfire, scarlet and orange and gold, violent and brilliant. The air hung heavy with the colors. Iakinthu stood at the bow and gazed unhappily at the beautiful, frightful spectacle. The legends—she had always considered them legends, with little truth among the fancy—of the last conflict between Mother Moon and her imprisoned lover had ended with sky-fires like this one.

That was a thousand years ago, she told herself. How could it happen again, in this day and time?

Uinthi joined her. "We're nearly there. Nearly at the land of fire."

"Fire indeed," Iakinthu said. "The sky's on fire, as well as the land."

Farther back along the deck, Aranthau asked for a change. Uinthi ran to help.

The sail dropped and the ship's speed fell away. As Aranthau jumped onto the railing, Iakinthu scanned the sea. She was wary of great mysterious predators, or ordinary sharks, or who knew what creature, in this new, strange place.

Aranthau dove. His shadow disappeared very near the surface, and everyone grew silent.

High above, the mast drifted back and forth. Paissu perched there, gazing toward Aranthau, gazing behind them to search for their pursuers.

I'm so proud of you, young dancer, Iakinthu thought. The ship rolled and yawed on the long swells, the tip of the mast wrote complicated messages against the darkening sky, and Paissu followed the writing with grace.

She took joy in Paissu's exuberance and fearlessness. Paissu, she thought, will be a renowned dancer.

Aranthau climbed up the side of *Flying Fish*, gleaming, dripping, his hair in tendrils down his back. He wrung it out and tied it up. It would be scratchy and stiff tonight. Along with her wish for dry land, Iakinthu wished for enough fresh water for a bath in a deep tub.

The companions whipped the sail back up the mast. It caught the wind, filled, and drew the ship forward. Paissu stayed where she was.

"Still there?" Aranthau called up at her.

"Just the same," she cried over the rhythmic flap of the sail's edge. "Did you see them?"

"Too noisy," he shouted. "Too much mud." He turned to Iakinthu. Startled by the strain in his face, she brushed her fingertips against his cheek.

"What did you see?"

"Death. Heat. Water opaque with ash. The land of fire even burns the sea."

She held him. He bent down to press his forehead against her shoulder. He trembled, though the air was warm, the long red rays of the setting sun were warm, even the water was warm. Iakinthu tried to remember when she had stopped feeling cold.

"Can I see our way through the fire?" Aranthau said. "Every living thing is fleeing, if it can, or dying. Perhaps we should have chosen the land of ice."

"It's too late," Iakinthu said. "If we turned back, how would we pass through the ice and take Rhenthizu to his mother and return home in time for Maranti to have her baby? Besides, cold water is too hard on you. And we'd have to pass the pirates."

He raised his head, smiling sadly.

"I meant it as a joke," he said. "But is that what you expect of me? To get Maranti home by winter?"

"So her baby can be born at home."

"This baby may have to be born among Rhenthizu's people," Aranthau said. "Or among the Maisusutha. Or even at sea, where Maranti chose it."

Paissu danced above the sail, imagining that she rode the back of a bull. In a while she would climb down, and Iakinthu would watch her do her exercises, handsprings across the deck, backbends over Iakinthu's strong, gentle arms. Sometimes she balanced on the rail around the deck and walked, spun, ran along the smooth wood, all the way around the ship. It was like riding Surefoot, standing up, at a gallop. She enjoyed it, and the companions of *Flying Fish* smiled to watch her.

She hoped Issiia was taking good care of Surefoot, as Paissu was doing her best to care for *Flying Fish*.

Does Issiia even know how to take care of a pony? she said to herself. My sisters will teach her, as Aranthau teaches me. Dragon Claws will watch out, even if she's still angry at Kilinkizu.

For now, Paissu stayed at the top of the mast. She was the smallest of the companions, the one who could climb highest. She corrected herself: Bdarde could climb this high, but did he deign to? Deign to help *Flying Fish* escape?

Do I think of him as a companion? Paissu said to herself. He is a pirate.

For a long time she thought he was afraid to climb, but then she saw him late one night coming down from her own favorite perch. He saw her watching him and ran away, and now, to her relief, he stayed on deck.

He sneered at her, doing women's work. Of course she did women's work—what else would she do, being a woman? Paissu thought Bdarde lucky to be with the Idaeans, who allowed their men to do women's work.

Would you ever see a man riding one of the People's horses, the way Aranthau rides *Flying Fish*? she said to herself, and laughed at the idea. Aranthau was lucky too. Men could ride ships. If they rode horses, they would surely hurt themselves.

The sun touched the western horizon, bright in her eyes, hot on her skin, falling faster each day. It glowed scarlet through the clouds, its light fracturing into streaks of red and orange and gold. To the north, the pirate ships faded into the twilight. In the east the sky darkened. Straight overhead the sky was still so blue it made the sea look gray.

Paissu balanced easily on the bow rail of *Flying Fish*, scooping up Rhenthizu's lentil stew with chunks of Maranti's much-improved campbread. The ship sailed across the calm water, propelled by a fresh breeze that ruffled Paissu's hair.

"Slave food," Bdarde whispered from the shadows beneath the bow.

He meant to startle her; she glanced at him and ignored him. She smiled to herself. He could go hungry if he thought he could hunt a deer from *Flying Fish*.

"That's what you are," he said. "A slave, taken from your village. "Do you ever eat meat? Do you drink from a golden cup?"

"Does anyone on *Flying Fish*? Why would we want to?"

He climbed the rail and sat astride so he could hold it with both hands.

"You'll hurt yourself," Paissu said.

"They're going to sacrifice you."

She frowned at him.

"They did it before, and they'll do it again."

Now she laughed at him, knowing laughter would make him jump down from his dangerous-to-boys perch and run away.

She jumped to the deck, rinsed her bowl with sea water, and climbed the mast.

The mast shuddered.

Is it a storm we're sailing into? Paissu wondered. She glanced toward the serene, darkening east. In the last light she picked out one of the pirate ships as it crept into view, then fell away again beneath the horizon.

Paissu wished the storm would rise up and drive them so far over the horizon she would never see them again.

Could I ever admit it to Iakinthu? she said to herself. Admit they frighten me? I am of the People, who never shrink from battle.

She turned her back on the pirates and watched the sunset instead. The ship sped on. The clouds, glowing with sunset colors, streaked from a thick dark plume. A thunderhead?

As she watched, another great cloud of dust and smoke rose heavily into the air, roiling and churning, scarred by lightning bolts that stitched its edges and illuminated its depths. She was glad the lightning was safely far away, but thought she had better climb down before the storm came closer.

Before she could descend, more lightning and a rumble of thunder shook the air. She clung to the mast, holding tight, flinching with each new clap of sound. The noise grew and grew and grew, till she thought it would continue forever, continue so loud it would knock her from her perch, or bring the lightning to fling her down. She dared to raise her head.

Fire rose beneath the climbing plume, red as coals. A black wall spread across the horizon, hiding the fire. Lightning crashed against the blackness. The rumbling of the air shook Paissu to her bones.

"Aranthau," she whispered, then called, "Aranthau! I see the fire!"

The plume of smoke and ash billowed high, rising and tumbling faster than any storm-cloud Rhenthizu had ever seen. It was thick and gray, like some immense creature that should crawl underground rather than fly. It rose. It spread. Its mass gathered and increased, though the wind pulled at it and covered the horizon with its substance and darkened the sky with its dust.

Ash and hot pebbles scattered across the sea, across the deck of *Flying Fish*. Rhenthizu dragged on a rope, pulling a bucket of water up the side of the ship and over the rail. He dashed the water onto the deck, wetting it down, dousing the heat of the pebbles in tiny spurts of steam. The companions soaked the deck, the sail, the sides of the ship, themselves. They pulled down the curtains of the stern cabin and carried them below.

Aranthau stood at the bow, a wet linen cloth wrapped around his face.

Uinthi worked beside Rhenthizu, bareheaded. Rhenthizu wished he had time to run below and get a headcloth, but he thought he should be as stoic as Uinthi.

Sharp gray specks fell, turning to warm, gritty mud on the wet deck. A rain of pebbles fell like a sudden squall, bouncing and sizzling. Several scattered across Rhenthizu's shoulders, hard and hot. He gritted his teeth.

"Ow!"

Nearby, Paissu clapped one hand over her mouth to stifle her cry. Her shoulder bore a red mark from the hot pebble that had bounced across the deck.

She stared at Aranthau, but Aranthau's attention remained on the mountain-storm before them. She ran to climb the mast, slipped, caught herself, nearly bumped into Rhenthizu.

He sat on his heels before her.

"Brave Paissu," Rhenthizu said, "will you attend Maranti in my place?"

She glanced toward Aranthau.

"Can anyone, even sharp-eyed Paissu, see through this cloud?" Aranthau said. "The Eldest Daughter may need you."

Could she refuse such a request from Aranthau? She scuffed through the debris, leaving footprints in the slurry of seawater and ash. She went below.

Iakinthu brought Maranti a cup of water. The air belowdecks pressed close and sharp and hot.

"You're hovering," Maranti said. "You're fluttering. Does it suit you, Iakinthu?" She had lost her usual good humor. Her linen robe clung to her, and her hair hung in damp curling tendrils.

"Come away from the window," Iakinthu said.

Maranti snorted. "Will the pirates see me from this distance?" She shrugged and opened her robe, baring her breasts and her belly, which had begun to show a smooth roundness.

Iakinthu kept her silence. She was embarrassed to admit, even to herself, that she wanted Maranti to avoid seeing the volcano. To stay out of the volcano's presence and perception.

"You'll be safer here," she said. "The passage will be dangerous."

"Why should the companions face the danger, while I avoid it?"

"Because you're Eldest Daughter, and I vowed to take you home." She sat by Maranti and took her hand. "Dear Maranti, I wish I had taken you home before we came on this voyage." Her vision sparkled with unexpected tears.

Maranti smiled. "Would you have left Rhenthizu with me?"

"Would I be here—would my ship be here—if Rhenthizu had wished to stay forever in Kunusu?"

"So you see," Maranti said. "We're meant to be here."

Iakinthu sighed, and Maranti managed a laugh.

Paissu ran into the cabin. Ash smeared her face and arms and made gray speckles on her kilt.

"Rhenthizu asked me to attend you," she said, "since he has to steer. Otherwise, he'd be here."

"I hear him," Maranti said, gesturing upward, though Iakinthu thought she only imagined she could hear his bare feet on the deck overhead. "How did you get so dirty, out here where it's so clean?"

"The dirt falls from the sky."

They went together to peer out the stern window. Iakinthu resisted the urge to draw them back into the shadows.

"Is it snow?" Maranti asked.

Everyone from Fair Island knew volcanic ash when they saw it, but Maranti came from Kunusu, where the explosion of mountains existed in history and legend.

"Snow is white," Iakinthu said, "and it melts, instead of sticking, when it touches your skin."

"Go and get some water," Maranti said to Paissu, "and I'll help you wash."

Iakinthu was content to leave them involved with small domestic tasks. She climbed the ladder to the deck, surprised by the dimness of the light. A thick gray haze hung in the sky. The ominous steaming mountain loomed on the horizon, much nearer than when she went below. Gazing at it made her shudder.

She tried to laugh at herself, but failed. Maranti must stay below while they passed the mountain. She feared what might happen if Maranti glimpsed it, or if it glimpsed her.

Outside, the air was nearly as close and hot as belowdecks. The smell of the mountain's breath sharpened. Pulling her headcloth over her mouth and nose, Iakinthu struggled against gagging.

She joined Aranthau at the prow of her ship. She slid her arm around his waist. His skin felt gritty with dust. Again she wished for a bathtub, hot water, a sponge of lavender soap, a jar of new olive oil.

He glared at the mountain.

"A terrible fight," he said.

"It's only a mountain," Iakinthu said, pushing away her own dread. "A mountain, like any other."

"Except that it might bury us in ash and stone." Aranthau glanced quickly at her, then returned to squinting at the dust-gray water. They might have been sailing across a desert.

"All the dolphins have fled." Aranthau signaled to guide the ship around a raft of pumice, nearly invisible against the ash that covered the water.

"Maybe the mountain will sink the pirate ships," Iakinthu said.

"I suppose it depends on who wins the fight."

A hot flush spread up Iakinthu's breasts and neck and face. Sweat gathered at her hairline and collected beneath her breasts.

Alarmed, Aranthau pressed the back of his hand against Iakinthu's hot cheek, above the protecting veil of wet linen. She thought the fabric ought to be steaming from her heat.

"Did I intend to anger you, my dear?" he said. "A poor joke."

Iakinthu wiped the sudden sweat from her forehead with the damp end of her headcloth.

"When did I trouble myself over a joke?" she asked. "Even a joke about Mother Moon and her consort. It's the change...and only warm seawater-mud to jump into instead of a cold stream." She put her hand over his, twining their fingers together, pressing his hand against her face. "Your hand is cool," she said. "Your body comforts me."

She stood with him in the prow of her ship. They peered into the failing day. The companions went belowdeck in small groups to eat cold food, uneasy in the mountain's shadow, uncomfortable in the stinking air and drifting ash. Everyone wore damp veils to protect their breathing, and most wore headcloths to protect their hair.

Night fell, an eerie dark gray. What starlight probed through the clouds washed over the ash. The sea looked like land. *Flying Fish* moved erratically forward, now catching the wind, now struggling against it.

The mountain rumbled. *Flying Fish* entered its treacherous channel. Great piles of ash and pumice rose along the shore of the blasted channel, and layers of ash covered the opposite shore.

The wind, equally treacherous, wandered around the horizon, first cool from the distant open sea, then hot from the land. The rhythmic snap of the sail's edge lost its beat. The ship wavered in its course and lost its way, and rolled heavily among the swells. The sail fluttered, nearly filling, going slack. Floating pumice bumped and rubbed against the planks.

Aranthau gazed at the channel, at the mountain; he looked over his shoulder, back into the gray sea and the gray sky, seeking their pursuers. Iakinthu thought she saw a flicker of sail above the horizon.

Aranthau climbed the rail to stand above the deck.

"Companions, to me!" he shouted.

His call moved down the deck, belowdecks. The companions gathered from all over the ship.

Rhenthizu staggered on deck, blinking groggily with sleep. Iakinthu had last seen him sprawled insensible at Maranti's side, while Maranti sponged his forehead and sore palms with lavender water.

Now all the companions stood before Aranthau, pressing around Iakinthu. She took comfort in their presence and in their strength.

"We must take up the oars," Aranthau said. "The mountain threatens us, and the wind fails."

Iakinthu touched her fist to her forehead, like all the others, acknowledging his right to ask this of her.

When did I last salute someone from my own land? she wondered, trying to remember.

Aranthau gave her a look of astonishment, that she would offer him such an honor. She thought, He deserves it.

The companions ran below to open the oar-ports and ship the oars. Iakinthu joined them, dreading the next few hours. Aranthau touched her arm. She stopped.

"Will you handle the steering oar?" he asked. "Rhenthizu must help row."

"I will," Iakinthu said, grateful to him, embarrassed to be so grateful that he had saved her from the punishing job of rowing.

Iakinthu turned to make her way to the stern, and nearly ran into Maranti.

"I asked you to stay below," Iakinthu said.

"Aranthau called us."

"And I made a request of you."

"It's hot and close--and dark—and I wanted to see!"

"You'll have plenty to see on this journey. You're better free of this sight."

Maranti searched Iakinthu's face, taking note of the smudges of ash, the headcloth, the wet veil.

"The sight endangers you," Iakinthu said softly.

"Are you as much a heretic as you pretend?" Maranti chuckled, with a twinge of sadness. She stole a single glance at the rumbling mountain, a glance that made Iakinthu wince.

"I'm your adviser and your protector. Let me advise you and protect you." Iakinthu noted Maranti's rough kilt and plain vest, her hair tied away from her face. "I advise you to leave the rowing to the others."

"Am I of any use at all?" Maranti cried, and ran below.

Distressed, wanting more than anything else to follow Maranti and talk to her, Iakinthu hurried to the steering oar. As the oars scraped through their locks and the blades cut through the ash and pumice and found the sea, she took the smooth-worn handle from Rhenthizu, who hurried below. The ship's bulk pressed against her hands, heavy and slow without its sail.

At the bow, Uinthi swung the depth-line and dropped the weight into the water, sounding the bottom of the channel. Iakinthu searched for Aranthau, and found him climbing the mast. Someone must be lookout, but as a shower of stones clattered across the deck, and a drift of ash followed it, making her eyes water, she wished he had given the task to someone else.

The oars clashed, rattling together out of sequence. Keeping ahead of the pirates required the sail, the best speed; how could the companions practice with the oars? A second stroke went little better, and *Flying Fish* moved with painful sloth.

A clear pure voice rose up from the lower deck, and the beat of a drum accompanied it. Maranti sang and played the beat. The companions dipped the oars and stroked, raised the oars, and returned. The ship crept forward, gained speed, and steadied. The rowers caught the rhythm and rode it, sending the ship deeper into the channel, closer to the smoking mountain, pushing *Flying Fish* through the pumice and ashy water like a plough in a wet field.

Rhenthizu flung a bucket over the side. It splashed into the sea, tilted, filled with water and tiny floating pebbles. He dragged it up and poured it over his head, wetting down his hair, his skin, the deck. His arms burned with the effort of rowing, of pulling up the heavy bucket. He threw the bucket again, sluiced the deck again.

In the distance, the cloud bulged and thickened and spread wider at the top of its column. Lightning burst from cloud to cloud, illuminating the dense ash from within. Another rumble, the roar of the mountain, crashed over the ship and set it shivering. Rhenthizu recalled the earthquake of his coming of age ceremony. He shivered, too.

He pulled up the bucket and carried it to Aranthau.

"Against the heat," he said.

Aranthau took a moment to respond.

"Yes," he said. "Yes, thank you." He bent his head for Rhenthizu to pour the water over him. It dripped from the corners of his headcloth, from the exposed curling tendrils of his hair.

"Uinthi," he said.

Uinthi hurried to them, lugging a bucket, splashing the water across the prow, washing the mud from *Flying Fish*'s eyes.

Aranthau nodded toward the exploding mountain.

"The mountain was quiet, a year ago," Uinthi said, responding to his unspoken question. "The passage was wide and still. A morning's walk, if you could walk on water."

"Some say he can," Rhenthizu said.

"Will I risk Iakinthu's ship to this?" Aranthau asked softly. "Can *Flying Fish* walk across mud?"

Aranthau blew out his breath in annoyance. He stared into a sea gray with floating, fallen ash. Rhenthizu feared he would dive in, despite the danger, to try to talk to the sea.

Aranthau sighed. "I'm deaf and blind here. The sea is silent to me. Will you help me guide *Flying Fish* through this trial?"

"That's why I came with Iakinthu," Uinthi said.

Aranthau glanced back along the deck of the ship, where the companions toiled with buckets and brooms, sweeping the mud from the deck, sluicing it from the sail before the weight of ash and water ripped the fabric or cracked the mast.

Aranthau sent below for another bolt of linen. He cut it into clean headcloths and facecloths to protect them all, to help them breathe. Rhenthizu dipped his cloths into fresh water, covered his head and shoulders, tied the mask over his mouth and nose. For a moment he pulled the material over his entire face, but the linen obscured his vision. He pulled it down again. He wondered if he would be able to see through Sheng silk.

Soon all the companions looked like bandits, their foreheads and bodies smudged with ashy mud and sweat and seawater. Rhenthizu took another turn at the steering oar, careful to follow Aranthau's directions exactly. He felt alone, for he was accustomed to being near Maranti, to hearing her laugh, to catching the occasional waft of her rose perfume. Instead, ash sifted slowly over the bare spot on the deck, the dark spot usually protected from the sun, where the stern cabin had been taken away.

He was glad she had gone below. But he missed her.

Small gray rocks dotted the sea, floating like muddy bubbles, some large enough to drum against *Flying Fish*'s side. A hot blizzard of dust and ash swept past Rhenthizu, peppering his back and legs. He squinted, trying to keep the particles out of his vision. His eyes watered, and his throat stung with the sharpness of the air. The smell nearly gagged him, and he struggled with nausea.

When Rhenthizu had himself under control again, he saw that Aranthau was signaling wildly. His voice disappeared in the rumble of the mountain and the crack of lightning and the quick hisses of steam from the ocean. Rhenthizu pushed the steering oar hard, forcing *Flying Fish* into much too sharp a turn. The sail shivered; the ship leaned. Rock grated against the side of the ship, sharp and heavy. *Flying Fish* shuddered as Rhenthizu steered to its limit. The grinding raked toward the stern. Rhenthizu flinched, as if the rocks were scraping his own side.

The ship turned sharply and lost the wind. The sail flapped and the ship wallowed in the long swells, but the groan of rock against wood ceased, and the ship turned free.

Rhenthizu expected a rock, a tiny atoll. It was an island: a floating island, a great raft of pumice stones bound together by a mortar of mud and ash and heat. It floated astern, tilting back and forth as the swells rose and fell beneath it. Seaweed trailed from beneath it, growing from its bottom, and straggly plants clung to its surface. One white blossom, dingy with ash and dried salt, drooped on its stalk.

Iakinthu climbed on deck. "The hold is dry," she called to Aranthau. "The planks held."

Aranthau waved to her and disappeared down the side of the ship. Iakinthu ran to the railing. Strange to see Aranthau hanging on a rope rather than diving, but Iakinthu was glad he had chosen a safer way of inspecting the side. He passed his hands over the planks, tracing the long scrape, searching for deeper damage.

He submerged in the opaque water. They might have been sailing on the Nile at flood, so much mud colored the sea. Iakinthu watched anxiously for Aranthau to surface. She was used to being able to see him when he dove.

He broke the surface, flinging his hair out of his eyes with a sweep of ashy water. He climbed back to the deck, his eyes tearing.

Iakinthu dipped a cup into the jar of water and poured it over his face.

"Fresh water—!" he said, protesting.

"There's fresh water, or there's mud," she said.

He picked up a length of torn linen, wrung it in more fresh water, and gave it to her as a mask.

"The island scraped the planks, but they're solid, and the seams are holding," he said to the companions. "We had better put the ship back on course."

Rhenthizu snatched his attention to the steering oar. The companions shifted the sail. The hot wind touched them, steadying the ship.

All that day, they passed pumice islands, strange floating bits of disconnected land, some lush with a season's vegetation, some as barren as a desert. Now and again a seal lay on an island and raised its head with deep sad eyes.

Rhenthizu's eyes ached from the flame of the setting sun. His arms ached from holding the steering oar. As twilight fell, Aranthau jumped from the prow and strode to the stern.

"Drop the sail," he said, and the companions complied.

"We can go a little longer," Rhenthizu said. The last red streaks of sunset had faded, leaving the sky gray and ugly, starless, mysterious, and the sea the same color. Behind them, the volcano rumbled and glowed, glowered and shivered.

"Can I see where we're going?" Aranthau said. "Can I keep us from sailing over an island, in the dark? One of these false islands—or a real one? We're surrounded by islands. And the companions need food and rest."

"What about the pirates?"

"What about them?" Aranthau said. "Can they see better than I? Perhaps they'll chase us in the dark and run themselves aground."

Chapter Eighteen

The soft gray ash filled the sky, turning sharp and grainy when it touched Iakinthu's skin. She pulled her headcloth down, but every sigh of hot wind, every surge of *Flying Fish* responding to the rowers, scattered tiny shards into her eyes. She blinked, letting tears flow.

I must be a sight, she thought with a small smile, as are we all. Her lips were dry and sore.

At the prow, Uinthi took the measure of the water and called the depth to Aranthau above. Aranthau clung near the top of the mast, exposed and vulnerable. Iakinthu had to watch him, to see his signals. Frightened by the mountain, the constant rain of ash, the shallow water, the danger to her lover, she gripped the steering oar hard.

Was I ever frightened in the dancing field? she said to herself, or the first time I crossed the Sunset Sea, sailing into the unknown?

I was immortal, then. We're all immortal when we're young.

An enormous belch of smoke and ash bellowed slowly from the mountain's mouth, rising high and spreading toward the ship. The constant rumble of the volcano, felt as much as heard, surged and roared like a living thing. Maranti's song and the beat of her drum slipped through it, and the rowers stroked on without faltering. Uinthi cried out the depth again. At Aranthau's gesture, Iakinthu eased the ship toward deeper water.

A section of the mountain's flank gave way, sliding slowly, inexorably, into the sea.

Aranthau shouted from above, signalling frantically. At first she thought she misunderstood him, for the scream and rush of steam overwhelmed his voice. He signaled again, desperate but certain and clear. She put her whole weight and strength against the steering oar, turning the ship hard and fast across the channel, toward the mountain wreathed and concealed in clouds of steam and smoke — toward the surge of water rolling toward them.

The turn threw the rowers off their rhythm, but Maranti's voice and the touch of her hand to the drum collected them again. *Flying Fish* plunged ahead, struggling toward the approaching bulge of water. It rose like a flowing hillside.

"Uinthi!" Iakinthu shouted. "Come away from the prow! Uinthi!"

The wind of their progress pulled her words back. Instead of shouting again, she gathered herself and filled her lungs and cried out the long triumphant whoop of the bull-dance field.

Uinthi spun around in amazement. Iakinthu laughed despite the peril, feeling once again the wildness of her youth.

Has Uinthi ever heard me make that cry? she said to herself. Have I made it, in as many years as Uinthi has been alive?

The young Maisusutha responded to her gesture and ran down the deck to her side.

"Are you tired? Do you want to switch places?"

"Get that rope and bring it here," Iakinthu said. She sought out Aranthau, halfway down the mast and descending quickly. "Aranthau, hurry!" Uinthi brought the rope.

"Good. Leave it here. Now, go below, tell everyone to brace themselves, tell the rowers to keep rowing—for their lives."

Uinthi ran, responding to the intensity of Iakinthu's charge.

Aranthau jumped to the deck and hurried to Iakinthu, scooping up the rope and looping it around her, around the sternpost, and around himself, binding them to the ship.

"Go below!" she said.

"*Flying Fish* will need us both."

The headcloths muffled their voices.

The bulge of water rolled toward them. *Flying Fish* plunged toward it, crossing the channel, struggling toward the deeper middle and toward the mountain. The ash and smoke grew thicker. Iakinthu coughed, struggling to breathe. Aranthau brushed the ash away from the linen over her mouth and nose, for it had covered the weave and blocked her air.

Secured by the rope, they held the ship steady.

A scatter of pumice pecked at Iakinthu and fell to the deck, landing softly in the coating of ash. We might as well have chosen ice, Iakinthu thought wildly. My ship looks like it was trapped in a gray snowstorm!

The steering oar felt firm and easy in her hands. She could manage it by herself. She wished Aranthau would go below. Ash crowned his headcloth and stuck on his eyebrows.

Flying Fish stroked toward the gathering wave.

For a moment, Iakinthu thought they would succeed: ride right over the traveling bulge of water and come down safe on the other side. But the water beneath them was still too shallow. The wave rode up along the shelf, rising, growing. Its smooth top reached half the height of *Flying Fish*'s mast. The face steepened. It reached as high as the point of the mast. *Flying Fish* climbed against it, along the front of the rising wave. The deck sloped steeply, and pebbles rolled along the ash layer, making shallow tracks. The wave rose higher, its smooth crest just out of reach. Iakinthu gasped and clutched the steering oar hard. She and Aranthau sent the ship straight up the slope of water. If her ship turned now, the wave would swamp it. Aranthau held as tight as she. They used all their strength to keep the ship steady between them. On the lower deck, the companions rowed desperately, and Maranti chanted and beat the drum.

The ship's prow rose. The earth pulled Iakinthu backwards. She clutched the steering oar to balance herself as much as her ship. Rope chafed her ribs.

As the wave began to break, *Flying Fish* shivered. Iakinthu waited in dread for it to slip backwards down the face of the wave, caught and pressed under and capsized. She moaned. Froth, and foam, and water mixed with ash and pumice washed over the prow and down the deck, filling her eyes and nose and mouth with warm sea water and grit.

Flying Fish leaped over the crest of the great mass of water, plunged through the crest of the wave and fell down the far side. It landed, crashing flat. Sea water blasted up around it, coming at Iakinthu from all sides. The ship's planks shuddered. The mast shivered and swayed. Iakinthu could hardly breathe.

Flying Fish moved smoothly ahead, streaking across peaceful water.

Maranti hesitated in her song. The oars faltered.

"Keep rowing!" Aranthau shouted. "For all our lives!"

Iakinthu felt the exhaustion in each stroke, but Maranti picked up the rhythm again, and the valiant companions drove themselves to a final effort.

Iakinthu looked back.

The huge wave rose so high it hid the land. It rushed on and on, beyond the beach and the shore, onto dry land. Stones crashed and rumbled, trees cracked and exploded, and the water rushed to eat up the land.

The wave crashed down, as loud as the eruption of the mountain.

As the wave rushed back from the shore, baring the tumbled mess of the land, carrying trees like so many twigs, the pirate ships sailed into view. Iakinthu gasped, they were so near. Out of arrow distance, but far closer than they had ever been before. Each ship rode on two ranks of oars, and Iakinthu thought, When have I ever seen a pirate ship with so large a crew?

The rush of water overwhelmed her hearing; she barely made out Aranthau's shout.

"Help me turn—we must turn, up along the channel!"

She pushed, and he pulled. *Flying Fish* turned slowly west again, away from the steaming ruin of the northern bank. Iakinthu risked one glance backwards. The pirate ships turned sharply, trying to evade the wild water of the retreating wave. The water drew back and back, exposing the ruined forest, the stripped beach, the empty floor of the channel, blasted out so recently that it lacked sea life, even seaweed or barnacles.

The pirate ships struggled on the retreating wave that *Flying Fish* had barely escaped. The double ranks of oars flashed, again and again, but the rowers flagged, their strokes uneven, missing the surface in the roiling of the water.

"Aranthau, look!"

The smallest ship of the pirate fleet faltered and lost its speed. Its rowers had fallen out of rhythm, tangling the oars on one side. The ship shivered sideways, propelled by the other rowers. It struck diagonally into the retreating wave. Prow-down, it slid over the crest of the wave and inexorably along its trailing edge.

Iakinthu imagined she heard the crash and the screams even over the long low roar of water across bare ground, even over the threatening rumble of the mountain. She imagined the rowers crushed and dying, stranded on the barren sea-bottom to be drowned when the wave returned. Slaves, their lives thrown away at will by the pirates. She gasped, horrified and amazed. Aranthau, too, stared in wonder at the disaster.

"Thank you, mother," he whispered. "Please take the others, too."

A great cloud of acrid smoke roiled over the water, cutting off their sight of the two remaining pirate ships, stinging their eyes, burning their lungs.

But they had passed the smoking mountain; the tide, rising, pressed them toward the end of the channel, faster and faster as the passage narrowed. A hot rank wind blew from the mountain's slopes. Aranthau fumbled at his ropes, at the knots tied awkwardly and in haste, and finally jerked out his knife and cut himself loose. He ran to the hatchway as Iakinthu struggled to hold the ship on a steady course. Her arms burned, and her back ached.

"Every other rower," Aranthau shouted to the companions belowdecks. "Ship your oars—a wind has come to fill the sail."

Half the oars pulled clattering into the ship.

Rhenthizu staggered out on deck. His short straight hair, wet with sweat, stuck out at all angles. He pulled his filthy headcloth over his hair, across his face. His linen kilt clung to his hips, sweat-soaked to translucence. The other companions followed him, still gasping, their hands sore and blistered and their hair in wet limp curls on their necks and shoulders. Sweat darkened Kilinkizu's bright hair.

The companions of *Flying Fish* moved as quickly as they could to raise the sail, to catch the volcano's hot wind and ride it out of the stinging air, the sharp ash, the unpredictable showers of pebbles. They all shook with weariness. Iakinthu knew it because she trembled, too.

The wind caught the sail, filled it, and pressed the ship forward. Maranti's song, so steady for so long, faded to silence. The drumbeat stopped. The rest of the oars rose from the sea, flung gobbets of ash-muddied water into the air, hesitated, and withdrew into the body of the ship.

The companions on deck slumped where they stood, collapsing in exhaustion.

The wind dropped; another blast of hot ash and pumice swept over the ship. *Flying Fish* crept through the sea, pushing aside the layer of hot mud and pumice. Pebbles spattered across the deck, sizzling in the puddles or scorching damp wood dry. The companions staggered up, again, to save *Flying Fish* from burning.

"Rhenthizu!"

His boat cloak sailed toward him, flung from the main hatch. It unrolled in the air and flapped like a huge bat. He lunged and caught it, soaked it with a bucket of sea water, swung it around his shoulders, and fastened the clasp. He soaked his headcloth again, wrapped it over his face, and pulled up the cloak's hood. Now he was hot and wet, but the falling stones stopped burning his back; the scent of burned hair left the acrid wind.

He flung the bucket back over the rail and hauled it up and splashed the water onto the deck, pulled the bucket up, and threw it back, endlessly. Time meant nothing but the burn in his arms and shoulders, the continuous fall of ash, the pelting of stones.

All the Idaeans struggled to keep the deck and the sails wet. Each bucket drawn from the sea contained less water and more sizzling pumice. Rhenthizu worked in a blur of grit-filled air, tears, and mud. If he pulled his head scarf across his eyes to shield them, the linen grew dark with mud; if he removed it, his eyes filled with stinging dust.

What difference does it make? he thought. The clouds blot out the sun — it might as well be twilight.

"Rhenthizu, lean down."

Uinthi set down the bucket, scooped out the skin of rubble to expose the sea water, and poured it over Rhenthizu's hood and cloak.

"You were about to start smoking."

The heat across his shoulders eased to a damp warmth. He pulled up a new bucket of water, skimmed the ash from the surface, and poured it over Uinthi.

With a great screech of wood against stone, *Flying Fish* shuddered to a halt. The mast reverberated. The companions staggered; they fell; the rail caught Rhenthizu and kept him from plunging overboard but bruised his side and knocked the wind out of him. Gasping, he listened with dread for the crack of breaking wood, but the mast held.

Aranthau broke the shocked silence. "Companions, lower the sail!" He ran to the bow. Uinthi sprinted after him, and Rhenthizu, staggering, followed.

Aranthau peered through the falling ash. "My father's parts!" he muttered.

Rhenthizu pretended the obscenity passed without his hearing it. He might have shouted some curse himself, but his throat was too sore to shout, and what point was a whispered curse?

"Did we run aground?"

"The ground ran aship," Aranthau said.

The ship's flank had scraped against the shore of an island, but instead of riding up on the beach, *Flying Fish* had shattered a layer of crust.

The pumice island, larger, older than the others they had passed, was held together with solidified ash, seaweed, barnacles, tangled clumps of mussels. The shore rose to shrubs, to small tangled trees, to a thick canopy of jungle, all covered with the gray powdery ash, the leaves trembling with the welter of falling stones.

The sea lay quiet all around them, covered with a desert of floating stones. Pressed by the light air, *Flying Fish* creaked and scraped against the island's shore, digging the gash deeper. Each movement raked a new curved wound through the paint. The sail thudded down and the awful screech of wood on stone eased.

Aranthau threw a line over the side, swung himself over the rail, leaped to the ground. Rhenthizu followed. The foamy pebbles crunched beneath his feet, forming a slippery layer on the hard-packed crust of the island.

Above them, Uinthi shouted through cupped hands, shouted again, in a language new to Rhenthizu, then ran halfway down the flank of the ship with the line and leaped the rest of the way to the floating island.

Rhenthizu, Uinthi, and Aranthau pushed at *Flying Fish*'s side, struggling to free the ship from the bite of the broken shore.

The island trapped them. Rhenthizu slipped on the crushed ridge of beach. He could hardly tell where island ended and sea began, the water was so thick with stones and the air so heavy with ash. Everything was the same gray. He strained against the ship's side. He knew what Aranthau must be deciding: More people to the shore, risking the ship to fire; send the companions into the rigging to raise the sails, hoping the light, wandering air would help free them, risking both the ship and the sails to fire.

A movement at his side made Rhenthizu start. He blinked, trying to focus his stinging sight. Beside him, a strange creature settled in to push at the ship's side. Several more joined them, gathering at the bow where the island gripped hardest.

Is it a creature? Rhenthizu thought. It's a person. They are all people.

A thick stiff mat, folded at one end to form a head-covering, spread over the person's back and almost to the ground. All Rhenthizu could see was feet and hands, feet in thick sandals, hands helping push at *Flying Fish*'s side. Each of the islanders wore the protective mat. Pumice bounced harmlessly from it, and ash scattered over its surface.

"One, two," Aranthau called. "Push!"

Rhenthizu strained against the ship's side.

"Stop. Again. One, two—"

As Aranthau spoke, Uinthi chanted in the same rhythm but different words, and the island people pushed in rhythm with the Idaeans. By the third "Push!" they too shouted with Uinthi, and *Flying Fish* shrieked back from the shattered beach, a handsbreadth, an armslength.

Water splashed between the ship's side and the shore. The narrow gap widened. Rhenthizu slipped, twisting around. His legs plunged into the water. He flailed for a handhold in a moment of panic, clutching at loose pebbles. The ship could crush him if it rolled.

Aranthau and Uinthi hauled him onto the beach.

"Get on board," Aranthau said. *Flying Fish* moved slowly out of the gash it had cut in the land. Thanks to the island people, it was free. Soon it would be out of reach.

Rhenthizu stepped into Aranthau's interlocked fingers. Aranthau lifted, and Rhenthizu sprang, vaulting over the rail. Uinthi followed; Aranthau grabbed the line and walked himself up the side.

The gap widened between *Flying Fish* and the floating island. On deck, the exhausted companions paused long enough to cry out in relief and gratitude. Uinthi leaned over the rail, waving to the island people, calling out to them again. They waved back, only their hands protruding from the protective mats. They pulled back into shelter, ran up the beach, ran through the shrubs. They disappeared into the jungle, their mats like the carapaces of gray-steaked gold beetles.

"What did you say to them?" Rhenthizu asked.

"I said thank you. I said I hoped we would meet again."

Lightning flashed in a net across the ash clouds, and thunder rumbled over the sea.

The rain began.

Chapter Nineteen

The companions on deck slumped where they stood, despite the ash beneath them and the rain falling on them. The rest of the companions, still below on the rowing deck, must have collapsed in their places, spent from their long efforts, from the last few moments of forcing the ship forward with half the rowers attending to the sail.

Iakinthu clutched the steering oar, her sight blurred by ash and tears. Smoke and clouds obscured her path, and she could only hope she was steering in the right direction. The rain slowly cleared the air.

Uinthi hurried to the prow to continue measuring the water's depth. Paissu followed, lugging a jar of wine. She came first to Iakinthu and poured the cup full. Iakinthu drank it, unmixed with water, and smiled gratefully. Paissu peered up at her, only her dark eyes visible below the headcloth and above the smudged mask.

"Thank you, little Paissu," she said. "I'm proud to have you as my student."

Paissu blinked, and ran away to give wine to Kilinkizu, to Uinthi, to Aranthau and Rhenthizu and to all the other companions.

Aranthau came to Iakinthu, set down and unfolded a camp chair, gently unbound Iakinthu from the stern post, and seated her on the chair while he took over steering. She was too tired for even a token protest, and sat with her arms resting on her knees and her head down. The unmixed wine crept up on her, making her vision sparkle even when she closed her eyes. She let her tears flow to wash the ash in rivulets down her face.

Rhenthizu slumped in exhausted misery. The stinging stench of the air continued, despite the rain. The long tail of the headcloth covered his back and shoulders. The wine, drunk too quickly, roiled in his stomach. He was ravenous but doubted he could eat. His hand stung from blisters and salt water and the sharp ash. His arms quivered with fatigue. His back and shoulders ached fiercely. He feared his legs would fail him if he stood.

"Rhenthizu."

He raised his head. Paissu offered him another cup of wine.

"Thank you." He drank, too tired to ask for water. The soft scent and the rich flavor reminded him of summer and grapes and celebration and home.

"You did well today," he said. Paissu had carried water to the rowers and the deckhands through the long flight from the mountain, all by herself. He wondered where Bdarde was through all this.

But of course he wants the pirates to come and take him, Rhenthizu thought, perplexed by the boy, as always. To take him and beat him to make a man of him. The men who had beaten Rhenthizu had made him a terrified, silent child, and he still had nightmares about them. The nightmares had become rare after Iakinthu saved him, but they hovered.

"Thank you," Paissu said shyly. She spoke easily with Iakinthu, with Maranti, with Kilinkizu, and was becoming accustomed to the men and boys.

We're strange to her, he thought. Did she ever see any men besides One Hundred Three and his apprentice, before joining us? Or did she think us all bandits, pirates, and the creatures who took Bdarde-who-was from us?

He sipped again from the cup. Rain splashed into the wine.

He gazed around at the ship. Its plunge through the crest of the enormous shore wave had briefly washed the deck clean, but the ash glazed it with another layer of mud.

"Are you all right?" he asked Paissu. "I thought I saw you fall."

"I only stumbled," she said. "When the ship jumped through the wave."

The ash had turned to bloody mud over her skinned knee.

"Iakinthu will put lavender water on it, and that will help."

She nodded, took the empty cup, and went around to the other companions.

Maranti climbed from the dimness of the lower deck.

A sudden confluence of wind and water, a sudden change in the air, a confused swirl of rain, and *Flying Fish* sailed out into clear air and calm sea.

Rhenthizu rose shakily and looked around in amazement. The ash cloud lay behind the ship, a roiling gray wall; beneath it, mud and floating pebbles created a barren, floating landscape. Ahead lay the horizon, sharp and perfect.

Aranthau guided *Flying Fish* to catch the new breeze. The sail flapped once, spraying mud, then billowed heavily. Its erratic flutter returned to the rhythmic pulse of its diagonal edge.

Rhenthizu stared in wonder at Maranti, who gazed at the changed weather as if it were only what she expected, only her due. She crossed the deck and sat beside him and took his hand.

"We've reached the other side of the world," she said.

The warm air caressed Iakinthu's face. The shade of the stern cabin protected her from the sun and heat, and her ship rolled gently on a new sea. Iakinthu dabbed lavender water onto the blisters on Kilinkizu's palms.

"Your poor hands," she said.

"They'll heal."

"Of course they will," Iakinthu said, inhaling the soothing resin scent. Lavender water was unequalled in its healing properties. Even Paissu's skinned knee was healing cleanly.

The companions had worked hard and long to free *Flying Fish* of ash and mud.

"Can you give us our lesson?" Iakinthu asked.

Kilinkizu laughed with surprise. "We escaped a volcano, a shore wave, and pirates—perhaps we escaped the pirates—and we're the first Idaeans ever to see this sea, these islands. And you want your lesson?"

"Of course. Will skipping it slow the pirates? Will skipping it cause another eruption?" She wrapped a bit of clean linen around Kilinkizu's hand, protecting the blistered palm. "Will skipping it help your hands?" she asked, more gently.

"I can write. I can give you your lesson. I can even draw." She turned her hands over. "It would be hard to sew. The blisters would weep and stain the cloth."

"Should you sew when your hands hurt? Let them rest and heal."

Aranthau climbed on board, dripping and naked, his hair all in tendrils down his back.

"What did you see?" Iakinthu asked. "What did you hear?"

Above, the sail caught a faint new breeze. It steadied *Flying Fish* in the long, low swells. The ship crept forward, the wind strengthened, the ship sped over the water like its namesake. At the steering oar, Rhenthizu guided it into deep water, following Aranthau's words of direction.

"I was nearly blind," Aranthau said to Iakinthu. "Nearly blind, nearly deaf—the mountain set a barrier against me."

"Against you?" Iakinthu said. "Or against the pirates? You brought us here safe. The pirates—they lost at least one of their ships. Perhaps they're all lost."

Aranthau gazed behind them, along the wake of *Flying Fish* written in the clear water, into the haze that spread out around the mountain's cloud of ash and steam. The edge of the crater glowed red and hot.

"They lost one," he said. "But two still follow us."

Chapter Twenty

Paissu spotted the strange craft first. She stared at it a moment, wondering what she saw. It was bigger than any whale. She always watched the whales, entranced and amazed by their size, their grace. The other companions of *Flying Fish* thought whales a rather ordinary sight, so now she watched in silence and kept her awe to herself.

As the fiery mountain receded, the strange jumbles of floating rock and barnacles and seaweed and scraggly plants appeared less and less frequently.

The sun, low on the horizon, glowed red and gold and hindered Paissu's sight. She realized that the bright golden fire shone from the raft, not from the sun: the sunlight reflected from a flat golden roof. People lined the raft's sides, paddling, and several low square sails helped it wallow along.

"Aranthau!"

He climbed to join her, moving more slowly than usual. Everyone moved slowly, aching and exhausted from their flight from the mountain's explosion, favoring their blistered hands. Paissu's scraped knee still itched and stung, despite Iakinthu's lavender water. For a whole day, Maranti had spoken only in a hoarse whisper, her throat sore from chanting the rowing count. Iakinthu's lavender and honey was bringing her voice back.

"Look." The raft's course would touch that of *Flying Fish* before sunset. As she watched, its lookout spotted her and stood up and pointed.

Aranthau called to the deck. A moment later Uinthi joined them and gazed toward Paissu's discovery.

"Do you know them?" Aranthau asked. "Do you speak their language?"

"Do I know everyone in the world, Aranthau?" Uinthi said. "I've heard of sailing craft like that one. If its people speak the trade language, I can speak to them."

"Should you?

"Are we in dispute with them? They'd show us the finest hospitality. Besides, we should warn them of the pirates."

Aranthau gave Paissu's hand a squeeze, and Paissu nodded her acknowledgment of his appreciation. He and Uinthi returned to the deck, leaving Paissu to watch the change in *Flying Fish*'s activity. Their course shifted slightly, to more easily meet the raft; everyone rushed around making themselves presentable. Paissu wished she had a beaded shirt like Uinthi's or a kilt of Egyptian linen like Rhenthizu's or an embroidered vest like Kilinkizu's. Her clothes from back home, of leather and wool, were very plain compared to Idaean finery, and besides they were too hot to wear in this climate. She had managed to wash most of the ash streaks out of her kilt. If she had time she would put on her claw necklace.

"Aranthau," she called. "They're turning, they're paddling toward us. Can you see?"

He stood at *Flying Fish*'s bow, his gaze as intense as the ship's. He raised a hand in greeting.

The raft turned ponderously. Its square sails came down, more hindrance than help when the raft moved across the wind. The chant of the paddlers reached them faintly across the waves. The sound gave Paissu a brief pang of homesickness for the chants of her sisters and her mothers around the campfires at night. Idaean singing still sounded strange to her.

"Paissu, come down!"

Before obeying Iakinthu's call. Paissu searched the sea behind her and around her. If the pirates' ships were out there, the distant haze and ash concealed them. Could they sail hidden in that darkness for long? Paissu could believe they would breathe that heavy air, that stinging dust, as long as it took to make a capture.

She shinnied down from the mast and joined Iakinthu.

Iakinthu Gephyra wore a tiered skirt of Egyptian linen. A wide band of sea-purple bordered each flounce. Her formal vest revealed her breasts, and a necklace of delicate gold leaves circled her throat. "What will you wear, little Paissu?" Iakinthu said. She wiped Paissu's face and fingers and palms with a scrap of wool cloth dipped in oil, sponging away the last smudges of ash and dirt. "There, that's better."

She led Paissu to the stern cabin, where Uinthi helped Maranti arrange her hair. Maranti held the boat snake, petting it to calm it amidst the commotion.

"Put this on, my dear." Iakinthu gave Paissu a new kilt, so fine and light Paissu hardly believed it was wool. In the shade of the stern cabin, it shone as bright as mountain snow. Gold threads wove a wheat design into the border, and the fringe was sea-purple. Paissu flung off her grubby kilt and wrapped the beautiful new one around her waist. Iakinthu tied it with white cords.

Then, to Paissu's surprise, Kilinkizu held out her spring vest, brightly embroidered with saffron crocuses and dragonflies.

"You may wear it today," Kilinkizu said, "because I know you like it and will take care of it."

As Kilinkizu held the vest for her and tied its fastenings, Rhenthizu came running up from belowdecks with a heavy handful of gold and turquoise and curved claws: Paissu's gift necklace from Dragon Claws.

"Just in time," Iakinthu said with a smile.

She lowered the necklace over Paissu's head and arranged it at her throat. Paissu stood quiet. Everything she wore was so fine, so proper for meeting new people.

Iakinthu led the way to join the other companions on the deck of *Flying Fish*.

Maranti and Kilinkizu wore formal tiered dresses; the others wore bright-dyed vests and kilts with fashionable belts and knots. Even Bdarde had been washed and combed, though his sullen look remained. Several companions carried lily-axe staffs. The blades turned and moved like golden butterflies.

Iakinthu gazed at them in satisfaction.

"We're presentable," she said. "And doing very well, I think, for a ship full of people who just survived a sea-wave."

The raft gleamed from its golden roof. As the sun sank farther, torches flared, reflecting all around the golden house.

The huge logs that made up the bed of the raft floated high in the water despite the house and the heavy gold and the multitude of paddlers.

Aranthau spoke softly; the companions reefed the sail. *Flying Fish* slowed. The raft paddled closer. It was longer than *Flying Fish*, wide abeam. It carried bundles and baskets of supplies and cargo, cages of bright birds or small creatures— Can they be rats? Iakinthu wondered. The boat snake raised its head and flicked its tongue, tasting the air, questioning it about new prey. Herbs and bushes and even a few trees grew from great baskets of earth. A small village occupied the raft, protected by a moat made of the sea.

A line of men strode to the leading edge of the raft. They wore fantastic headdresses of glorious feathers, gold, and jade, and long loincloths of intricately woven and brightly dyed material. Their earlobes hung low with enormous earrings of jade or gold.

"Their ears must hurt," Paissu whispered.

The men carried clubs with gold-ringed handles and massive jade heads, and knives of translucent green obsidian.

The leader who stepped forward wore a long robe of multicolored fabric and a pectoral of gold that was richer and more perfectly worked than any Pharaoh had ever worn.

Iakinthu stood at the prow of her ship, gazing in wonder at the incredible raft and its people and its glorious excess, and at its leader.

"I've come from Idaea," Iakinthu said. "I am Iakinthu Gephyra, bridge between people, and I offer our friendship."

The leader remained silent.

Iakinthu tried again, repeating herself in Rhenthizu's language.

The leader on the raft listened impassively, arrogantly. Silently.

Iakinthu tried a third time.

"Egyptian?" Uinthi said, glancing at her sidelong.

"Pharaoh believes it to be the original language," Iakinthu said. "I promised I would test her idea."

The leader spoke a few words, her tone commanding.

Iakinthu waited, hoping Uinthi understood.

"Her words are strange to me." Uinthi frowned, blew out a breath of frustration, then spoke. Iakinthu understood only the proper names. Apparently the leader understood even less. Uinthi tried another tongue.

The people of the golden raft stared at them as if they were some strange creatures or an apparition. The leader scowled.

"Do I know every language of every people?" Uinthi said softly, sadly.

The leader of the raft village barked a command.

One of the leader's attendants came pushing through the line, dragging with her one of the paddlers, who followed, head down, clutching his paddle. He knelt at the leader's feet, knees and elbows on the deck and his head bent, and he spoke in a whisper. The leader's lady in waiting prodded him with the butt end of a feathered spear. The paddler spoke a little louder. Uinthi leaned over the ship's rail, straining to hear. He spoke again.

They exchanged a few sentences.

"It's very difficult to hear him, when he speaks to the ground," Iakinthu said.

"He's frightened," Uinthi said. "He comes from a mainland city, but he's..."

Iakinthu understood that Uinthi was searching for a delicate way of saying he was a slave.

"He's...in the service of...the great king Jade Stingray, and his daughter, Lady Jaguar."

"We bring greetings from the Idaeans, from the people beyond the Sunset Sea," Iakinthu said, wondering what they called the sea from which, in their land, the sun would rise. Uinthi spoke her words to the cowering man, and he whispered them to his mistress. "The companions of the Eldest Daughter of Mother Moon greet the court of the great king and offer our respect to him and to Lady Jaguar."

"You may accompany us," Lady Jaguar said: the paddler translated her words, and Uinthi translated the paddler's words into Idaean. "Join us, returning to the home of my father, the great queen Blood Jaguar and her consort the great king Jade Stingray, after his procession, to acknowledge him, and celebrate, and feast."

Iakinthu considered, if only for a moment, declining the invitation and sailing away to continue her own voyage, but the first encounter with any new civilization was far too important to squander or spoil. Besides, to refuse would be rude.

"We're pleased to accept your invitation," Iakinthu said. "And we hope you and Jade Stingray and Blood Jaguar will condescend to accept our gifts of friendship."

Iakinthu sat with her companions among the courtiers of Lady Jaguar. Uinthi sat on Iakinthu's left, prepared to translate. The poor paddler, who had the honor and misfortune of knowing a trade language, crouched shivering at the feet of Lady Jaguar, making himself very small and still clutching his paddle.

Maranti sat on Iakinthu's right, and Rhenthizu beside her. Kilinkizu sat a little behind them, her drawing desk open on her lap.

Their seats were sections of the same type of log that formed the body of the raft, light-colored and lightweight, large but easy to move.

A cloth of exquisite softness, softer than rare Kashmiri wool, woven with delicate patterns of earth colors, covered each seat. Iakinthu stroked it gently. Observing the wealth of these people, their lavish possessions, the quality of their craftsmanship, she felt a moment of doubt and apprehension: Did she have anything to trade that would interest them?

The courtiers kept their faces so impassive it was easy to imagine they were ignoring their guests. But they watched her, taking the measure of her and her companions, even as she indulged her own curiosity about them.

She gazed frankly at Lady Jaguar.

Her gold and jade and feather headdress towered over her, the feathers quivering as if alive. Her wide forehead sloped back. Enormous jade spools depended from her earlobes. Iakinthu wondered if some hidden strap supported them. A jade axe lay across her knees, cushioned by the long, intricately woven, exquisitely dyed robe. The material took colors as brilliant as Sheng silk, including a uniquely intense red.

Beside Lady Jaguar sat a member of the nobility, equally elaborately dressed. Iridescent feathers streamed from his headdress. Jade plaques of pure soft green formed his necklace. He wore a heavy, ornately worked gold ring in his prominent nose.

The raft ploughed ahead through the night, moon and luminescence lighting the way. Always, Iakinthu remained aware of the dark doorway of the gold-roofed house. It faced the stern, like hatches on sensibly constructed boats, only a few paces from where she sat. She imagined the great king Jade Stingray sitting inside, watching everything, listening. The only thing to hear was the water and the soft chant of the paddlers. Lady Jaguar and the king's other attendants remained silent, so the Idaeans did as well. Iakinthu noticed that the courtiers avoided looking toward their sovereign, but she was Idaean and gazed where she would.

The darkness inside the gold house also remained silent and still.

~

Iakinthu had visited many courts with rituals of greater or lesser strangeness. She was impressed by the ability of their hosts to sit motionless for hours, waiting, as she supposed, for their king. When she found herself nodding off, she thought, I should retire from the game of diplomacy.

She was about to speak, to move, to stand up, when Maranti rose and broke the silence, pressing her hands to the small of her back.

"Bad manners it may be," she said, "but I must move, and I must pee!"

Lady Jaguar snapped a few words to the paddler, who like everyone else had remained motionless, though his was by far the more uncomfortable position. In his kneeling crouch, he translated, trembling, and relayed Uinthi's reply.

"Ah," said Lady Jaguar, her sympathy perfectly comprehensible.

She rose and offered her hand to Maranti. Maranti grasped it, her sealstone bracelet glinting in the early light.

Rhenthizu took Maranti's other hand, to attend her as she followed Lady Jaguar and several of her attendants to the raft's stern. Iakinthu gestured to Kilinkizu and Uinthi and Paissu to come, as well.

"And bring him," she said softly.

The paddler cringed. Lady Jaguar toed him gently and gave him leave to move. He staggered when he rose, and when Uinthi helped him, Lady Jaguar snorted with disdain.

They trooped to the stern, where rush screens and pots of leafy bushes concealed a latrine, a hole bored through the great raft's logs to the water. The sea continually washed it clean.

Without ceremony, Maranti hiked up her skirts and squatted over the hole, letting Rhenthizu hold her hand to steady her.

A moment later she said, with relief, "That's better."

"Lady Jaguar says, The boys may pee over the side," Uinthi said. "She means Rhenthizu—and me. Will I shock her, do you think?"

"How often I pee now!" Maranti exclaimed. "How inconvenient! But at least it saves me bleeding."

One of Lady Jaguar's attendants handed Maranti a white wad.

Maranti took it. "Thank you," she said. "What's it for?"

The noblewoman replied before either Uinthi or the paddler had a chance to translate Maranti's question, and her answer was clear before the paddler interpreted her words or Uinthi translated.

"To clean yourself."

"Oh." Maranti used it for its intended purpose and then was left with the wad of white material. She glanced around, looking for a net or basket.

The Lady's attendant made a peremptory gesture of explanation. Maranti let the material fall into the latrine hole, and the sea carried it away beneath the raft's logs.

Iakinthu had learned years ago, at the Egyptian court where rituals could go on for hours, always to take advantage of an opportunity to relieve her bladder. She did so now, a bit disconcerted by the sea gliding along so close beneath her, gently splashing.

Lady Jaguar's attendant gave her a wiping cloth; she used it and discarded it, thinking, This type of cloth is new to me; I will have to investigate it later.

Kilinkizu spread her tiered skirt around her and peed with complete modesty.

Paissu hesitated by the latrine hole. Rhenthizu and Uinthi, understanding her shyness, turned their backs. She quickly used the latrine, wiped herself, and rejoined the Idaeans.

"We shall see if I shock her," Uinthi said, hiked up her long shirt, pulled aside her loincloth, and peed like a girl.

"I thought you were a man," the Lady said, in a matter-of-fact tone.

"Usually I am," Uinthi said.

The Lady laughed. "And very handsome, either way." Her stern expression relaxed; the laugh connected her to their small group.

Iakinthu took the moment to introduce her other companions, making a game of it, repeating her name, then Lady Jaguar's, nodding toward the noblewoman. Lady Jaguar said her own name, correcting Iakinthu's pronunciation, and said, "Iakinthu." Iakinthu said, "Maranti," and nodded toward the Eldest Daughter.

When Iakinthu's turn came again, she said her name, bent down, and gently touched the paddler-turned-translator, who still huddled at Lady Jaguar's feet.

"Tell us your name, valued translator."

Lady Jaguar frowned, taken aback, and her attendant drew in a sharp breath.

Uinthi translated for him. He replied in a hesitant whisper, his head down, his shoulders hunched.

"Is that a proper name for a valued translator?" Uinthi said.

"What did he say?" Iakinthu asked.

"Can I pronounce it?" Uinthi replied. "I'll try to tell you later."

Understanding that Uinthi was embarrassed by what Lady Jaguar had called the translator, Iakinthu said, "With your permission, Lady Jaguar, may we call him He Who Bridges Words?"

"You may call him anything you like," Lady Jaguar said. "He hardly needs a name of his own."

"It's difficult to hear him, bent all over like that," Maranti said. "May he sit up?"

"What a strange request," Lady Jaguar said. "He may raise his head a handsbreadth from the deck, so you may hear him more easily."

Bridges Words, trembling to be spoken of, to be spoken to, to be noticed at all, obediently raised his head, while remaining crouched on the deck.

"May I sit?" Maranti said.

Lady Jaguar gazed at her speculatively, then raised one eyebrow at Rhenthizu. She looked him up and down, pausing at kilt level, taking his measure.

"Ah," she said. "I understand. Lady Maranti, you must have some nourishment." She spoke to an attendant, who giggled and hurried off, light-footed despite her elaborate ceremonial costume and her gold and jade jewelry. The screen of leaves closed behind her.

"But, my Lady Jaguar, should we return to attend your king?" Maranti asked.

Lady Jaguar, with an approving nod for Maranti's good manners, said, "Our king was always sensible when his wife was with child. Unlike some men." She smiled. "Our king is…very patient."

She led them away from the latrine to the starboard edge of the raft, where they sat on bolts of bright cloth in the moonlight. The breeze played in the sails, and the stroke of the paddlers whispered in the night.

Lady Jaguar's attendant returned. She placed a carven jade pot on the deck, raised an even more elaborately sculpted jade pitcher, and poured a perfect arc of steaming water into the pot. She knelt, poured the contents of the pot into the pitcher, rose, and again poured the liquid, now dark and frothy. She repeated the process several more times, never spilling a drop.

When the tan froth threatened to spill over the green edge, she stopped, knelt, lifted the pot and sipped from it, then presented it to Lady Jaguar.

The steam carried the fragrance to Iakinthu, an earthy scent with a hint of wine and a startlingly sharp touch. Her mouth watered, her eyes watered.

Lady Jaguar drank deep. Her attendant received the jade receptacle and offered it to Iakinthu. Iakinthu bowed her head in appreciation. Eager as she was to taste the source of the tantalizing smell, she attended Maranti. If Iakinthu drank first, before the Eldest Daughter, Lady Jaguar might be offended, when her attendant had proven it safe for her, and she had proven it safe for Maranti.

Besides, Iakinthu thought, why poison us, when we are outnumbered and alone with them?

Maranti drank without hesitation.

"Oh!" she said. "Oh, Iakinthu, drink."

A bitter sharp flavor flowed across Iakinthu's tongue. She savored the warmth, the dark earthiness, the intoxication. When she swallowed, the aftertaste stung her lips, her tongue, her throat. She breathed in the scent. She licked the trace of foam from her lips.

The attendant took the jade cup from her. Iakinthu felt an undiplomatic urge to snatch it back.

Lady Jaguar arched her eyebrow at Uinthi as her attendant poured the drink into jade cups.

"Are you a woman now, or a boy?"

"Am I peeing?" Uinthi said.

Lady Jaguar laughed and allowed her attendant to give a jade cup to Uinthi, who drank, then wiped away the froth, backhanded.

Lady Jaguar nodded toward Rhenthizu. "Let him drink, as he's with us, but he must keep it secret from the other men."

Rhenthizu drank. He coughed and gasped. He wiped his lips and was about to wipe his eyes when the attendant hurried forward with a square of delicate white cloth.

"Very good," he said doubtfully.

Lady Jaguar laughed again. "Men! They think cacao is sacred to men, they think they should keep it to themselves, and they think they should trade cacao beans for gold or weaving or jade, till the essence dries up and floats away as dust. How foolish!"

The attendant passed jade cups around. Rhenthizu, always polite, sipped, but barely.

"What is it?" Iakinthu asked.

"Cacao," replied Lady Jaguar. "Food of the gods."

Iakinthu could well believe it.

"And," Lady Jaguar added in a matter-of-fact way, "it will settle your stomach, my young guest, which I believe may be a benefit to you."

"Thank you, Lady Jaguar," Maranti said.

"We shall return," Lady Jaguar said when they had finished. She strode toward the king's house, her ladies in waiting hurrying behind her.

Iakinthu bent and touched the translator on the shoulder. He flinched and ducked his head.

"I am Iakinthu Gephyra," she said, "the Bridge between People, and, to me, you are He Who Bridges Words. You have part of my name. That forms a bridge between us. Stand up and walk with my companions."

When Uinthi translated, he obeyed. Iakinthu handed him her jade cup. He still clutched his paddle and he still kept his head down, gazing at the cup.

"You may have some of my share," Iakinthu said.

He drank quickly, surreptitiously, and pushed the cup back into her hand. One of the attendants snatched it away, and when she thought Iakinthu's attention had returned to Lady Jaguar, she flung away the beautiful cup. It splashed and sank.

Iakinthu had seen such behavior before. The more extreme the hierarchy, the more likely it was.

Iakinthu led the Idaeans after Lady Jaguar, giving Maranti her arm.

"Is it true?" she asked. "About the cacao?"

"It is," Maranti said. "The cacao sits easily in my stomach, unlike anything I've eaten or drunk for days."

"It's bitter," Rhenthizu said. "And my tongue still stings."

Maranti laughed. "You may give me your share any time Lady Jaguar condescends to serve it to us."

"Willingly," Rhenthizu said.

They followed Lady Jaguar back to the king's house and took their places on the carven log seats. Lord Smoke Stingray, who had remained in exactly the same position as when they left, looked stern, but then he had looked stern before they rose from the gathering.

The lightening sky burst into dawn. This far south the sky had little dawn or dusk. It moved from dark to daylight with barely a moment of crepuscular dimness.

Waves washed upon sand with a quiet shushh. A shoreline rose from white beach to enormous green trees climbing the hillside. The curve of beach glowed in sunrise. The forest beyond was a vivid, exotic green, casting its long shadow onto the sand. Birds cried.

The sun rose.

Its light reflected in brilliant gold from the entire hillside. Iakinthu blinked, dazzled, and when her eyes accustomed themselves to the brightness, the hillside became a stepped pyramid, flat-topped, supporting a square, windowless, looming house.

Gold sheathed every surface.

Staring in amazement, Iakinthu thought of Pharaoh's pyramid. But Pharaoh covered only the tip of her tomb, the last few courses of stone, in gold. This pyramid shimmered and gleamed and glowed from its base to the roof of its house.

The people standing on the long course of stairs to the top gave her a measure of the pyramid's scale, and she was impressed.

The sails fell; the raft drove inexorably onto the beach, grinding its great breadth against the shallow-sloping sand. It moved so slowly it barely jarred its passengers when it halted. Attendants ran to the prow with smooth-planed boards, placing them to create a ramp from raft village to the home of the great king.

Behind the raft, *Flying Fish*'s sails folded and its anchor splashed into the water. Aranthau would wait, and watch, and worry.

On the beach a procession waited, dressed in garments of sheer magnificence: gold and jade, bright red loincloths and shoulder capes, and fantastic headdresses of feathers and streamers.

Two of Lady Jaguar's attendants hurried to drape her in an iridescent feather robe that fell from her shoulders to the ground and trailed an armslength behind her. She and Smoke Stingray walked together toward the door of the raft's central house. The feathers of the robe and the cascading feathers of their headdresses shimmered in blue and green touched with gold.

Bridges Words whispered to Uinthi, fear permeating the softness of his voice.

"He humbly suggests we join the procession to honor the great king on his return," Uinthi said.

"Then we shall take his advice, with our appreciation," Iakinthu said. She rose, along with the other Idaeans, picking up the gifts they had brought. She would watch and wait till she understood exactly who the gifts should go to and how they should be parceled out.

A dozen attendants hurried into the raft's central house. Drums and flutes sounded from within.

Lady Jaguar and Smoke Stingray and all their attendants fell to their knees and bowed as low as Bridges Words had done. He tried to fling himself to the deck as was his habit, but Rhenthizu and Uinthi gently took his elbows so he remained standing.

"Do Idaeans kowtow to the Sheng?" Iakinthu said. "Do we prostrate ourselves to the Black Sea warlords? We salute our equals, with respect."

The attendants reappeared, emerging with a palanquin that flung gold light from every surface. Five young women followed the bearers, two beating drums and three playing flutes in an eerie tune.

Fine red cloth permeated with gold dust shaded Jade Stingray. Gold dust fell at the carriers' every step. It wafted past the Idaeans; it glittered on the deck.

Iakinthu squinted at the shadowed figure of the king. He sat still and silent in his carry-chair, the feathers of his headdress swaying with the chair's motion, escaping from the chair's open sides, catching gold dust on the iridescent plumes.

Beside her, Uinthi made a startled sound. Surprised, Iakinthu squinted at the returning king.

Ah, she thought, I wish I still had young eyes.

But finally she saw what Uinthi saw.

The great king, rather than being dressed in ceremonial garments, was wrapped in bright cloth and adorned with jade and gold. The red wrappings covered his body, his arms and legs, all but his face.

Jade Stingray was a mummy.

Iakinthu had spent years, on and off, in Egypt, discussing treaties and trade with Pharaoh. The conversation had always turned toward her pyramid and her death goods. She gave orders about them to her minister;

she described the details endlessly to Iakinthu, blithely unaware that the Idaeans disdained to take their riches into the afterworld. Iakinthu had even traveled down the Nile with Pharaoh's court, accompanying the carved and painted sarcophagus of a minor member of the royal family, killed in a hunting accident, on his way to the transshipment point to the Valley of Kings.

But this was the first time Iakinthu had seen the bare face of a mummy.

The wrappings left the king's face exposed. It was quite horrible, wrinkled and darkened, its lips pulled back from yellowed teeth, its eyes sunken and dried. Its hair — its wig — was long and thick and black and glossy, dressed with oil and feathers, a bizarre contrast to its dried, tanned face.

Lady Jaguar and Lord Smoke Stingray followed their king along the deck of the raft, down the ramp, onto the beach.

Iakinthu followed, bemused by the revelation of the king's state. She wished she could take Bridges Words off in private and question him. That, of course, would have to wait.

She stepped from the ramp to the beach. She had been so many days at sea that the solid ground rocked beneath her. She made herself remain steady. Light sparkled in the corners of her eyes, a sign of exhaustion.

The great king's attendants greeted him; they turned to the golden pyramid.

The Idaeans followed their hosts up the golden stairs. The gold leaf was polished into the stone so that it flowed across every smooth plane, into each corner and every tiny crack or flaw, following contours so closely that the substance of the pyramid could have been solid gold.

Iakinthu lost count of the steps. She felt hotter and hotter as they climbed, as the morning sun warmed the air and the ground and reflected from the gold-covered stone. The effect was that of walking toward a source of heat, as if the king's house at the top of the hill of gold glowed like an oven.

She glanced toward Maranti, concerned, but the Eldest Daughter climbed like a young gazelle, faintly polished with sweat. Sweat dripped down Iakinthu's forehead. She wiped it away before it fell into her eyes and smeared her kohl.

The Idaeans moderated their pace to stay with her. She appreciated their courtesy, but the necessity of it embarrassed her. By the time they reached the top, her legs ached and her head spun with fatigue and hunger. The drums pounded through her, and the high-pitched notes of the flute pierced her hearing.

On the flat top of the pyramid, an area as large as a dancing field, the palanquin carriers knelt and lowered the chair gently. The drummers and flute-players increased the tempo of their playing. The cacophony nearly drowned out Lady Jaguar, and, more important, Bridges Words' whispered translation.

Lady Jaguar faced the golden palanquin, spread her arms wide, and spoke.

"My revered mother, we've brought your husband, my honored father, home from his progress through his lands and oceans, and we bring food and gifts and visitors."

To Iakinthu's surprise and relief, the musicians fell silent. For a moment the only sounds were the calling of birds strange to her and the whisper of the wind through leaves. The golden pyramid was so tall it overtopped the forest. The intense green canopy of the trees spread out like an ocean, shimmering in waves as the breeze passed across it.

The soft notes of a single flute, in a much lower register, drifted from the golden house. The player emerged from the shadows of the house, leading the way for a second palanquin. Its carriers brought it out onto the wide forecourt. Its ornaments were the most elaborate of all. Strings of gold bangles jingled to the pace of the bearers, long scarlet feathers arched like a crown around the edge of the red cloth roof, and the pillars and bed of the carrier glowed with the soft green of jade. Poles of polished dark red wood supported the contrivance.

While the first palanquin had made do with eight carriers, this one required twelve to bring it the short distance from the darkness of the house to the shining forecourt. The carriers knelt and lowered the chair to the ground.

A second figure sat within it, nearly hidden from Iakinthu's view, only its wrinkled face visible.

It moved.

Iakinthu started, then, embarrassed, stood very still. An ancient woman rose from her seat and descended. She was frail, laden with gold, and Lady Jaguar and Lord Smoke Stingray hurried to help her themselves rather than ordering an attendant or even a member of their court, to perform the service.

Iakinthu put her fist to her forehead in salute to the mother and touched one knee to the ground for a moment. The other Idaeans followed suit and let Bridges Words be when he flung himself to the ground like all the other attendants.

Chapter Twenty-One

With tiny, uncertain steps, Lady Jaguar's mother took a central place, heading her own court, facing the court of her husband Jade Stingray. The great queen's flute player decorated the air with mournful notes. Four of her ladies lifted a red cloth over her head to shade her. The sun cast scarlet shadows over her face.

"Rhenthizu," Iakinthu said softly, "give me the Egyptian linen."

Rhenthizu pulled the bundle of fine white cloth from his carrier bag. Iakinthu unfolded it and gave one corner to Uinthi, one to Rhenthizu, one to Bridges Words. She raised the fourth corner, and the Idaeans lifted the linen panel to shade their Eldest Daughter. Maranti smiled at Iakinthu and shifted her position a few steps. Iakinthu followed, to keep the shade cloth centered, and found herself and her companions all protected from the fierce and rising sun. She touched Maranti's hand in appreciation of her courtesy.

I complained about the cold among the Maisusutha, Iakinthu thought. I should have kept my words to myself. The air here is like a blanket of steam!

Bridges Words kept up a whispered translation.

"My great queen, Blood Jaguar, my honored mother," Lady Jaguar said. "You look so well."

"I look like a wrinkled old woman," Blood Jaguar said. Her quavery voice sharpened. "Which is what I am. When I die, smooth my face with clay so people will know how beautiful I was."

"I will, mother. Everyone knows you're a great beauty. Will you die soon?"

"Yes. Soon. Then you will go away to conquer your own lands. Will I ever see you again?"

Lady Jaguar smiled tightly.

"My husband wants his dinner, and I want my gifts, and who are these strange people?"

"Visitors, who bring offerings to acknowledge you and Jade Stingray."

"Come along, then," said the old lady, and hobbled to her palanquin.

Iakinthu dreaded climbing down the pyramid, but instead of descending, the chair carried the great queen around her golden house. Behind it stood a structure with open sides and a roof thatched with long green leaves. Blood Jaguar dismounted and took her place on a cushion on the golden floor. Her attendants set out more cushions. The great queen waved toward them, gesturing for her visitors and her court to join her. With her companions, Iakinthu sat gratefully. The green roof moderated the heat, and the pavilion caught a faint sea breeze.

Then Jade Stingray entered the pavilion.

Iakinthu wondered if the mummy had been tanned, or stuffed, or smoked and dried, to preserve him. When the carriers brought him in, a musty odor of decay wafted through the pavilion. Maranti looked queasy.

"Do you suppose Lady Jaguar would give me more cacao?" she said softly, with little hope.

The carriers set King Jade Stingray beside Great Queen Blood Jaguar. He had been her husband in life; he was still her husband in death. This surprised even Iakinthu, who had seen many death customs in many parts of the world.

Lady Jaguar and Smoke Stingray faced them, court attendants on one long side of the pavilion, Idaeans on the other. Iakinthu was grateful that the pavilion was so large, with open walls, for the mummy was several paces away, and the sea breeze carried his oppressive odor across the forest's green canopy.

The attendants brought in a feast, on platters of gold or jade and baskets woven of gilded reeds. The fragrance of maize made Iakinthu's mouth water. She watched Lady Jaguar to follow the proper etiquette; her companions watched her. The attendants served them. She recognized maize, and beans, and squash; a red round fruit and slices of a soft green fruit were new to her.

The attendant serving the Idaeans hesitated when she came to Bridges Words, but at a stern glance from Iakinthu, she set a plate before him as if he were an acknowledged person.

Everyone waited as the food steamed gently and fragrantly before them.

They all must be as hungry as we are, Iakinthu thought. They had sat waiting for the return of their great king throughout the night, and they had missed the benefit of cacao.

The attendants withdrew, and the ladies-in-waiting served Blood Jaguar with their own hands. They laid the platters on stands of carved jade and finely painted pottery. The eldest of them knelt and presented her with a long-handled gold spoon. A moment later one of Lady Jaguar's ladies presented Lady Jaguar with a similar spoon, of jade and silver.

Queen Blood Jaguar scooped up a spoonful of stew and fed it to her husband. The meat fell from Jade Stingray's stretched lips; the dark sauce reddened his teeth and dripped down his chin. An attendant wiped his face gently.

Lady Jaguar and her consort strode along the length of the pavilion to mirror her mother's actions, feeding stew to the mummy of her father. Smoke Stingray performed the honored task of wiping the dead king's leathery lips.

Queen Blood Jaguar fed her husband three or four bites, then handed the spoon to her lady and gestured for Jade Stingray's plates to be taken away.

"My husband is satiated, and he proclaims the food good and free of poison. He bids us enjoy the feast."

She picked up a bit of rolled maize flatbread and ate it. With that signal, all the members of the court set to feasting.

Bridges Words whispered, gazing longingly at the plate before him.

"Bridges Words says we may eat now," Uinthi said.

"And you," Iakinthu replied to Bridges Words. "You, too."

Uinthi translated his reply. "I may be killed, but any day I might be killed. Perhaps this day will be worth it." He scooped up some of the stew in a bit of flatbread and savored it, closing his eyes.

"People of his station seldom eat meat," Uinthi said. "This is a week's worth of food for Bridges Words."

"Tell him to eat slowly," Iakinthu said in Maisusutha. "If he throws up his dinner, our Eldest Daughter might, too, and that would be poor diplomacy."

The feast went on into the afternoon. Iakinthu's mouth burned from the spices. The flatbread took away some of the heat, as did the maize gruel everyone drank. She thought she would have grown to like the fiery dishes if she had tried them when she was younger, but she found herself yearning most undiplomatically for yogurt, bread, and a flask of wine.

Jaguar's attendants and Queen Blood Jaguar's attendants carried jars and pitchers into the space between the two courts. They poured cacao into a froth and served it in golden cups, but only to the men of the first rank. The woman who served the Idaeans bowed to Rhenthizu and presented him a cup. Uneasily, she handed a cup to Bridges Words. She ignored Maranti and Iakinthu, as the attendant serving Jade Stingray ignored Lady Jaguar. Queen Blood Jaguar's lady put the cup before the husband-king, then waited to wipe his lips and chin when the great queen held the cup to his mouth and poured in the cacao.

When the attendant came to Uinthi, she hesitated.

Iakinthu had visited lands where women shared possessions, responsibility, and authority; she had visited places where women suffered as possessions. Iakinthu herself had been called "he" and treated as a man because a ruler wished to keep up his trade with Fair Island. And of course she had spent time with the People. Sometimes her diplomacy had been strained.

Now she watched the attendant's confusion and thought, most undiplomatically, it serves you right, if you have no idea how to treat my Uinthi properly.

Uinthi smiled at the attendant, leaving the decision to her. The attendant held out the last cup, then hurried away into the crowd of servants. Perhaps, if the nobles thought she had erred, they would be unable to distinguish her among all the servants. Iakinthu thought she would recognize her again—but there were so many servants.

Uinthi turned to Maranti, but Rhenthizu had already surreptitiously poured most of his cacao into the empty cup that had held her maize gruel. Maranti drank, closing her eyes and savoring the cacao as intensely as Bridges Words savored the meat.

What transgressors we are, Iakinthu thought. My grandmother would approve, I think. She would sometimes keep our customs and abandon diplomacy.

Uinthi poured half the cacao into Iakinthu's cup. Iakinthu smiled, patted Uinthi's hand gently, and drank. The intoxication differed from that of wine or poppy or tobacco, but it did intoxicate her. She wondered what Aranthau would think of it.

Behind her, Bridges Words burped and set down his empty cup.

"I may be killed," he said again. "But today is a good day."

When the feasting finally ended, not long before dusk, Queen Blood Jaguar called Lady Jaguar to her; a moment later the lady came to Iakinthu.

"The great queen my mother and the great king my father wish to welcome you."

Iakinthu walked with Lady Jaguar; the other Idaeans followed, holding carefully wrapped gifts.

Maranti slipped around to Iakinthu's right, so Iakinthu headed the group.

"You are Iakinthu Gephyra," she said softly. "Here, you're our leader."

The sea breeze touched them with a cool breath as they crossed the space to the great queen. Iakinthu glanced out over the wide top of the gold pyramid, across the beach and past the raft, to the sea beyond, and *Flying Fish* anchored offshore. Aranthau sat on the bow, waiting, watching.

"Jade Stingray, my father, Blood Jaguar, my mother, this is Lady Iakinthu Gephyra, from Fair Island, come from far away to do you honor."

"Honored king," Iakinthu said, as if she were talking to a living person, "honored queen, thank you for your hospitality."

"My husband welcomes you," Blood Jaguar said. "Come and sit with us and tell us your story."

Lady Jaguar guided Iakinthu to a place of honor facing the queen and king. The fetid odor of his decaying body and bits of food from past meals settled over her. She took shallow breaths, and was glad when Rhenthizu maneuvered Maranti so she would be upwind of the mummy king.

"We come from a small island," Iakinthu said. "Fair Island has fertile farms, and places where people gather. Your pyramid is as grand as any I have ever visited."

"This old thing?" the queen said. She gestured dismissively. "You should have seen my husband's court when he was younger. You may read his history." She nodded toward a tall stone pillar, rising gold from the pyramid top, intricately carved all over, with a central figure of a powerful young man. Iakinthu tried to see the similarity between the carving and the shriveled mummy, but her imagination failed her.

Kilinkizu will want to read the history, Iakinthu thought. She'll want to see the writing, she'll want to learn it, even if it's as eerie as the paintings on the pottery.

"We had many more people to attend us," the queen said with regret bordering on bitterness. "More festivals, more celebrations, a larger army, and supplicants who wished us to help them please the gods."

"Mother," Lady Jaguar said, "everyone honors you and tells your stories."

"Daughter," the queen said haughtily, "our state is much lowered, and you must recognize it." She peered at Iakinthu. "How far away is your island?"

The translations faltered over the sea and the distance, and in the midst of trying to sort out the tangle, Uinthi said without a change of tone, in Idaean, "Bridges Words says to keep our island secret. He says the queen is disappointed because Fair Island is very far away, but Lady Jaguar and Smoke Stingray might still mount an assault on us."

"He says that, does he?" Iakinthu said in an equally mild tone. "I'd like to hear more of what he has to say. Should we distract the honored king and queen with baubles and wine?"

"I think we should," Uinthi said, "though I hate to think of your good wine dribbled away."

"We'll make the sacrifice."

Bridges Words spoke to Uinthi in a soft and urgent tone.

"He says to give the gifts to Smoke Stingray."

Iakinthu raised her eyebrow, for in most of the lands she had visited, etiquette demanded she give presents to the highest-ranking person in her company. On the other hand, she had also learned to appreciate good advice.

Particularly, she thought, advice from someone in whose interest it is to protect my own interests.

Maranti picked up the folded length of Egyptian linen. She rose gracefully, carried the linen to Smoke Stingray, and placed it in his hands.

He accepted it, immediately turned to his wife, and placed it in her hands. "A gift for your honored father."

Lady Jaguar accepted it, then approached her grandmother.

"A gift to my honored father."

Queen Blood Jaguar accepted it.

Iakinthu waited with some amusement to see if she would pass it along to some other honoree, perhaps going back down the hierarchical scale. Iakinthu had seen her gifts passed along before, but this was the fastest transfer yet.

"My husband wishes me to have it." Blood Jaguar placed the linen in her lap. "It's good to know young people today appreciate what's proper." She picked up a corner of the linen and inspected it closely. "Very fine weaving. What does the design say?"

As far as Iakinthu knew, the design said only that it was very thin and very fine and comfortable in the heat. She wished she was wearing her Egyptian robe right now, but the tiered skirt was more proper, and it had pockets.

"The design is sacred to Isis, goddess of growing things," Iakinthu said, making up the story. Who knows? she thought. It could be true. "It's the fabric of garments worn by Pharaoh and by Pharaoh's most important councillors, in Egypt, a great civilization to the south of my home, where they build pyramids as tall as the pyramid of Queen Blood Jaguar, but Pharaoh's pyramid shines with polished stone rather than gold."

Blood Jaguar accepted the explanation and the implied compliment with a nod.

Uinthi gave Smoke Stingray a jar of sweet almonds, and Rhenthizu presented him with an amphora of wine. Maranti placed a necklace of gold, with intricate flowers of lapis and carnelian, around his neck, where it nearly disappeared against the heavy gold of his pectoral. All these presents ended up with Blood Jaguar. She let Lady Jaguar place the necklace around her throat, where it gleamed and glittered, and the flowers trembled with her breath as if they were made of petals, and the wind was touching them.

Smoke Stingray opened the jar of almonds. He drew out an almond in its shell and squeezed it, puzzled.

"Let me shell it for you," Rhenthizu said. He pulled apart the outer husk and cracked the inner shell with his strong fingers. He handed the almond to the great queen.

"The almond has great powers of health," Iakinthu said. "We eat it on long voyages. It protects sailors from bloody-mouth. And it tastes good."

"Bloody-mouth is unfamiliar to me, and this is too hard for my old teeth," Blood Jaguar said. She gave the jar to Lady Jaguar, who crunched a nut between her strong teeth, then husked and shelled another.

"It does taste good." She looked more closely at one of the unhusked almonds, the fuzzy parted husk, the half-hidden shell. "I think they are sacred to women," she said with mischief in her voice, "and only women should eat them."

She laughed; Iakinthu laughed, wondering if Lady Jaguar would overlook it if Smoke Stingray ate some of her almonds, as he overlooked her drinking some of his cacao.

Smoke Stingray pried the wax stopper from the amphora with a wickedly sharp obsidian knife. He sniffed the wine and wrinkled his nose.

"Has it gone sour?" he asked.

Offended at the insult to her household's finest wine, Iakinthu took the amphora, poured wine into a gold cup, and sipped it. It touched her tongue with summer, with the bite of heat and the sweetness of grapes.

The queen took the cup and poured wine into her husband-mummy's mouth. It dripped out; everyone ignored his inability to swallow except the attendant who wiped up the drips, who also was ignored.

Queen Grandmother tried the wine. "How unusual," she said. "I think it would benefit from some chili."

These western people should appreciate wine more, Iakinthu thought, but she kept her thoughts to herself. She wished she had drunk more of the gift wine, as she preferred it to maize gruel. And it was a good vintage.

"Smoke Stingray," she said, "here's a talisman of my country."

Iakinthu drew a small leather pouch from her pocket and opened it. She drew out a tiny, delicate ice-jade model of a dancing bull, his dancer springing over his back. The sculpture, of the finest Sheng quality, caught the light and spread it softly through the figurine.

She put the dancing bull into the prince's hands.

Smoke Stingray cupped it and regarded it closely. All the other gifts he had presented immediately to Lady Jaguar for her mother to give her father, barely deigning to give them a glance. He looked at the dancing bull wistfully. He placed it in the palm of his hand — his hand dwarfed it — and touched the bull's head, stroked its horns, ran his fingertip along the graceful curve of the dancer's body.

Lady Jaguar whispered something, her voice as sharp as a whisper could be, and Smoke Stingray came to his senses, handing over the bull dancer.

"What is this creature?" the great queen asked.

"It's a bull," Iakinthu said. "A male—"

"I can see that," Blood Jaguar said drily, for the carving was quite accurate, and the parts of a bull were noticeable. "We've heard stories of enormous creatures in the far north. But I thought they were only stories, imagined, or told of the gods." She peered at the figurine more closely, noticed the human dancer was a girl, then glanced at Maranti. "Is this you?" She turned to Uinthi, and said in a low voice as if only Uinthi would hear, "Should I ask you?"

Uinthi looked a bit put out to be identified again as a woman, but perhaps Lady Jaguar had pointed out Uinthi's nature to the great queen.

"The dancer is Iakinthu," Uinthi said.

"When I was their age," Iakinthu said. "Now I keep the mothers of bulls and train young dancers like Paissu."

"Did you bring one of these creatures in your strange boat?"

"They're too big for such a long trip," Iakinthu said. "They pine for their island."

Blood Jaguar sighed. "I'm too old to go to see these marvels. I'd pine for my island." She gestured to Smoke Stingray; he knelt at her feet. She took his hand and gently placed the figurine in his palm. "You're young. You might travel so far."

Uinthi added to the translation, "Bridges Words says we must decline to take him or Lady Jaguar to our country because they'll raise an army and conquer our land. They want new land and foreign people to rule."

"Ah," Iakinthu said, understanding: The mummy kings held the land and the people and the riches of their kingdoms even after their deaths, and their offspring inherited only the right to go and conquer other places.

"It will be many months before we return home," Iakinthu said. "We're seeking the home of my given child Rhenthizu."

Blood Jaguar looked Rhenthizu up and down. "He comes from somewhere else," she said. "His people are unfamiliar to me. Perhaps Lady Jaguar and Smoke Stingray could help you find them."

Uinthi added to the translation, "Bridges Words says—"

"Tell him I understand," Iakinthu said. She would hardly do Rhenthizu's people an honor by bringing a conqueror to their land. "And say to him that if he becomes any more nervous, the wily queen will understand he's telling us more than she wants us to know."

The sun had moved completely across the sky. It fell toward the green and forested horizon, its rays still hot and bright, and sank into darkness with barely a flare of sunset. The night closed in, hot and humid. Torches flared around the pavilion. Four attendants carried a large brazier into the pavilion. The heat and smoke poured out of it.

"Thank Queen Blood Jaguar for her hospitality. Lady Jaguar will understand— Maranti—"

Bridges Words spoke to Uinthi rather than translating, and Blood Jaguar gave him a sharp, angry look.

"We have to stay for the ceremony," Uinthi said. "Bridges Words says it would be a terrible insult to leave now."

"Very well, but Eldest Daughter is tired, and so am I."

Lady Jaguar gave her a nod of sympathy. "I understand. But the gods and the ancestors require sustenance. Tonight I will feed them."

And here I thought, Iakinthu said to herself, that what we were doing all day was giving sustenance to the ancestors.

In the humid heat, the smell of the mummy intensified. Maranti's goldstone complexion lost its usual glow in the face of growing exhaustion and revulsion, and even Iakinthu, who had endured—and enjoyed—ceremonies, rituals, and parties that went on for days, wished for her quiet cabin and the touch of Aranthau's cool hands.

Lady Jaguar rose and strode to the center of the pavilion. Her ladies attended her, bringing a cushion, a red leather pouch intricately embroidered, and a bowl filled with white strips. Papyrus? Iakinthu wondered. It fluttered: paper.

Lady Jaguar took her place before the brazier. From the pouch she drew a length of cord. Iakinthu squinted to see it better, to understand what the ritual involved. Bits of gold glittered along the cord's length.

Jaguar opened her mouth, thrust out her tongue, and brought the end of the cord to her lower lip. Then, to Iakinthu's surprise, she threaded the end of the cord into her tongue, into a slit that till now had been invisible.

She drew the cord up, and the first bit of gold touched her.

It was a thorn, wrought in gold, polished sharp. When it passed through the slit in her tongue, it pierced the flesh and came through the top of her tongue smeared with blood.

She leaned over. One of her ladies held a strip of paper to catch the blood as it flowed from her mouth, and when blood darkened the paper, the lady placed it in the brazier. It sizzled and burned.

Beside Iakinthu, Maranti gasped, then silenced herself and sat rigid, her eyes open but focused far into the darkness. Iakinthu took her hand; Maranti squeezed her fingers gently. Rhenthizu held her other hand, and swallowed hard and clenched his jaw.

The Idaeans and the court of the great queen and the mummy king sat in polite or reverent silence until Lady Jaguar pulled the last thorn through her tongue, bloodied the last strip of paper, and gazed serenely at the fire as her lady burned her sacrifice. Heat gathered in the pavilion, as if the paper released intense power by its burning, as if the land breeze gathered all the heat of the day and carried it to the top of the pyramid.

Sweat soaked Iakinthu's jacket and plastered her hair to her forehead and dripped between her breasts. She might as well be in a Maisusutha sweat bath, waiting for a vision, saying to Thamenthu that she preferred visions from poppy smoke to those of rock steam, and Thamenthu teasing her about the softness of the Idaeans, too civilized for their own good. She swayed and caught herself, hoping only she had noticed her lapse.

The sparks of the burning paper flared and died. All the court of Blood Jaguar and Jade Stingray knelt to Lady Jaguar. She rose, reflecting the light of the guttering torches from her skin, from her jewelry, gold on gold. She strode to her place, her step strong and sure.

She glanced at Iakinthu. "The universe will survive for another circle of the calendar," she said, her words only slightly contorted by her swollen tongue, translated smoothly by Bridges Words and relayed by Uinthi. "I fed it. I am the sustenance and the savior of my people and the land of my mother and my father."

Could I speak at all, Iakinthu wondered, after such a trial?

Iakinthu drew a glass vial from her pocket and offered it to Lady Jaguar.

"If you drink it, it will ease the pain," she said.

Bridges Words hesitated, and Lady Jaguar snapped a word at him: Translate!

When he obeyed, she frowned for a moment, then smiled at Iakinthu, joyful and confident.

"I hold the pain to my breast," she said. "The universe draws life from my blood and from my pain, and speaks to me." She held out her hand. "But I would like the little jar. It's very pretty."

Iakinthu put the purple glass vial in Lady Jaguar's hand, thinking, How appropriate, that to color glass purple, the artisan must add gold.

She rather wished she had drunk the extract of lavender and poppy herself before handing over its glass container.

Chapter Twenty-Two

Aranthau waited on the beach with the ship's boat, ready to take them aboard when they ended the long golden descent. Iakinthu's legs ached. Rhenthizu and Kilinkizu flanked Maranti, each holding one of her hands, solicitous despite her assurances.

Would the Maisusutha consider my Maranti too soft and civilized for her own good? Iakinthu thought, fiercely proud of the Eldest Daughter. They would honor her.

She hiked up her long skirt and waded into the surf, careless of her sandals, grateful for the coolness of the water.

"Shall I swim?" she asked Aranthau.

"Let me row you," Aranthau said. "The bay has sharks, and skates with long stinging tails."

"Stingrays," she said.

He touched her cheek, laying his cool hand against her skin. She leaned into his touch, grateful for his strength. She took his hand and kissed his palm.

He helped her into the boat; Rhenthizu and Kilinkizu performed the same service for Maranti and clambered in after her. Uinthi and Paissu jumped in. Bridges Words hung back on the beach.

"And who is this?" Aranthau asked, looking Bridges Words up and down.

"Bridges Words is our honored translator." Iakinthu held out her hand to him. "Will you come to my ship?"

When Uinthi relayed Iakinthu's question, Bridges Words glanced nervously toward the raft, where his king—his owner, Iakinthu supposed—had returned to his house, accompanied by lines of torches. He replied to Uinthi.

"He says, 'Tomorrow I may be killed, but today was a good day.'"

"I think that the life of a commoner is hard here, and the life of a possession even more difficult. Tell him, please, that he's welcome, and that I'll ask Lady Jaguar if he may come with us, if he wishes it."

Bridges Words listened, gazed at her curiously, and joined the Idaeans in the boat.

"What a day," Uinthi said. "Sometimes I thought I was in the sweat lodge, it was so hot! But, was I rewarded with so much as a small vision?"

"I thought the same thing," Iakinthu said. "And wished for a bit of poppy smoke."

On the water, the heat moderated. Aranthau stroked smoothly, pulling the boat toward *Flying Fish*. Bridges Words held out his hands, palms up, showing the heavy calluses, amazed that someone else was rowing.

"I thought to come and get you from that gold mountain," Aranthau said. "You were gone so long."

"I saw you," Iakinthu replied, "keeping watch."

"Have you seen such a ritual?" Maranti asked. "Anywhere in your travels?"

"Lady Jaguar's sacrifice was unique in my experience," Iakinthu said. She described it to Aranthau, who grimaced. "Will you ask Bridges Words what he knows about it?"

Uinthi tried, but their translator grew nervous.

He's tongue-tied, Iakinthu thought and had to keep herself from laughing, afraid she would offend him.

"Only kings and nobles can explain the workings of the sky and the world and the underworld, he says," Uinthi told her. "If even they understand the gods." Uinthi quirked one eyebrow. "He's frightened, Iakinthu. Maybe he'll tell us more if he comes to trust us."

"I'd be frightened, too," Iakinthu said, "if I thought that every day I might be killed."

"When you danced," Aranthau said, "fear was the farthest thing from your mind, and you might have been killed at any moment."

"I chose to dance," Iakinthu said. "Did Bridges Words choose to be… commanded?"

Aranthau shipped the oars and let the ship's boat slide through the water to *Flying Fish*'s side, where it barely touched the planks before its forward motion ended. Paissu grabbed a line and ran up the side; she dropped the rope ladder to them. The rest of the companions gathered at the rail to greet them.

They were home.

The morning had already turned scorching when Iakinthu woke.

When have I slept so late? she asked herself. And then: When is the last time I stayed awake from night to morning to night?

The People and the Maisusutha danced till they were tired; Pharaoh performed many rituals and propitiations but always kept her comfort in mind. The people of Blood Jaguar and her daughter were another thing entirely.

Lady Jaguar's sacrifice was the most extreme Iakinthu had ever witnessed. She hoped Bridges Words would consent to tell her if last night had been an ordinary ritual or an extraordinary one.

Aranthau had slept beside her, but he usually rose at dawn, and dawn was long past. Iakinthu sat up slowly, aching and still tired. She thought of going back to sleep, but instead rose and dressed in a plain kilt and closed vest.

On deck, her companions had rigged a sail across the deck, to provide some shade. Maranti cooled herself with a feather fan, and Paissu sat in her favorite place near the top of the mast, watchful as always, ignoring the sun.

I must weave her a hat, Iakinthu thought. She wondered if the island of Lady Jaguar grew proper reeds for weaving. Her people used pottery and cloth rather than mats and baskets, and she smiled to herself at the idea of the noble Lady Jaguar weaving.

Toward the bow, Kilinkizu and Bdarde spoke together in low voices, but their bodies and expressions gave evidence of another argument. Iakinthu wished she could find some happiness in the boy, but whenever she saw him she wished he were somewhere else, and Kilinkizu grew sadder and more troubled each day. The pirates had ruined his spirit, murdering him as they had murdered his sister.

I wonder if Lady Jaguar would perform a ritual to bring him back, Iakinthu thought. Or, better, if Idaeans could return to one of our rituals, deliberately forgotten for a thousand years.

The boy flung himself away from his mother, strode a few paces down the deck, saw Iakinthu, scowled, and disappeared belowdecks.

And he may stay there, she thought, if he prefers being hot and uncomfortable to being in the breeze, however slight.

She smiled at Kilinkizu and crossed the deck to embrace her. Her numerator smiled shakily.

"What will I do?" she said. "He's so angry."

"He needs a proper grandmother," Iakinthu said, though the last thing she wanted to do was stand in the place of Bdarde's grandmother. "Perhaps Dragon Claws will take him."

She laughed, and even Kilinkizu giggled at the thought, before she sobered again.

"If Dragon Claws were still speaking to me," she said sadly. "She's angry, too." She sighed. "Bdarde thinks he needs to be beaten and starved, to make him into a man."

"Oh, what kind of man would that be?" Iakinthu said. "A man like the pirates, like the barbarians. Who would want such a man?"

"His…king," Kilinkizu whispered, avoiding, as she did, a profanity.

"That person belongs to the barbarians," Iakinthu said. "You—and Bdarde-who-is—belong to Fair Island."

Kilinkizu touched her fist to her forehead in assent.

"And now I'm hungry," Iakinthu said, "and I'll think about Bdarde later."

Rhenthizu listened as Uinthi and Bridges Words conversed. Every so often he thought he recognized a word, but he finally decided he was imagining that the southern trade language lived somewhere in his distant memory. He would have to learn it anew.

Uinthi leaned back, elbows on the deck, hair down, sidelocks braided, wearing an Idaean kilt and a Maisusutha beaded vest, a combination that struck him as odd but suitable. His hair, too, refused any fashionable curl.

"What does he tell you?" Rhenthizu asked.

"He tells me to be wary."

Rhenthizu glanced across the water toward the island, where raft and shore alike remained quiet and still. Lady Jaguar's people, the great queen's people, must be as tired today as the Idaeans.

"I already am," Rhenthizu said. Tired as he was, he had fallen asleep only after he saw that Aranthau, always protective of *Flying Fish* and his crew, had asked several other companions to watch the raft and the shore.

"He says the Jaguars will come to our home and take our land, because Lady Jaguar has none of her own to rule."

"Will she paddle her raft across the Sunset Sea or even to the land of the Maisusutha?" he asked. He doubted the raft would be seaworthy; it was a coast-bound craft.

"He says Lady Jaguar might take us for sacrifice."

Rhenthizu shivered. "I like my tongue the way it is," he said.

"If Smoke Stingray had been the one to spill his blood last night, his tongue would have stayed whole. He would have spilled his blood from his penis."

Rhenthizu shifted his position. Uinthi watched him close his legs and raise his knees, protectively, and laughed sympathetically.

"I felt like doing that when he told me." Uinthi grinned and shrugged. "Their gods are demanding," he said, and made himself sit cross-legged on the deck, more relaxed but more vulnerable.

"Their whole world is demanding," Uinthi said. "It demands their blood, or it will end."

"Does it demand our blood?"

He asked Bridges Words a question; he replied intently.

"Any day, we could be killed."

"Our new friend's favorite phrase," Rhenthizu said.

"For him it's surely true."

"As it is," Rhenthizu said, "for any slave."

Uinthi translated for Bridges Words, who gave Rhenthizu a long and thoughtful look.

Paissu was the first of *Flying Fish*'s companions to see the movement on the raft.

"Aranthau!" she called down. "They're coming to us."

Below, on deck, all the companions grew alert. Aranthau strode to the bow to watch the activity on the beached raft. It had nearly floated free earlier that morning as the remarkable tide rose, but its people had merely checked the lines and went back to sleep, and the raft settled when the tide went out again. Still, Paissu saw why they had beached it without a worry. On the shore she was accustomed to, the tide was too gentle to free so big a craft.

Lady Jaguar's people put canoes over the side, loaded them with packages, and held the largest canoe steady so Lady Jaguar and her consort could take their places.

Paissu wondered how they could move in their elaborate clothing and headdresses. She wished she could see and hear them better, but she stayed at the top of the mast and kept her eye on the big raft. It had many men on it, and in Paissu's experience that usually meant trouble.

Iakinthu put on her best jewelry while the canoes cut through the water toward *Flying Fish*. She could have changed her clothes, but the heat was so oppressive that she remained in kilt and vest.

"Let me arrange your hair, Iakinthu Gephyra," Kilinkizu said, distressed that Iakinthu was skipping both formal dress and henna. Henna took a long time, but clothes were easily changed.

"Please," Iakinthu said, and stood obediently while Kilinkizu brushed her hair with an oiled brush, braided and coiled it at her nape with a butterfly pin, and arranged her sidelocks in long curls.

"Will you make note of our visitors?" Iakinthu asked. "Draw them, note their interests—?"

"Of course," Kilinkizu said.

Wearing her sealstone bracelets and her dragonfly necklace, Iakinthu hurried back on deck. A faint breeze eased the heat.

She conferred with Aranthau; when Jaguar's canoe reached *Flying Fish*, he threw down the ladder.

"Lady Jaguar and her consort may come aboard," Aranthau said.

Bridges Words' reply to Uinthi came out in a squeak, he was so distressed by the order.

"They'll be offended," Uinthi said. "And you're scaring Bridges Words."

"Allow them a few attendants, my love," Iakinthu said. "Their state is important to them, being without land as they are."

"Very well," he said reluctantly. "They may bring two attendants."

"And two guards," Bridges Words suggested. "Please, my lord."

Aranthau assented to the negotiation. His order went to Uinthi, to Bridges Words, to Lady Jaguar, who frowned.

"We welcome you with friendship and gifts," Iakinthu said, "as you welcomed us. Come on board my ship. You may trust my hospitality."

"How will we bring our gifts," Lady Jaguar said, "without attendants to carry them?"

"We have baskets," Aranthau said drily.

"Very well," Lady Jaguar said, and Iakinthu understood her before Bridges Words and Uinthi translated.

Iakinthu was beginning to understand a few words of Lady Jaguar's language, a few words of the southern trade language that both Uinthi and Bridges Words spoke as they conveyed her welcome, and Lady Jaguar's cautious assent.

I wish I could learn new languages as quickly as when I was younger, she thought. And I wonder how accurate Bridges Words' translation is? How many honorifics and qualifications must the poor man add out of fear?

The guards climbed first, scrabbling up the ladder against the side of the ship, reaching the deck, flanking the ladder to protect their mistress and their master as they followed, equally unfamiliar with ladders and the sides of ships. Two young women came carefully after them. Iakinthu was glad the bay was mirror-still.

"Where are the baskets?" Lady Jaguar said. Iakinthu laughed and set two of the companions of *Flying Fish* to help bring up the packages.

"Come, sit in the shade." Iakinthu led Lady Jaguar and Smoke Stingray to a spot beneath the awning. Maranti, waiting in a camp chair, added her welcome to Iakinthu's.

The noble visitors took their places, and their two young attendants sat on the deck behind them.

The guards, too, ignored the chairs set out for them, standing instead behind Lady Jaguar and Smoke Stingray. Iakinthu noticed the axes they carried on their belts, the heads intricately carved blades of jade, heavy enough to do damage no matter their ceremonial appearance. The attendants also carried knives in heavy gold sheaths, with the gleam of obsidian showing between the woven straps of the grips. Headdress feathers brushed the awning.

Will we give them reason to use their weapons? Iakinthu said to herself. Mine is a visit of diplomacy and trade.

She noticed with pleasure that Jaguar wore the purple glass vial as an ornament on a gold chain around her neck, and that Smoke Jaguar likewise displayed the bull dancer.

Lady Jaguar is very clever, Iakinthu thought. The hold of *Flying Fish* carried several crates of glass vials and vases, less elegant than those in her cedar chest but well suited to be filled with lavender flowers and stopped with wool.

She poured two cups of wine and offered one to Lady Jaguar.

"A different vintage—"

Bridges Words hesitated, confused.

"From a different year?" Uinthi suggested; Iakinthu nodded.

"Made in a different year, from different fruit—you might like it better."

Jaguar sipped the wine politely, then took another sip.

"Much better," she said.

"It can make you dizzy," Iakinthu warned. "So be careful."

"Ah, like—"

Uinthi stumbled over the word, tried again, shrugged, and converted it to Idaean.

"She says wine must be like balithi, and Bridges Words says balithi is a honey drink, but I must say it right."

Bridges Words tried to correct Uinthi's pronunciation; he tried to keep from laughing at the mangled word.

"You're speaking Idaean," Iakinthu said, "and Idaeans will know it as balithi."

One of Lady Jaguar's attendants hurried away and soon came back with a painted jug. Iakinthu finished the last drops of her wine and accepted a cup of balithi.

"Only a little," Maranti said. "I can get dizzy all on my own these days." Uinthi spoke; Bridges Words explained, and the attendant smiled at Maranti and poured a few drops of balithi into her cup.

"Iakinthu," Uinthi said, "what of the stories of poison honey…?"

"And what of honey medicine?" Iakinthu said. "If Lady Jaguar wishes us harm, she and Smoke Stingray have more people than we do. Does Bridges Words think they mean us harm today? Do you trust him?"

"I do, but he's too frightened to speak of some things."

"When you can, find out why, and what he's most frightened of. For now, the place of Iakinthu Gephyra is to drink with her guest."

She bowed slightly toward Lady Jaguar. Lady Jaguar nodded once, sharply, in acknowledgement. They raised their cups and drank.

She expected it to be sweet like honey, but it tasted tart, with a strange undertaste. She let it linger on her tongue. It carried specks like dust, the source of the aftertaste. It reminded her of the texture of cinnamon tea, which had enjoyed a considerable fashion when Aranthau brought the spice back from the east. His voyage had earned its cost and more with the cinnamon bark alone.

"Oh," Iakinthu said, as the effects of the drink swirled around her. "Much stronger than wine," she said. She did feel dizzy, and in the corners of her vision the creatures decorating Lady Jaguar's accoutrements and painted vases moved and danced, climbing off their painted surfaces and gamboling across the deck. The symbols on the edge of her robe flew up into the air and circled Iakinthu's head as if they were constellations and she were the North Star.

Bridges Words drank his balithi down before Lady Jaguar could object to his being served with it.

Lady Jaguar is jealous of her privileges, Iakinthu thought. She keeps them close, rather than distributing them. And of course Bridges Words is still her possession.

She tried to remember if she had told Bridges Words that she intended to make him a free man, but the gamboling little monsters on the deck distracted her, and the circling stars made her dizzy.

"Do you see those?" she asked Lady Jaguar, pointing at the pitcher, which now was plain undecorated pottery, letting her finger drift after the creatures.

"I see new land, my own land, for me and Smoke Stingray to rule," Lady Jaguar said. She gestured out to sea, then let her hand fall into her lap. She laughed sadly. "Can you tell me, Iakinthu from far away, of new land and new people who would bow to our authority?"

"I know of people whose kings are cruel and careless of their wellbeing," Iakinthu said. "They might give their loyalty to kinder rulers."

The creatures on the deck had stopped dancing. Now they were fighting, and their blood spattered across the deck. Iakinthu watched from far away.

The attendant tried to refill her cup, but Iakinthu declined. She felt dizzy, somnolent, nauseated.

"Have more," Jaguar said, taking her own advice, gazing out at the imaginary island she yearned for.

"I beg your pardon," Iakinthu said, "but it's new to me, and I must get used to it."

Bridges Words giggled. Uinthi gazed into a cup, tears flowing.

"Uinthi, what is it?"

Uinthi might have answered, but Bridges Words spoke first, and Uinthi straightened and resumed translating.

"He says, Today he may be killed, but he's lost all his fear."

"You should beat him," Lady Jaguar said, "when he speaks out of turn."

"Do Idaeans beat each other?" Iakinthu said. "Sometimes we wrestle."

The creatures on the deck wrestled, and then they ran around playing a game, using the head of one of their number as the ball.

Iakinthu shivered.

"Kilinkizu," she said, "can you draw those creatures? Maranti, you're better off drinking wine or cacao."

"I have monsters of my own to draw," Kilinkizu whispered.

"Are *you* all right?" Maranti asked.

"I wish the creatures on the deck would put their heads back on and climb back onto their pottery," Iakinthu said.

Everyone looked at her, but Lady Jaguar nodded.

"Balithi gives her the gift of a vision."

"I prefer poppy," Iakinthu said. "Or even the Maisusutha way." She added quickly, "Tell Lady Jaguar I thank her for the vision."

She had to force herself to stay awake. Lady Jaguar downed a third cup of balithi, and a moment later fell into a doze, her chin on her chest, a drop of blood on her lip. She snored softly, safe in the care of her bodyguard and her attendants.

Iakinthu called for, olives, cheese, and wine. She chose yet a different vintage, heavier, darker, in hopes that Lady Jaguar would like it better than the light, flowery wine that the great queen had suggested mixing with chile, or the recent vintage Lady Jaguar had replaced with balithi.

Kilinkizu sat near Iakinthu with her writing-box on her lap, making quick sketches and notes with a glass pen and several vials of colored ink. Lady Jaguar sampled the Idaean food, occasionally glancing at Kilinkizu. All the while, the companions of *Flying Fish* brought one basket after another of packages from canoes, stacking them behind Lady Jaguar and Smoke Stingray.

"Why have you come here?" Smoke Stingray asked, looking at Aranthau.

"To trade, to make alliances." Iakinthu answered him. Aranthau had many talents—among other things, he was an excellent bargainer—but Iakinthu was the diplomat.

"And," she said, "to reach the Untamable Ocean, which lies to the west. Do you know it?"

"Of course," he said, arrogantly.

Jaguar glanced at him quizzically. "We know *of* it," she said. "That one has seen it." She nodded toward Bridges Words, and said, casually, "Do you want him?"

"He's of some use to me," Iakinthu said with equal ease, "until I learn his language."

"I give him to you," Jaguar said.

Smoke Stingray snapped out an objection, and Bridges Words, head down, whispered unnecessarily, "He's angry." He raised his head, apparently startled, at Smoke Stingray's low comment to Lady Jaguar. "He thinks you would give more than nothing for me." He lowered his head again. "But he might kill me today to show you he cares nothing for your riches."

"Did he say that?" Iakinthu asked. "That last?"

Uinthi said, "That's what Bridges Words thinks. Smoke Stingray only thinks Lady Jaguar gave you something without being sure she'd get something in return."

"We will have to make Lady Jaguar's kindness worth her while," Iakinthu said.

Lady Jaguar pointed with her chin toward the stern cabin, where Maranti had retired to rest. Rhenthizu sat nearby, mending a sail.

"Your daughter," Lady Jaguar said, with an implied question.

Iakinthu decided to let Lady Jaguar think Eldest Daughter was a term of relationship rather than a title.

If I tell her of our goddess, do I want to know what she'll tell me of her gods? Some other day, perhaps.

"She's tired," Iakinthu said. "As were we all at her stage."

"Yes, that's true." Lady Jaguar gestured for one of her attendants. "We'll make cacao for your captain and my consort," she said. "My attendant does it very well."

Iakinthu watched the performance, the ritual, carefully, enjoying the precise moves, the water's curve into the pitcher, the curl of steam, the change from clear water to brown froth. The young attendant knelt and poured cacao into two drinking cups. She offered one to Smoke Stingray; with a jerk of his noble head he ordered her to give the first cup to Aranthau, their host, before he accepted the second for himself.

After they had drunk, Lady Jaguar said, "Now, your Aranthau will show my consort his ship, and we will talk."

Uinthi said, "Lady Jaguar said 'big canoe,' according to Bridges Words. Bridges Words knows what a ship is. Has Lady Jaguar ever seen one?"

"Our Bridges Words has undiscovered talents," Iakinthu said, and in the same tone replied, "It's my ship, Lady Jaguar, but I'm proud to give Aranthau its tiller and its sails."

"Yours? Very well, no matter," Jaguar said despite her surprise. "They'll see your ship, and you and I will visit with your daughter."

She waved off the difficulty the two men might have in speaking to each other, without Bridges Words. "They'll point. They'll understand each other well enough." She claimed Bridges Words, ordering him to follow, as if she had forgotten giving him to Iakinthu.

Rhenthizu rose when they approached. "She's asleep," he said softly.

"I'm only dozing." Maranti pushed herself up on her couch and ran her fingers through her loose hair. It curled around her face, over her shoulders, over her breasts. "Is that cacao I smell?"

Lady Jaguar smiled as her attendant came forward with the pitcher, still half full. The other attendant brought Lady Jaguar a chair. "The men drink it as a ritual. We'll drink it in friendship."

Unwilling to be outdone, several of the companions of *Flying Fish* brought chairs for Iakinthu and Kilinkizu, for Uinthi and Bridges Words. Bridges Words sat gingerly. Iakinthu wondered if he would abandon the chair for the deck, but he sat back in it and looked pleased.

I wonder, Iakinthu thought, if he's thinking, I may be killed, but it's a good day.

She sipped from her cup, enjoying the complicated taste and the pleasure it gave her. Like Queen Blood Jaguar, who thought wine might be improved with chili, Iakinthu thought the cacao would benefit from the addition of some honey.

"Thank you, Lady Jaguar," Maranti said. "I was wishing and dreaming for another cup of cacao."

"It's very good for you."

Iakinthu noticed that Lady Jaguar was building up a reserve of obligations. It was past time to discharge some of them.

"Rhenthizu," she said, "would you bring me the small cedar trunk from my cabin?"

He touched his fist to his forehead and vanished belowdecks.

Iakinthu absently scooped up a fingerful of honey from the tray of olives, almonds, honey, and dried fruit that one of her companions had set nearby. She let it flow into her cup and swirled it around. She licked the honey from her finger and sipped her cacao with the honey still on her tongue. The honey made the chili milder and moderated the bitterness of the cacao.

She closed her eyes and savored the drink. It made her feel less tired.

Lady Jaguar husked and shelled an almond and popped it into her mouth. "Sacred to women," she said, smiling.

"Dip one in honey," Iakinthu said, pointing to the dish, which was painted with small bright bees that shone up through the golden honey.

Lady Jaguar looked closely at the dish. "Ah," she said. "You too have the royal lady." She munched an almond covered with honey. "Very good."

Uinthi passed an almond covered with honey to Bridges Words. They both licked the honey from their fingers and laughed. They talked softly together; Lady Jaguar glanced at them with disapproval.

Should they speak only when they're translating and serving her? Iakinthu wondered. That's what Lady Jaguar believes.

"The royal lady is the bee," Uinthi said, "but this is the first time Bridges Words has tasted honey. He'd like more."

"He may have as much as he likes," Iakinthu said. "And I will be grateful if he helps us negotiate for fresh food and water."

Iakinthu passed him another almond, dripping with honey. He spoke to Uinthi while he was still chewing it.

"Would you say that again?"

Iakinthu understood Uinthi because Bridges Words swallowed the almond and said exactly the same thing a second time.

"He says you should ask for more balithi. He stole some once—we'll keep that from Lady Jaguar, because she'd want to punish him even though he...serves you now—and he lost all his fear for two whole days."

This interested Iakinthu considerably.

"Tell him I will, but before I accept more presents—or ask for more balithi—I'll give some." She thought, I'm used to trading partners who covet Idaean wine and pottery and worked gold and olive oil. Here on the other side of the Sunset Sea, they have pottery to rival ours; they have honey drink instead of wine. They have more gold than I've ever seen. And they have cacao. I hope they'll covet something I have to trade.

Rhenthizu rejoined the group, carrying a small wooden chest painted with saffron crocuses.

"Thank you, my dear," she said.

She drew aside the fluffy raw wool that cushioned the contents of the box. The scent of cedar and lavender rose around her. She always added lavender to packing material, even when the cargo was immune to insects.

"What is that smell?" Lady Jaguar sounded both curious and eager.

"Lavender." Iakinthu handed her a puff of lavender-impregnated wool.

Lady Jaguar put it to her nose and breathed deeply, savoring the scent like a Sheng amber-buyer or a broker of wine.

"That is very pleasant," Lady Jaguar said. She sniffed it again. "Is this the hair of a creature? What creature smells like this?"

Iakinthu reached into the bottom of the chest and scooped up a handful of lavender. She handed the dried flowers to Lady Jaguar, who rubbed them between her fingers and breathed the scent with pleasure. Iakinthu found this promising.

Iakinthu drew out a purple glass vase, four fingers tall, delicate, the product of her favorite glassmaker in Kunusu. She presented it to Lady Jaguar.

"Thank you for your hospitality."

Lady Jaguar took it formally and with delight. She held it up to the sunlight and gazed through it.

"Purple obsidian!" she said. "Where do you find it? How do you form it like this without breaking it?"

"The artisans in my homeland know how," Iakinthu said. "They keep the knowledge as their deepest secret."

"I thank you for it," she said, "and my necklace." She touched the gold-chained vial around her neck. She sniffed the wool puff again. Her hands rather full, she poured the lavender flowers into the vase and pushed the wool in, to hold the flowers in and transmit the scent.

Through the afternoon, Iakinthu did her best to stay awake in the heat, even when Lady Jaguar dozed. She had been persuaded to drink another cup of balithi and now rather wished she had followed Aranthau's lead in declining it.

Kilinkizu sketched Lady Jaguar while she slept.

"I want some of that red dye," she said, nodding toward Lady Jaguar's robe. "Will it make ink, I wonder?"

"They paint their stone carvings, so it must make paint." Uinthi gestured toward the island, where tall rectangular stones flanked the path to the golden pyramid. "They're carved and painted. Very complicated. We had to keep walking past them, though I wanted to stop to look."

"And one of Lady Jaguar's attendants drew on paper the whole time we were up there," Iakinthu said, remembering the small quiet figure with brushes and paint pots. "Would I have noticed her if she had been sitting in the dark? But she sat beneath a torch, for the light."

"Was she drawing? Or writing?"

"I think the two may be very much the same thing for Lady Jaguar's scribe."

"May I talk to her scribe?"

"When she wakes, we'll ask her." Iakinthu glanced toward the deck, where the pottery creatures had been playing. Now they sat beneath Lady Jaguar's chair, busily scribbling on blocks of paper. Go away, little creatures, Iakinthu thought. You are the strangest vision I have ever seen.

They jumped up, ran to the cacao pitcher, leaped at it, and dissolved onto its surface. Iakinthu's dizziness faded.

"Would Lady Jaguar like henna, do you think?" Maranti said. She stretched out her hands, showing the faint patterns on her palms. "I want a new design. This is so faded."

"When she wakes, we'll ask her," Iakinthu said again, but she let Lady Jaguar doze on. She gazed at their visitor, taking in the fine weave of her red robe, the brocaded edge of complicated signs, her jade necklace and heavy earrings. She had left off her complicated headdress, which Iakinthu supposed she must wear only for ritual occasions.

Lady Jaguar suddenly sat up straight, her eyes wide open.

"I'm awake!" she said, a bit belligerently.

"Of course," Iakinthu said. "As are we all. Thank you for the balithi. The experience was unique."

"Where are the men?" Lady Jaguar asked.

"They went below," Iakinthu replied. "I'm sure they're comparing... ships." She and Maranti laughed; Uinthi snorted and translated and waited for Bridges Words to relay the comment, and after a moment Lady Jaguar joined the laughter. Kilinkizu continued to draw, and Rhenthizu gazed past them all, pretending Iakinthu had spoken without a double meaning.

Uinthi asked Bridges Words a question; he replied at some length.

"Show Lady Jaguar her portrait," Uinthi said to Kilinkizu. "Bridges Words says she likes to have images of herself carved into stone, so people will know she rules as her father's regent."

With some hesitation, Kilinkizu turned the quick sketch toward Lady Jaguar. The lady looked at it and drew her eyebrows together. A small pucker appeared on her long, smooth brow.

"Tell her my red paint is the color of iron rust, of henna, while hers is the color of sunsets and the plumage of fabled birds."

"Ah," Lady Jaguar said, taking the comment for a compliment, as it was meant. "The likeness is acceptable."

Maranti showed Lady Jaguar her palms, with the faded red-brown henna designs. Lady Jaguar took her hand gently and traced the spiral.

"Does your skin grow this way? Is it a tattoo?" She frowned. "It's the wrong color for a tattoo, and too pale."

"It's a decoration," Maranti said. "This is the color of henna. I put it on, and enjoy it, and it fades, and I put on a different design. Would you like to see?"

They sent for henna and linen strips. Extravagantly bored, Rhenthizu said, "It's my turn at lookout," and practically leaped away to relieve Paissu from her perch atop the mast.

Rhenthizu gestured for Paissu to join him on deck. She clambered down the mast.

"The island is quiet, the golden hill is quiet, the big raft is quiet," she said.

"They serve a dead man," Rhenthizu said. "What can anyone do for a dead man?"

"I'd rather be burned," Paissu said, quite sensibly.

"So would I," Rhenthizu said. "Go get something to eat and something to drink and have a rest. Thank you for looking out. You're very observant."

"What are Iakinthu and Uinthi doing?"

"Painting Lady Jaguar with henna."

Paissu ran off toward the stern.

Rhenthizu continued to the bow. As he passed the hatch, Smoke Stingray's forbidding bodyguard climbed up and glared around as if expecting a war party; Aranthau and Smoke Stingray followed, talking back and forth as if they understood each other, Aranthau pointing out features of the ship, Stingray replying, gesturing at the raft.

Kilinkizu's rude little boy followed them, talking at the same time. Rhenthizu preferred to think of him as the rude little boy rather than as Bdarde-who-is. He missed Bdarde-who-was. He understood that giving the boy her name was meant to honor her, but he wished Iakinthu had thought of some other honor for his friend.

"What did he say?" the boy demanded, pulling at Aranthau's kilt.

Aranthau ignored him, in the way of Idaeans to ill-mannered children. He straightened his kilt.

"Why are you talking to him when he understands nothing you say?" the boy demanded.

Smoke Stingray glared at the boy. Rhenthizu thought he might like to see what happened if the boy pulled at Stingray's elaborate loincloth, but then again, perhaps the consequences would be quite serious.

"Why are you *listening* to him when you understand nothing he says?"

Rhenthizu sighed. The boy was working himself up to one of his tantrums. Perhaps he will come with me to the bow and help with the lookout, Rhenthizu thought, turning back toward Aranthau and Stingray, hoping to distract the young Bdarde.

"You're both stupid, stupid, stupid!"

Stingray picked the boy up by his armpits, lifted him past the gunwale, suspended him over the sea, and dropped him.

The boy yelped, more with surprise than with fear. When he hit the water, he screamed, a scream cut off when the sea gagged him.

Aranthau dove in after him.

Can the boy swim? Rhenthizu wondered, as he ran to throw a line and float over the side. Pirates should know how to swim, but so should Idaeans, and how many Idaeans know how to swim?

Rhenthizu had always been surprised by how few of his shipmates thought it worth their while to learn.

Kilinkizu ran to the bow, blobs of henna spattered across her skirt, one hand wrapped with a linen strip.

"What happened?" she cried, flung off her skirt, and dove in after Aranthau and the boy without waiting for an answer.

Aranthau knifed beneath the surface. Kilinkizu splashed after him. Rhenthizu held the line so the float would be in reach when they came back into the air.

"What happened?" Iakinthu hurried to his side, followed by Lady Jaguar and the rest of Maranti's henna party, all with strips of linen around their wrists or hands. Paissu jumped onto the rail and was about to dive in, but Rhenthizu caught her by her vest and hauled her onto the deck.

"Can you help by jumping on top of them?" Rhenthizu said. "Wait, stay, help me pull them up."

"Can he swim?" Paissu said with disgust. "Did the pirates let his mother teach him to swim?"

"Where are they?" Iakinthu asked. "They've been underwater for a long time. Can Kilinkizu swim?"

"All the People can swim," Paissu said. "I told you, the pirates should have left him with his mother."

"You're right, little Paissu," Iakinthu said. "They should have had your wisdom."

Kilinkizu surfaced, gasped, and dove again.

Bdarde suddenly appeared, his head and shoulders rising above the water as if he were breaching like a whale, as if he had been pushed into the air. A dark shape moved beneath him, raising him to safety. The boy splashed back into the water, thrashing and crying and sputtering. Rhenthizu expected Aranthau or Kilinkizu to appear beside him, but the lithe shadowy shape dove deeper and vanished.

Rhenthizu threw the line.

Paissu pointed. "Did you see?" she whispered.

Kilinkizu surfaced next to Bdarde, trying to keep him afloat despite his struggles. A moment later Aranthau appeared, barely out of breath. He supported Bdarde from the other side. Bdarde coughed and thrashed around, trying to free himself.

"Be still!" Kilinkizu said. "The sea returned you."

"Do you want to drown?" Aranthau said.

Bdarde thrashed some more. Aranthau let him go. Bdarde kicked and screamed and jerked himself from Kilinkizu's grip and sank a second time.

"Stay here to catch him," Aranthau said, and dove. He brought the boy back into the air. They tried to hold him. He was tiring and breathless, but he struggled and fought them.

"Stop it," Aranthau said, guiding him toward the float. "If you sink a third time, the sea will own you."

Bdarde cried and coughed and choked in fury and fear. Exhausted, he went limp.

Aranthau sat him on the float, wrapped the boy's hands around the line, and steadied him as long as he could reach him. Rhenthizu pulled Bdarde up the side, trying to feel sympathetic for the boy's humiliation and the bumps and scrapes the side of the ship inflicted on him.

Maranti and Uinthi threw a rope ladder over the rail so Aranthau and Kilinkizu could return to the ship with more dignity.

Iakinthu reached down and lifted Bdarde onto the deck. He sat down hard, coughed out water, snarled some ugly and unintelligible words, and threw up on Smoke Stingray's feet.

The lord stepped back with a shout of annoyance. The bodyguard lunged forward— Could he think to attack the little boy? Rhenthizu wondered. He and Iakinthu moved at the same time, standing shoulder to shoulder, pushing Bdarde behind them, facing Smoke Stingray and his bodyguard.

"Serves you right!" Rhenthizu said, pointing at Stingray's feet.

"What happened?" Iakinthu asked again.

"He threw Bdarde overboard."

"For shame!" she said to Stingray. To the bodyguard, she said, "Fetch the water bucket to clean my deck." She pointed to the bucket, and he understood before Bridges Words and Uinthi could translate. Bridges Words stood at the edge of the group, trying not to laugh at his former owner, and Uinthi was occupied giving Aranthau a hand over the rail of *Flying Fish*.

Lady Jaguar stepped between Iakinthu and Stingray and asked him an angry question. Her attendants hovered in the background, twittering like frightened birds, and her bodyguard glared from person to person, baffled. Stingray's bodyguard hurried back with the bucket and poured the water on his lord's soiled feet, splashing Lady Jaguar's spotted fur ankle-cuffs and the brocade hem of her robe.

She snarled at him. Horrified, he fell to his knees and bowed his head in submission to her anger and her will.

Bridges Words shouted something.

Lady Jaguar and all her people froze and stared at him, more in astonishment than obedience.

Uinthi, gripping Kilinkizu's hand, helped the numerator over the rail to safety, then hurried to Bridges Words.

"He said, 'Stop,'" Uinthi said. "'Everybody stop.'"

"Good for him," Iakinthu said. "Can you ask everyone to be calm, or do we have to fling ourselves on this poor man to keep him from being killed?"

She bent down, took the bodyguard's trembling hand and raised him to his feet.

"Fetch another bucket of water," she said, "and this time pour it more slowly."

For a moment Rhenthizu thought the man would throw himself at her feet in gratitude and supplication, but Iakinthu kept his hand in hers till he understood her translated words.

Kilinkizu knelt beside Bdarde, patting his back as he coughed up more water, gently exploring his scrapes and cuts. Her long bright hair straggled around her face and down her back; the henna wrap had come off and all but a faint trace of the new henna design on her left hand had washed away.

Bdarde stopped coughing, and his breath came easier. He shrugged his mother away. Kilinkizu went stiff with hurt. Aranthau sat on his heels beside them.

"Your mother saved you from drowning," Aranthau said.

"You saved me. She's a woman. Women just get in the way."

"The sea saved you," Paissu said. "It spat you out, it refused you. And Kilinkizu kept you from sinking again."

Aranthau rose. Bdarde surreptitiously hid behind him, clutching his leg.

"I jumped in the water with my mama when I was a little tiny baby, and then I could swim," Paissu said. "If the pirates left you with your mama, you could swim now, too."

"Enough for now, Paissu," Iakinthu said. "Correct though you are."

Rhenthizu had been aware all this time of the conversation between Lady Jaguar and Lord Smoke Stingray, and though the words themselves were unknown to him, the tone was clear enough: the lady wanted to know why her consort had overstepped the bounds of hospitality, and he was defending himself to her. Rhenthizu could hardly blame him; he suspected every companion of *Flying Fish* had wanted to do exactly what Stingray had done.

Stingray's tone changed; he spoke over Jaguar, and his meaning was clear before Bridges Words and Uinthi translated: "Throw him overboard again, and this time leave him there."

"When my father finds me," Bdarde said, his voice rising till his voice reached a high and angry pitch, "we'll come back here and find you and kill you."

Smoke Stingray laughed.

Bdarde burst into furious tears, tried to stand, and staggered. Aranthau caught him and picked him up and carried him belowdecks, saying, "Warm porridge and sleep."

To Iakinthu's surprise, Bdarde-that-is clutched Aranthau around the neck and hid his face against his shoulder.

Kilinkizu stayed where she was, staring at the puddles, her hands in her lap, discouraged and bedraggled.

"You, too, my dear," Iakinthu said. "Warm porridge and a rest. And a cup of wine. Or two."

"Paissu's right," Kilinkizu whispered.

"What?"

"I saw..." She reached into her bodice to touch her reading stone, to be sure it had not slipped away into the sea. "I see more clearly underwater, but what did I see? Can I believe what I saw? When I reached for Bdarde, I grasped water. I thought Aranthau had saved him. Did Aranthau save him? Aranthau thought it was me."

"It was the sea," Paissu said again. "The sea picked him up and threw him out. Why would the sea want him?" At Kilinkizu's expression of despair, Paissu blushed furiously, ran across the deck, and climbed the mast.

Maranti helped Kilinkizu to her feet, picked up her henna-spattered skirt, and, when Kilinkizu balked at going belowdecks where Aranthau had taken her son, the Eldest Daughter took her to the stern cabin and drew the curtains around them.

Iakinthu gazed at the remaining group: Lady Jaguar, still angry, Stingray, unrepentant, Bridges Words, delightedly amused, Uinthi, watching with customary reserve, and Rhenthizu, calmly coiling the line and pulling up the ladder.

Lady Jaguar scowled at Smoke Stingray, then composed herself and spoke briefly to Iakinthu.

"I bid you good evening," she said, through the dual translation of Bridges Words and Uinthi. "We may speak again tomorrow." With that, she crossed the deck, followed by her attendants, who helped her over the side to the waiting boat.

Smoke Stingray watched her go, spoke a few more arrogant words, and followed her. In a moment the visitors had gone, and the deck was quiet. Iakinthu sighed and sank down to the deck. She glanced at Uinthi, at Bridges Words, waiting for the translation. Bridges Words knelt, bowed, pressed his forehead to the deck, and spoke. Iakinthu could barely hear him. She drew him gently up to face her.

"The lord said, You should give us that boy to make into a person. You've neglected the rites. You've spoiled him. But there's still time."

"Is that what he thinks." Making Bdarde a given child had occurred to her, of course. What a relief it would be to miss his crying and complaining. He was like a young tomcat in a bag, spitting and screaming to escape, so outraged he clawed anyone trying to free him. She doubted Smoke Stingray or Lady Jaguar would improve his fate.

Chapter Twenty-Three

The deck prism filled the cabin with dawn light. Iakinthu woke from a sound sleep, grateful to be rested after the previous day. Has any diplomatic meeting I've ever had been as ridiculous as the visit of Lady Jaguar and Lord Smoke Stingray? she said to herself. And now I wonder what today will bring.

She rose, flung on a kilt and jacket, and went on deck to see about breakfast. Uinthi and Bridges Words sat side by side, eating porridge and speaking softly together. Paissu sat on the gunwale, listening intently. Nearby, Aranthau poured steaming water into a jug. The unmistakable scent of cacao rose from the jug. Iakinthu's mouth watered.

"Aranthau, my love, you are a magician."

He smiled. "Do you suddenly believe in magicians?"

"I must, if you could trade with Lord Stingray for cacao."

"I had able assistance." He gestured toward Uinthi and Bridges Words. "I believe Lord Stingray and I each think we outfoxed the other in our trade."

"What did he want?"

"Henna for Lady Jaguar. The interruption yesterday annoyed her."

"He may have my share," she said.

"Good," Aranthau said. "He has it, and we have several jars of cacao. Bridges Words has shown me how to tell real cacao from counterfeit, and how to judge the quality."

"Bridges Words is beyond price," Iakinthu said sincerely. Bridges Words glanced up, hearing his name, and Uinthi translated for him. He nodded to Iakinthu, accepting her compliment in his own glum way.

Iakinthu picked up two cups of cacao, gave one to Uinthi, and offered the other to Bridges Words. After a moment, he accepted it, declaimed a few words, and hunched over the cup with his head bowed. He sipped, surreptitiously.

"He says, 'Tomorrow they may kill me, but today I will drink cacao from the hands of a great lady,'" Uinthi said.

Iakinthu realized how Bridges Words might have interpreted her offhand comment.

If I put a price on a man — even if I put him beyond price, she thought, then he is a possession.

"Uinthi," she said, "have I told Bridges Words he's a free man?"

"Did you tell me?" Uinthi said. "Could you explain to him, without me to translate?"

"Then, my dear, please tell him he's free. And express to him my sorrow that I neglected to tell him for so long."

Uinthi spoke briefly to Bridges Words, who remained crouched on the deck, his face hidden as he bowed his head in supplication.

He asked a question; he looked up at her, his raggedly cut hair falling over his eyes.

Uinthi spoke, then repeated the words so Iakinthu could understand. One more language I should learn, Iakinthu thought, feeling tired.

"You're free," Iakinthu said. "Of course you may leave. You are welcome to remain with the companions of *Flying Fish*, but you may go wherever and whenever you please. You may become a companion of *Flying Fish*, if you wish."

Bridges Worlds leapt to his feet and spoke energetically to Uinthi, emphasizing his words with gestures. Cacao splashed from his cup to his wrist. He paused long enough to lick the drops from his skin and put the cup on deck, then continued speaking. Uinthi listened, head cocked to gather in entirely what he was saying.

He fell silent, intent on Uinthi's response.

"I understand," Uinthi said, in the trade language.

Iakinthu said softly, "I understand 'I understand,' but you must tell me the rest."

"We must flee," Uinthi said.

"What are we fleeing?"

"I'll spare you most of the details. Bridges Words can be...most eloquent when he chooses. Lady Jaguar and Stingray plan to take the hearts of the companions, except Aranthau —"

"How do I come to be so honored?" Aranthau asked, his tone dry.

"They recognize you as captain, as navigator. When they have conquered Iakinthu and sacrificed her and all of us, you will submit to them and sail *Flying Fish* to Fair Island, which they wish to rule."

"So much for hospitality," Iakinthu said. "Is everyone aboard?"

"Kilinkizu went ashore to visit with Lady Jaguar's scribe," Uinthi said. "She took young Bdarde with her to spare Aranthau his attention."

Iakinthu paused long enough to pick up her cup of cacao and sip from it. It was still too hot to drink. She sighed and reluctantly put it down. She glanced toward shore, toward the shining golden pyramid, hoping to see one of Lady Jaguar's canoes returning with Kilinkizu. The lagoon remained still.

"We had better go and fetch them."

Iakinthu took time to dress in a seven-tiered skirt with borders of sea-purple. She put on her jewelry: gold bangles, her sealstones, gold spiral earrings, a necklace of delicate butterflies with shivering wings of carnelian, jade, and topaz.

She fanned herself as a flash of heat overtook her, flushing her skin. Sighing, she thought, Must I sweat all over my best clothes?

A splash of lavender water cooled her face and neck. She climbed to the deck and stood facing a wisp of breeze. Aranthau stowed parcels of gifts into the ship's boat.

Uinthi touched her arm.

"Let me and Bridges Words go alone," Uinthi said. "We—"

"—might be kept hostage," Iakinthu said. "Do we want Lady Jaguar to have more hostages?"

"She might keep you."

"When she wants us, she'll keep us, if we move too slowly. But can you imagine her raft catching my ship? We'll visit, ply her with gifts, ask her to dinner tonight, fetch Kilinkizu, and fly away into the morning." She turned to Bridges Words. "Will you come with us when we flee?"

Bridges Words raised a quizzical eyebrow when Uinthi told him what Iakinthu had said. She hardly needed Uinthi's translation to understand his reply.

"Will I stay with Lady Jaguar, as her slave, who might be killed on any day, or will I ride this craft away, a free man? What a difficult decision!"

Iakinthu laughed and followed Paissu down the rope ladder. Aranthau reached to help her into the ship's boat.

"My captain, my love, please stay with *Flying Fish* and be ready to flee as soon as we return."

Aranthau frowned but avoided an argument which he must lose. Iakinthu nodded at him in gratitude. Her dread increased with each passing moment.

Aranthau glanced at Paissu and Rhenthizu. "Guard her well," he said.

"Of course we will," Rhenthizu said.

"Someone must carry the gifts," Paissu said. "Would it be proper for Gephyra Iakinthu to go unattended?"

"Quite correct," Iakinthu said.

Aranthau stepped off the boat and onto the ladder, helped push off, and watched as they rowed toward King Mummy's island.

Iakinthu sat in the stern of the ship's boat with Paissu while Rhenthizu and Uinthi rowed and Bridges Words perched in the bow, puzzled but pleased by his status as passenger. He raised his hands to the sky and shouted a few words.

"What did he say?" Iakinthu said, though this time she had picked out a little of his declamation.

"You know what he said," Uinthi said, breathing hard, rowing hard.

"'Today they may kill me—'" Iakinthu said. "And after that?"

"'—but I will enjoy riding in freedom.'" Uinthi grinned wryly. "I believe our new friend perceives the world with precision."

The sun had climbed well above the horizon, and people hurried about on shore.

"I must pay my respects to Lady Jaguar," Iakinthu said. "Uinthi, please fetch Kilinkizu. Can Bridges Words tell you where to look for her? Where Lady Jaguar's scribe might be?"

"We will find her," Bridges Words responded.

"What about you?" Uinthi said. "How will you speak to Lady Jaguar?"

"I'll speak with her as Aranthau spoke with Lord Smoke Stingray," Iakinthu said. "We'll understand as much as necessary."

Iakinthu reached the top of the gold pyramid, soaked in sweat and fondly remembering the cool beaches of the Maisusutha.

Will I ever wish to be too warm again? she wondered. She touched her hair, which had responded to the heat and humidity by curling into tighter lovelocks.

Her younger companions had paced her courteously though they could have leapt up the stairs like young agrimi. When they neared the top, Uinthi and Bridges Words slipped away. Paissu stayed to attend her.

Lady Jaguar strode from the king's gold house, followed by her attendants, who straightened her headdress and her robe as she walked. Iridescent feathers fluttered around her head. The mummy king's fetid, musty scent clung to her until one of her ladies wafted scented smoke toward her with an iridescent bird wing. The smoke swirled around them all, rising in sweet clouds from a decorated clay bowl.

"My Lady Jaguar," Iakinthu said formally, inclining her head.

"Iakinthu Gephyra," replied Jaguar. When she continued, Iakinthu interpreted her words and tone. "What a pleasure to see you again, and so early in the morning, missing any invitation or messenger, and before I am properly dressed." She delicately plucked the stopper from the glass vial around her neck, inhaled the lavender scent, and stoppered the vial again.

"Your dress is magnificent." Iakinthu's tone was of honest sincerity, for Lady Jaguar's robe was as finely made as the best Egyptian linen, and her jewelry as finely wrought as Iakinthu's, though more massive.

"How may I serve you?" Lady Jaguar said.

Iakinthu smiled, thinking, Would Lady Jaguar serve me? But the translation is adequate.

"Please let me serve you," Iakinthu said.

Paissu came forward with the gift, a beautiful pot painted with octopods and fishes. As any of the People would, she offered it directly to Lady Jaguar. The Lady gave her a quizzical glance and gestured for one of her attendants to take it.

"Please accept my invitation to dine this evening." In the lady's language, Iakinthu said, "Food. Sunset."

Jaguar repeated the words, correcting Iakinthu's accent.

"Food," Iakinthu said again. "Sunset."

Lady Jaguar made a sound of agreement, approval, either of Iakinthu's improved speech, or of the invitation; it made little difference which, as the lesson would end soon and the dinner was entirely imaginary.

Lady Jaguar continued at length, speaking of balithi.

She is saying, Iakinthu thought, that she will bring a pot of her horrible drink, because she prefers it to good Fair Island wine. Thinking about its taste and effect nauseated her.

A shriek interrupted Lady Jaguar, who frowned and looked across the pyramid's platform.

Uinthi, Bridges Words, Kilinkizu, young Bdarde, and Lady Jaguar's little scribe Hummingbird approached, in an unruly group. Kilinkizu and Bridges Words each held one of Bdarde's hands and did their best to pretend he came along willingly. Bdarde made this impression difficult to maintain.

"I was drawing," he shouted. "You wanted me to draw and I was drawing, and I want to draw and I want to stay here. I hate your boat."

Uinthi held several pieces of bark paper. "And very nicely did you draw, too. Kilinkizu will be able to teach you your letters, maybe even your numbers, you're so talented."

"Girls' work!" he shouted.

"The People leave it to men," Paissu exclaimed. "But women should know it too!"

"Indeed we should," Iakinthu said when they came close enough to hear her over Bdarde's rude shouting. "And all of us are grateful to Kilinkizu for teaching it to us." Would that she could teach the boy to speak softly, Iakinthu thought. He gave her a headache. Suddenly she shivered in the dense heat and knew that the increasing headache had a different cause than the little boy's bad manners.

"My drawing's still wet," Bdarde said. "You'll smear it. You'll wreck it. Give it to me!"

"I'll give it to you when you have a free hand," Uinthi said.

"Bdarde must go back to *Flying Fish* until he calms down," Iakinthu said. "*Flying Fish* is a ship, little Bdarde, not a boat. Would your sire the great mariner approve of such a mistake?"

Kilinkizu blushed at the vulgarity of Iakinthu's statement. I am sorry, Iakinthu thought, my dear Kilinkizu, but sometimes diplomats must be less than diplomatic in order to make themselves understood.

"Bdarde must return to *Flying Fish* until he's calmer," Iakinthu said again. "Kilinkizu, please take him to the ship and put him to bed."

For a moment she feared Kilinkizu would object and argue with her in front of Lady Jaguar. Instead, Kilinkizu dropped to her knees before the scribe Hummingbird and embraced her shoulders. They spoke together, each in her own language.

"Thank you, dearest Hummingbird. I hope we can visit again."

Hummingbird stretched up to kiss Kilinkizu's forehead. Uinthi whispered a translation of her reply. "Your scribe-line is most beautiful, my friend Kilinkizu."

Bdarde, one hand freed, tried to snatch his drawings from Uinthi.

"Give them to me!"

"I might if you would stop shouting," Uinthi said.

"I'll shout at you if I want, you're a fake boy, I can ignore you, I can do whatever I want."

Uinthi burst into laughter. Iakinthu felt entirely irritated.

"My lady Jaguar," she said, "my deepest apologies for this boy-child." She sighed. "Do we know how boy children can be sometimes? He is overtired and requires rest." To Kilinkizu she said, "Please, my dear, take him to the ship's boat."

Kilinkizu touched her fist to her forehead, kissed Hummingbird's cheek, rose, and with Bridges Words holding Bdarde's other hand, led the sulking little boy down the pyramid's shining gold stairs.

"Food," Iakinthu said to Lady Jaguar. "Sunset."

"I will bring the balithi," Lady Jaguar said.

Flanked by Uinthi and Paissu, Iakinthu faced the long climb down the golden stairs, anxious to follow Kilinkizu to the bottom of the pyramid, where Rhenthizu waited with the boat at the edge of King Mummy's Island.

Paissu sat beside Iakinthu in the ship's boat, concerned for her given mother, proud to have been chosen to attend her, glad to be gone from the golden pyramid. She scowled at Bdarde, who whined and cried, then abruptly fell asleep, having exhausted himself. Kilinkizu held him in her lap.

Bridges Words muttered something; to her surprise, Paissu understood what he said. He spoke in a mix of Idaean and the trade language. Paissu had been listening to Uinthi and Bridges Words and felt pleased with herself that her attention was rewarded.

"He would be best left as a present," Bridges Words said, "and the pretty vase retrieved."

Paissu rather agreed with him but would have felt sorry even for Bdarde if he were left with Lady Jaguar.

Some Idaean will have to be a given child to Lady Jaguar, Paissu thought, and one of Lady Jaguar's will come to the Idaeans, to seal a peace. Would the Idaean survive? She shivered, thinking of Bridges Words' description of what would happen to all the companions of *Flying Fish* if they failed to escape now.

When you are dead, Paissu thought, you are dead. Still, I am glad to be a given child to Iakinthu Gephyra.

Paissu poured some water into her hand and patted Iakinthu's forehead with her damp palm. She glanced at Uinthi and Rhenthizu, wishing they could row faster, but they plied the oars as hard as they could in the pressing heat.

"Thank you, Paissu," Iakinthu whispered. "May I have a drink?"

Paissu held the flask to her lips. Iakinthu drank, but the flush remained on her cheeks, and the heat of her skin touched Paissu's fingertips.

"Are you ill?" Paissu asked, troubled. In their short acquaintance she had come to think of Iakinthu as strong, strong as Dragon Claws.

"I am," Iakinthu said softly, surprising Paissu. The People denied illness and pain, sometimes until too late. "The cold fever has afflicted me since my girlhood in Egypt. I hoped it would spare me on this trip."

The steady rhythm of the oars slowed, and the boat settled into the water, sidling softly against the flank of *Flying Fish* with a hollow bump. Bridges Words flung the bow line to Aranthau. Kilinkizu woke Bdarde, who grumbled sleepily.

Paissu held Iakinthu's hand and noticed that her fingers were cold. Uinthi and Rhenthizu moved to attend Iakinthu, but Paissu motioned them back.

"Iakinthu must ride the boat to the deck," Paissu said.

The other members of the boat party, knowing of Iakinthu's recurring illness, acquiesced. Even Iakinthu acquiesced. Rhenthizu and Uinthi called for the lines that would raise the ship's boat.

Kilinkizu led Bdarde to the ladder.

"I want to ride the boat, too," he said.

"Climb," Kilinkizu said, her patience at its limit, "or swim."

He grudgingly climbed, and Kilinkizu followed him to the deck.

Paissu hugged Iakinthu, steadying her, as the companions hauled the boat up. Iakinthu rested her head on Paissu's shoulder, her breathing shallow.

Was I ever afraid with the People? Paissu thought. We rode over rough land. We brandished spears and swords. We chased away raiders and bandits with bow and arrow. But now with the peaceful Idaeans, I was frightened of the glowing giant squid, I'm frightened of Lady Jaguar, I'm frightened that Bdarde might have told the truth — she pushed that thought away — and I'm frightened that Iakinthu might die.

The boat swung over the rail and onto the deck with a thump. Aranthau vaulted in beside Iakinthu. Paissu drew back so he could support her.

"Help me attend her, little Paissu," Aranthau said. He helped Iakinthu to stand, and Paissu slipped beneath her other arm.

"How quickly can we flee, captain my love?" Iakinthu whispered.

Without Aranthau and Paissu, she would have fallen. She fainted.

Chapter Twenty-Four

Iakinthu wondered where she was, what she was doing. Chills, then fever, wracked her aching body. Sweat soaked her, and the sweat chilled her more deeply. A cool cloth stroked her forehead. The scent of lavender coiled through the smell of sickness.

Flying Fish sailed on, surrounding Iakinthu with the shusssh of the sea, the creak of timber and line. A breeze of cool salt air touched her skin, sending her abruptly into another fit of shivering. She knew Aranthau's touch from long dear familiarity, and the warmth of his body beside her. He held her; he bent over her and kissed her and blew poppy smoke into her mouth. She breathed it gratefully. The aching eased.

She dreamed. A great scrape of sand on wood sent her rushing, in her dream, to the deck, afraid *Flying Fish* had run aground.

"Rest, sleep," Paissu whispered, holding her hand, preventing her from rising. "It's all right, everything is all right. *Flying Fish* left Lady Jaguar far behind."

She slept again. She woke again, shivering again. *Flying Fish* swayed in a motion strange to her. Where are we? she wondered. Are we adrift in a windless sea? When has Aranthau ever allowed *Flying Fish* to drift becalmed?

As if she had called him, Aranthau supported her head with his strong rough hand.

"Drink," he said.

Iakinthu opened her eyes. Aranthau held a cup of regional design, its figures dancing elegantly across the surface. She saw them through a haze of poppy smoke.

Poppy is better than balithi, Iakinthu thought. The drawings stay on their cup instead of dancing away. They would dance on my nose and on my forehead if the cup held balithi.

"Drink," Aranthau said again. "It's a remedy for shivering."

She sipped, nearly spat it out, swallowed hard. She trusted Aranthau, but the drink tasted worse than balithi, with a bitterness that she tasted all the way down, a bitterness that broke through the heavy overlying sweetness.

"What is it?" she whispered. Her lips were dry and cracked beneath the lavender and beeswax salve. "Where did it come from?"

"It's cinchona," he said. "The guides helping *Flying Fish* to the Untamable Ocean traded for it."

"Bitter."

"Yes."

She squeezed his hand, grateful to him for tasting it before he would ever ask her to drink it, grateful that he could drink it and avoid ill effects.

"Sleep now," he said.

The next time she woke, she felt much better. The wracking ache had dissipated. Both chill and fever had vanished. She was hungry and thirsty. She tried to rise and failed, then peered around the cabin.

"Iakinthu!" Paissu exclaimed, her voice soft.

"I'm here," Iakinthu said. "May I have a cup of wine?"

Paissu grinned and leapt up and unstoppered the wide-bottomed wine flask. She poured out the wine, mixed it with a little water, brought it to Iakinthu, and held it to her lips.

Iakinthu savored the wine's cool purple taste. She touched the cup, but her hands shook.

"Oh, I hate this weakness!" she said.

"I'll help you," Paissu replied. She gave Iakinthu another sip of wine and put her arm around her shoulders.

Iakinthu put her hand on Paissu's.

"What's the matter, dear Paissu?"

Paissu hesitated.

"Your hand trembles," Iakinthu said.

Paissu gazed into Iakinthu's eyes.

"Do Idaeans sacrifice children?"

Instead of denying it, instead of asking her where she had gotten such an idea— Where else but from Bdarde?— Iakinthu took a deep breath. "A thousand years ago, in times of terrible danger, that happened. Sometimes, when Mother Moon and her companion have terrible quarrels..."

"The People sometimes quarrel. But do we sacrifice each other? Do we sacrifice given children?"

"Oh, my dear." Iakinthu hugged Paissu and was glad to feel her stop shaking and relax in her arms. "If a child were ever sacrificed again, they would be Idaean. And they would choose. They would consent."

Paissu brought Iakinthu's hands to her lips and kissed them.

"May Mother Moon and her companion stop quarreling," Paissu said.

A sacrifice, Iakinthu thought, makes them quarrel more. They create chaos and destruction. Does Paissu want to know this?

Paissu sat up straight, her composure recovered, her worries erased, and grinned.

"Take another sip of cinchona," she said, "and then I'll go tell Aranthau you're awake."

"Where are we?" Iakinthu asked. "The sea is so quiet— Can we be becalmed?"

"You'll be so surprised when you see where we are," Paissu said. She helped Iakinthu sit up straighter and put another pillow behind her. "Are you too warm? Are you chilled?"

"I'm just right," Iakinthu said, smiling. "Thank you, my dear."

Paissu ran out of the cabin, her footsteps pattering on the deck. Iakinthu lay back on the pillows, already exhausted, determined to stay awake.

When she opened her eyes again, Aranthau sat nearby, suddenly with her.

"Did I see you come in?" she asked.

"I let you sleep," he said. He had tended her through the cold fever several times over the years. He put his hand to her forehead. "You'll be better soon."

"Paissu promised me a surprise," Iakinthu said.

"Yes," he said. "Are you strong enough to go on deck?"

"With your help, I might be."

He helped her sit on the edge of her bed; he brought a clean kilt and jacket and helped her dress. Iakinthu rose, shaky, determined, tottering—am I an old woman, now? she wondered—to the ladder, and dragged herself upward.

Aranthau climbed close behind her, steadying her against the slow strange sway of *Flying Fish*. Bright sunlight spilled through the hatchway. Iakinthu blinked against the light.

I should have worn my kohl, she thought.

Paissu and Rhenthizu helped her onto the deck. A breeze touched her, hot and damp.

Flying Fish moved, but its sails were tightly furled. Lines reached up all around the gunwales, like a rope fence, so many she found it hard to see through and past them, but the sails' sheets lay coiled and wrapped. Iakinthu's sight accustomed itself to the bright sunlight that seared in past the fence of rope.

She gasped.

Flying Fish was flying.

"Can I believe this?" she said. "Am I dreaming again?" Her knees wobbled, and she sank toward the deck. Aranthau caught her, steadied her, guided her to a camp chair secured to the deck in the shade of the enormous shape that hung above her ship.

It resembled a giant swollen fish, bulging in the middle, pointed at each end. A net of thick cords restrained it. The fence of rope connected its net to the net that cradled *Flying Fish*. The marvelous cloth of its skin gleamed with a pattern of scales in red and blue so bright she had to look away. Then she had to look again. Bands of hieroglyphics stretched across the scales, as if the drawings danced. The tip of *Flying Fish*'s mast plunged into a huge bolt of red cloth that protected the belly of the great floating thing from the sharp wooden spear.

"What is it?" Iakinthu watched it, frightened. "Will it fall?"

"Our hosts call it balunu," Aranthau said. "I say it wrong. Uinthi," he called, "come and tell Iakinthu how to address this great flying thing."

Uinthi and Bridges Words turned from the bow, where they had been leaning over the gunwales looking out over the land, enthralled.

"Iakinthu!" Uinthi ran down the deck, ignored the sway of the ship in the wind, knelt beside Iakinthu, and touched fist to forehead.

"You're well!" Uinthi said.

"I'm better," Iakinthu said. "That bitter drink helped me."

Bridges Words followed, nonchalantly gripping the ship's rail as he walked. When he reached her, she was amused that he remained standing and failed to give any salute to her. Freedom had taken him over and changed him. Iakinthu kissed Uinthi's forehead and smiled at Bridges Words.

"Will you tell me the proper word for this great air-floating thing?" she asked them.

"Balunu," they both said at once. The word sounded exactly the same as the word Aranthau had said.

"Balunu," she repeated.

"Balunu," Bridges Words said again.

Iakinthu sighed. "I could hear the proper word when I was younger," she said. "But now, I hear everything in Idaean. How does it fly?"

"It's wonderful," Uinthi said. "The skin is so smoothly woven that it will hold water or air. They lay it on the ground and fill it with smoke—"

Bridges Words said, "Air," in perfectly understandable Idaean. "Hot air."

"With pipes of gold and that ruburu stuff. It fills up like a pufferfish and rises into the sky."

"That is wonderful," Iakinthu said. "Are we at the mercy of the wind?" She understood enough about sailing, from many years with Aranthau, to know that steering a ship depended on the difference between air and water, keel and sail. The balunu had only air. Could it do anything but drift with the wind?

"I'll explain it later," Aranthau said, "but now you should rest."

Iakinthu thought to resist, but Aranthau knew her limits after an illness as well as she did—and was more likely to respect them. He thought only to prevent a relapse.

"All the cookfires are out, but I'll bring you some wine and bread," Rhenthizu said.

"Thank you, my dear." She took Aranthau's hand. "I would rather rest on deck than climb down the ladder," she said. "In the stern cabin." She frowned. "But where is everyone? Where's Maranti?"

Rhenthizu laughed. "Many of our companions were well pleased when our hosts said everyone must leave the ship to lighten its weight. We stayed to attend you, but everyone else is walking."

"In this heat?" Iakinthu exclaimed.

"Kilinkizu is with Maranti, and will watch to see if she tires. Our hosts will call the ship down if she prefers to ride." He grinned again. "She much prefers to walk."

Aranthau helped Iakinthu to her feet and slipped one strong arm around her, supporting her as she walked slowly to the stern cabin.

I'm moving like an old woman, she thought. Am I ready to be an old woman, to retire? Perhaps I am.

Rhenthizu brought wine, water, bread, and sweet almonds to Iakinthu. He sat beside her in the stern cabin, feeding her bits of bread and sips of wine, glad that she was recovering.

"Thank you," she said, after all too little. "That's enough." And in a moment she slept again.

He joined the others at the bow of *Flying Fish*, where the fence of rope ended and gave them a clear view. Buoyed by the balunu, *Flying Fish* sailed the air. Moving south, it followed a wide path cut through the jungle. A faint, hot north wind helped it, but a hundred people below toiled along the path, pulling it forward. They drew it by ropes attached to the balunu's netting. A few more held ropes tied to the cleats on *Flying Fish*'s deck, steadying the ship against the whim of the wind.

"You knew of this," Rhenthizu said to Uinthi. "Before we ever came here."

"Would you have believed me?"

"I would have marveled and waited to see."

"Did I believe it myself, before I saw it?" Uinthi grinned. "It was this adventure, or a long, long sail."

"Into storms and cold," Bridges Words said, speaking Idaean. "It's a place where you might freeze in a moment, and..." He glanced at Uinthi and spoke in the trade language.

"And few travelers return."

Rhenthizu leaned on the gunwale and gazed across the land, following the path below toward the distant glint of the Untamable Ocean.

"They need oxen, or horses," Rhenthizu said.

"A horse would balk at that path," Paissu said. She pointed ahead, where the path rose in a hundred, a thousand steps, climbing a peak from which streams fell to form the lake they were passing.

"The nearest horse is eating grass in the meadows of the People," Uinthi said.

"What's a horse?" Bridges Words asked.

"A creature who will pull burdens for you."

"If you ask nicely," Paissu said. "Horses prefer being ridden."

Bridges Words gave her a quizzical look.

"I suppose if using people to pull stone up a pyramid is good enough for Pharaoh," Aranthau said, "using people to pull the balunu is good enough for our hosts."

Rhenthizu leaned over the gunwale, searching out the companions of *Flying Fish,* and Maranti. They were walking directly beneath the ship, taking advantage of its shadow. The sun was overhead, the shadow below, so his friends were out of sight. He had reassured Iakinthu, but he did worry about Maranti. Usually fearless, she had taken one look at the swelling balunu with its woven dancing creatures, the netting, the ropes, and declined to stay on board. Most of the other companions agreed with her.

To his delight, she appeared from beneath the ship, looked up, and waved to him.

"Rhenthizu!"

"Maranti!"

"I wish you were down here!" she shouted.

"I wish you were up here!" he replied. He glanced at the heavy ropes leading from *Flying Fish*'s deck cleats to the ground.

I could go down, he thought, but could I get up again before *Flying Fish* landed?

He liked to swim, he liked to sail, more than he liked to run or walk in the heat of the day. Maranti waved again, and he waved back, and she strolled back underneath *Flying Fish* to walk in its shade. He admired her grace, her beauty, her strength.

The balunu carried *Flying Fish* southward, across the narrow stretch of land that barred them from the Untamable Ocean. The afternoon wore on, and the sun crept westward, till it dropped beneath the lower flank of the balunu and shone full force on the deck. Rhenthizu arranged the sides of the stern cabin to protect Iakinthu from the sun. She slept on. This illness caught her every few years.

It might take her, he thought. It does take people.

As a child, he had watched and marveled to see her dance with Terebinthu in the bull-dancing field, catching Terebinthu's sweeping gilded horns and leaping to his back, springing to the ground as he galloped snorting and spun to run at her again.

Was I ever afraid when I watched her dance? he thought. But I am afraid when I see her so ill.

Aranthau brought a flask of cinchona water, knelt on the deck on the other side of Iakinthu's pallet, and roused her gently.

"It's so bitter," she said. "Must I drink it? I'm only tired. The cold fever has gone."

"Bridges Words says you should," Aranthau replied. "For a few more days. It will ward off the shivering."

"Very well," she said. "But I must have wine after."

Aranthau smiled and supported her as she drank and wrinkled her nose at the taste.

Rhenthizu went belowdecks, sliding down on the polished rails of the ladder, to fetch a qeto of wine from the cool lower cargo deck. When he entered the cargo space, he found it uncomfortably hot.

Of course, he thought. The sea keeps it cool, and we are in the air and beaten by the sun.

He wondered if the heat would wreck the wine.

But everyone we meet prefers their own drink, their own path to insight, he thought. Balithi or cacao, tobacco or fasting. I think we will wish we had brought more empty glass vials.

He took the wine to Iakinthu, who drank it gratefully without a word about its warmth.

The sun sank lower; the oppressive heat eased slightly, and the balunu's tight skin loosened within its net.

The guides of the balunu stopped. Without the pull of the ropes, *Flying Fish* hovered. The balunu sank, and *Flying Fish* with it. In a movement like that of a dance troupe, the guides drew *Flying Fish* quickly toward the lake that stretched far westward, gleaming red and gold with the light of the setting sun. They pulled hard, moving along two long piers, dragging *Flying Fish* with them.

Flying Fish hit the water between the piers with a startlingly solid splash. Its timbers creaked. The ship rolled, pitched, and steadied. Iakinthu grasped Rhenthizu's hand.

As soon as *Flying Fish* touched the water, the guides of the balunu pulled powerfully on the ropes and drew its sagging belly safely away from the padded tip of the mast. The balunu deflated. The rope fence drooped across *Flying Fish*'s deck as the balunu sank and touched the shore.

"Excellently sailed," Aranthau said. "I'd like to see how they do the voyage with one of Lady Jaguar's rafts."

Because of course they must carry the rafts across this land all the time, Rhenthizu thought. Have they ever transported a ship like *Flying Fish*?

Their hosts had asked a pretty price to float the ship across the land. They tasted the wine, shrugged, politely offered balithi to their guests and possible customers. They preferred their own ceramic pots to the amphorae of the Idaeans, their own cloth to Egyptian linen. And indeed their cloth was very fine.

But they marveled over Idaean glass and accepted a price of three boxes of vials, two at the beginning of the trip, one at the end.

The companions of *Flying Fish* used the ropes draped from *Flying Fish* to the balunu as a path, climbing them to return to the ship. Maranti came to the stern cabin, hugged Rhenthizu, and bent to kiss Iakinthu.

"You look so much better!" she said.

"I am," Iakinthu said, "though all I do is sleep. You look well, too," she said, a little surprised.

"Of course I am! How fast could *Flying Fish* sail through the air, when it had to be pulled every step? We strolled and watched the birds. You must see a hummingbird! A real one, I mean."

Rhenthizu took her hand, and she squeezed it gently.

"I know hummingbirds from the Maisusutha," Iakinthu said. "They are wonderful."

Kilinkizu climbed over the gunwale. Her bright hair was dark with sweat. Bdarde followed, as deflated as the balunu-skin, too tired to engage in his usual complaints and whining. As if by chance, he approached Aranthau, who picked him up and cuddled him, very much as he had cuddled Omempau when she was a child. Bdarde fell asleep. Iakinthu felt a surge of unexpected pity, even affection, for him.

Head Guide arrived last. She strolled toward Aranthau, picking her way easily across the rope-covered deck. Uinthi and Bridges Words joined her, translating as she spoke. Rhenthizu was getting used to the double translation and picking up some of the trade language.

"What did you think of your voyage?" she asked. Though Bridges Words understood her, to Rhenthizu her language sounded entirely unfamiliar, entirely unlike Lady Jaguar's, entirely unlike the language he had spoken as a child.

"I marvel at it." Aranthau said again, "Well sailed."

"I like the shape of your ship. It moves through the air much more easily than the cargo rafts. We will do business with you any time."

"We must go," Aranthau said, "and then we must come back."

Head Guide grinned. "Where do you come from?"

Bridges Words hesitated before translating, and likewise Uinthi passed on the question with some reluctance.

"Will you tell her?" Rhenthizu said, trusting Uinthi to keep his comment untranslated. Had they met another group of people who wanted to take them over, torture and sacrifice them, and sail *Flying Fish* away to conquer Fair Island?

"From a very long distance," Aranthau said. "From a very powerful land."

It was unusual for an Idaean to brag about the power of Idaea, however true it was. Rhenthizu thought it an excellent idea in this time and place.

"Ask your queen to send more visitors—and more glass!" Head Guide said cheerfully. "Now I must speak to you about tomorrow."

Paissu thought rain would fall that night, though the sky remained clear and the Starpath glowed overhead. The air itself oppressed her, and it was smotheringly hot belowdecks. She thought of climbing the mast.

Could I get to the top of that great bolt of cloth? She thought she might, but then she would be caught if it rained.

She spread her sheepskin underneath the ship's boat and curled up to listen to the night—the faint creak when *Flying Fish* swayed, whispers and snores of the companions, the eruption of some great gronking creatures from the jungle.

The other companions of *Flying Fish* slept where they could, belowdecks in the heat or crowded into the bow or on either side of the stern cabin or even on the ropes that covered the deck.

On shore, the guides slept in thatched-roof shelters. Cooking fires glowed here and there. For the guides, this was only another trip.

The light of the Starpath faded. Paissu peeked out from beneath the ship's boat. Clouds had gathered, dark and close. A few raindrops pattered on the oiled silk of the boat's cover. Paissu grabbed her sheepskin and climbed into the boat, under its cover, as the storm began. Rain fell so hard it sounded like a waterfall, a stream gushing over *Flying Fish* and across the deck. A burst of lightning, so close its thunder sounded against the lighted landscape, cracked across the sky. Paissu could barely see the thatched shelters, and the glossy surface of the lake roiled into twisting patterns where the rain struck it.

The storm lasted only a little while, and then the clouds dispersed, and the Starpath reappeared. The world fell silent and dark, cooking fires drowned. As Paissu fell asleep, the gronking of the invisible jungle creatures began again, softly.

Head Guide came aboard well before dawn. It was a moment before Rhenthizu roused Uinthi and Bridges Words to translate, but everyone already knew they must awaken, break their fast however they could, and climb down to the shore.

"It is time," Head Guide said. "Yesterday we traveled a gentle path, and the balunu moved easily along it. But today we climb, and the balunu must float higher than the peak. Your craft must be as light as possible."

"I must stay on board," Aranthau said. "Could I ever leave Iakinthu?"

Though Iakinthu was much improved, she was far too unsteady to leave the ship, much less climb the slope that faced them. Head Guide grumbled, but her inherently cheerful nature returned when Aranthau gave her a purple glass vial for herself, one with a stopper of ground glass.

"We will manage," she said, "because the balunu is strong and powerful, and your craft cuts through the air."

So Rhenthizu and Uinthi and Bridges Words must join the walkers, while Aranthau and Paissu remained with Iakinthu.

Only Bdarde held back, jerking at Kilinkizu's hand when she led him toward the ropes. He pulled away and ran to Aranthau.

"You should let me attend you," he said.

"Should I?" Aranthau replied calmly. "Do you address your king this way? Does he attend you?"

"She gets to stay on board," Bdarde said, pointing at Paissu. "Why does she get to stay on board? She should walk, like a woman, and I should ride like a man."

"Come with me, Bdarde," Kilinkizu said, taking his hand and refusing to let him pull away again.

"Could you make yourself useful?" Aranthau said. "Then you might have a turn on *Flying Fish* today. But you disobey your mother, and Iakinthu is sleeping."

"She's an old woman and she should—"

Kilinkizu covered his mouth, holding it shut to silence him.

"Be quiet," she said. Her cheeks flamed with anger and embarrassment. "She's your queen, and you'll treat her with respect." Awkwardly, still covering Bdarde's mouth, she herded him to the gunwale, picked him up, and put him on the path of ropes. He crouched and grabbed them and edged toward the ground.

Iakinthu would argue about being called queen, Rhenthizu thought, but if it makes little Bdarde stop his insults, then Kilinkizu may call her queen or Pharaoh or Mother Sun as far as I care.

He imagined again that they might have left the little boy with Lady Jaguar as a given child.

We might have traded him for Kilinkizu's friend Hummingbird the scribe, Rhenthizu thought, and Kilinkizu might be more content.

Maranti joined him, followed his gaze, and sighed. "The pirates spoiled him," she whispered. "Perhaps Aranthau will bring him back."

She leaped easily onto the gunwale, stepped onto the rope path, and strode across it as if it were solid alabaster. Rhenthizu followed.

On shore, the gold pipes rang against each other like bells. Fires lit the pre-dawn shore, roaring and blowing their hot air into the pipes and into the balunu. Its flanks swelled. Standing out of the way of the guides with Maranti, Rhenthizu watched the preparations for the day's flight, fascinated.

"What a din!" Maranti exclaimed. "Sailing is more peaceful."

"Some voyages are all storms and cold," Rhenthizu said.

Maranti pointed along the line of the path, barely visible in firelight and false dawn. "Head Guide says we'll sail through a mountain pass today. I hope mountain storms spare us."

"Sailing through a mountain pass," Rhenthizu said. "That sounds like one of the songs of Bdarde-that-was."

"Oh, it does," Maranti said. "One of her adventures!" Tears filled her eyes and spilled down her cheeks. "I miss her so."

"I, too." He glanced around, saw Kilinkizu nearby, and wondered: Will the boy ever take our musician's place? Or conduct himself in a way to honor her?

He put his arm around Maranti's shoulders, and she hugged his waist. She sniffled and delicately wiped away tears with her fingertips.

"Pharaoh's engineers could dig a canal," she said. "And a tunnel."

"A hundred years ago," Rhenthizu said. "Pharaoh's Canal is filling with sand now, Tuola said. She said she could barely sail through it. And have you ever heard of the engineers of Egypt building a tunnel?"

"They need new blood and a new job," Maranti said. "If I were Pharaoh—" She let her words trail off.

"You're Eldest Daughter," Rhenthizu said. "Being Pharaoh as well might be difficult."

"Then we want our own engineers," she replied.

They watched as the balunu inflated with new hot air. Workers pumped great bellows to urge the flames to increasing heat. The guides held the balunu near the ground, straining against its yearning to fly. At Head Guide's command they allowed it to rise, pulling the ropes from the ground in long arcs.

In the stern cabin, Iakinthu sat on a tied-down camp chair, flanked by Aranthau and Paissu. They stayed well away from the snaking connecting ropes. The ropes dragged across the shore, across the lake's edge, over the gunwale. The balunu rose, narrowly missed the mast with its buffer of cloth, and loomed overhead. The rope fence formed; the balunu tugged at *Flying Fish* but failed to lift the ship.

"Iakinthu!" Uinthi said, greeting her from the pier at *Flying Fish*'s stern, accompanied by Bridges Words. "Are you well?"

"I'm better," Iakinthu said. "I'll be well soon."

"Another day of adventure," Bridges Words said.

Iakinthu wondered if he meant it but suspected he spoke from the depths of his dry humor.

Striding up the pier, Head Guide joined them. She folded her arms and gazed frowning at the balunu and at *Flying Fish* and at the connecting ropes. The balunu strained toward the sky, making the ship rock and sway.

"I am unhappy," she said, and waited for Bridges Words' translation. "I am unhappy with the strain on the connecting ropes. My lady Iakinthu, could you walk today?"

Aranthau began to speak in her defense, but Iakinthu answered.

"When I was younger, I might have recovered from the cold fever so soon," she said. "But now my ship must carry me. Most of my companions will walk with you."

"I would be happier if your ship were lighter." Head Guide gestured toward the peak before them, a looming dark barrier.

"A shame they refused our wine as payment," Iakinthu said to Aranthau. "*Flying Fish* would already be lighter."

"Perhaps they'll take some as a gift," he said.

The winch lifted one of the great amphorae of wine from the hold. Iakinthu covered her eyes. With difficulty, the companions maneuvered the cargo net past the rope fence and lowered it to the pier.

"Another," Head Guide said, and Iakinthu did wonder if this lightening of the craft might be a common occurrence, and who benefited from the abandoned cargo.

When *Flying Fish* was lightened by the weight of a second great amphora, Head Guide nodded once, sharply.

"Now we must hurry," she said. "The balunu flies highest before the heat of the day."

"Please give your workers the wine," Iakinthu said. "It's a good vintage."

"Someone may drink it," Head Guide said doubtfully. "If they're thirsty enough. Perhaps adding some chili..."

Iakinthu started to scowl but decided to laugh instead.

The guides loosened their ropes, and the balunu floated higher. It pulled *Flying Fish* out of the lake so fast and hard that Paissu gasped and clutched the support of the stern cabin. They rose and rose and rose, much higher than the day before. *Flying Fish* shuddered and swayed. It took all the strength of the guides below to steady it.

Head Guide called out an order. They set off, tramping along the path toward the peak.

Paissu looked over the stern. From this height, the guides looked very small as they walked along pulling the long ropes. Torches lit their way along the path and cast their shadows, straggly, dark-against-dark. The storm had cooled the air. The great staircase rose before them, looming; the peak glowed green, catching the first rays of the rising sun.

A cheerful song rose from the guides.

Aranthau brought Iakinthu bread and cheese and a net of small green fruit. He patted a cushion so Paissu would join them.

The bread was dry and chewy. Aranthau gave her a fruit from the net.

"A benefit of bribes," he said. "Head Guide liked her glass so much she gave me fruit. These are guayabo."

"They're good," Paissu said around a mouthful of the fruit's tart sweet flesh. She crunched the little seeds.

"They are, but I'll be glad when we have our cooking fires back," Iakinthu said.

"Late today, Head Guide told me," Aranthau said. "We'll reach the sea. It's as hard to climb down the stairs as up."

Dawn touched the balunu, the ropes, and *Flying Fish*. Aranthau frowned.

"What's the matter?" Paissu asked.

"The dawn touched the peak before it touched us," he said.

Paissu thought for a moment. "Does that mean *Flying Fish* is lower than the peak?"

"Yes," Aranthau said. He stood, went to the gunwale, and gazed at the land moving beneath them, still dark and shadowed with the torchlight.

"We will have to trust Head Guide," Iakinthu said.

"What choice do we have?" Aranthau said, his tone grumbly.

Quick as light the sun rose over the horizon and brought full day and the heat of morning upon them.

Paissu looked at the deck and gasped. Red spots and streaks, as bright as blood, covered the smooth planks.

Aranthau spat out a word Paissu had yet to learn, but his tone was clear. His gaze followed the stain up the mast, to the bolt of red cloth on the top of the mast. The rainstorm had soaked it and carried its dye down the mast and across the deck.

He touched the deck; he strode to the mast and drew his hand down its surface. His fingers came away red.

"Will it ever come out?" he said.

Rhenthizu was glad of the wide path and its stone surface. The jungle pressed in from both sides, so dense he imagined he could see it grow. They had already passed one work gang, cutting back the jungle before dawn, chopping the branches with obsidian axes.

Now it was full day. The heat built. The air closed around him, as thick as water. Sweat dripped down his face and sides and stained his belt and the waist of his kilt. His hair, grown out only a finger's length, felt sharp and sticky.

Maranti strolled along beside him. She was sweating, too, and she had pulled her long curls up off her neck, twining her hair into a knot with a string of pearls. She smiled at him.

"I'll be glad to reach the sea," she said. "The Untamable Sea! You can give me a swimming lesson."

"Braving sharks would be worth it, for a cool swim."

They reached the stone steps.

The steps led endlessly upward, a flight a hundred times longer than the golden steps of King Mummy's island. Rhenthizu had climbed those easily when he kept pace with Iakinthu. After a hundred steps his legs ached.

The guides barely slowed as they climbed, and they had *Flying Fish* to pull as well. As the path rose, the ropes slanted; the guides pulled them in and coiled them, and now they must carry the weight of the extra rope.

Flying Fish glided along at a steady height, a height below the peak of the ridge. Rhenthizu watched the path of the ship, worried.

They reached a plateau, a wide paved terrace cut into the slope. A short stone wall edged the terrace. On the other side, the wall cut down toward the jungle, vanishing into a tangle of a hundred shades of green, a thousand colors of flowers, an iridescent hummingbird that buzzed, rose straight into the air, and vanished beyond the balunu's curved flank.

The second crew of guides ran forward and relieved the first crew, all at once instead of a few guides at a time. The hand-off went so smoothly that the fresh crew barely paused at the terrace. Above, *Flying Fish* and the balunu glided past, casting a great shadow over guides and companions. Paissu waved from the stern. Rhenthizu returned her salute as cheerfully as he could.

He resigned himself to more climbing, though his legs trembled. But the guide crew that had been relieved paused on the terrace, sitting on their heels, opening leaf-wrapped packets of corn flatbread, cutting guayabo into pieces and sharing it around.

Uinthi and Bridges Words joined Rhenthizu and Maranti, returning from the head of the guide crew, with news from Head Guide.

"We're to stay here till the signal," Uinthi said.

Rhenthizu frowned. "While *Flying Fish* leaves us behind."

"Yes. But Head Guide was definite."

"And cheerful." Bridges Words paused, frowning for words, then spoke to Uinthi.

"Head Guide does this every day," Uinthi said. "Would it be to her honor to break a client's craft?"

"Has she been honored with a craft like *Flying Fish?*" Rhenthizu replied.

"All the more reason to transport it safely," Bridges Words said. "A great achievement travels fast."

"By balunu?" Rhenthizu said.

"By runner." He paused again, sighed in frustration, and let Uinthi translate.

"Runners are faster than a balunu. And easier to direct."

"The roads spread all out," Bridges Words said, spreading his hands, fingers extended.

Like the resting crew, they sat on their heels and brought out bread and cheese and wine. Rhenthizu found himself caught between sitting with *Flying Fish* to his back, or in his sight. He decided he would be more content if the ship were in his view.

Rhenthizu picked off the moldy bits of bread and scattered them to the wind. Perhaps a bird or a lizard would find them appetizing. He preferred bread hot from the oven or the baking coals, and cheese from the ship's cool hold. He wondered if their store of cheese would be ruined by the heat of sailing through the air. He drank from his wineskin, glad of the dark taste, anticipating its effect.

All the time, he watched *Flying Fish* as it came closer and closer to the peak. The balunu rose above the ridge, but *Flying Fish* was on a straight course into the slope.

"Uinthi," he said, "what exactly did Head Guide tell you?"

"Does Bridges Words know all the terms for sailing the balunu?" Uinthi replied. "Head Guide laughed at our doubt."

"Do I want to laugh right now?" Rhenthizu said.

"Head Guide is different from Lady Jaguar," Maranti said. "Lady Jaguar wanted our ship. Head Guide wants our business."

"I wish I were with the ship," Rhenthizu said, watching it move farther away and closer to the peak.

Behind them, Kilinkizu labored up the stairs to the terrace. Rhenthizu watched her with concern. She was as agile and strong as any of the companions, but Bdarde hung back, dragging on her hand, draining her strength, whining like a mosquito.

Kilinkizu approached them hesitantly.

"Come share our bread and wine," Uinthi said, patting the paving stones beside her. Kilinkizu smiled tiredly and joined them, sinking to the ground.

Uinthi stroked her arm and handed her a slice of cheese and a chunk of bread that he tore from the less moldy side. Kilinkizu separated it into two pieces and offered half to Bdarde, who scowled.

"I want meat," he said. "Meat is what men eat."

Rhenthizu, Uinthi, and Bridges Words all laughed at him. Bridges Words said something and Uinthi laughed again.

"What did he say?"

"Can I translate? It's very clever, but would you like to hear it? He made a joke about a nearby city whose men eat men."

"I hate you," Bdarde said, and stamped away.

"He may kill me someday," Bridges Words said. "But today I will eat his bread."

Kilinkizu handed him Bdarde's portion, and Bridges Words crammed it into his mouth. He had a habit of eating as fast as he could.

I used to eat like that, Rhenthizu thought. Could I believe that Iakinthu would let me have whatever I wanted?

He tore off part of his bread and cheese and handed it to Bridges Words, who gave him a startled look and ate it so fast Rhenthizu feared he might choke. He washed it down with wine, which he had become fond of.

"Everyone says that the People eat men," Kilinkizu said. "In all my time with them, did I ever see that, or taste human flesh?" She grimaced and took a bite of the bread and cheese, a gulp of the wine. "But we hunted. We grew so tired of meat that we'd ride to a farm under a shield of peace to trade fresh meat for fruit and porridge."

She drank more wine.

"The People had a story," she said. "Of a band of People who traveled far from their land to rescue the son of the great-grandmother of Dragon Claws —"

"The son?" Rhenthizu asked, startled.

"The People love their sons," Kilinkizu said, offended, "and weep when they part. May I finish the story?"

"Please," Rhenthizu said, "and please forgive my interruption."

Kilinkizu nodded and continued.

"Their journey was so long, and across such desolation," she said. "Could they carry enough food, or find a place in the desert to hunt? They were hungry and thirsty, but they continued their quest. The goddesses loved them for their bravery, and replenished their packs with bread that never molded, bread that sustained them for a day with a few mouthfuls."

Rhenthizu raised one eyebrow but refrained from commenting that he wanted the recipe for magic bread.

"I'd like some of that magic bread," Uinthi said.

"Young Bdarde would prefer magic meat," Bridges Words said. In their exhaustion, and perhaps with a little too much wine, they all found his comment terribly funny. They laughed, even Kilinkizu, and found it difficult to stop. From across the terrace, Bdarde glared and turned his back.

When finally Rhenthizu stopped laughing, gasping for breath, he said, "Poor Bdarde has missed his dinner, and a story. Did the heroes rescue the great-great-great-grand..." He paused, trying to figure out the relationship of the lost boy to Dragon Claws. He failed. "Did they rescue the boy?"

"Yes, after many trials, and the goddesses rewarded them by transporting them home on a cloud, like the balunu."

Rhenthizu almost asked why the heroes had to walk across the desert and endure many trials, even with magic bread, if the goddesses could have sent them to the boy on a magic cloud or sent the boy home on the same magic cloud in the first place, without the need for any trials at all.

Would there be a story to tell, he thought, if the goddesses were so obliging? The goddesses must have wanted to see what Kilinkizu's heroes would do. The goddesses must have wanted to know the story for themselves.

He leaped up with a shout. He pointed toward *Flying Fish,* which had been in his sight the whole time.

A flap fell away from the balunu's side, pulled loose by a rope, and a cascade of sand and rocks fell from the opening, as if the ship of the air were emptying its bowels. The flow narrowly missed the stern of *Flying Fish* and fell to the ground well behind the guides, well in front of the terrace where the guide crew and the companions rested.

The balunu rose, lighter now, raising *Flying Fish*. The guides slowed, letting the balunu catch them, letting the guide ropes stretch almost vertical, so pulling the balunu forward was much more difficult, and keeping it under control took great skill.

Tiny in the high distance, Aranthau stood at the bow and Paissu clung halfway up the mast, and even Iakinthu rose from her chair to clutch the stern rail and watch as her ship skimmed just above the peak.

Chapter Twenty-Five

Iakinthu wondered if she were dreaming or hallucinating. Did I drink more balithi? she thought. Or cinchona? But the nasty tastes remained only in memory. She clutched the stern rail, shivering, looking down at the peak. *Flying Fish* skimmed over it with a few armspans to spare. The shadow of the balunu shielded her from the beating sun.

"Iakinthu."

Aranthau stood behind her. After he spoke her name, he touched her gently on the shoulder. She turned away from the stern rail, glad to stop staring down, to the distant path where the guides walked, to the all-too-near peak now behind them.

He embraced her.

"Come," he said. "Come and rest."

"What else have I done but rest since we took leave of Lady Jaguar?"

He smiled. "We are well away from Lady Jaguar's ambitions," he said. "Look."

He pointed forward.

Beyond the edge of land, beyond the harbor where the balunu dock sprawled, the sea extended to the horizon.

"Is it the Untamable Ocean?"

"Can I know, for certain sure, before I swim in it?" Aranthau said. "But I believe it is."

She let him settle her beneath the stern cabin's awning. He brought her cinchona water sweetened with honey; she drank it gratefully despite its bitterness and soon felt its effects.

"I'm so tired of being ill," Iakinthu said.

"I know," he replied. "And the companions of *Flying Fish* miss you. What is a ship without its leader?"

"Its captain will care for it," she said.

"And its young given child," Aranthau said, nodding toward Paissu. She clung to the red-stained mast in the shadow of the balunu, gazing toward the sea, as comfortable high above the deck as she was on solid ground.

"She'll make such a dancer," Iakinthu whispered, and fell asleep.

The guides pulled ahead, bringing *Flying Fish* out of the reach of the jagged stone peak. The second crew and the companions followed, walking into the sun, waiting for the heat to ease.

The trail narrowed. On one side, a stone wall rose above the reach of Rhenthizu's fingertips, holding back the steep hill. Opposite, another stone wall stretched down into the jungle.

Rhenthizu avoided looking down. The drop into leaves and branches, so unlike the surface of the sea, made him dizzy. Ahead of him, Maranti climbed barefoot up the stone stairs with her sandals dangling from one hand. She negotiated the trail more easily than he did, and yet he worried.

He looked up and forward to *Flying Fish* sailing through the air toward the sun. Paissu, in silhouette, still halfway up the mast, raised her hand to wave. Rhenthizu waved back, wondering if she could possibly see the companions among the guide crew.

He followed Maranti around a gentle bend in the trail and gasped. He found himself gazing into the endless Untamable Ocean.

"It's wonderful," Maranti said. "Is it wonderful?"

"It is," Rhenthizu said. The sight of the sea made him happy. He wanted the companions back on *Flying Fish*; he wanted Iakinthu to be well; he wanted to fulfill Iakinthu's traditions and be finished with this voyage and on his way back…home. Fair Island was home.

The trail descended and disappeared. The two stone retaining walls became one, and stone stair treads projected from the wall, secured by only one narrow edge, leading downward as they floated above the steep slope that fell into the valley.

Rhenthizu hesitated, to the disgust of one of the guide crew, who hissed at him from close behind. Rhenthizu understood the unknown word: Go on!

Maranti had already descended half a dozen steps, as sure on the floating stairs as she had been on the perilous climb. One hand on the stone wall, wishing for handholds, Rhenthizu stepped downward.

Finally, after the sun had touched the sea and cast its golden path across the water and disappeared beneath the horizon, Rhenthizu and the companions reached the shore. Cacophony surrounded them as the path guides handed the balunu ropes over to the landing guides. The balunu bowed to its guidance, dipping low over the landing dock, lowering *Flying Fish* into the water. Landing guides swarmed onto the lines to release the net from the balunu and haul it from beneath the ship.

The companions cheered, adding their voices to the splash of waves, the creak of lines, the roar and crack of furnaces preparing for the balunu's return trip. A great raft piled high with cloth-wrapped, rope-secured packages rode low in the water, waiting its turn to fly across the peninsula, and its paddlers stared at *Flying Fish* in silent amazement.

Rhenthizu held Maranti's hand as they crossed the beach. Sweat ran down his sides. His loincloth was soaked.

Maranti pushed back her sweaty hair. "I want to bathe," she said. "I want to be covered all over with olive oil, and I want you to scrape it off." She glanced sidelong at him, at the loincloth made translucent by his sweat and grinned. "And I will do the same for you, though you are very alluring as you are."

Her compliments lifted the exhaustion from him and made him strut. He wanted to fling off the loincloth and run splashing into the sea, pulling her with him to cavort like a man enchanted by a sea goddess. But the water around the landing dock, like the water in any busy harbor, carried trash and filth of every sort.

The companions gathered, waiting impatiently for *Flying Fish* to be secured to the dock. Kilinkizu joined Rhenthizu and Maranti, Bdarde in tow. For once the little boy remained silent instead of spouting his usual complaints and insults. He had wilted like a cut flower, of heat and exhaustion.

"I so want to swim," Kilinkizu said. "But the water is disgusting."

"Soon," Rhenthizu said. "Soon we'll be on *Flying Fish* and away, and Aranthau will find us a place free of garbage."

"And free of sharks," Maranti said, hopefully.

Vendors of food and drink clamored around them. Hunger and thirst sent pangs of longing through Rhenthizu's body, but they were pangs for bread and wine instead of chili and maize gruel.

"Does anyone offer cacao?" Maranti asked.

"Cacao is the drink of the gods," Rhenthizu said. "Only for ceremonies."

"I am Eldest Daughter," Maranti said, haughty for a moment. "Everything I do is ceremonial." At his look of surprise, she burst into laughter. "Do we have a single thing to trade, even for maize gruel?" she said. "Everything is on *Flying Fish*, and our carry sacks are full of moldy crumbs. Come, let's go aboard and ask Bridges Words to show us again how to make cacao."

"You may have my share," Rhenthizu said, as he always did.

Paissu ran across the beach to the companions. "We skimmed the peak," she cried, "so close I almost touched it."

"I saw you," Maranti said. She knelt, and Paissu fell into her embrace. "I would have been frightened, all that way in the sky."

"It was fun!" Paissu said.

"Is Iakinthu better?"

"She's still very tired, but she can get up, and she can eat," Paissu said. "She said she would rather have walked. But flying was fun," she said again.

"How did you come to us, before *Flying Fish* is moored?" Maranti asked.

"Oh — I jumped," Paissu said. Seeing the companions crossing the sand, she had naturally slipped between the supporting ropes, leaped from the gunwale to the dock, and run to the beach.

She led the way, through the noise of furnaces and the ring of golden tubes, through the smell of hot ruburu, past the colorful collapsed skin of another baluṇu waiting to take shape and lift into the sky, and onto a dock built of heavy logs twined with thick rope.

The landing guides wrestled a gangplank from the dock to *Flying Fish*, but Paissu took a running start and leaped to the ship's side, grabbing the rail and vaulting onto it. She ran along the railing to the stern, to Iakinthu, who watched her with fond pride.

"Iakinthu, the companions are coming!" Paissu cried. "And we can sail away!" She leaped to the deck, to Iakinthu's side.

Iakinthu took one look at the companions, returning wearily to *Flying Fish*, and sent them all to scrounge a quick meal of cheese and olives and sweet almonds, then to fall exhausted into sleep. Though Aranthau was anxious to sail away, the companions must have some rest.

Iakinthu took Aranthau's warm calloused hand as he sat beside her to keep watch while the landing guides freed *Flying Fish* from the balunu. Head Guide arrived with a team of workers to remove the bolt of red cloth from *Flying Fish*'s mast.

Bridges Words and Uinthi, both drooping with exhaustion, joined Iakinthu and Aranthau.

"Will you sleep?" Iakinthu said.

"When Head Guide is paid," Uinthi said, gazing up at the mast, where Head Guide's workers wrestled with the sodden cloth. Its red dye leaked over their hands and down the mast, dripping another layer of scarlet onto the wood. Aranthau frowned.

"Will we negotiate?" asked Bridges Words.

"Head Guide brought a strange craft whole across a dangerous path," Iakinthu said. "I'll pay her what we agreed, glass and lavender and oil, and hope she gets some good from our abandoned jars of wine."

She regarded Bridges Words.

"And you, my friend? What have you decided?"

He barely needed Uinthi's translation. "Can I find my people? Did Lady Jaguar kill them all?"

Iakinthu stretched out her hand to him. Hesitantly, he took it, then dropped to one knee before her and, in the Idaean way, touched his fist to his forehead.

"Iakinthu Gephyra, who shared your name with me, may I sail away with you?"

"I'll be glad to have you among my companions," Iakinthu said.

IV
The Untamable Ocean

Chapter Twenty-Six

Its fresh water replenished, its deck bright with fruit and maize and chili pods in bulging nets, its mast stained red and its sails spattered with the dye as if with blood, *Flying Fish* sailed out of the balunu harbor and into the Untamable Ocean.

At a safe distance, in clean water deep enough to protect the ship from the tides, Aranthau called for the sail to furl and the anchor to drop, and he followed it into the water in a long deep dive.

Even after all the years, Iakinthu worried when he dove so deep and long. As always, she was relieved when he breached from water to air and splashed down like a dolphin. He climbed the side of *Flying Fish* and stood naked on the deck, dripping seawater. Iakinthu sponged him with olive oil, and scraped away the salt and anointed his long hair.

"What did you see, my love? What did you hear?"

He gazed westward.

"The Untamable Ocean," he said. "So wide that the whale calls fade to whispers. Could we carry enough food, enough water, in *Flying Fish*, to sail across it?"

"Our next voyage," Iakinthu said, thinking, My beloved Aranthau would take great joy in such a long sail. But I would dread it. "Perhaps. For now, shall we search for Rhenthizu's people?"

Flying Fish carried Iakinthu and the companions along a coast that stretched forever beside them. Iakinthu yearned to approach the golden hills and great headlands. Curls of smoke and the glow of campfires drew her with the promise of new people, new friends, new trading partners.

Who may want anything but our good Fair Island wine! she thought.

But everything Uinthi had discovered about Rhenthizu's people and everything Aranthau learned about the Untamable Ocean pointed to a land much farther north. So they sailed on.

Early one morning, when the day was still cool but dawn spilled across the land onto the sea, Iakinthu rose from her sleeping shelf. Beside her,

Aranthau opened his eyes, like most ship captains able to go from sleep to wakefulness in a moment. She brushed her lips against his forehead.

"I'm going to walk, my dear, while it's cool. Go back to sleep."

He touched her cheek; he smiled; he fell asleep again before she had tied on her kilt.

Climbing to the deck, she thought, A few days ago this ladder would have defeated me.

And then she laughed at herself because she had to pause several rungs below the hatch to catch her breath and rest.

Paissu, silhouetted against the brightening sky, leaned down from the deck and extended her hand.

"Iakinthu Gephyra." She whispered, wanting to let the other companions sleep undisturbed. "May I walk with you?"

"Thank you, my dear." Iakinthu took Paissu's hand, glad of her young strength, her shoulder to lean on, Paissu's attention to any roll of the ship that might steal Iakinthu's balance. This was the longest she had taken to recover after a bout of the cold fever. She was glad of the cache of cinchona bark in her healing stores.

Flying Fish rode the dawn sea in long leisurely tacks, guided by the companions of the night watch.

"Oh," whispered Paissu in a long amazed sigh. "Oh, look!" She pointed.

A great spout sprayed above the surface of the sea. Glad for once of her increasing far sight, Iakinthu spotted the blue whale. It paused between water and air, breathing, then dove and flipped its tail and disappeared.

Aranthau, wide awake, tying his loincloth, strode across the deck and joined Iakinthu and Paissu.

"What do you see, little Paissu?" he said.

She pointed west, beyond the first blue whale. Iakinthu squinted.

A forest of whale-spouts covered the sea, rising, falling, moving through the water toward *Flying Fish*, toward the coast. A hundred—a thousand? Iakinthu lost count.

"What do you hear?" Aranthau asked Paissu.

"I *see* them. I hear their breathing." She looked up at him. "What do you hear?"

"They speak a new language," he said.

Bdarde ran to Aranthau, making a great racket. How can he make so much noise, Iakinthu wondered, irritated, with his bare feet on the deck?

"What is it?" he shouted. "Who's yelling at us?"

"They're singing," Aranthau said. "Do you hear them?"

"What ugly singing," Bdarde said. "What are they singing about?"

Aranthau smiled. "Sex."

Bdarde made a face and turned away.

The other companions joined them, watching the great gathering of whales swim toward *Flying Fish*. Iakinthu glanced at Aranthau, wondering how to avoid being in the midst of the behemoths. He gazed at them, calm. She took on his reaction, trusting him to care for her ship.

"Where are they going?"

He nodded toward the distant coastline. "A great gulf with warm water and protection from storms."

Any entrance to the gulf lay too distant even for Iakinthu's longsighted vision, but Aranthau's knowledge of their surroundings always proved true.

The first whale swam across their bow, surfacing, spouting, descending. Several others followed, and then the enormous pod surrounded *Flying Fish*, before, behind, and beneath. Uinthi and Rhenthizu joined them and leaned over the rail, amazed by the size of the creatures, longer than *Flying Fish*. Despite herself, Iakinthu braced for a crash. One whale after another slipped beneath her ship and swam smoothly on. Her ship sailed smoothly on as well, untouched by creatures that could have sunk it with a casual flip of the tail. One did flip its tail, showering the companions with cold sea water. Iakinthu gasped.

"It's..." She caught her breath, overwhelmed by the smell.

"Smelly," Aranthau said. "They sing to each other, they smell each other."

"Their smell is...very loud."

The great whales passed beneath and around *Flying Fish*, spouting and singing, swimming toward the distant coast and the inlet to a shallow sea where they would play and commune and mate and give birth.

Flying Fish ran along the coast, day after day, catching strong winds and delicate winds, and a current of warm water that sped it northward. Lines of smoke occasionally wrote in the air, calling Iakinthu to put in to land and create new bridges with the people of the fires. But the coast here was too golden, too dry, to be the land of Rhenthizu.

When I was younger...Iakinthu thought. I have been an honorable bridge between people. Will Rhenthizu's people be my last meeting?

Iakinthu walked the deck every day, needing less and less to lean on Paissu's shoulder.

"Will I dance with bulls, Iakinthu?" Paissu asked one morning.

"Of course you will, if you wish it."

"Will I be too old to learn? We've been gone a very long time."

"You're learning already," Iakinthu said. "The best dancers learn to dance in the rigging when they're very young, like you. If you danced with a bull now, you would barely reach his horns. Best to grow a little taller."

Paissu stretched to her tallest. She had grown, even since joining the companions of *Flying Fish*. Iakinthu thought that in a year or two she would reach Iakinthu's height. Iakinthu was one of the smaller bull dancers, but as far as she was concerned, she was the perfect height.

"Come and eat with us," Kilinkizu called softly. Paissu and Iakinthu joined her and Bdarde, who for once was quiet as he scooped porridge into his mouth with his fingers. When Iakinthu was settled on a camp chair, Paissu ran across the deck and bounded up the mast. In a moment she was at its peak, moving gracefully around the scarlet tip.

"I worry," Kilinkizu said softly.

Iakinthu smiled. "I rejoice," she said. She could choose to worry, but what good would that do? Worry, cautions, would hurt Paissu's pride and confidence.

Chapter Twenty-Seven

The rain began. The golden coast turned green.

As *Flying Fish* slipped north along the coast, rain pelted against the sails, across the deck, through the woven roof and walls of the stern cabin. Maranti stayed below deck, wrapped in a woolen boat cloak, feeling the effects of her pregnancy.

Glad to be recovered from the cold fever, Iakinthu took her turns at steering and lookout, her hair dripping cold water down her neck. Aranthau stalked the deck, pausing at the bow at each round. Rivers and streams from the coast obscured his underwater sight with muddy runoff. Paissu, watching with sharp young eyes from the mast, was his invaluable aide.

Rhenthizu came to relieve Iakinthu at the steering oar just before twilight, with the setting sun peeking from beneath low gray clouds on the Untamable Ocean's distant horizon. The light turned suddenly golden. Rhenthizu put his arm around Iakinthu's shoulders and pointed east. A rainbow stretched across the coastline. It doubled, tripled, the colors changing from brilliant to ghostly.

Flying Fish stayed in deep water but in sight of the coastline. Iakinthu watched the green hills and beaches pass by, and the great stone headlands march along like great creatures in stone armor. Intrigued by the occasional plume of smoke, she yearned to stop and meet the people of the forested coast.

She wondered if anyone on shore saw *Flying Fish*; she wondered if they wondered about her as she wondered about them. But she let the ship continue onward, only asking Aranthau to mark the smoke streams in his memory, on his infallible picture of the lands and sea new to Idaeans. On the way back home, they might explore and stop to meet new people.

Paissu spent her time dancing with the wind and the sea, watching the long beaches and tall headlands pass by. Aranthau trusted her to warn of any unusual sight or danger. When Iakinthu tired, he accompanied her belowdecks and sat with her, confident in Paissu's attention.

Iakinthu wished all her strength would return. She lay wrapped in a boat cloak in her bed, soothed by Aranthau's warm hand against her palm. He brought heated wine and sweet almonds, and she dozed.

~

Above the deck and the ship's companions, and Bdarde scowling up, Paissu watched. She liked to walk barefoot along the yardarm, balancing as *Flying Fish* moved beneath her. It's like riding Surefoot, she thought, and wondered how Issiia-now-Fire-from-Cold-Ashes and Surefoot were getting along; she wondered if Issiia had found her own name or continued to use the name borrowed from Kilinkizu.

She is very brave, Paissu thought. She expected Kilinkizu to be with the People, with her, and instead Kilinkizu is here with me. And with Bdarde. She wondered if Kilinkizu regretted her choice.

"Come up, come up!" she called to Bdarde. "It's fun. It's like flying."

"It's girls' work," he shouted. "Would I do girls' work? I'm a boy!"

"Too bad for you," she said. "How boring! Do you ever do anything fun?"

"Do warriors have fun? We train with spears. We fight. We kill men and we fuck women and make them have our babies."

The companions on deck studiously ignored his rudeness, his insults, his obscenities.

"Too bad for you," Paissu said again, unperturbed. "Is that all supposed to be fun?"

"Girl! Girl! Girl!" he shouted.

This was the last measure of disappointment for Kilinkizu. She strode across the deck and took Bdarde's hand.

"Paissu is busy doing important work, girls' work," she said. "Come with me and leave her alone."

He tried to twist away from her but she led him firmly to the bow.

"I want to attend Aranthau."

"Aranthau is attending Iakinthu," Kilinkizu said. "What need has he of you?"

"Women's work!" Bdarde exclaimed. "What man wants to do women's work?"

"A man who is proud," Kilinkizu said. She stroked his hair; he ducked away. "If everything is women's work, what's left for men to do?"

They passed out of Paissu's hearing before she had to hear his reply. She returned her attention to the ship, the sea, the land.

Far ahead, waves crashed against great rocks.

"Rhenthizu, Rhenthizu!" Paissu called.

"I hear you, little Paissu," he called back from his place at the steering oar. "What do you see?"

"Rocks ahead." She pointed.

Rhenthizu guided *Flying Fish* to deeper water, avoiding the danger. Paissu held tight as the ship heeled away from shore to pass the hazard.

The rocks looked like the heads of stone giants, peering out to sea, back to land, indifferent to the waves and to the incoming tide slowly covering their faces. Paissu shivered. They might be drowning, she thought. Drowning to death, then coming back to life when the sea recedes again. Over and over.

She looked away, scanning the beach, the forest, the headland...

...where a tiny shape stood at a rock projection's peak. For a moment Paissu thought it might be a deer, facing her, then realized it was a human person, staring motionless, amazed, at *Flying Fish*.

Paissu waved.

Slowly, the figure raised her hand in salute. Her hair whipped around her face, her shoulders.

A song floated over the wind. Paissu listened, entranced.

Aranthau appeared from belowdecks and climbed to join her, seeking out the source of the singing.

"Did you hear?" Paissu whispered, amazed by Aranthau's having heard the song from inside the ship. "Do you see?"

"I hear, and I see." He spoke as quietly as she did.

The song was soft and bright, barely skimming the waves. Paissu wondered that the other companions moved about on deck, oblivious to the melody, but she feared a shout to them would interrupt the singer and cause her to flee. Aranthau remained silent as well.

Together, Paissu and Aranthau watched the figure till it faded into the distance; Paissu listened till the song drifted away. She lowered her hand.

"Good sight," Aranthau said. "You are my eyes—and now my ears—when I attend Iakinthu."

"I'll watch. And listen," she said. "Will Iakinthu be well?"

"The cold fever affects her more each time it takes her." His somber expression worried Paissu. He sighed. "I should have kept her from steering. But who can overcome Iakinthu's will?" He shook off his distress and said,

"Iakinthu will be glad to know about new people to meet. We're farther from home than any Idaeans have traveled."

He made his way hand-over-hand down a line to the deck, then disappeared below.

The long evening vanished into dusk. *Flying Fish* slowed, its sail partially reefed, its course farther from shore. Paissu climbed down the mast, tired and hungry, still song-entranced. She was glad to see Iakinthu sitting near the brazier and Maranti with her, and Rhenthizu stirring a pot of soup. Kilinkizu joined them, followed— Of course, Paissu thought—by Bdarde, who trudged along with his head down. When Aranthau sat beside Iakinthu, Bdarde made his way to Aranthau's side, looking at him with worship. For all Paissu's admiration for Aranthau, she wondered that the little boy disregarded his mother. Paissu sat beside Kilinkizu, amused that Bdarde gave her an angry glare. Perhaps he's jealous, she thought, but it's his own fault. Kilinkizu put her arm around Paissu and gave her a fond squeeze.

"Paissu saw a siren," Aranthau said. "And heard her song."

"Tell me of her," Kilinkizu said. "My sight would miss her. Should I have heard her?"

Aranthau hummed a bit of the song but stopped when Rhenthizu clapped his hands over his ears.

"If I had heard that singing," he said, "I would have followed it!"

"It's beautiful," Kilinkizu said, and Maranti nodded her assent.

"It's terrifying," Rhenthizu exclaimed. "How would I resist it? How did I miss hearing it?"

Paissu thought, I heard it through the air, and Aranthau heard it through the sea. Rhenthizu missed it because of wind and waves.

Rhenthizu ladled soup into bowls and passed them out, to the thanks of his companions. Except, of course, Bdarde. Paissu waited in anticipation of what he would say.

"Why do you serve us?" Bdarde said. "That's—"

"Oh, stop," Rhenthizu said.

"Are you my sire?" Bdarde said, as if he were an animal. "Are you my brother, to tell me what to do?"

"Be quiet!" Kilinkizu cried, embarrassed by his rudeness.

"If I offend you so," Rhenthizu said, "serving my friends, my companions, refuse your dinner and go hungry."

Bdarde pulled his bowl in close to his chest, afraid Rhenthizu would take it back. He shoveled a spoonful of soup into his mouth. Paissu did her best to avoid laughing at him when he burned his tongue with his greed.

Once it cooled a little, the soup, with bits of chili and fresh tomato—"Eat them soon!" Head Guide had advised—tasted wonderful.

Iakinthu dozed and woke, dozed and woke. Paissu slept nearby. Aranthau remained on deck through the night, guiding *Flying Fish* with his preternatural awareness of sea and sky.

It's always like this, Iakinthu thought, when the cold fever takes me. I recover enough to be bored, to have slept enough, I go back to being useful, and then I become too tired to do any shipboard tasks or even to study the lessons Kilinkizu offers us, or the language Bridges Words would teach me. And every time I'm sick, the tiredness lasts longer. I should be grateful that I have my life, but, oh, I am too tired.

Paissu snuggled down in her boat cloak, blinked, and smiled at Iakinthu.

"Can I fetch you anything, Iakinthu Gephyra?" she said softly.

"Thank you, little Paissu. I am content." Is that true? she chided herself. But the truth would trouble my young friend. "Did the siren frighten you?"

"She entranced me. But the men feared her."

"That's the way of sirens. If all the companions were men, *Flying Fish* might be broken on the siren's rocks."

"Aranthau would protect *Flying Fish*."

"Yes, he would. Even from a siren. My love is an extraordinary man." She smiled. "Go back to sleep now. You were extraordinary, too, dancing on the yardarm. When we get home, I'll take great pleasure and pride in helping you select a bull calf to dance with, to grow with."

"That will be fun," Paissu said.

Soothed by the sound of the water flowing past the side of *Flying Fish*, they both fell asleep.

Rhenthizu sat with Uinthi and Bridges Words, learning more of the trade language that Bridges Words brought with him. The words and the signs tickled the edge of his memory. I knew this language when I was a child, he thought, and I'm glad to recall it.

Uinthi said, "He says, 'This is how you say, I am sad. I am discouraged. I believe you are planning to cheat me.'"

Rhenthizu laughed. "And 'Tomorrow they may kill me, but today I will be sad and discouraged and cheated.'"

Bridges Words glanced at him sidelong. "You learn quickly," he said, and Rhenthizu understood him.

"And this makes me happy and encouraged, and you give me a great gift, and I wish you would be happy and encouraged too."

Bridges Words gazed at him for a long moment.

"I will try," he said finally. "Have I had any reason to be happy and encouraged? You—" he gestured to include Rhenthizu and Uinthi and *Flying Fish* and all the ship's companions "— have given me reason."

Paissu stood in her usual place, on the yardarm by the mast, watching the sea and the land, enjoying a moment of the sunshine that broke through the rain.

Will I see another siren? she wondered. But Aranthau had chosen to sail farther from land, so the beaches and headlands and forests lay softened by distance. People, even sirens, would be too small to see. *Flying Fish* would be, to them, a strange shape moving along the far horizon.

The wind freshened. Sudden clouds obscured the sun, moving in from the west. Rain slanted down, darkening the sea. Beams of light broke through the clouds, shining on the waves, then disappeared as the rain fell heavily. A gust brought cold droplets. She shivered. Rain soaked her hair and ran down her face. She blinked and wiped the rain from her eyes, and peered ahead into the blur of wind and rain and sea.

"Paissu! Come down." Aranthau stood at the foot of the mast, beckoning her. She thought to remain where she was, for she was one of the People, strong and capable. But if Iakinthu of the Idaeans was like Celestial Wind of the People, Aranthau was like Dragon Claws, and Paissu would do as either of them asked.

She shinnied down the mast, careful of its slick surface. The mast was wet, the deck was wet, Aranthau was wet.

"You are very wet, little Paissu," he said.

"As are we all, on deck," she said. "Cold food tonight, I think." Braziers burned on deck only. Fire was too dangerous to light below.

She wiped the rain from her face again, then laughed.

"Go below. Get dry. Iakinthu has asked Kilinkizu for a writing lesson, and asks if you will join them."

"Yes!" she exclaimed. "But—the watch?"

"Other companions can watch, though you are best." He smiled at her. "We're far from rocks and shores and tides. It may be that Bdarde will take a turn."

"He—" Bdarde would have one of his tantrums, Paissu thought, then realized that he might watch from the bow, or even climb the mast, for Aranthau.

And if he did, she and Iakinthu would be spared his grumpy presence while Kilinkizu taught them their letters. "Maybe he will!" she said.

She scampered belowdecks, where the ship held the warmth of the morning. She rubbed her hair with a linen towel, put on a dry kilt and vest, and hung her sodden clothes to dry.

Iakinthu looked so much better than yesterday, color in her cheeks, sitting straight at the study table, instead of slumped, her long hair dressed. A few strands of silver followed the curl of her black hair, beautiful in the cloud-dimmed light from the deck prism.

"Iakinthu Gephyra," Paissu said, touching her fist to her forehead in the Idaean way.

"Paissu, dancer," Iakinthu said, smiling.

Paissu leaped and turned full circle before her feet touched the ground again. Iakinthu and Kilinkizu laughed with delight.

On the table before her, Kilinkizu set out bits of paper, ink and pens, her reading stone, and a handful of sweet almonds in their shells.

"Today," she said, "we'll study numbers."

Paissu looked at her sidelong.

"Do you hear any rain? If the rain has stopped I should go back to being lookout."

Iakinthu glanced up at the deck prism, where the falling rain made the light tremble in watery waves.

"The rain," she said, "is still raining."

"What's wrong?" Kilinkizu asked.

"Would I wish to insult you?" Paissu whispered.

"How so?"

"I like your lessons," Paissu said. "I like being able to write my name, to point to it and say, 'This is me!' I think my written name is pretty."

"Numbers can be pretty, too," Kilinkizu said.

"Do I want to return to the People and become their numerator?"

Kilinkizu gazed at her somberly. "That's One Hundred Three's work, and then the boy's. Would you take his place?"

"What if he wants to ride with the People instead of counting our wealth in his little house? And only I knew enough to take his place?"

"He would have to ride astride, to keep up with the People. How could he do that without injury? He had better stick to men's work."

Both women, and Paissu as well, heard the echo of Bdarde's complaints about women's work. Paissu giggled, and Iakinthu caught her glee, and finally Kilinkizu laughed, too.

Iakinthu snorted and burst out into another peal of laughter. Kilinkizu wiped away tears, smearing her kohl. Paissu clapped her hands over her mouth, but she was still laughing.

"Oh, Kilinkizu, I am sorry. Should I laugh at your little boy? I should act like a sister."

"Better laughter than his anger. I think he would be angry if I told him he should learn to be a numerator, proper men's work." She stopped laughing. Her eyes filled with tears again. "Boys of his tribe have only brothers," she said.

Iakinthu clasped her hand, patted her arm. Paissu thought to exclaim that everyone must have sisters, born or given, but Kilinkizu's sadness kept her silent.

"Now," Kilinkizu said, serious again, joy and sadness both banished, "how many almonds are in my hand?"

She opened her hand, which was empty.

Paissu frowned. "The almonds are there." She pointed to the pile of unshelled nuts, tempted to take one and crack its shell and eat it.

"I will tell you of a wonderful insight that I learned in Hind," Kilinkizu said. She lifted her hand, still empty of almonds. "This is zero, sunya, kha."

Rhenthizu sat with Maranti in the stern cabin, protected from the drizzle by boat cloak and oiled silk. *Flying Fish* cut through the sea, its steering oar tied steady, its sails cupping the wind. The coast was a faint white line in the distance, interrupted by headlands, backed by forest, with a rampart of mountains beyond.

Rhenthizu slid his hand beneath Maranti's boat cloak and drew her bare foot into his lap. He pulled the stopper of the unguent bottle. The scent of lavender flowed out, softening the salt air's sharp sparkle. The lavender-infused olive oil flowed cold into his hand. He rubbed his palms together to warm it, then stroked it over Maranti's heel and instep and down to her toes. She sighed with pleasure and pressed her foot up between his thighs, teasing him gently.

He pulled the boat cloak around her foot to keep it warm and stroked the oil onto her other foot. When she touched him again, reaching and pressing softly with her heel, he drew in a long deep breath.

"My love," he said.

"My lover," she replied. "Will you please me?" She reached for him. He took her hand and slid up beside her, letting her cover them both with her cloak. Her warmth, her touch, her scent excited him. The rain pattered on the stern cabin's roof, surrounding them with a shield of sound.

Rhenthizu drew Maranti close. She kissed him and loosened his loincloth and drew his hand to her sex. He stroked and caressed her with his oil-slick fingers. She pressed against him, moved astride him, pinned his arms, touched her breasts to his chest. She encircled him, surrounded him, brought him to one climax, then another, and held him while she shuddered and gasped with pleasure.

They lay together in a fog, dozing, waking to touch each other. She stroked the scars on his back, and he allowed it.

"Rhenthizu!"

Aranthau's voice catapulted Rhenthizu from the warmth of Maranti's bed. He ran out into the open, tucking his loincloth back around him.

"Steer to deeper water," Aranthau called from the bow. In a moment Rhenthizu freed the steering oar and leaned his weight against it, feeling the resistance of water and ship. *Flying Fish* turned with a pitch and a yaw, then steadied as the ship came around to plough into the waves head-on.

In the dark and the rain, he peered around to find what Aranthau saw. But he found only the dark and the rain.

Aranthau walked from bow to stern, stopping once to lean against the rail, to look for other boats, to listen for people. *Flying Fish* came abreast of the shore fire. The flames blazed and sparked in the rain.

"What do you see?"

"A fire on shore, ahead. It's small. But its people might be night-fishing."

Maranti pulled aside the stern cabin's night curtains. "Is everything all right? Shall I help with the watch?"

"Stay dry and warm," Aranthau said. The rain dripped down his face, through his hair.

"I am quite warm," she said, smiling, and withdrew inside.

Flying Fish sailed far out to sea before turning to parallel the coast again. Rhenthizu wished they could stop and talk to the people on shore and ask about his own people. Uinthi had recommended going farther north before approaching land and, because Uinthi had toiled so long and hard in his interest, he accepted the advice.

Dawn shadowed the mountains, casting their images into the sky, and the rain paused as if the sun pushed it away. The other companions came on deck, yawning, firing the braziers to make camp-bread and to heat water and wine for breakfast.

Rhenthizu made cacao—less elaborately than Lady Jaguar's people did—for Maranti and took it to her with a slice of warm bread and honey.

She ate it hungrily and drank the cacao with relish. She offered the cup to Rhenthizu.

"It's for you," he said. The smell made him queasy.

She laughed. "It would be funny if all Lady Jaguar's men disliked it so and drank it anyway, and thought they succeeded in forbidding it to women, who like it."

"Kilinkizu would say it was the way of men," Rhenthizu said.

Maranti sobered. "For the men she knew before she came to be Iakinthu's given child, it was true. How unhappy they must all be."

Rhenthizu had to agree. "Will Bdarde ever learn happiness?"

"I wish I knew. He's awfully stubborn." She drained the cup of the last of her cacao, threw off the boat cloak, and leaped up. The early sunlight flowed through the silk curtains and played with color on her skin, blue and green and lavender as if she were an undersea creature.

Rhenthizu adored her with his gaze. She put on her vest and loincloth and kilt and looked down critically at the fit.

"I'll have to sew some new clothes soon," she said, smiling. "I'm glad I left my mirror belowdecks."

A little shocked at the idea of the Eldest Daughter making her own clothing, Rhenthizu held out his hands. "My stitches have been praised," he said.

"I'll be glad of your help," she said. "My stitches wander like a caterpillar."

Chapter Twenty-Eight

Paissu joined Aranthau at the top of the mast.

"Watch for deadheads," he said. "So much river, so much silt, so many logs." The silt made him as shortsighted underwater as Kilinkizu was in the air.

"I will," Paissu said, thinking, The deadheads are hard to find, the trunks of huge trees waterlogged and nearly sunk beneath the waves. If she was lucky, she would see a few tendrils of the fallen tree's roots, or the end of a long branch. But sometimes all that was left was the trunk, polished smooth by waves and sand, floating in wait beneath the surface.

Paissu took her place, watching for obstructions in the sea ahead. She pulled a rough rock from her pocket and shook it. It rattled. She had picked it up from the deck when the rock storm ended—that felt like so long ago!—and the fallen stones had cooled. It was spherical, just the size to fit in her hand.

"I've seen those before," Iakinthu had told her. "You only find them around volcanoes. This is the first that I knew for certain had fallen from the sky, from the volcano's cloud. If you break it open—"

Paissu had clutched the rock to her chest, protecting it, and Iakinthu laughed.

"Would I break open your shaker, my young friend?" she asked. "It's yours, it's safe. But when I had a dozen of them, I sacrificed one to see what was inside. What rattles is broken mud. I think that the mud falls into the volcano, and the volcano coats it with stone and blasts it from its mouth."

"I like the way it sounds," Paissu said.

The sea changed. From brilliant blue in sunlight or ominous gray beneath clouds, it turned a sludgy brown. When the first streaks of silt-filled water passed beneath *Flying Fish*'s bow, Paissu called Aranthau. He joined her and asked the companions to reef the sail till the ship was barely creeping along with enough wind to steady it.

"Good sighting," he said. "The Great River, which Uinthi and Bridges Words call the Wimahl, is ahead of us."

"Can you teach me how to know that?" Paissu asked.

"Can you swim?"

"All the People can swim," she said.

"Can you open your eyes underwater?"

"I can try."

"I can try to teach you," he said. "But here and now, it's too dangerous—and the water is too full of silt—to see anything."

Iakinthu walked the deck with Maranti, appreciating all the work that her companions had done to make *Flying Fish* presentable after its long voyage. The ship glowed as if new, its decks and rails polished to a satin sheen, its sails repaired with fine stitches. She noticed the corner Maranti had patched and realized Rhenthizu had silently and secretly repatched it. Maranti had the skills of a diplomat; she lacked the skill of sewing.

Iakinthu averted her gaze to keep Maranti from noticing her discovery.

"I am as new as my ship," she said. "I feel my old self again."

"And I'm a new self," Maranti said with a smile.

Aranthau came hand-over-hand down the sheet and landed on the deck beside them.

"Iakinthu Gephyra, shipowner," he said formally, placing his fist to his forehead.

"Aranthau, my shipmaster," she replied with equal formality.

"*Flying Fish* needs fresh water. It would be best to approach the shore now and find a stream or a spring, instead of waiting till we reach the Great River."

"But the Great River is fresh water," Iakinthu said, puzzled.

"Fresh water filled with silt and fallen trees and all manner of debris from the shore." He smiled at her. "Does Fair Island have a great river for you to compare? Does any great river reach the Idaean Sea? You know fast-flowing springs and clear streams."

She nodded, accepting his knowledge and experience. "Then we will find a clear stream, a fast-flowing spring, before we reach the Great River."

Flying Fish sailed slowly up the coast until Paissu called the sighting of a stream. It cut across the beach from forest to sea. She looked for people who might negotiate for water, but beach and forest edge remained deserted.

When the ship's boat splashed into the waves, Paissu clambered down to join Rhenthizu and Uinthi and Bridges Words. Rhenthizu and Uinthi took up the oars, while Bridges Words sat in the stern with a box of treasures. Paissu steadied an empty water jug.

They hoped to scout the stream, find themselves alone, sample the water and bring a jar back, then approach the shore with *Flying Fish* and fill all its water jars. But if people appeared, they hoped to trade treasures for water and friendship.

"We may be going into danger," Rhenthizu said to Paissu.

"Do the People fear danger?" Paissu replied, ready to be offended, ready to argue to stay with the scouting party.

"The People are very brave," Uinthi said. "But they know when to be cautious."

"So do you."

Uinthi laughed and pulled on the oar. "Keep watch, then, my young lookout."

"I will." She gazed at the beach, wondering if she might see and hear another siren.

Instead, two tattered figures ran from the forest and down the beach to the water's edge, waving desperately, in silence. Paissu pointed.

Cautiously, in case the strangers had hidden weapons or were decoys for an attack, Uinthi and Rhenthizu rowed the boat toward the beach. Bridges Words put the trade box between his feet and picked up a short bow. He held it mainly for show. Uinthi had politely given up trying to teach him to use a bow after his shot went so wide of the target that he lost one of the arrows. Rhenthizu had more patience but less success. Still, there was something to be said for having one passenger visibly armed.

Paissu touched the hilt of her knife and slipped off its leather tie so she could draw it easily.

Rhenthizu glanced over his shoulder again.

"Are they Sheng?" he said in disbelief.

Beneath the dirt, their ragged robes were fine silk of brilliant color and delicate, intricate embroidery.

The People told stories of the Sheng at the other end of the Silk Road, of their enormous ships ten times the size of *Flying Fish*. Do I believe in a ship ten times the size of *Flying Fish*? Paissu asked herself. I liked to hear the stories, but did I believe them?

"They are Nipunu, dressed in the robes of nobility," Bridges Words said. "I saw one of their ships when I was a little boy, before I was stolen off to Lady Jaguar. They came to trade for gold and jade. They have a perfect hunger for jade. When they saw purple jade, that's what they wanted most."

"Can you speak to them?"

"Have I spoken to the Nipunu since I was a little boy? I will try."

The boat skidded up onto the beach, nosing roughly into the sand. Uinthi and Rhenthizu shipped the oars. Rhenthizu relieved Bridges Words of his short Idaean bow. For now, the arrows stayed in their quiver.

Bridges Words spoke hesitantly, pausing to search his memory for words long unused.

The taller of the two Nipunu clapped his hand over his mouth and waved his hand down, down, signaling for quiet. He waded into the water beside the boat, heedless of his robes, and climbed in, leaving the younger, shorter Nipunu to scramble in behind him. They wore similar robes, they tied their hair in similar ways. Young Nipunu nobles, Bridges World said.

Paissu glanced at Uinthi, then at the taller of the Nipunu.

"*He* is a man," Paissu whispered in Uinthi's ear.

Uinthi replied too softly for anyone else to hear. "We will know who they are when they tell us."

Uinthi and Rhenthizu backed the oars to pull the boat away from the beach, then turned and rowed toward *Flying Fish*.

Paissu gazed at the two new people, who shivered with cold. She drew out a boat cloak and offered it to the younger Nipunu, who took it, bowing, then wrapped it around the older Nipunu's shoulders. Paissu was used to seeing gifts passed along, but usually the recipient spent a moment or two appreciating a gift. She wondered what the Nipunu would have done with a second cloak, but the rowboat carried only one.

Perhaps he is cold and will get sick, Paissu thought.

Paissu pulled out the lunch bag, drew out a loaf of camp-bread, and tore off a hunk for each of them. The younger of the two took a piece, gave it a puzzled look, sniffed it, nibbled it. Paissu tore the bread into chunks. She ate hers; Bridges Words ate his. The Nipunu ate theirs, slowly, carefully. Paissu decided they were unfamiliar with bread. Or perhaps they feared poison— We could have speared them or left them on the beach! Paissu thought. Why would they fear poison now?

They rowed back in silence. On *Flying Fish*, Aranthau stood by the rail, gazing down at them, his arms crossed.

"Are they water?" he said.

After a moment, Paissu realized he was making a joke.

"They're frightened," she replied. "And cold."

"Ah. Cold, frightened water. Come aboard."

They all scrambled up the side, and the companions brought the ship's boat back to its place. The Nipunu collapsed to their knees on the deck.

"Could we leave them?" Rhenthizu said.

"We took their warning," Uinthi said.

"I see they are being chased."

They followed his gaze. A large canoe with a dozen paddlers raced toward them.

"I would have to employ considerable diplomatic skills to solve this," Iakinthu said.

"Set the sails," Aranthau told the companions. He glanced one more time at the fresh-water stream cutting the beach from forest to shore. "We will make do with rain," he said, "till we find another stream."

The canoe came on fast. Before *Flying Fish* had gotten properly under way, the canoe approached nearly within bow-shot. One of the men jumped to the tall eye-painted prow of the canoe, weapons in hand. The paddlers worked harder, shouting in rhythm, voices angry.

The sails saved the Idaeans, rippling and filling with wind, moving *Flying Fish* out of range and finally out of sight of the canoe. Once they were safe, everyone gathered around the Nipunu.

"I thought they were Sheng," Rhenthizu said. "But Bridges Words says different."

"They are Nipunu," Bridges Words said to Iakinthu. He explained about their voyages to obtain jade, his passing familiarity with their language.

Paissu watched them curiously. The older Nipunu knelt with shoulders squared, head up, expression stern. The younger Nipunu knelt, head down, watching surreptitiously.

"Speak to them, please, Bridges Words, my Gephyra companion. Find out who they are and how they came to be so far from home."

He spoke haltingly to them. First he pointed to Iakinthu and said her name and added a few words of explanation. The younger of the two Nipunu knelt at Iakinthu's feet, pulling on the older companion's robe to join in the obeisance. He resisted; Paissu thought he might fling himself before Aranthau instead of Iakinthu, which would be a terrible rudeness.

Aranthau would be embarrassed, Paissu thought. But I think Iakinthu would only laugh. Does she like being worshipped?

And of course Iakinthu reached down and drew the younger Nipunu up, just as the older Nipunu put his forehead to the deck.

"Our visitors are cold," Iakinthu said. "Bring bread and olive oil and warm wine. And camp chairs, and another boat cloak."

All these things were done. The Nipunu watched Iakinthu sit on a camp chair, but they remained kneeling. The younger Nipunu sipped wine before bowing and offering the cup to the older. He accepted the wine without a word or glance.

When Iakinthu offered dry clothes, both Nipunu declined, the older with a look of disdain at the rough wool, the younger reluctant, shivering.

"Perhaps they want Egyptian linen and gold jewelry," Bridges Words said sourly.

"You may ask them. We have both in the hold."

"I will ask them their names," Bridges Words said.

Wrapped in boat cloaks, holding cups of warm wine, they knelt facing Iakinthu.

Bridges Words spoke to them again. The younger answered him; the older gazed into the distance.

How rude, Paissu thought. Did we leave them to be captured, or did we save their lives?

"This one is Genji," Bridges Words said, "and that one is Murasaki." He pointed to the younger Nipunu.

"Welcome, Murusuku," Iakinthu said. "Welcome, Gunjusu."

Bridges Words repeated their names in their own language. Paissu heard the difference between what Murasaki said and what Iakinthu said, but Iakinthu repeated their names in the Idaean manner. Bridges Words shrugged in acceptance.

"Near enough for understanding. Their ship was blown off course and wrecked by a terrible storm. They lost a great trove of purple jade. They thought they would lose their lives, as many of their shipmates did. Murusuku believes a few others might have reached shore. A hope rather than a certainty."

He spoke again, listened, asked for repetition, signaled for a slower pace. Gunjusu sipped wine; Murusuku answered the questions.

"We gained the beach," Murusuku said, while Bridges Words translated. "We thought we were saved, but the people came out of the forest and took us away. They never hurt us, but they kept us under guard. I know a little of the trade language—"

At that, Bridges Words snorted in annoyance and spoke in an entirely different language, much more fluently than he spoke Nipunu. Murusuku looked at him, astonished.

"Iakinthu and I can speak to you, too," Uinthi said. Paissu understood as well, as long as everyone spoke slowly; she had been listening to the trade language when Bridges Words and Uinthi spoke it, learning it, studying it, though less formally than she studied scribing and numerating with Kilinkizu.

The conversation went more smoothly after Murusuku's revelation.

"We learned they planned to sell us as slaves. The people to the north keep slaves. They thought we would be valuable, being unusual. We wished we had kept the jade from sinking, for we thought we might trade it for our lives and freedom."

Murusuku looked straight at Iakinthu. Gunjusu stared, stony-faced, out to sea.

"Do Idaeans keep slaves?" Iakinthu said. "You are safe with us. Your freedom is safe with us."

Murusuku said a few words to Gunjusu, and Paissu realized he spoke little or nothing of the trade language and must be spoken to in Nipunu.

"We are the noble sons of a great family," Murusuku said.

Paissu kept her silence rather than asking any questions. Uinthi said they would know what they needed if the Nipunu chose to tell them.

"Our family would pay a great ransom for its oldest son. But if we were sold as slaves, we must perform seppuku to save our honor."

Iakinthu asked; Murusuku answered; the Idaeans were horrified. But Paissu understood. So did Kilinkizu. And especially Rhenthizu.

"Our visitors will want to rest," Iakinthu said.

Was it intentional, Paissu wondered, that Bridges Words and Rhenthizu conducted Gunjusu while Iakinthu and Uinthi stayed with Murusuku? Belowdecks, they entered the small compartment where Kilinkizu kept the ship's records. Here they could speak in private.

Murusuku knelt on the deck and bowed. Iakinthu sighed and prepared to join her on the hard deck, but Uinthi touched her arm.

"Let me." Uinthi knelt easily, facing the castaway. "Murusuku."

As Murusuku reluctantly looked up, Uinthi unlaced her leather shirt. Murusuku's eyes widened.

"I thought you were a boy," Murusuku said.

"Usually I am," Uinthi said as always if someone asked or noticed. "You are safe with us. If you are a son and brother, then you are a son and brother."

Murusuku hesitated. "I must remain as I am," she said.

"And Gunjusu?"

"He is the eldest son of the favored wife," Murusuku said. "My mother is newer, less favored. She hoped sons would raise her in our father's estimation. She is honored now. My sisters..."

"Are sons," Iakinthu said.

"Except my eldest sister, who was acknowledged a daughter when she was born. My brothers have wives, and when they want children, they go to our mountain house. When they come back, they have a baby, and who's to say who is mother, who is father."

"And you go to sea, adventuring, trading," Iakinthu said.

Murusuku hesitated, bowed, and said softly, "I am honored to be Gunjusu's attendant and food taster and negotiator."

"And brother."

"He believes I am his brother. Everyone believes I am his brother." Murusuku glanced from Uinthi to Iakinthu to Paissu. "Except you."

Astonished, Paissu thought, did Rhenthizu or Bridges Words notice? Or Aranthau?

She wondered about Aranthau. If I asked him, she thought, and he believed Murusuku to be son and brother, I might embarrass him! The People say men are easily embarrassed.

Despite the boat cloak, Murusuku shivered.

"Your clothes are wet and dirty and you are cold," Iakinthu said. "When you've slept, your clothes will be clean and dry and you will be warm."

Murusuku bent to touch forehead to floor.

"This is how Idaeans salute," Uinthi said, and touched fist to forehead. Murusuku mirrored the gesture, turning to Iakinthu.

Uinthi fastened the leather shirt laces.

Murusuku undressed beneath the boat cloak, handing out one silken kimono after another, each more elegant—and less dirty and bedraggled, though equally wet—than the last.

"Many layers," Uinthi said, when Murusuku handed out the fifth and last of the kimonos.

"My brother wears eight," Murusuku said.

"What is he concealing?" Iakinthu asked drily, then smiled. Uinthi and Paissu laughed, and after a moment Murusuku giggled, cut off the sound, and laughed in a deep voice that Paissu found most unconvincing.

"He demonstrates our family's wealth. And, for me, layers are... convenient."

Rhenthizu wished he could be in two places at the same time. Three places. First he wished to attend Maranti. Second was his duty at the steering oar. Third, he wished he could stand at the bow or climb the mast to see what lay ahead. Paissu was the best lookout, but even Paissu needed rest and food and her feet on the deck sometimes. And she was fascinated by the new visitors, especially Murusuku.

Paissu watched the younger noble son, narrowing her eyes when Murusuku attended and served and bowed to Gunjusu, frowning at the food- and wine-tasting before every meal, which Gunjusu waited for Murusuku to perform, taking it as his due.

Rhenthizu had to agree that worrying about poison was excessive. We could pitch them into the sea, he thought, and could they stop us? We could have left them behind to be recaptured.

He wondered if Paissu was falling in love with the exotic noble son. He wondered if the People ever did fall in love with men, or only took pleasure with them in celebrations or to get daughters.

She is much too young for that, he thought.

He returned his attention to *Flying Fish*.

Aranthau climbed down from the mast and joined him. A frown had replaced Aranthau's usual calm.

"I miss my sea sight," he said. "The Great River blinds me."

"You see it coming," Rhenthizu said.

"I see it, I hear it, I smell it, I taste it. It's like a thick wool curtain. I miss my sea sight."

It must be wonderful, Rhenthizu thought, to be able to know everything in the sea around you. Wonderful, and terrible when it goes away.

He touched Aranthau gently on the shoulder. Aranthau patted his hand.

Paissu reminded herself that Murusuku was a son and brother and could be in danger if anyone believed otherwise.

Murusuku blended smoothly with the rest of the companions, a life of being inconspicuous working to advantage. Gunjusu, on the other hand, became almost as irritating as Bdarde, all the more because he was grown up.

He's like the men the People tell funny stories about, Paissu thought, as Gunjusu knelt on the deck out of the wind and let Murusuku serve him and bind his hair and wash his kimonos, one at a time, for apparently it was beneath his station to wear fewer than seven robes, no matter how dirty they were. He seldom spoke to Murusuku except in a tone that anyone of the People would have refused to hear or acknowledge.

"What does he say to—to Murusuku?" Paissu whispered to Bridges Words.

"He says the silk is stiff and Murusuku should wash it better."

"Someone should tell him it's because of the salt water, and it's because of him that we missed the fresh water."

"Will Murusuku tell him? Will I?"

"He will have to wear stiff robes." Paissu giggled, and Bridges Words smiled his small infrequent smile. Gunjusu frowned but kept his gaze steady, away from Bridges Words and Paissu. He spoke again to Murusuku.

"He says he is meditating, bringing himself the patience of Hill Rock."

"'The rock would speak to Murusuku in a more respectful voice," Paissu said.

All day *Flying Fish* had been approaching Hill Rock. It kept getting bigger and bigger until Paissu thought they should call it Mountain Rock, though to her it looked like a woman's breast, the breast allowed its natural shape by a cuirass. The other breast would lie pressed beneath the water, out of the way of the archer's bowstring. She would call it Mother Rock, if anyone asked her.

The rock, whatever its name, however it would speak, rose from the sea separated from the beach by a narrow strip of tidewater. Attendant stones, one standing, one lying, flanked it. Paissu wondered if the tide—the tides were enormous in the Untamable Ocean!—would go out so far that it would expose the rock's base, so she could reach it from the beach and climb its steep sides, where seagulls nested.

Gunjusu waited for patience while Paissu listened for the Mother's voice. *Flying Fish* sailed past Mother Rock and continued north.

The rain returned.

Chapter Twenty-Nine

The mouth of Pharaoh's Great River Iteru had been as calm as Wimahl was treacherous. Wimahl's energy overwhelmed Iakinthu. Wimahl, the Great River, spilled out into the Untamable Ocean, carrying with it a burden of silt and trees and detritus. It crashed against rocks and sand bars, it created great sprays like waterfalls; it roiled in magnificent swirls. Rain and sea and river mixed, till *Flying Fish* crept through a shroud of water.

Aranthau tried to approach Wimahl's mouth, but thought better of it when *Flying Fish* rolled and pitched and yawed in the complex currents. He signalled to Rhenthizu to steer farther out to sea.

"Can the ship's boat enter the Wimahl's mouth?" Iakinthu asked.

"Would we ever see it again? It would be smashed on the rocks or pulled under by a whirlpool."

"We would have been better to welcome someone from the canoe that chased us, instead of our noble visitors," Iakinthu said uncharitably. "They might have known more of the route."

"They might have caught more slaves to sell," Aranthau replied, "if they outnumbered us."

"You are wise."

He smiled. "In my wisdom, I suggest we sail past the mouth of this Great River and approach a quieter shore."

"Bridges Words says people come to trade at the Great River, and Uinthi agrees. Rivers meet here. People meet here. Wars stop here."

"People get here some other way than here to there," Aranthau said, pointing to the deck, then to the Great River's mouth. "Or they know the obstacles." He grinned. "Or they can see through silt. My wisdom fails at silt."

Iakinthu took his warm, hard hand. She pressed it to her chest, to her cheek.

"You are the guide of my ship and of my companions," she said. "I trust your wisdom." She smiled back at him. "Even if it fails at silt."

And then, gradually appearing, a graceful canoe cut through the spray and the mist. Strong and calm, its paddler guided it toward *Flying Fish*. It slid through still water though waves crashed all around. Iakinthu watched in awe as it passed through the violence of the Wimahl's bar and entered the quieter sea.

She raised a hand in greeting and touched her forehead in salute.

A raised paddle was her reply. It dipped again on the other side, once, twice, three times. The canoe spun half a turn; the paddler gestured for *Flying Fish* to follow, and thrust his craft forward.

Aranthau glanced at Iakinthu.

"Yes," she said.

He knew, all her companions knew, that she would choose an invitation, though it might lead to danger. They all accepted her choice.

"Oars!" Aranthau shouted. "Rhenthizu!" He pointed, and Rhenthizu used all his strength to guide *Flying Fish* into the crashing waves. The companions ran to the oars. "Paissu!" Paissu, clinging to the top of the rain-slick mast, climbed halfway down where the motion was a little quieter. She paused, looking after their guide, tracing the currents and waves.

The rowing drum beat. *Flying Fish* pressed toward the river mouth. Iakinthu stayed with Aranthau, clutching the bow rail as her ship pitched through each wave, climbing the face and pounding down the other side. Spray soaked her. Aranthau signaled to Rhenthizu with one hand and steadied himself with the other.

"Log!" Paissu called from above. She pointed. Aranthau saw it, glanced quickly at the canoe, and followed it to keep *Flying Fish* steady on course. The log passed by, skimming just beyond the oars but never touching, spinning into a whirlpool and vanishing. Iakinthu gasped.

At the end of forever, *Flying Fish* pushed out into a river nearly as calm as the great river of the Pharaoh. The ship's sails caught the wind and pressed it against the current.

"Stop the oars," Aranthau called. The rowing drum signaled the change with a quick rattle, then fell silent. The oars retracted. The companions ran up on deck, covered with sweat, letting the rain wash them.

The guide canoe spun again and drifted along the current toward the ship. It slid around in another sharp turn and paused an armspan from *Flying Fish*.

Aranthau raised one eyebrow in appreciation of the paddler's skill.

"I am Iakinthu Gephyra, bridge between people," Iakinthu called, in Rhenthizu's trade language. "We thank you."

"I am Comucomulu, leader of the Kinuku, guide of the Wimahl, which welcomes you. I welcome you."

"We're glad of your welcome. Will you board?"

"I will."

Aranthau threw down a line.

Comucomulu secured his canoe to the line, then climbed the side of *Flying Fish*. All too late Iakinthu realized he was a man of age and wished Aranthau had offered him the ladder. Yet Comucomulu agilely walked up the slick planks and joined them on deck. His skin shone with the cold rain, and his braided hair dripped rivulets down his chest. He looked them all up and down, his one-eyed gaze taking in Iakinthu and Aranthau, Rhenthizu at the steering oar, Uinthi and Bridges Words, the companions of *Flying Fish* joining them from belowdecks, the Nipunu edging toward the stern cabin to stay out of the wet.

"You were to be mine," he said to Gunjusu and Murusuku.

Murusuku whispered the translation to Gunjusu, who stiffened and scowled. His hand went to his obi as if he expected to find a weapon. Comucomulu watched him with some amusement.

"They are among my companions now," Iakinthu said mildly. Will he take offense? she wondered, hoping to forge a friendly acquaintance.

"Hmph," he said. "Negotiating for them took a great deal of time. I discovered they were of little use, even for status, to my allies down the coast, so you are welcome to them. I hope they are of value to you."

"Come out of the rain," Iakinthu said, gesturing to the stern cabin.

"I'm accustomed to rain," Comucomulu said, but allowed himself to be guided under the canopy and seated on a camp stool. Iakinthu sat facing him, with Aranthau behind her, Uinthi and Bridges Words waiting nearby, their skills at translation unneeded.

Iakinthu asked for olives and almonds, bread and wine. In a moment Murusuku knelt before Comucomulu with a tray.

Comucomulu, like every other person on this side of the Sunset Sea, sniffed the good Fair Island wine and handed it back.

"Would you prefer balithi?" Iakinthu asked, put out as usual by the rejection of her good vintage.

"Balithi!" he exclaimed. "I've heard it drives people mad."

"It has…unusual effects." She sipped from his wine cup, glad of the warmth. Perhaps she should have offered cacao, but its preparation took time.

"Are you showing me there's no poison?"

"I'm drinking wine."

"Water is more to my taste," Comucomulu said. "And I like these little nuts." He crunched several almonds. "The cup is very beautiful."

Iakinthu swallowed the last mouthful of wine, drinking too fast to honor the vintage, shook out the last few drops, and offered Comucomulu the painted cup with both hands.

"Then you must have it," she said. "With my appreciation and admiration and gratitude."

He accepted it and looked at it more closely, squinting a little with his one good eye, smiling as he traced a delicate octopus's painted tentacles.

"Uinthi—" Iakinthu said, and before she could finish, Uinthi disappeared to take the steering oar from Rhenthizu, and Rhenthizu appeared in the stern cabin, all attention and surprise.

The scarred lid of Comucomulu's blind eye contracted as he blinked at Rhenthizu. "I thought you might be Akokulu."

Rhenthizu gazed at him in wonder. "Yes," he said. "I am."

Chapter Thirty

Rhenthizu stood trembling before Comucomulu. He touched his fist to his forehead. Then Iakinthu was beside him, guiding him to her camp stool to sit facing the leader of Kinuku and guide of Wimahl.

"This is my given child, Rhenthizu," Iakinthu said.

"Strange name for an Akokulu," Comucomulu said.

"He is a beloved member of my family. We seek his mother."

"Interesting customs your people have," replied Comucomulu. "Does he have two mothers?"

"Yes," said Iakinthu solemnly. "I am one."

"Perhaps the other is here." Comucomulu nodded upriver, where a scatter of temporary shelters dotted the northern bank and the smoke of campfires blended into the mist. "The Akokulu are here to trade."

Rhenthizu looked over his shoulder, following Comucomulu's gesture, though they were too far away to pick out any people.

Would I recognize my mother if I saw her? he wondered.

Comucomulu stood at the bow of *Flying Fish*, where the people on the riverbank could see him if the rain and the mist would only clear.

"You are wet," Iakinthu said. "May I offer you a boat cloak?"

"I'm accustomed to rain," Comucomulu said again. "But it's tedious, and you are wet—and cold—as well. I'll have to do something about the weather."

Iakinthu, standing to his right so he could see her, looked at him askance. Behind them, beyond the maelstrom of the Wimahl's mouth, the sun was sinking, a faint glow among rain clouds.

The light turned golden as the sun broke through the clouds. The rain stopped, and the mist dissipated into a perfect evening. Comucomulu spread his arms to let the slanting sunshine warm his back.

Before them, a double rainbow arced from horizon to horizon.

Canoes set out from the riverbank toward *Flying Fish*.

"Join me," said Comucomulu, drawing Rhenthizu up beside him at the bow. "Look for your people. What's your name?"

"Rhenthizu."

"Your Akokulu name," Comucomulu said impatiently.

"Can I remember?"

"He was very young when he came to me," Iakinthu said.

"Hmph." Comucomulu's left eyebrow rose, twisted by the scar. "Your mother's name? Your father's?"

Rhenthizu shrugged, distressed.

Maranti joined then and took Rhenthizu's hand. He squeezed it, glad of her presence.

Canoes surrounded *Flying Fish*. People called up to Comucomulu in a language unfamiliar to Rhenthizu. Comucomulu replied in the trade language.

"I'm their guest," he said, "and they are mine. They followed me bravely through the storm of Wimahl's mouth."

"Who are these new people?" One of the paddlers came right up to *Flying Fish* and knocked against its side. In a moment the ship reverberated with knuckles against planks, soft tapping or hard knocking.

"We are Idaeans," Iakinthu said. "Come to visit and trade."

Flying Fish floated quietly at anchor. As the Idaeans prepared to join Comucomulu on shore, the navigator approached Aranthau and gazed at him intently.

"I would prefer you to stay on board your ship," he said.

Aranthau sighed. "Very well," he said, a little annoyed by the stories that had apparently followed him around on this side of the world.

The rest of the ship's party headed for the beach.

Comucomulu and Rhenthizu paddled the navigator's canoe to shore, while Iakinthu and Kilinkizu and Paissu rowed the ship's boat and Uinthi and Bridges Words paddled the light Maisusutha canoe. A fleet of Comucomulu's people, curious and welcoming, surrounded the canoes and the ship's boat.

"We'll meet in informal dress," Iakinthu said, "like our host." They left behind the double-bladed axes and the Egyptian linen and seven-flounced skirts. Instead they wore everyday kilts and vests. Iakinthu's leather pouch held presents.

On shore, children ran to Comucomulu, swarming him with cries of welcome.

"Grandchildren," he said as he picked up one of the youngest, a toddler still unsteady on her feet. "Say 'welcome' to our guests."

"Welcome, welcome, welcome!"

Rhenthizu went down on one knee to be nearer their height and touched his fist to his forehead. Kilinkizu joined him, then Uinthi and Paissu, also saluting. The children looked curiously at Paissu, who met their gazes, raised her head, and howled like a wolf.

They laughed and mimicked her. Rhenthizu was surrounded by a small human wolf pack, and beyond them adults as curious as the Idaeans. They looked like him, unlike the Idaeans, however welcoming, however loving, Iakinthu and her people had always been to him.

Paissu howled again. Rhenthizu laughed with delight, and in a moment the child-wolves stopped howling and began to laugh, and the Idaeans laughed, and the people of the Wimahl laughed.

Before Rhenthizu even noticed that Comucomulu had disappeared, the leader and guide returned, changed entirely. His wind-tangled hair now gleamed smooth, rebraided and anointed and decorated with shell. He wore leather leggings, a necklace of enormous claws, and a woven blanket in tones of gray and white and brown across his shoulders.

"Ah well," Iakinthu said from behind Rhenthizu, "we can bring out the lily-axes some other time." In her kilt and closed vest she moved through the crowd of child-wolves and Comucomulu's people and presented him with a blue flask of transparent glass, full of precious rose oil.

"Thank you for your guidance," she said. "You cared for my ship as I would, as my captain Aranthau would. We're all grateful." She drew the stopper from the flask, inhaled the scent, touched a drop to her wrists and throat, and offered it to him.

Comucomulu inhaled.

"That is beautiful," he said.

Iakinthu stroked a drop of rose oil onto his wrist, replaced the stopper, and gave him the flask. He secreted it in a leather bag fastened to his belt.

A succulent smell enveloped Rhenthizu in powerful memories.

Wukanushu, he thought. Wukanushu, the great fish, sustenance of my people. Have I thought of it since I became an Idaean? Have I tasted it since I was a little boy?

Comucomulu led the Idaeans to a shelter, to a fire where silver sides of fish sizzled against planks.

"Wukanushu," Rhenthizu said.

Comucomulu repeated what Rhenthizu said, the word a little different from the way Rhenthizu spoke it.

"Yes," Comucomulu said.

"I remember it."

"Who could forget wukanushu?" Comucomulu said.

"I forgot many things. I hope to remember them now. Leader, guide—"

"Call me 'Grandfather.' That's who I am, to everyone of your generation."

"Grandfather," Rhenthizu said, easily using a word the Idaeans would avoid. "I will. Thank you."

"Come, sit, eat."

"I'm eager to visit my people. You said they're here—?"

"They camp farther up the Wimahl. It's too late tonight. Too dark. Tomorrow, in the morning, we'll visit."

Rhenthizu could only comply. They sat near the fire, enjoying the smell of the cooking fish, until it was ready to eat.

Protected from the rain, they feasted.

Iakinthu had trained herself to eat anything, everything, whether or not she enjoyed it. She felt about wukanushu the way Comucomulu felt about Idaean wine. It was too heavy, too strong-flavored, too rich. She wanted bread, olives, almonds...and a cup of wine. She was tired; she wanted her bed on *Flying Fish*; she wanted Aranthau beside her. She should be excited that Rhenthizu would visit his birth people soon; otherwise, why had she brought him so far? But she feared he would choose to stay with his mother and she would lose him. Maranti would lose him, or Iakinthu would lose Maranti.

I will still have Kilinkizu, she thought, dear Kilinkizu who defied her People to stay with me. She had good reason. Does Rhenthizu?

She rose, her knees creaking. Clouds gathered overhead. Rain threatened.

She sought out her companions: Rhenthizu, sitting near Comucomulu, speaking intently; Uinthi and Bridges Words, happily eating wukanushu, surrounded by younger members of Comucomulu's group; Kilinkizu, peering closely at her sketch on a piece of papyrus; Paissu with the pack of little wolves.

"It's time to bid goodnight to our new acquaintances," she said. "Paissu, to me, please."

Paissu ran to her, followed by her new friends. "Iakinthu, may they visit *Flying Fish?* They would like to see it."

"Tomorrow, if their mothers allow it," Iakinthu said, stroking Paissu's hair.

Paissu's momentary disappointment vanished in her usual good cheer. "That's better!" she said. "Easier to see, easier to climb the mast."

"That's sensible," Iakinthu said. "Paissu, would you ask Rhenthizu if he'll come back with us?"

Uinthi and Bridges Words wiped their greasy fingers on handfuls of grass and crossed the river beach to join Iakinthu at the ship's boat.

"So many new words!" Bridges Words said, happier than Iakinthu had ever seen him. "Will I learn them all before I die?"

Iakinthu laughed. "You have many, many years to learn new words," she said, "and I'll value your every year and every word." It pleased her that he smiled.

She put her arm around Uinthi's shoulders, thinking, wukanushu might be very good for my dear Uinthi.

"Will you take me to *Flying Fish?*" she asked them. "I want a familiar place to sleep."

"Of course," Uinthi said.

Kilinkizu rolled her papyrus and put away her charcoal sticks as Rhenthizu joined them.

"I'll stay on shore tonight," Rhenthizu said, "with your leave, Iakinthu. Comucomulu has things to tell me."

"Of course, my dear," she said, restraining herself from saying, Maranti will miss you. "But do you have a boat cloak to keep you from the rain?"

"I was accustomed to rain," he said, "when I was a little boy, and it would be good to get used to it again." He touched his fist to his forehead. "Sleep well."

When Rhenthizu returned to the campfire, Comucomulu had disappeared.

"He went to go to sleep," said one of Paissu's young wolf pack.

Did I offend him? Rhenthizu wondered. I told him I would say good-night to Iakinthu. I thought he understood I would come back.

"Maybe we should all do the same," he said.

"We're wolves! We hunt at night!" They all ran away in their pack, howling.

Without even a boat cloak, Rhenthizu walked along the river shore. Campfires faintly lit his way.

How far is the camp of the Akokulu? he wondered. It would be best to visit them with Comucomulu, to be properly introduced, but…

He continued walking. The fine mist changed to misty rain. His hair, his vest, his loincloth grew damp. The rain intensified. His boots squelched. He thought of Maranti, snug in wool blankets and sheepskins back on board *Flying Fish*. He wished they were sharing that warmth.

Growling startled him. Had Paissu's wolf pack followed him?

A pack of white dogs, shorter than his knee-height, ran out of the darkness to surround him, barking and growling and nipping at his boot-strings. Rhenthizu stopped.

"Hush," he said. "You'll wake people."

To his surprise, they quieted. One sniffed at his toes. Another stretched out its front legs in a play-bow, its tongue lolling. A third rolled onto its back, exposing its belly and its furry balls.

A human figure ran out of the darkness and the rain.

"Bad dogs, bad dogs!" The words were in the language of Rhenthizu's birth rather than the trade language he had spoken and listened to all day. "Come away, come away, leave him alone."

"They're all right," Rhenthizu said, a little awkward in his speech. "We were making friends."

"They're bad dogs. They should stay in their pen. They should stay out of the mud so I can spin their fur."

Her voice touched him.

"Will I help you return them?" He peered at her through the darkness, the rain, wishing for more light. All the campfires were behind her, sizzling and sparking as the rain put them out.

"You're wet and cold," she said. "Why are you away from your camp?"

"I'm becoming accustomed to rain again," he said. He searched for the right word to use to address her, failed, fell back on Idaean. "Lady, will I help you? Did I meet you with Comucomulu?" Was that why her voice sounded so familiar?

"Shoo them along, then," she said. "But why is a friend of Comucomulu helping an old slave?"

She held out a treat to one of the woolly-dogs, who snapped it up greedily and danced around her feet. Another woolly-dog shouldered in for a treat, and the first dog snarled and nipped. In a roil of white fur like a moving blanket, the woolly-dogs followed her. Rhenthizu brought up the rear, shooing them as she had asked, wishing he had a blanket made of their woven fur.

Their pen stood under a shelter of poles and reeds with eaves wide enough to keep the rain off Rhenthizu, the woolly-dog keeper, and a fire. The keeper herded the dogs into the pen and fastened the gate behind them. They ran around and around, reminding Rhenthizu of lambs. He smiled at the thought of growling lambs. They settled, and a moment later they all slept.

"Come here, get warm." The woolly-dog keeper herded him like one of her charges, taking him closer to the fire. When she poked the coals into flames, he saw her more clearly.

"Who are you?" he whispered.

"I told you, I'm an old slave. Does anyone know an old slave's name?"

He wished he did know it. He wished he remembered her name, and his own. His legs went weak, and he stumbled to the ground, kneeling before her, touching his fist to his forehead in salute, bowing his head.

"You are my mother," he whispered.

She fell utterly silent. She touched his hair. Her hand trembled, and drew back.

"Go," she said, softly, intensely. "Go!"

He raised his head. She was gone. Even her shadow had disappeared, vanished in the dark and the rain.

Rhenthizu stumbled along the river shore, back toward Comucomulu's camp. The rain fell hard, obscuring his sight, sizzling in campfires. Darkness surrounded him. He felt his way. The quiet flow of the Wimahl helped guide him. Shivering, he thought that he would become accustomed to rain more slowly than he wished.

Will I know when I reach Comucomulu's camp? he wondered. He would recognize the guide's canoe, if he could only see it.

He wanted to turn back, to try to follow his mother, to speak to her, but she had commanded him to leave her. She must have good reason. She said she was a slave. Rhenthizu had the Idaean horror of slavery, and memories of being a child at the mercy of his owners. His mother might be in danger for speaking to him.

Might I put her life at risk? Should I ask Comucomulu?

He decided against that.

A light glowed through the mist on the river: a torch, surging with each quiet slice of a paddle.

"Rhenthizu!" Uinthi's voice carried softly across the water.

"Here!" he said, keeping his voice low.

In the torchlight, Paissu waved and Uinthi let the canoe scrape gently onto the shore.

I might have walked right past it, he thought.

He joined Paissu and Uinthi, glad of familiar faces.

"We thought you would be wet," Paissu said. She and Uinthi sheltered under oiled silk. She lifted a parcel, also wrapped in oiled silk. "We brought you a cloak."

"My dearest friends," he said gratefully. "May I go back to *Flying Fish* with you?"

"Of course," Uinthi said. "I will even let you paddle."

He laughed.

They returned to the ship in silence, Rhenthizu glad of the torchlight and the exercise of paddling and the company of his friends, his new given sister of the People, his childhood companion. He could tell them what had happened when they reached the ship and could speak belowdecks without their voices carrying over the water.

If we spoke Idaean, Rhenthizu thought, would anyone understand?

But— Rhenthizu thought of Bridges Words who knew Nipunu and young Lord Murusuku who knew the trade language of Rhenthizu's own people—who could ever be sure? Best to wait.

Back on board *Flying Fish*, they went belowdecks out of the rain. Rhenthizu wrapped himself in the boat cloak even though he had stopped shivering.

Maranti looked out from the sleeping cabin.

"Did you find— Oh!" She saw Rhenthizu and smiled with relief. "My love."

They went to Kilinkizu's workroom to talk in private, doing their best to keep drops of water from spattering her drawings and the drawings of Bdarde-who-is, tied to the bulkheads. Maranti sat beside Rhenthizu and drew the cloak around them both.

"I'm all wet," he said.

"Do I care?"

He put his arm around her; she put her arm around him, sliding her hand gently across his back.

"Tell us," Uinthi said.

He told them.

"Your mother!" Maranti exclaimed. "You've found your people!"

"She said she's a slave," Uinthi said. "Would she be a slave among her own people?"

"I remember that my—" He was about to say "father," but hesitated, wanting to spare Maranti any embarrassment, wondering if Paissu would even know the word. "My people owned slaves, but they were from other tribes." He passed his hand across his eyes. Am I trying to remember? he wondered, or trying to forget?

"Rhenthizu," Uinthi said, her tone serious, "if your mother is enslaved, can she return to her people?"

"She was frightened," he said. "So frightened. Was she afraid of me?"

"She was afraid *for* you."

Rhenthizu waited.

"My brother, you're used to Idaean ideas. Iakinthu freed you and welcomed you into her family. She hopes to return you to your born family so you may choose to stay with them, if you wish it." Uinthi took a deep breath. "If your mother is known to be a slave, can she return to her own people and be accepted?"

"If we free her—"

Uinthi shrugged. "Maybe. Free her, honor her, make her wealthy. With enough gifts, enough diplomacy..."

The rain intensified, pattering onto the deck above them, trickling through the scuppers.

"Iakinthu's diplomacy," he said.

"Maybe," Uinthi said again. "She's solved many difficult encounters."

"Why would my mother fear for me?"

"She saw you. She recognized you. She knows what happened to her and to you. Everyone on this river knows by now that we're here, from a long distance, and looking for your born family. Could you return to them, in honor, if they believe you're a slave?"

"Do I look like a slave?" he asked angrily.

"You do if you take off your vest," Uinthi said quietly.

He flushed. He seldom thought of the scars, but sometimes they pulled at his back and reminded him of the bad times.

Maranti tightened her arm around him. He laid his cheek against her smooth hair. He wished he knew what to do.

"She's protecting you," Uinthi said. "So you can return to your father."

"Instead of his mother!" Maranti exclaimed.

"Maybe she hopes I'll protect her," Rhenthizu said.

"Maybe she does. But for now I hope you'll follow her caution."

"Until I know more. Until I understand more or remember more." He wondered how much he could remember from before the bad times.

The smell of wukanushu, the feeling of familiarity among Comucomulu's family...

"Good," Uinthi said, and suddenly yawned. Paissu's head drooped. Maranti yawned too, and in a moment they were all yawning.

"Time for sleep," Maranti said.

In the morning, Rhenthizu rowed Iakinthu to the river shore, accompanied by Uinthi and Paissu and Kilinkizu, all more formally dressed and protected by silken rain cloaks. Uinthi and Paissu carried their bows; Kilinkizu brought her drawing box. The rain misted across the river, obscuring the distant far bank.

Comucomulu met them at the water's edge. His grandchildren ran to Paissu and surrounded their new friend, greeting her with growls and howling.

"Be human people today," Iakinthu said gently, and they quieted to whispers.

"There you are," Comucomulu said to Rhenthizu. "I wondered where you went."

"I thought you had gone to sleep," Rhenthizu said. "So I did the same." More wukanushu cooked nearby. His mouth watered at the smell.

"Yes, indeed," Comucomulu said. "I'm older than I used to be. I like nights for sleeping." He cocked his head to peer more closely at their rain cloaks. He wore a blanket around his shoulders, woven so tightly that the rain beaded on its surface. "What are you wearing?"

"Rain cloaks, made from the silk of the Sheng," Iakinthu said. "Rhenthizu brought one for you, to thank you for your guidance." She drew out a folded rain cloak, silk dyed a brilliant blue and thickly impregnated with oil. The cloak lacked the embroidery the Sheng were so well-known for, because the holes the needles made damaged the waterproofing. She handed it to Rhenthizu who offered it to Comucomulu.

Comucomulu accepted the new gift, opened it out, held it over his head, let it droop across his shoulders. The blue silk flowed around him in the breeze.

"Beautiful, sky-colored." He glanced up, peering from beneath the edge of the silk. "On some other day than today."

"I'm glad to know," Iakinthu said, "that you sometimes have blue sky."

Rhenthizu made himself stand still and quiet. He would rather have fidgeted, demanded that Comucomulu take him to the Akokulu, asked how to free his mother. Instead, he waited for Iakinthu's diplomacy.

"Come and eat," Comucomulu said. "Then we'll visit the Akokulu camp."

Iakinthu walked along the river shore, glad of her sturdy boots. She wore a seven-tiered skirt and her best dragonfly necklace, to honor Rhenthizu and his people, but her rain cape concealed her dress and jewelry. She glanced behind her to the west, where the weather came from, and saw only more clouds.

Rhenthizu walked silently beside her. His attention was on the shelters along the shore.

He's looking for his mother, of course, she thought.

Maranti, questioned as she persisted in helping Iakinthu dress for this excursion, had told her about Rehnthizu's encounter with his enslaved mother. The encounter troubled Iakinthu. Rhenthizu's mother had reason to fear, for herself and for him.

Would her owner claim Rhenthizu, her son, captured with her, as a possession?

Rhenthizu touched her elbow and nodded toward a fence built of withes, where a pack of woolly white dogs snuffled and growled over their morning meat. The people of the camp gathered to watch them pass, curious about the strangers. Rhenthizu scanned them, but his mother remained out of sight.

Iakinthu feared he might sprint up into the camp. She took his hand. It trembled.

They passed small canoes and great canoes, carved and painted with wonderful monsters. Comucomulu nodded at the great canoes.

"Soon they'll all be filled with smoked wukanushu, food for the whole year. Everyone will go home, and I'll have a great deal of work to do to guide them all back to the sea."

"I admire your skill," Iakinthu said, "and my captain Aranthau thinks you're the most accomplished navigator he's ever met or heard of in all the world."

Comucomulu accepted the compliment stoically.

"I've heard of canoes that cross the ocean," he said.

"Their navigators are very accomplished," she said, "and they face great storms and great distances. But do they face the Wimahl?"

"Maybe I'll try crossing the ocean someday." His hand mimicked a boat crossing waves. "Guide the last great canoe out of the river, and keep going."

People paddled the small canoes upriver, slicing through the rain and mist.

"They're going to the fishing platforms. Here, we're all at peace, even if at home we're at war."

"I'm always glad of peace," Iakinthu said.

"Do your people wage war?"

"In the time of my many-greats grandmother," Iakinthu said.

"Did she win?"

"Yes."

"Did you enslave your enemies?"

"Our enemies…were annihilated."

"Ah. You are fearsome warriors."

"We prefer peace." She thought of the pirates, with a sharp stab of grief and regret for her murdered friends. *Flying Fish* had outdistanced the pirates, and she hoped they had been lost in the Sunset Sea. "That's a story for another time."

"Winter is the time for stories," Comucomulu said.

Rhenthizu stopped with a gasp. His hand gripped Iakinthu's harder.

"I recognize…"

The camp was similar to the others along the river shore. Dressed differently than Comucomulu, the people wore cloaks of closely woven bark, and conical hats of wonderful design.

The people in the camp approached Comucomulu's group, welcoming the guide and leader, curious about the visitors.

The fishing party was mostly young men and boys, with a few older women and men.

They might remember Rhenthizu, Iakinthu thought. They might be related to him. His father might be among them. If he is, the question of Rhenthizu's mother becomes even more complex.

The eldest woman greeted them. She was taller than Iakinthu, with a few strands of gray in her long black hair.

"Good morning, Comucomulu," she said. "Have you come to visit?"

"To introduce new friends to the Akokulu," he said.

He extended his hand toward the Akokulu elder. "My lady of the Moon and Water, Kuwayupituchu of the Akokulu, meet Iakinthu Gephyra of the Idaeans and her son and her attendants."

Iakinthu touched her forehead in salute. "I am very glad to meet you, Lady Kuwayupituchu," she said in the language of Rhenthizu's birth. She nodded toward Rhenthizu, Uinthi, Kilinkizu, and Paissu, speaking their names.

"Welcome," said Kuwayupituchu. "Come in out of the rain."

They crowded into the largest of the shelters, where a small fire drove off some of the damp and the smoke collected beneath the thatch.

"You should visit us at home, where we can host you properly," Kuwayupituchu said. She called for smoked fish and fresh berries.

Iakinthu decided to use the high etiquette of Pharaoh. "We are honored to be in your presence," she said. "No matter where we meet."

"Where do you come from?" Kuwayupituchu glanced from one to another of the Idaean party.

"We come from the other side of the world," Iakinthu said. "The other side of the Sunset Sea." She smiled. "Uinthi might call it the Sunrise Sea."

Uinthi laughed. "The Maisusutha have another name for it, but the sun does rise from the sea, where I come from."

"Are you Nipunu?" Kuwayupituchu asked in a doubtful tone. "Are you Sheng?"

"I'm Idaean, from Fair Island. Uinthi is from the Maisusutha. Kilinkizu and young Paissu are from the People, the most accomplished horse-riders of the world, and Rhenthizu —"

"Rhenthizu is one of us," Kuwayupituchu said. "Though his name is unfamiliar to me." Her pause invited him to explain.

"I was lost when I was very little," Rhenthizu said, his voice quiet. "I lost my name in the wilderness."

"That happens sometimes," Kuwayupituchu said, "when you're lost and raised by sea wolves. You may have to return to the wilderness of the sea to find it."

Iakinthu was content to replace the slavers with wolves, an altogether more acceptable group of beings. Sea wolves were new to her, but she could imagine Rhenthizu running and swimming with them.

As she had fallen back on the etiquette of Pharaoh, she took up a metaphorical way of speaking.

"Rhenthizu is my honored given child, given to me by the sea wolves and brought up in my household." She smiled at him and took his hand. "He wished to visit his birthplace, his birth-people, so I've brought him."

"A long journey," Kuwayupituchu said.

"The longest I've ever been on, and it's the business of Gephyra of Kunusu to go on long journeys. This journey is my pride and my pleasure."

Kuwayupituchu looked approving. "Do you know your clan?" she asked Rhenthizu.

"My clan is Idaea, by way of wolves."

"We come from wolves," Kuwayupituchu said, "so it's good they found you. Now, if it had been bears…we might never have seen you again."

"I'm glad it was wolves instead of bears."

Iakinthu could practically feel Paissu, behind her, yearning to howl.

Kuwayupituchu delicately picked up a berry and savored it.

"Tell me," she said, "what is a rider, and what is a horse? Is it a kind of canoe?"

Kilinkizu made a few quick strokes with her charcoal on papyrus. Iakinthu caught her breath. The drawing was, unmistakably, Issiia, on Paissu-who-was-Minnow's pony Surefoot.

"Oh," Paissu whispered, looking over her shoulder, and Iakinthu felt the same.

Iakinthu passed the drawing to Kuwayupituchu.

"A noble creature, and very patient," Kuwayupituchu said. "And a beautiful child."

"My granddaughter," Iakinthu said, smiling with pride. "A given child to the People, as Paissu is a given child from the People to me."

"I gave Surefoot to her," Paissu said, "so she can keep up with Grandmother Celestial Wind and the other People."

"She'll take good care of her." Iakinthu put her arm around Paissu and gave her a gentle hug.

"Did you bring horses with you? I would like to see horses."

"Our journey was too long," Iakinthu said. "A horse would be most unhappy on board a ship, without a place to run or growing grass to eat."

"I'll imagine the creature and remember your drawing," Kuwayupituchu said to Kilinkizu.

"You may have it, if you like it," Kilinkizu said.

"Thank you," Kuwayupituchu said, pleased.

"Will you visit my ship, my *Flying Fish*?" Iakinthu gestured downriver. "It's only a little distance, or it will come to us."

"Does it fly?"

"It's named after a fish that flies."

"Creatures that consent to carry you on their back, fish that fly— I'd like to see such things."

Iakinthu thought it would be interesting to have a given child who was her own age. That could make the relationships as complicated as they were with the People.

"You might travel with us, if you liked."

"To the other side of the world?" Kuwayupituchu frowned thoughtfully. "Thank you for the invitation. I'll consider it, with advice from the other elders." She glanced outside the shelter. "We'll have rain all day, unless Comucomulu consents to change it for us."

"I did that yesterday," he said. "I'm tired. We're accustomed to rain."

And so Kuwayupituchu sent her young men off to fish, though they grumbled—behind her back—that they wanted to see the giant canoe everyone was talking about.

"Later," she said, perfectly aware of what they were saying. "The ship will wait. The fish will swim past your fishing spot, and spawn, and die. Catch some of them first." She put on her wonderful patterned basket-hat, gestured them back out into the rain, and set off for *Flying Fish*.

Again, Rhenthizu looked for his mother as they passed her camp; again, she remained out of sight. Again, Iakinthu took his hand and squeezed it with reassurance.

Kuwayupituchu led the way along the shore, striding along, cheerfully greeting everyone they met. Iakinthu and Comucomulu could barely keep up with her, and the younger members of the party stayed behind her out of respect.

"*Those* people," she said when they had passed the camp of the woolly-dogs. "If I met *those* people anywhere else, I'd kill them." She spoke in an entirely matter-of-fact way.

"Are they…unfriendly?" Iakinthu asked.

"We're at war. Always."

Rhenthizu passed the woolly-dog camp, finding it difficult to maintain his composure. Trust Iakinthu, he said to himself. She will help find a way to rescue my mother.

Their party arrived at Comucomulu's camp, where *Flying Fish* lay at anchor off the river shore, and where several people waited for Comucomulu, to ask for his guidance out of the Wimahl's treacherous mouth.

"I must go," he said, sighing heavily. "Can I ever do what I like? I must help all these people." He climbed into his graceful canoe and paddled away, toward a trio of enormous cargo canoes waiting to begin their journeys home.

Kuwayupituchu watched him go. "If I give him a great present, he may train one of my children to be a navigator."

"That would be a wonderful thing," Iakinthu said. "He dances with the water."

"A handsome way of putting it," Kuwayupituchu said. "He would like that description. May I have permission to repeat it to him? May I tell him you said it?"

"Of course, if it would please him."

Flying Fish's boat scraped against the river shore. Aranthau, having seen his companions return, had come to collect them.

"Can we all fit?" Iakinthu asked.

"If we're friendly," Aranthau said, smiling. He moved over so Rhenthizu could take the other oar, and they rowed back to *Flying Fish*, the ship's boat heavy in the water.

They climbed to the deck. Bdarde ran to Aranthau. "Aranthau, Aranthau, Aranthau, why do you always leave me behind?"

Rhenthizu sighed. He wished he liked the boy better.

I suppose I should try to learn his language, Rhenthizu thought. But it's so harsh.

"What's that noise?" Kuwayupituchu asked. "Is that a language? It sounds like a moose calf bellowing."

Rhenthizu stifled a laugh, but it was true. The language of Rhenthizu's birth, the language Kuwayupituchu was speaking, sounded like the soft twitter of birds, while the language Bdarde was speaking did sound like bellowing. Young, untrained bellowing.

"Do you understand?" Aranthau said to Bdarde.

Kilinkizu understood, and blushed with embarrassment.

Kilinkizu's mood changed. Kuwayupituchu had made her happy by appreciating her drawing, and she had collected a pouch full of flowers and leaves and stones that she was eager to draw. Now she looked sad, and embarrassed. Then she squared her shoulders and said, "Bdarde, will you help me draw these leaves and stones?"

He looked from her to Aranthau, who gestured toward Kilinkizu. "You may show me your drawings later," he said, "if your mother allows it."

With a glance over his shoulder toward Aranthau, Bdarde quietly followed Kilinkizu.

A moment later, Maranti ran up the ladder from belowdecks and came to Rhenthizu. He took her under his rain cape. She hugged him. He put his arms around her, breathing in her rose-tinted scent, basking in her warmth.

"I missed you so," she whispered.

"And I, you." It was true, though they had been apart only since dawn.

"Come out of the rain," Iakinthu said, "and meet Lady Kuwayupituchu, of Rhenthizu's clan."

Maranti tensed in Rhenthizu's arms. "Your clan!"

Maranti feared that he would choose to stay here with them. Fear was so foreign to her that he was startled to see it. He accompanied her to the stern cabin.

"Eldest Daughter," Iakinthu said formally, "please welcome Lady Kuwayupituchu of the Akokulu, from whom Rhenthizu was lost, then saved by wolves."

"I'm honored to meet you," Maranti said. "Rhenthizu is my dearest friend and companion."

Kuwayupituchu gazed at her, and Rhenthizu had the instant impression that his new kinswoman knew everything.

"You are Iakinthu's eldest daughter?"

"I'm Eldest Daughter of the Idaeans. My greatest pride and honor was to be elected to the position."

"She graces our journey with her presence," Iakinthu said.

Iakinthu showed Kuwayupituchu to the camp chairs in the stern cabin. Iakinthu's companions and Kuwayupituchu's people crowded in. Rhenthizu was so tired from staying awake most of the night that his vision sparkled around the edges.

Iakinthu offered Maranti the center chair, out of respect; Maranti declined it out of equal respect, and the understanding that Iakinthu and Kuwayupituchu must negotiate, perhaps to decide on the possibilities of Rhenthizu's future. She guided Rhenthizu to the chair beside Iakinthu and sat beside him. He was glad of the warmth of her hand.

As if on command, Murusuku appeared with a tray of almonds and olives and a flask of wine.

"My young Lord Murusuku of the Nipunu anticipates my wishes," Iakinthu said, by way of introduction.

Murusuku bowed in acknowledgment. Kuwayupituchu nodded in reply. "I heard about you. You've joined the Idaeans, I see."

"I'm honored to be accepted among them."

"And lucky," Kuwayupituchu said.

"Comucomulu enjoyed the almonds," Iakinthu said. "He preferred to leave aside the wine."

Kuwayupituchu drank some, pretending to like it.

"Iakinthu Gephyra," Murusuku said, "the lady might like cacao."

"An excellent idea." Iakinthu said, surprised, to Lord Murusuku, "You know of cacao? How to prepare it?"

"I do. The water's hot. I'll bring it."

They sat through the performance of preparing cacao as Murusuku poured it from flask to flask till it frothed.

"A little chili only." Murusuku sipped from the cup, handed it to Iakinthu, who sipped from it as well and politely offered it to Kuwayupituchu, who raised one eyebrow and accepted it.

She sipped and licked her lips thoughtfully. "I like that," she said. "It sparkles on my tongue." She handed the cup to Maranti, who took a gulp rather than sipping it. Rhenthizu pretended to drink the stuff.

"Cacao is from the south," Iakinthu said, "a gift from Lady Jaguar, who also was kind enough to allow Bridges Words to accompany us." She nodded toward Bridges Words, who had come to gather with all the companions of *Flying Fish* in a half-circle around the stern cabin.

Soon everyone was passing around cups of cacao.

Rhenthizu noticed that Kuwayupituchu chewed on an almond before sipping from the cacao cup. He tried that himself and found the combination more pleasing than cacao alone. Perhaps if he added some honey...

He considered the combination of olives and cacao and decided that would be a mistake.

"May I ask your advice, Lady Kuwayupituchu?" Iakinthu said after a polite interval.

Kuwayupituchu finished the last of the cacao in the cup and allowed Murusuku to pour more.

"You may," she replied.

"Rhenthizu, my given child, has gifts for his family."

"Ah. Is he wealthy?"

Iakinthu gestured around her, at *Flying Fish*. "A share of our trade belongs to him. He'll have presents when he meets his family, for himself and for them. For you." She opened the pouch on her hip and drew out a scarf of delicate Changthangi wool from farthest Hind, dyed with the finest, richest shell-purple. It lay weightless across her hands as she offered it to Lady Kuwayupituchu, who accepted it graciously.

"I wear mine around my neck. It keeps off the cold wonderfully well."

Lady Kuwayupituchu stroked it and wrapped it around her throat.

"Light as a cloud," she said, "and the color of sunset."

Iakinthu smiled, liking the description.

"We must speak together," Kuwayupituchu said.

Iakinthu understood: she wanted privacy.

Aranthau understood as well. "Come and let us show our guests around *Flying Fish*," he said to the companions, and Bridges Words translated his Idaean into the trade language.

Aranthau led the guests away, with Bridges Words to speak for him, leaving Lady Kuwayupituchu unattended, with Iakinthu, Rhenthizu, Maranti.

Lady Kuwayupituchu drew closer.

"I know who you are," she said to Rhenthizu.

Rhenthizu straightened in surprise.

"You're the right age. *Those people*—" She said the words in the same contemptuous tone she had used to refer to the woolly-dog group. "—raided our village. We killed as many of them as they killed of us. When we drove them off, some of our people were...lost. Now I know they were saved by the sea wolves." She nodded toward Rhenthizu. "You are one of those lost people."

Kuwayupituchu accepted Iakinthu's metaphorical explanation of Rhenthizu's presence as her given child, given to her by sea wolves. They were all content to leave slavers out of the story entirely.

Iakinthu drew another gift from her pouch: a blue silk bag containing a dragonfly pin whose wings trembled delicately at any motion. She leaned toward Kuwayupituchu and fastened the dragonfly to the new scarf.

Kuwayupituchu touched the trembly wings and laughed with delight. "It might fly away at any moment," she said.

She paused, then turned to Rhenthizu and spoke to him again.

"I'll take you to our village. Your father will be glad to see you, after so long," she said. "And your mother..." She hesitated. "Perhaps she's still living with the sea wolves."

"Thank you, Lady," Rhenthizu said, his voice carefully steady. "I remember only a little of that time. I wish I knew more...about my mother. I wish I could remember my name."

"You want a new name," she said. "You want to forget that older time."

Iakinthu thought, This has been one of my better negotiations.

She knew what Rhenthizu's name would be. He would go out alone, he would fast, he would wait—so much easier to make use of poppy, she thought, but the people in this land prefer the harder task—and return to her.

He would be Sea Wolf.

Chapter Thirty-One

Lady Kuwayupituchu departed for her camp, taking Rhenthizu with her. "He's invited to join a fishing party," she said cheerfully. "His father was a great fisherman in his youth, so he must learn to spear wukanushu. And in a few days, we'll go home with our exchanges, with our food for the winter, and with Rhenthizu."

Maranti watched him go, disconsolate.

"Will I lose him, Iakinthu?" she asked.

"It's possible," Iakinthu said, wishing she could dissemble for Maranti's benefit. "It's always possible, when I return a given child. Uinthi went back to the Maisusutha —"

"To explore for you. To search out Rhenthizu's people!"

"Yes. But I missed Uinthi so. As I miss Issiia. As Kunusu misses you." She kept any hint of scolding out of her voice.

"Kilinkizu stayed with us," Maranti said hopefully.

"I'm grateful to her for making that choice. What would I do without her?"

Belowdecks, Iakinthu wrapped herself in a dry cloak. The relentless rain had penetrated even the heavy oiled silk of the cloak she had worn that morning. Soon all their clothes would be soaked.

Outside, the ship's boat bumped gently against the side of *Flying Fish*, returning from Lady Kuwayupituchu's camp. Uinthi knocked on the ship's flank.

Iakinthu returned to the deck.

"Are you ready to go to shore?" Uinthi held the oars, and Paissu sat in the bow as navigator, as lookout.

"The boat is working hard today," Iakinthu said.

"So are we!" Uinthi exclaimed, smiling.

Iakinthu walked along the river shore toward the woolly-dog camp. Uinthi and Paissu followed with carry-bags full of gifts. Iakinthu wondered which of her offerings would be welcomed or even acceptable; the people here so often surprised her.

They stopped several paces from the camp, near the dog pen. The little creatures rushed toward them, barking frantically, pushing their black noses through the withes.

Paissu howled softly, and the woolly-dogs ran to the other side of the pen, yelping. Paissu laughed.

"I wish they were sea wolves," she said. "I'd like to meet the sea wolves."

"I hope we might," Iakinthu said.

"Wolves run with the People," Paissu said. "They can run almost as fast as a horse. But they're land wolves. I wonder how fast the sea wolves can swim?"

"We'll find out," Iakinthu said, hoping that she could avoid swimming with the sea wolves, wondering if they would welcome Rhenthizu. Claiming to know them could prove dangerous.

In the shadows behind the woolly-dog pen, a woman stood silent and watchful. She pulled a plain woolen cloak over her head to conceal her face.

The other people in the camp noticed their visitors and came down to the river shore to greet them.

"You are strangers," said a young woman acting as leader of the group.

"Strangers who hope to become friends." Iakinthu took a cup painted with bluebirds, similar to the one that had pleased Comucomulu, from Paissu's carry-bag. She offered it. "I am Iakinthu Gephyra, of Fair Island."

The young leader said her name.

"I'm glad to meet you, Alukuwusu," Iakinthu said.

Alukuwusu repeated her name. Iakinthu tried again.

Alukuwusu smiled. "That will do, I suppose. Iakidthu Gephyra."

Iakinthu found the accent charming.

Alukuwusu grew solemn. "You are friends with Kuwayupituchu."

"I understand that everyone is friends, here on the Wimahl shore."

"Everyone is at peace, which is different from being friends."

"Ah. May we all be at peace, then?"

Alukuwusu hesitated, accepted the cup, and looked at it closely. "These birds are new to me."

"They live on Fair Island."

"Do they sing?"

"Beautifully."

"Come out of the rain," Alukuwusu said.

"We're becoming accustomed to the rain," Uinthi and Paissu said together. They laughed, and Alukuwusu joined in. Iakinthu smiled, but her new cloak had already begun to fail at keeping her dry. Her knees ached.

Alukuwusu led them to a shelter, where a small fire drove off some of the damp. They walked past the shadowed figure behind the woolly-dog pen without acknowledging her presence.

She must be Rhenthizu's mother, Iakinthu thought. She must be. Is she looking for Rhenthizu? Yearning to see him, or fearing to see him?

Alukuwusu offered Iakinthu a beautifully carved stool. She sat, gratefully, though she wished she could pick it up and inspect the powerful images.

She let the damp cloak slide from her shoulders. Paissu came to her side and put her arm across her shoulders. "You're chilled, Iakinthu," she said.

"I'm accustoming myself to the rain," Iakinthu said, trying to smile.

"The weather is usually better this time of year," Alukuwusu said. "You must have a blanket and some food." With a gesture she produced both: great slabs of wukanushu straight from the fire, on a trencher carved and painted with fish; and a blanket woven with energetic geometric designs.

Iakinthu found the fish rather overwhelming, but she was glad it was hot, and the blanket was the equal of Fair Island wool.

"Wonderfully soft," she said, stroking it. "And warm. Thank you, Alukuwusu."

"You must have it as a gift," Alukuwusu said. "A fishing camp is the wrong place for Potlatch, but a good place for giving small presents." She looked again at the bluebird cup.

"Is a fishing camp a good place for trade?"

"Yes," Alukuwusu said. "This time of year, we came to trade for wukanushu. We go home with enough for the year."

"How is this made?" Iakinthu asked, stroking the blanket again.

Alukuwusu glanced at the woolly-dog pen. "Our dogs have the best fur of anyone's," she said with pride. "We bring them here to feed them fresh fish, which makes their fur cast off the wet."

"Back at home, and on the sea, I'll be grateful to have a cloak that casts off the wet."

"Will you trade for cloaks?"

"Would you trade for woolly-dogs?"

Alukuwusu frowned thoughtfully. "Then would you need our cloaks?"

"We come from so far away," Iakinthu said. "How can I know when we might return? My cloak might wear out before then."

"You would have to be very hard on it," Alukuwusu said, pretending to be offended.

"I'll use it as gently as I can." Iakinthu stroked it a third time, appreciatively. She imagined a flock of woolly-dogs rushing across a field at her family's farm, imagined Terebinthu tossing his head at their barking, gamboling with them the way he gamboled with Woof. She smiled at the thought.

"I'd consider a trade," Alukuwusu said. "They do, after all, have puppies."

In the end, the negotiation for a dozen woolly-dogs was more difficult than the negotiation for Rhenthizu's mother. Iakinthu drove an easy bargain, but drew it out to avoid suspicion of her true intentions. When they had agreed, Uinthi and Paissu had empty carry-bags, and Iakinthu had promised three copper ingots. She suspected Alukuwusu coveted the copper most, though she disguised her preferences well.

"We are agreed," Alukuwusu said. "My slaves will come for the copper."

"We are agreed." Iakinthu added, "May we hire the caretaker long enough to learn how best to keep the woolly-dogs?"

"Oh, she's only a slave," Alukuwusu said. "You may have her."

The woolly-dogs ran around the deck yapping and growling till Rhenthizu's mother spoke to them sharply. They gathered around her feet and quieted into a living, breathing rug. Bdarde came running out.

"I heard dogs!" he said, sounding delighted. "Dogs—" He stopped, staring. "Are they *puppies?*"

"They're dogs," Iakinthu said.

"They're too small," Bdarde said.

Iakinthu felt glad that he was speaking their own trade language instead of the trade language of Rhenthizu's kin.

"Who *are* you?" Rhenthizu's mother said. It was the first time she had spoken since Alukuwusu gave her to Iakinthu, since Alukuwusu's people paddled away with their canoe low in the water for the weight of copper.

Remembering her mistake with Bridges Words, determined to do better this time, Iakinthu said, "I am Iakinthu Gephyra, of Fair Island, and you are free."

"Free?"

"You were Alukuwusu's slave. All my companions are free."

"I'll always be a slave. Once you are enslaved, you are always a slave. Even if you're free."

"Are you a slave if you're rescued from the sea wolves? If you come back to your home wealthy and honored, with your grown son who is a prince of another country?"

Rhenthizu's mother whispered something. Iakinthu suspected it was Rhenthizu's name, but she agreed with Kuwayupituchu that his childhood name was best forgotten.

"Where is he?"

"He's gone with Kuwayupituchu's fishing party to learn to spear wukanushu," Iakinthu said. Suddenly she felt exhausted. She drew the cloak of woolly-dog fur tighter around her.

"Please," said Rhenthizu's mother, "tell me who you are."

Iakinthu took her belowdecks, where it was warm and dry, and told her who she was. And who Rhenthizu was.

Rhenthizu carried an enormous wukanushu, slung in a net, up the side of *Flying Fish*. As a guest of the fishing party, he had speared it himself. He looked forward to cooking it and sharing it with the companions. His stomach growled. His clothes and hair were soaked.

The young men, naked, had stood on wooden platforms projecting over the river. Rhenthizu had hesitated, then flung off his kilt and finally his vest.

He waited for any comment about the scars on his back. One of the fishing party glanced, then quickly looked away.

Doing his best to believe in his own story, Rhenthizu said, "Wolves play rough."

"A tattoo would preserve the touch of the sea wolves for you. My auntie, back home, could make a superb design."

"I would be honored," Rhenthizu said, meaning it.

He reached the deck of *Flying Fish* and stopped, astonished. A pack of little woolly-dogs slept together in a makeshift enclosure. He looked around. The stern cabin was empty, its canopy sagging with rain. He dropped the fish, the net, the fish spears that his new friends—his new kin—had given him. He slid down the ladder. Belowdecks, he blinked while his vision got used to the dim light. Low voices, laughter, came from the sleeping cabin.

He stopped in the doorway. All the companions—Idaeans born and given, the Nipunu lords, Bridges Words—sat together on the sleeping platforms.

His mother sat among them.

She saw him. She rose. She took a hesitant step toward him.

He crossed the cabin, joined her, embraced her.

"My mother," he said in his birth language.

"My son," she replied.

Chapter Thirty-Two

"You must have new names. You must visit the sea wolves and receive their approval to return with us." Kuwayupituchu said. "If they agree, you may return to our village." She and Iakinthu had embraced the idea that Rhenthizu and his mother had joined the sea wolves, who had helped raise him then allowed him to be a given child to Iakinthu.

"But who was given child to the sea wolves?" Rhenthizu asked.

"I suppose we'll find out when we meet them," Iakinthu said, wondering if perhaps they would find an Idaean sheepdog swimming happily with the sea wolves. Woof sometimes bounded into the sea, though she seldom got her thick long hair completely wet. Iakinthu tried to remember seeing Woof swim instead of only standing in the gentle waves and barking at seaweed.

It was time to seek out Comucomulu and ask him to guide *Flying Fish* across the river bar, back to the sea.

"Mother of Rhenthizu," she said, "will you help me choose suitable gifts for Comucomulu?"

The great canoe of Kuwayupituchu accompanied *Flying Fish* along the coast. Rhenthizu helped paddle, such a different experience from that of rowing. He joined in the chants. The sea sprayed over him; the rain washed away the salt. The tall stark headlands and crescent beaches and dense forests passed them by. Elk herds crossed grassy dunes.

Flying Fish sailed like a ghost, half-hidden by spray and mist and the ever-falling rain. Whenever the mist cleared for a moment, Paissu waved from her lookout perch, or Maranti stood barely shielded by the stern cabin's canopy. Rhenthizu wished she would go where it was warm and dry.

Kuwayupituchu sat in the canoe's stern, wrapped in furs, her gaze as sharp as that of the creatures carved into the bow of the canoe. Sometimes, when another paddler took Rhenthizu's place, she patted the bench next to her, and he climbed over the mounds of smoked fish to sit by her side in silence.

The great canoe lay much nearer the water's surface than the deck of *Flying Fish*, exposing its passengers to the chop of the sea.

The gush of a spouting whale cut through the chanting. A black dorsal fin sliced up through the water, then another, and another. Black whales, their sides white-splashed, surrounded the canoe. Rhenthizu gasped. Though these creatures were smaller than the southern whales that had passed them, they swam much faster, much closer, and had bigger teeth.

One spouted an armslength away. It dove. Its black-and-white body glided beneath the canoe.

The paddlers shouted in excitement. One youth grabbed up a spear.

"Would you spear a sea wolf while it played?" Kuwayupituchu said, just loud enough to be heard. "Besides, this part of the sea belongs to others."

The spear fell with a clatter.

The sea wolves spouted again, arched into and out of the water, and sped away.

"Sea wolf?" Rhenthizu whispered. He had understood the sea wolves to be wolves. He imagined these sea wolves taking him on their backs across the Sunset Sea, all the way to become Iakinthu's given child. He preferred that story to his memories.

"These are the sea wolves of the sea," Kuwayupituchu said, understanding his confusion. "Your visit is to the red sea wolves, who move between the land and the sea. We call them sea wolves of the land."

That evening as the sun dimmed toward the horizon, they reached a beautiful rocky cove between tall headlands. The paddlers drove the canoe gently onto the round beach rocks. *Flying Fish* anchored just offshore and dispatched the ship's boat to join them. Uinthi helped Rhenthizu's mother to dry land.

Wet land, Rhenthizu corrected himself, embracing her. Does it always rain in the land of my home?

"This is the territory of the red sea wolves," Kuwayupituchu said. "The sea wolves of land. They allow us to visit, as we allow them to travel past our villages. We build longhouses in our land. They build dens in theirs."

Rhenthizu was glad to know that this stretch of beach lacked war canoes to chase *Flying Fish* and demand the return of the Nipunu lords.

"Will we go back to *Flying Fish* for the night?" Rhenthizu asked. "I miss Maranti."

"As she misses you," said Uinthi. "Lady Kuwayupituchu, shall Rhenthizu go back to *Flying Fish*?"

"He wants his new name," Kuwayupituchu said. "And he might as well find it now."

A squall of rain spattered them. Lady Kuwayupituchu's companions had already gathered driftwood to start a fire, to get warm, to cook wukanushu. Rhenthizu's stomach growled.

Rhenthizu's mother walked up the beach, past the pile of driftwood, toward the dunes and the line of dark trees.

Kuwayupituchu pointed. Along the crest of the dunes, a group of small wolves stood watching, their fur red in the fading light.

"They welcome you," Kuwayupituchu said.

The wolves disappeared into the forest.

"Mother...?" Rhenthizu called.

"I, too, need a new name," she said.

Rhenthizu shivered. The tall spruce's boughs drooped nearly to the ground, dripping constantly; he sat on dry needles, leaning against the tree's trunk, breathing its scent, protected from the rain but cold. He wondered how long till daybreak. The sun would have to rise some way above the horizon before its light would touch the western edge of the forest, if its light could penetrate the endless clouds.

His stomach growled. His quest required a fast, so he had walked past the fire and the companions of Kuwayupituchu who teased him and offered him bits of smoked fish. He laughed, too, and waved them off, however much he wanted to accept the food.

He wished for the sun and light of Fair Island; he wished for bread and wine and olives. He wished for a fire, a warm boat cloak, the touch of Maranti's hand. He sighed.

In the distance, the red sea wolves howled. Their song raised his hair.

I wish I had known you, he thought. I wish...

He reminded himself that the wolves had given him to Iakinthu. He imagined the long journey with the wolves, who occasionally, inadvertently, scratched his back to blood, but who fed his toddler self and snarled at the approach of bobcat or cougar or bear looking for a small tasty meal. He allowed his fantasies to erase the memories of the real journey.

For three days, he sat beneath the spruce tree and dozed and dreamed and fantasied.

On the evening of the third day, dizzy with hunger, he walked along a narrow trail through the forest. Salal bushes crackled as he passed, breaking the eerie singing silence. A fallen tree lay covered with moss, saplings sprouting from its surface. Its death had created a space where sunlight could touch the ground, where bushes and moss and ferns now grew, where the saplings of great trees would soon sprout. He surprised a deer, which bounded away, tail flashing.

Rhenthizu sat on the soft moss of the mother log. Sunset barely penetrated. A patch of light touched his feet.

An animal flowed out of the forest, into the light.

It was the most beautiful creature he had ever seen, surpassing the grace of the horses of the People, the elegance of Mother Moon's serpents, the strength of Iakinthu's Terebinthu. It moved like water. The sunset light shined its black fur.

"Hello, creature," he said.

It rose on its hind legs. It stood, and rose and rose, till it was taller than he was, and it shared its name with him.

By the time he reached camp, full darkness lay across the forest, the dunes, the beach. The fire glowed.

The rain stopped.

He made himself walk steadily, however shaky his legs.

His mother sat on a driftlog by the fire. The low flames made the shadows of the bare tree roots quiver like many-fingered hands.

She gestured; he sat beside her. She handed him a piece of smoked fish. He ate it.

"Thank you," he said, feeling better.

"Who are you?"

"I am Fisher."

She smiled. "A rare name, from a rare being. A good name."

"Who are you?" Fisher asked.

"The wolves came to me that first night," she said. "I saw their eyes, glowing, from what light who can say? They licked my face and lay near me, warm as fire. They brought me fish and berries, and showed me the stream where I could drink." She smiled. "Mother Wolf, red as sunset, showed me her puppies, and I told her about my woolly-dogs and my lost son, brought back to me in health and strength." She patted his hand and squeezed his fingers. "Mother Wolf shared her name with me. I am Red Sea Wolf."

Rhenthizu — I must remember to be Fisher, he thought — squeezed her hand in response.

"We are going home," Red Sea Wolf said. "Will you tell your companions who you are?"

Fisher stood, pulled a burning branch from the fire, and walked down the beach. The sea's gentle waves spread across the sand. He waved the torch. An answering light came from *Flying Fish*; Uinthi glided toward him in his canoe.

The canoe kissed the sand. He pushed it around, climbed in, careful of its bark skin, and took one of the paddles. He and Uinthi returned to *Flying Fish* in silence.

All the companions waited on the deck of the ship. Maranti was first to greet him, then Iakinthu and Paissu, then Aranthau, Bdarde a shadow behind him, and Fisher was surrounded by all the companions of *Flying Fish*. He and Maranti stood in side-by-side embrace.

Iakinthu looked up at him. When did I grow so much taller than she? he wondered. She's always been a towering figure to me.

She smiled at him and brushed her hand across the top of his head where his hair was growing out.

"Who are you?" she asked him.

"I am Fisher."

She blinked in momentary surprise, then collected herself. "Welcome, Fisher, my twice-given child."

"Fisher, my love," said Maranti.

"And the mother of Rhenthizu, the mother of Fisher?"

"She is Red Sea Wolf."

Iakinthu laughed and wept. "Two wonderful names!" She smiled. "Go, sleep, both of you. Maranti hardly rested while you were gone."

Maranti took Fisher's hand. Together they went belowdecks.

Paissu climbed the mast. Full dark enclosed her. She considered the last few days. Maranti and Iakinthu had begun to despair of Rhenthizu's return, but Paissu had known he would find his name in the correct way.

She wished she had gone into the forest, too, to find a new and more grown-up name, but Iakinthu tasked her to stay with Maranti.

Some other time, Paissu said to herself. Can one of the People have too many names?

Strangely enough, Paissu felt shy of Rhenthizu now that he was Fisher. Is he still my given brother? she asked herself.

She felt less shy of Rhenthizu's — Fisher's — mother. Perhaps it was that now she had her own name, a wonderful name, too, which had taken away her fear and shame.

Splashing below broke through her reflections. Bdarde had jumped into the sea, seeking attention. Kilinkizu and Aranthau dove in after him. The sea shone with ghostly light. It covered Kilinkizu when she rose to breathe, creating a sea goddess. On her third breath she came up with Bdarde in her grasp.

He's glowing, too, Paissu thought, but he's a little sea demon. Then she thought of his drawings, tied to Kilinkizu's wall beside Paissu's own flowing script.

I'm glad he likes something, she thought.

Reluctantly, Bdarde climbed the rope up the ship's side. Kilinkizu and Aranthau followed.

"You should leave me with the sea people!" Bdarde dripped a puddle of luminescent water.

Iakinthu wrapped him in a boat cloak, then made to do the same with Kilinkizu.

"Am I cold?" Kilinkizu said. "The water felt warm."

"The water is freezing!" Iakinthu said. "Did I ever feel such cold water as the Untamable Ocean?"

"I saw him," Kilinkizu said, staring, squinting, at Bdarde. "Underwater, I saw him."

"He's covered with sea-light," Iakinthu said. "As are you." She drew a dipper of fresh water from the water-jug and held it for Kilinkizu to wash off the salt and the glow.

"I saw him clearly," Kilinkizu said.

Paissu understood. Kilinkizu, on land, in air, was going blind. Underwater, she could see. Paissu questioned how this was possible, but if Kilinkizu said it, Paissu believed it.

"Too bad," Bdarde said. "If you were blind, I would have got away."

The adults stared at him in shocked silence.

"You would have drowned," Iakinthu said, nearly losing her infinite patience. Aranthau looked as if he might pick the boy up and throw him back over the side, as Smoke Stingray had done. He turned and walked away. Bdarde made as if to follow, but Kilinkizu put one hand on his shoulder and gazed at him in silent disappointment.

Paissu was sorry Bdarde was too young to challenge. She was sure any of the People could best any of his house at wrestling, or riding, or archery, but it had to be fair; they had to be well-matched. She muffled a giggle at the idea of an archery competition with Bdarde. One of the People half his age would beat him at archery. She wondered what he had been brought up to do by the pirate Kilinkizu had speared. He must know how to do something.

"My father should have killed you," Bdarde said to Kilinkizu. "They said you were disobedient, which meant I would be disobedient too, so they beat me. Did I ever cry? I was always obedient. I was always respectful. To my *father*."

"Speak in a civilized manner," Aranthau said, his back still turned. Bdarde looked, despite his protestations, like he might cry.

Kilinkizu did cry. Tears streaming down her face, she fell to her knees and embraced the boy, who stood stiff and angry.

Iakinthu stroked her wet hair.

"I was disobedient," Kilinkizu said to Bdarde, holding his shoulders and looking him in the eye. "I *was* disobedient. My disobedience saved me. My disobedience created you."

Horror dawned. Bdarde shook off her embrace and ran away into the darkness. Paissu waited for another splash, another angry shout. Instead, Aranthau sighed and followed him.

Iakinthu sat on the deck beside Kilinkizu.

"Tell me," she said.

Kilinkizu took a deep breath, then breathed out fast and hard.

"When the pirate king took me...I told you I was happy and proud. Could I make him happy? Only cruelty made him happy. He counted my days, waiting for me to stop bleeding."

Iakinthu gave a short cry of laughter. "What men count women's days? That's women's business."

"He wanted a son. He said I was taking too long. Wasting his valuable seed. He threatened to give me to one of his men. Could they be any worse? Maybe they could."

Paissu stayed very still, very quiet, afraid that if they noticed her they would send her out of earshot.

"One night I stole away. I ran to the beach. Did I mean to drown myself? *Can* I drown myself? I love the sea. The sea embraces me. Then I heard the singing. I returned at every chance. Sometimes they caught me—" She hesitated. She shrugged away the memory. "The singer came to me, walking right out of the water, glowing like the moon." She sang a few notes, making Paissu shiver.

Did Fire-from-Cold-Ashes ever sing? Paissu asked herself.

"I loved him. I *loved* him." She shrugged again. "And then the pirate king moved camp, to lay waste to some other village, inland and far from the sea.

"And I had Bdarde. And the pirate king was..." Her tone changed, to contempt. "...He was very proud." She glanced toward the bow of *Flying*

Fish, where Bdarde had fled, where the boy's voice and Aranthau's deep soft words alternated.

"What Bdarde could have been..." She stopped. "Maybe he *will* go back to the sea."

Iakinthu stroked her hair again. She understood.

"Go, sleep," Iakinthu said. "Today has been long." She glanced up at Paissu. "You, too, little Paissu. Time for sleep."

Chapter Thirty-Three

Fisher held the steering oar steady. Paissu stood watch. Iakinthu and Maranti and Red Sea Wolf sat in the shelter of the stern cabin. Fisher's lover and his born mother and his given mother spoke softly together. Iakinthu translated. Maranti and Red Sea Wolf tried out words of each other's language. Aranthau surveyed the sea from the bow of *Flying Fish*.

The rain faded to a damp mist. Clouds loomed over the sea and the land. *Flying Fish* followed the great canoe of Kuwayupituchu, full of Fisher's new friends, toward Fisher's born home.

Fisher smiled. The world was perfect to him. He would be happy to sail forever, to cross the Untamable Ocean all the way to Hind, through Pharaoh's canal, and home to Fair Island. He wondered if Kuwayupituchu might guide her canoe in the same direction.

But the canoe turned east, *Flying Fish* following, into a great wide passage between an enormous island to the north and the mainland to the south. They left the Untamable Ocean behind, entering quieter waters that could change suddenly to high seas and storms.

Uinthi joined him. "Shall I spell you?"

"I'm content," Fisher said.

"I'd be content if the sun would shine."

Fisher grinned. "Comucomulu would say, 'I'll have to do something about that.'"

The sun broke through. The rain stopped. Inland, the clouds dispersed. Fisher gasped.

The mountains rose to high snow-covered peaks.

Fisher remembered. "I've seen those mountains before," he said. "They are still as big as when I was small."

"Did I believe the tales of such great mountains?" Uinthi said in wonder. "I do now."

Iakinthu and Red Sea Wolf and Maranti came out of the stern cabin into the sunshine.

"What a glorious land," Maranti said, shading her eyes to gaze around at the sea, the shore, the forest, and the mountains.

Three elegant longhouses stood along the shore. As Kuwayupituchu's great canoe approached, one of the paddlers stood and called out. People hurried to greet them and to watch the new ship that accompanied her.

Aboard *Flying Fish*, Iakinthu watched with satisfaction as her companions prepared for the return of Rhenthizu — Fisher, Iakinthu reminded herself — to his born family.

Must I give him back? she wondered. I've already returned him to his mother, or returned his mother to him.

"What if we turned around and sailed away?" she said to Fisher.

He embraced her. "Red Sea Wolf wishes to return. She wonders if her… companion…wishes to see her again."

He meant his father; Iakinthu appreciated his delicacy, his speaking in the Idaean way.

"What does Fisher wonder?" Iakinthu asked.

"I wonder who I would have been."

"You were my Rhenthizu, and now you are Fisher, your own." She looked him up and down. He wore his purple-striped loincloth, washed clean in fresh water, and his embroidered vest. His hair was growing out, black and straight. Iakinthu resisted the urge to curl it around her fingers. She sprinkled fine gold powder on her kohl and painted his eyes.

Maranti stood apart, wrapped in a boat cloak despite the sunshine, solemn, her gaze on Fisher. Iakinthu approached her, but Maranti stepped back.

"Will Egyptian beauty keep my companion by my side?" she asked. "He will decide, one way or another."

Though Fisher was too far away to hear her quiet voice, surrounded by friends who wished him well and laughed and chatted, he left the group with light touches and thanks and joined Maranti.

"Will you come with me?"

"I'll wait for you," she said. "Until you've made your choice."

He took her hand. She drew him to her and embraced him, then kissed him quickly and let him go.

"Your born family will honor you," she said. "Remember that your given family loves you, too." She gave his hand to Iakinthu, then retired to the stern cabin.

Iakinthu led him back to the companions.

Uinthi stood by, wearing white deerskin, smiling at the friend of his childhood. Bridges Words watched, uncertain of his place in this ceremony but dressed in a kilt of Egyptian linen and earrings of gold wire and tiny glass flasks that clinked musically when he moved. Paissu was the picture of the People, in pants of a herringbone pattern, recurved bow over her shoulder and quiver at her hip. Iakinthu gestured with the pot of kohl and brush. Paissu came to her, raised her face to Iakinthu, and let her paint her eyelids.

Iakinthu painted all her companions, even those who would stay behind with Aranthau on *Flying Fish*, even Lord Gunjusu and young Lord Murusuku, already resplendent in their clean, bright kimonos. They would surely be a decoration to Fisher's escort, as exotic as flamingoes or the parrots of Lady Jaguar's land.

Kilinkizu came to Iakinthu and arranged her lovelocks, which she had earlier dressed and curled. Iakinthu painted Kilinkizu's eyelids, putting a long, gold-flecked black streak beneath the startling blue of her eyes to conceal the crease of her squint. She handed the kohl to Kilinkizu. Kilinkizu painted Iakinthu's eyelids.

"Red Sea Wolf, will you wear kohl?"

Red Sea Wolf hesitated, then agreed. After only a few days with the Idaeans—or perhaps her change had begun after a few hours with the sea wolves—she was confident and brave. Her long hair spread down her back, gleaming with oil, a few gray streaks marking her maturity. Iakinthu added an extra measure of gold dust for her. The people here used little gold, perhaps finding it of no value compared to shell and cedar, but it was handsome on her, gleaming around her dark eyes.

Finally Iakinthu painted Aranthau. He seldom wore cosmetics, saying that the sea would splash off any paint, but he knew Iakinthu liked to see him adorned, so he allowed it on special occasions.

"What about me?" Bdarde said to Aranthau. "I want gold, too!"

"Kohl belongs to women," Aranthau said. "You must request it from Iakinthu Gephyra and ask permission of your mother."

"I deserve gold! Do I care about women's paint? I should have it without begging!"

Kilinkizu's fair skin colored in embarrassment. "Since you prefer to remain unadorned, instead of celebrating your uncle's homecoming, you must remain on *Flying Fish*," she said.

"He may stay with me," Aranthau said. Bdarde's frown faded.

Iakinthu kept her time and attention for Fisher. He bent his head to her. She drew a flask of lavender oil from between her breasts, swirled it gently, and poured the warm gold-flecked fragrance onto Fisher's hair and over his shoulders.

Kuwayupituchu's great cargo canoe paddled up beside *Flying Fish*.

"Shall we go ashore?"

"We are ready."

Iakinthu handed Red Sea Wolf into the ship's boat and joined her on its center seat. Fisher's gifts were already loaded, and the golden lily-axes. The companions lowered the boat and Uinthi's canoe and swarmed down the sides of the ship to clamber aboard. To Iakinthu's surprise and approval, young Lord Murusuku joined them, though Gunjusu remained behind.

I know which of them is the braver after experiencing one capture by the people of the Untamable Ocean, she thought.

The boat surged forward with the power of her companions' oars. The cargo canoe and Uinthi's light canoe, carrying Uinthi and Bridges Words and Paissu, flanked them. Iakinthu turned to wave at Aranthau, even to Bdarde, who stood barefaced at the rail. She settled onto the boat's seat to watch, with pride, as Fisher stood in the bow, returning to his born family.

The ship's boat scraped onto the shore.

With the companions, Fisher leaped out into the shallow water to drag the boat higher so Iakinthu and Red Sea Wolf could step out dry-footed. Uinthi's canoe slipped up beside them, and Kuwayupituchu's heavily loaded cargo canoe landed with a grinding crunch.

Fisher strode out of the cold water and stepped onto the land of his birth.

Iakinthu and Red Sea Wolf joined him. The companions gathered behind them, bearing the gold-headed ceremonial staves. Kuwayupituchu stood off to the side with her companions, watching the Idaeans quizzically.

Fisher expected the people of this village to know that the Idaeans were approaching, the same way Comucomulu had known of the Nipunu. He wondered if they knew who he was; he wondered if they would accept him. His arrival was different from Kilinkizu's homecoming, which had been planned and expected and was a long-established ceremony. He had been taken and rescued, offered to the sea wolves and returned, rather than given as she'd been. Now he was brought back, and he still must decide what to do next. That decision waited. First he must face the present.

The creatures on the carved door-pillars of the central longhouse stared out, so unfamiliar, so strange, that Fisher wondered if they welcomed him or wished him away. He realized—remembered—recognized—that they were wolves. They gave him more confidence. The sun glowed bright, illuminating the beach and leaving the longhouse's interior dark.

Between the door-pillars, a shadow appeared. The villagers lined the path from the longhouse to the shore.

The shadow stepped out. Tall and powerful, wearing an intricately woven patterned hat and a cape of woolly-dog fur and necklaces of shell and turquoise and onyx and mica, he stopped in the sunshine and waited.

I have my answer, Fisher thought, observing the resplendence, about whether he knew of me.

Fisher approached, flanked by Iakinthu and Red Sea Wolf, followed by the companions of *Flying Fish* in all their finery. He felt dizzy, as if he had tried poppy again, enveloped by the powerful fragrance of Iakinthu's lavender oil.

"Welcome home, Kuwayupituchu. I hope your voyage was successful."

"Thank you," Kuwayupituchu said, and Fisher heard his father's name for the first time since he was taken. "I think you'll be pleased. These are my guests." She nodded toward Iakinthu. "Iakinthu Gephyra, of the Idaeans."

"Welcome, traveling captain," said Fisher's father to Iakinthu.

"Thank you for your welcome, Talishu-Bikulu," Iakinthu said, speaking his name as if he were Idaean.

He glanced at Fisher's mother. "I know you," he said in a sharp tone.

"Do you?" she replied. "I knew you in a different life. I am Red Sea Wolf. This is my son, whom you also knew in a different life, who now is Fisher. We're returning from the sea wolf people, with our visitors from the other side of the world."

Now I'll find out, Fisher thought, if he'll say, You were taken as slaves, never mind the wolf people, go away, you shame me. If he says that, my decision is easy, my decision is made for me.

Fisher stepped forward and offered his father an ivory carving of Iakinthu and Terebinthu, Iakinthu vaulting over the great bull's back, the red-and-white bull arching his neck and bellowing as if in life, his horns gilded.

"I've heard of this creature, this bison," Fisher's father said. He accepted the carving; he ran one finger along the gold horn. "Do you wrestle to capture it?"

"We dance with them," Fisher said. "My given mother Iakinthu danced with the bull, with Terebinthu."

Fisher's father said, "I've danced with the killer whales, standing on Mother Whale's back. But that's a story, and stories are for the season of rain."

Fisher wondered if this land had a season that lacked rain.

Talishu-Bikulu stroked the gilded horn again and glanced at Iakinthu. "Welcome, dancer with great creatures." He turned toward Red Sea Wolf. "Welcome, Red Sea Wolf, my companion in another life." He gazed at Fisher. "Welcome, Fisher. Welcome home, my son."

Paissu thought everyone let out their breath at the same time. Maybe, she thought, they'll all float up into the sky, they had held so much breath for so long.

She was glad for Rhenthizu — Fisher, she must remember to think of him, now that she knew others changed their names like the People. She wondered what her own next name would be. Something exciting, like Dragon Claws, or worthy of stories like Fire-from-Cold-Ashes.

Paissu would do for now, while she was Idaean.

She glanced toward Kilinkizu, who watched her given brother, her son's uncle, with fondness. Kilinkizu moved off to the side of the gathering, sat on a huge gray gnarl of driftwood, and brought out papyrus and sticks of charcoal. Squinting even in full daylight, she sketched.

The companions planted the lily-axes on the beach. They unloaded the boat, arranging Fisher's gifts before him, piling gifts for Red Sea Wolf equally high: bolts of Egyptian linen and Fair Island wool, flasks of lavender and rose oil and poppy, twists of tobacco, jars of sweet almonds and of cacao, ingots of gleaming copper. Lady Kuwayupituchu, too, received copper ingots in thanks for her aid and wisdom.

"My artisans will transform them," she said, "and the masks will tell stories this winter."

Paissu noticed that Iakinthu had left the amphorae of Idaean wine in the hold of *Flying Fish*. Everyone in this land preferred their own drink. She wondered what they would think of cacao and hoped *Flying Fish* would still have some when they sailed away.

Young Lord Murusuku knelt at Red Sea Wolf's feet, bowing, offering her a packet of scarlet silk. Paissu recognized it as Murusuku's innermost kimono, the one with the most beautiful and intricate embroidery, of lion-dogs and gryphons, celestial dragons and white clouds.

"Such a gift," Red Sea Wolf said. "Thank you, my dear Lord Murusuku." She allowed the young lord to open the kimono and hold it for her to put on, to straighten the collar and tie the obi and spread her long hair down her back. The Idaeans, Talishu-Bikulu from her former life, and Fisher all murmured their appreciation and approval.

Finally, Iakinthu presented Fisher and Red Sea Wolf each with a knife of sky-iron in a sheath of leather reinforced with earth-iron. Drawing the blades made a wonderful fierce sound.

"My gifts from the Idaeans are yours," Fisher said to Talishu-Bikulu.

"This winter's Potlatch will be the source of many stories," Fisher's father said.

The sun set against dazzling pink and orange clouds. The sky turned indigo, then black and star-studded. Sparks mimicked the stars. Mother Moon rose, one day this side of full.

Fisher's two families rejoiced. Fisher, Iakinthu, and Uinthi kept busy translating between Idaeans and Akokulu. Paissu and Bridges Words, still learning the Akokulu language, helped as best they could.

They feasted on wukanushu and almonds, camas and shepherd's bread, cacao. Paissu thought it very funny that most of the women liked the cacao and most of the men, like Fisher, preferred water. Lord Murusuku prepared the cacao and served it and, unlike the other men, drank it. Kuwayupituchu's companions brought out an intricately carved square wooden box full of water and clam shells the size of two cupped hands with which to dip and drink the water. Paissu wondered how they had made the beautiful box watertight without staining its seams with pitch.

Drowsy with poppy, Iakinthu sat beside Kilinkizu on the driftlog. Its water-smoothed curves created a comfortable bench, softened by her boat cloak. Kilinkizu leaned against her, her head on Iakinthu's shoulder, asleep. Snuggled against her other side, Paissu dozed.

A breeze touched the papyrus, fluttering it. Iakinthu caught the drawings before the air could take them away. The sound, the movement, wakened the numerator.

"All's well, my dear," Iakinthu said. "Go back to sleep. Or we may go into the longhouse, or back to *Flying Fish*."

Kilinkizu took the drawings, blinking at them in the light of the moon. She drew in the Idaean manner, true to life or story, but the Nipunu embroidery influenced her as well. Her figures moved with graceful curves, like living things. Fisher-the-man danced on the page, while fisher-the-creature played at his feet.

"So beautiful," Iakinthu whispered.

"I have to imagine what I used to see." Kilinkizu sighed. "And I imagined Bdarde-who-was, playing her lute." She showed Iakinthu another drawing, Idaean and Akokulu people dancing, Bdarde-who-was barely visible in the background, a visitor from another world. "Would the lute go well with drum and flute?" She dashed away a tear, smudging her kohl. "Will Bdarde-that-is ever play the lute?"

"He's a stubborn little boy," Iakinthu said. "And he likes to draw."

"So he does," Kilinkizu replied, in a moment of appreciation.

Aranthau, glowing with sea-light, rose nearly silent from the waves. He hurried up the beach to Iakinthu.

"The Northerners," he said.

Knowing the sea above and below, how had he missed their sailing ship? They had snuck up the coast while *Flying Fish* lay at anchor in the Wimahl; then the underwater mud-cloud of the Wimahl's mouth had concealed them.

"Did I think they could follow us so far?"

Aranthau believed he had failed his ship's companions.

"I thought to tell Thamenthu about them," Iakinthu said. "But I was grieving for the companions of *Dolphin*, for Bdarde-that-was. Instead of warning her, I boasted that my companions defeated them."

Thamenthu of the Maisusutha would be on guard; her young warriors would delight in driving off invaders, but what about Lady Jaguar? What about Head Guide and the balunu herders? She had to think that the Northerners missed Lady Jaguar and her people, or escaped as *Flying Fish* had escaped, or they would be sailing back to their own lands, conquered and enslaved.

They must have negotiated with Head Guide to cross from sea to sea, but what might have happened at the end of the journey?

She rather wished the Northerners *had* come upon Lady Jaguar, without the advice and help and warnings of Bridges Words.

Paissu looked up from her sleeping nest.

"The Northerners?" In the manner of the People, she moved from a doze to sharp attention, gripping her knife.

"Can you find Red Sea Wolf and Lady Kuwayupituchu?" Iakinthu rose from the drift-log, moving slowly to ease her aches. "I must speak to them. Warn them and ask their advice. Kilinkizu and I will gather the companions."

Fisher, holding hands with Maranti, approached Red Sea Wolf, who sat near a bonfire sipping from a cup of cacao. Her favorite woolly-dog snored softly at her feet.

"My born mother." He dropped to one knee before her and touched his fist to his forehead.

"My found son," she said, smiling. She held out her hand to Maranti, who grasped it softly. They had already become fond of one another. Fisher wondered if he would have to leave his born mother behind or watch Maranti sail away on *Flying Fish*. Or if all three of them would stay in this new land, or all three sail back home.

I still think of Fair Island as home, he thought.

"Will I be Rhenthizu, or will I be Fisher?" he said.

Before they could discuss his question or even think about it, Paissu ran into the firelight.

"The Northerners," she said. "Two ships. Aranthau says the Northerners are coming."

In the chaos of the gatherings, the explanations, the warnings, Kilinkizu and Red Sea Wolf stood together in silence. Each knew of the other's past but only a few words of the other's language.

Paissu returned to them, her hand on the hilt of her sky-iron knife.

"I'll protect you," she said. "But I wish I had Surefoot."

"Thank you, brave Paissu." Kilinkizu put her arm around Red Sea Wolf's shoulders.

Following Kilinkizu's lead, Paissu put her arm around Red Sea Wolf's waist. Fisher's mother shivered against her shoulder and gripped the hilt of her new sky-iron knife.

Fisher joined them, looking grave.

"Another war party," Red Sea Wolf whispered, gazing at Fisher. "To capture us, to separate us when we're so recently reunited."

"Where—" said Fisher.

"How did they—" said Kilinkizu.

"Can I know?" Paissu said. "I tell you what Aranthau told me. What he heard from the sea. Would I doubt Aranthau, who sang the kraken away to save my life?"

Chapter Thirty-Four

Iakinthu sat in the bow of the ship's boat, wearing her finest seven-tiered skirt and embroidered vest, her hair dressed into lovelocks with lavender oil, her eyelids heavy with kohl. Her golden dragonfly earrings quivered.

Her companions rowed her toward the great ships of the Northerners. The northerners' ships' boats rowed toward her, making her glad that Uinthi and Bridges Words and Paissu accompanied her in Uinthi's canoe, and Fisher flanked her with his new brothers in a powerful war canoe. Standing warriors filled the Northerners' boats, armored and armed.

"I wish I had let Dragon Claws make my armor," Kilinkizu said, squinting into the bright ocean where the Northern ships rolled at sea-anchor.

"Should we negotiate in armor?" Iakinthu said mildly.

"Do I mistake the sun glinting on bronze?" Kilinkizu said, with an edge in her voice.

Despite her failing sight, she was correct. All the warriors stood with upright spears. The Northern negotiator stood in the bow of his boat, his armor reflecting the sun, a spear upright beside him, its sky-iron point shining darkly. A long sword in a gold scabbard hung at his hip.

"Do we ever expect Northerners to know manners?" Iakinthu said.

At the bark of an order, the approaching Northerners stopped rowing. The boats skewed in the waves. The negotiator stumbled to his seat with a clank of armor.

"Back your oars," Iakinthu said. Her companions did as she asked and held the boat steady against the low waves.

Iakinthu and the Northerner regarded each other.

"I am Iakinthu Gephyra, bridge between people," Iakinthu said.

"What bar-bar-bar is that old woman speaking?" the negotiator said.

Iakinthu put her hand gently over Kilinkizu's, rather concerned that Kilinkizu would treat the negotiator the same way she had treated the captured Northerner back on Siurthi's *Dolphin*.

"She said she bows to your power, Master Superior," said a young man sitting behind the negotiator.

Iakinthu let them believe she lacked any knowledge of their language, difficult as it was to keep from laughing.

"Will you translate for me, Kilinkizu?" she said. "To prevent any misunderstanding."

"Yes, Iakinthu," Kilinkizu replied, well aware that Iakinthu knew the Northerners' language because Kilinkizu had taught it to her.

"You've followed us a long way," Iakinthu said.

"Surprised, are you?"

"Are the Northerners known for seafaring?"

"We're known for conquest."

In the war canoe, Fisher softly translated, his voice barely audible over the touch of the waves. His new friends listened, then laughed. Each one had a powerful bow, a fang-studded club.

The Northerner glared at them, gripping his spear.

"Where is our king's son, our prince, the heir to our empire? Where is his guardian?"

"You left them behind on *Dolphin* when you fled," Iakinthu said. She wondered if she should pretend the dead man and Kilinkizu's son had returned to Kunusu in Siurthi's ship. She preferred to tell the truth, though she could spin a falsehood with the best of them. The truth was easier to remember.

When Kilinkizu translated, her voice trembled.

"You have our prince," the Northerner said. "The people you've visited have described him to me. A proper warrior, who commands his due."

What a way to describe Bdarde-who-is, Iakinthu thought. Though that helps explain him.

"As for his guardian, my brother—did you murder him?"

Iakinthu tightened her grip on Kilinkizu's hand.

"Is their king with them?" Kilinkizu whispered, too softly for the negotiator's translator to hear.

"Speak a proper language, girl!"

"Speak like a civilized person," Iakinthu said.

Kilinkizu repeated Iakinthu's reply in a strong voice, the trembling wiped out by anger.

"We prefer to discuss this subject with your king."

He laughed.

"Would our king leave his subjects ungoverned to chase you around the world?"

"They would be relieved if he did," Kilinkizu whispered.

"Do you stand in his stead?" Iakinthu asked. "Will you introduce yourself?"

"Introduce myself to women?" he said, sneering. "What woman can speak my name? You may address me as Master Superior."

"Then I must address you as Nameless," Iakinthu said, well aware that her choice was an insult.

All the men in the Nameless boat brought their spears to point at Iakinthu, but Nameless himself raised his hand to stop them.

"Give us our prince. Perhaps we'll allow you and these others to live."

In the war canoe, Fisher left out the threat. The Akokulu were ready for conflict or trade. Conflict would prove their bravery; trade would provide wealth. Fisher was by upbringing an Idaean, and would choose trade over conflict. Whether Nameless would allow his men that path was another question entirely.

Would Kilinkizu forgive me, ever forever, Iakinthu thought, if I gave Bdarde to them, paid a killing-price for the death of their warrior, and let them sail away?

The idea tempted her.

"Iakinthu Gephyra," Kilinkizu whispered, reading her thoughts. "He's mine, to save from them."

Iakinthu sighed.

"I've accepted Bdarde—your prince—as my given child," she said to Nameless, pausing to allow Kilinkizu to translate. "He'll grow up in my household and learn the ways of diplomacy. When he comes of age he will return to you, and stay with you if he chooses." She wished she could say, "I will return him to his mother," but that would be an untruth. She had already returned him to his mother.

"Is this how Idaeans behave?" Nameless snarled at her. "Stealing a prince—Murdering his guardian?"

"His guardian offered him to me," Iakinthu said. "He said your king had many other princes and could do without this one."

Nameless stared at her, horrified.

"Is this true? Is he easily replaced?"

Nameless remained silent. Could he admit his king had only one son? And that one, according to Kilinkizu, not even his own.

I could tell Nameless who Bdarde's father really is, she thought, but I doubt that would end our confrontation in an acceptable manner.

Nameless shouted "Go about!" Fury distorted his words, but his rowers understood. Perhaps he spoke to them only in anger, and they were used to it. They spun the boat so quickly that the standing warriors staggered; a few sat down heavily, clutching their spears.

The ship's boat, Uinthi's canoe, and the Akokulu war canoe returned to the beach, to the longhouses.

"If they attack, we'll defend and defeat," Talishu-Bikulu said. "If they threaten, we'll take their boats and make slaves of them." Everyone in the village and Iakinthu's companions stood encircling the discussion, listening attentively. Fisher whispered a translation to the companions; Uinthi whispered in turn to Paissu and Bridges Words.

"Can they be bought?" Lady Kuwayupituchu asked.

"My son is beyond price to them," Kilinkizu said.

"They prefer killing to trade," Iakinthu said.

"And they are preparing for exactly that," Kilinkizu added. "They attack at false dawn and celebrate their victories as the sun rises."

"How do you know this?" asked Lady Kuwayupituchu.

"I was one of them." She cut off her explanation, which came perilously close to telling the Akokulu she had been a slave. "I prefer being an Idaean."

"What do they do if they're defeated?"

"They die," Kilinkizu said.

"That would suit," said Talishu-Bikulu.

Kilinkizu smiled grimly.

"Do you ever return given children?" Kuwayupituchu asked Iakinthu.

"Always," Iakinthu said. "The given child agrees to be given and returned." She suppressed a sigh. Did Bdarde ever agree to anything? Once in a while, if Aranthau asked him.

"I mean, before they come of age?"

"Ah. That would break our traditions."

Talishu-Bikulu and Kuwayupituchu understood.

"Did his father agree to this?" asked Talishu-Bikulu.

"His father sent him away with a guardian who offered him to us in exchange for his own life." That was close enough to pass as truth. "His mother—" Iakinthu nodded toward Kilinkizu "—allowed the boy to join my household and take an Idaean name."

Talishu-Bikulu frowned at the guardian's decision. Lady Kuwayupituchu raised an eyebrow. "I wonder if your negotiations are usually more... diplomatic."

"Usually they are," Iakinthu said. "Bdarde's guardian neglected his gifts."

"He lacks a ransom."

"True."

"Can *you* be bought?"

"When a given child comes of age, I give the given child and the mother gifts. As I gave gifts to Fisher and to Red Sea Wolf." Iakinthu said, "Do I need more riches?"

She wanted to talk to Aranthau, who remained on board *Flying Fish*, along with Bdarde. Her ship lay at anchor close to shore. Enough companions remained aboard to crew *Flying Fish* if the Northerners approached. The Akokulu war canoes stood ready, even eager, for a fight.

Iakinthu wanted to return to her ship, to stand with her captain and her companions. She wanted a diplomatic solution. She had brought Fisher home to his mother, but she had also brought war.

A low roar spread across the water. Iakinthu rose, startled, thinking, When did Aranthau ever sound the conch trumpet?

"We must go," she said. "That's Aranthau's warning of danger. We must return to *Flying Fish*."

"Are the Northerners coming back?" Kilinkizu asked, puzzled, squinting toward two black-sail ships, which remained steady off-shore.

The conch trumpet sounded again, a short series, more intense than the first.

Aranthau blew a warning that everyone knew, but which had last been sounded a thousand years ago from the sea near Knossos.

The villagers, too, understood approaching danger all too well. Women gathered children and the elders and led them from the shore, where small waves grew and approached, out of time with the tide. The Northerners forgotten, dismissed as a much smaller risk despite their armor and weapons, they crossed the beach and climbed up the slope and disappeared into the forest.

The companions ran toward the ship's boat and Uinthi's canoe; some waded into the water to swim the short distance to *Flying Fish*, the men hesitating with a gasp when the frigid water reached their crotches, the women pausing a moment when the water touched their breasts. Talishu-Bikulu's young people followed, equally excited, leaping into canoes: war canoes, cargo canoes, fishing canoes, shouting and gesturing for Fisher and the other companions to hurry, to join them, to get away from the beach into deep water.

Chapter Thirty-Five

Will I be Fisher, or will I be Rhenthizu?

Fisher used his moment of indecision to embrace Red Sea Wolf.

"If we're defeated—"

She brushed his short hair back with one hand. Her other hand gripped the hilt of her sky-iron knife.

"I want to see you with your hair long again," she said. "I want to see you adorned with shell and masked as a wolf."

"Run to the wolves," he said. "They'll keep you from the Northerners. I'll come to find you if I can."

"*When* you can." Standing straight, Red Sea Wolf guided Paissu to Fisher's side. "*Flying Fish* needs its lookout."

"But I promised—" Paissu said.

"To protect me. Best done by standing with your companions."

Lady Kuwayupituchu hurried to them. "My friend, you who are now Red Sea Wolf, we must hurry to high ground." She could read the waters of the familiar strait as well as Aranthau. "Unless you have a flying canoe that we can ride to the top of a cedar tree."

"That would be quite wonderful," Red Sea Wolf said. She squeezed Fisher's hand in farewell, accepted Lady Kuwayupituchu's hand, and struggled up the bank. They paused only long enough to open the pen of woolly-dogs. Surrounded by a carpet of running white fur, they followed the other villagers into the forest.

Taking Paissu's hand in turn, Fisher ran for the shore. Paissu joined Uinthi and Bridges Words in the little canoe; Fisher joined his new people in one of the war canoes, and all together they paddled for deep water.

Iakinthu hauled herself up the side of *Flying Fish*, too alarmed to wait for a more decorous return.

Aranthau helped her onto the deck as the rest of the companions swarmed up the sides and to their places, ready to weigh anchor, to work the oars, to unfurl the sails if the breeze freshened.

"Oars!" Aranthau called out. "Leave the sails!" He sprinted toward the steering oar. "We'll go to the middle of the strait." Iakinthu followed.

Bdarde appeared from nowhere. "What was that awful noise?" He glared at Iakinthu as if she had sounded the conch trumpet, though Aranthau kept it, depending from his belt. "What *is* that awful noise?"

Aranthau looked down at him, startled. "Can you hear it?"

As answer, Bdarde clapped his hands to his ears. "It hurts! It hurts!"

"The Northerners —" Iakinthu said. In the distance, the Northern ships plunged toward shore, seeing an easy victory as the Idaean ship and the canoes abandoned the village, and its people fled.

They think we are fleeing them, Iakinthu said to herself.

"We must get *Flying Fish* into deeper water. Mother Moon —"

The water receded from the shore, faster than any tide.

Kilinkizu reached the deck.

"It hurts!" Bdarde cried again. "It hurts!"

"I know," she said. She flinched as a sound apparently imperceptible to Iakinthu washed over her. She knelt before Bdarde and spoke softly to him, holding his shoulders gently.

He listened.

Aranthau stroked the boy's hair. "Will you do as your mother asks?"

Bdarde's eyes filled with sudden tears.

"Will I ever see you again?"

"Someday," Aranthau replied. "Somewhere in the sea."

Uinthi and Bridges Words and Paissu climbed onto the deck. As they hauled the canoe up the side, Bdarde jumped to the rail, almost as elegantly as Paissu, and dove into the sea, while Kilinkizu snatched the canoe's line from Uinthi's hands and dove after him.

Uinthi shouted in surprise and anger. Paissu stared in disbelief. Bridges Words watched, impassive.

Iakinthu cried out. She ran to the rail, too late to catch them, to stop them. Kilinkizu propelled Bdarde into the canoe, then leaped like a dolphin to join him, nearly capsizing the light little craft. She paddled furiously toward shore, desperately overcoming the receding sea.

"We have to —"

"If we go back," Aranthau said, "*Flying Fish* is lost. All the companions are lost."

"But what's she doing?

"Returning to her true people."

Again, Iakinthu understood.

"And honoring Mother Moon," she said. Tears ran down Iakinthu's cheeks. "Oh, my Kilinkizu," she whispered. "My dear Kilinkizu."

Aranthau looked around. "Where is Rhenthizu?"

Iakinthu wrenched her attention away from Kilinkizu and the tiny canoe, which grew tinier as it struggled to reach the shore against the receding sea.

"He is Fisher now." Iakinthu wished to keep him, yet felt glad of his acceptance by his born people. She pointed to one of the war canoes, where Fisher's white vest marked him out among his kin.

"Fisher!" Aranthau shouted. "Mother Moon is coming! Deep water!"

Fisher raised his paddle to signal that he had heard, he understood, everyone in the canoes already understood. The story was in their blood and in their bones and for some, in their memories. All unknowing, the Northern ships plunged toward shore.

Paissu ran to the mast and climbed to her perch. The Northern ships sailed toward shore, toward the empty village and the prospect of loot, destruction, slaves. The warriors on the prow pointed toward *Flying Fish*, toward the canoes, laughing and shouting abuse. Paissu knew a little of their language; even she, used to bawdy talk and rough curses among the People, found their insults embarrassing. She wished Iakinthu or Aranthau, Fisher or Red Sea Wolf had had time to explain to her what was happening and why they were fleeing from a fight. She wished the enemy was within her bowshot.

The beat of Maranti's drum set the rhythm of the rowers. On deck, Iakinthu stood by Aranthau. They strained against the steering oar, pushing *Flying Fish* away from shore. The ship scraped the sea bottom as the water flowed away beneath it. Paissu clutched the shuddering mast.

What is this mysterious movement of the water? she wondered. Has anyone seen a tide like this?

But she was the only companion of *Flying Fish* who was mystified. She could explain anything about the behavior of horses, she could speak to Surefoot with her breath, but she still had a great deal to learn about the sea.

Flying Fish surged forward, freeing itself from the grinding rocks. The flotilla of canoes rushed ahead, into the safety of deep water.

Paissu scanned the shore. The exposed sea bottom revealed long strands of kelp, water-rounded rocks, shoals of oysters.

Kilinkizu pulled Bdarde along, then took him up and carried him, running, stumbling over the wet rocks. Uinthi's canoe lay abandoned behind them, and Paissu felt a pang for it.

Uinthi will miss it, she thought, for Paissu believed it would be lost forever. I wonder if he will forgive Kilinkizu? Maybe he understands why Kilinkizu took it. I wish someone would tell me!

Kilinkizu reached the gleaming beach beyond the sea stones. Instead of following the villagers into the forest, she angled across the crescent of sand toward the headland that defined its western edge.

Paissu glanced down toward Aranthau and Iakinthu, who stood together pushing the steering oar. Beneath *Flying Fish,* the water sucked backwards from the shore, its surface eerily calm, revealing kelp-covered stones, pools covered with bright anemones pulling in their tentacles, stranded flopping fish. The low roar of the water surrounded them, and Aranthau flinched, hearing sounds imperceptible to the other companions.

The Northern ships beached, grinding rough, and the Northerners scrambled to the stones. The ships listed as the sea fled behind them, but the Northerners were mad with fighting lust. Running, slipping, stumbling, they swarmed toward the village.

The roar of the conch trumpet spread out across the water. On deck, Iakinthu struggled to hold the steering oar steady while Aranthau leaned against it and blew the trumpet, again, again. Paissu understood it as a warning, an attempt to alert neighboring villages.

She wished she knew what he was warning them about and why the sea was behaving so strangely.

Iakinthu ran to the hatch and called down to Maranti to ease the pace of the rowing, then to stop. *Flying Fish* and the canoes had traveled far from shore. Rowers and paddlers alike gasped, exhausted. The companions staggered up on deck. The canoes surrounded the Idaean ship, bumping softly, fended off by paddles.

Still panting, sweat dripping, Fisher climbed to the deck. He embraced Iakinthu, then Aranthau, and ran to Maranti's side as she climbed from the rowing deck.

Everyone looked toward shore, Idaean and Akokulu alike.

The Northern ships listed crazily. One had fallen entirely on its side. The cries of the rowers, trapped, floated across the water.

The warriors heaped Akokulu possessions on the beach, plundering the houses of carvings, pelts, copper ornaments.

"Oh," Paissu said softly, as a trickle of flame ran along the eaves of one of the houses, then another, and a larger fire exploded at the base of one of the grand doorposts.

She looked away, blinking tears of grief for the carven creatures. The great wolf, holding up the people and the world, did her best to protect those above her, as was her right and her duty.

A flash of white and gold caught Paissu's gaze.

Kilinkizu stood at the point of the headland, holding Bdarde's hand, her other hand raised to the sky, to Mother Moon.

"Iakinthu," Paissu whispered, hardly able to speak, hardly able to believe Iakinthu would hear her. But Iakinthu looked up, and Paissu pointed. Seeing Kilinkizu, Iakinthu took a step forward as if she could walk across the water to her friend.

The great wave came.

Chapter Thirty-Six

After the long night, at dawn, Iakinthu stepped onto the beach. Quiet wavelets lapped the shore.

Drift-logs lay in jumbled heaps where longhouses had stood. The forest beyond mirrored the chaos on the beach, trees a thousand years old pushed over by the force of water, then tangled branch and root when the wave receded. Dawn cast violent shadows across the sand.

The wave had ripped the small windblown trees from the point of the headland where Kilinkizu had honored Mother Moon, her water-born son at her side.

They had vanished.

Iakinthu let her tears flow, seeing again the great wave climbing the headland and Kilinkizu giving herself and her son back to the sea.

Will she find her lover again? Iakinthu wondered. Or a new lover, from a different sea? I hope so, and I hope Bdarde too finds his peace.

She wiped her eyes with the back of her hand, smearing what was left of her kohl after the endless night.

The Northern ships had disappeared, dragged out to sea and shredded like paper boats. As for the Northerners, they too had been pulled away, screaming, out of reach of any rescue. Iakinthu grieved for their enslaved rowers, but thought nothing more about the Northerners themselves.

Her companions gathered around her. Every Idaean knew the story of Mother Moon's great wave that had saved Kunusu from invasion a thousand years ago.

Uinthi stood, shoulders slumped, with Bridges Words and Paissu.

"If I had caught her…"

"She did what she must," Iakinthu said.

"We'll sing about her," Paissu said.

"And so will we."

"Tomorrow we may die and all be sung about," said Bridges Words. "But today I will live."

The Akokulu joined them, pulling canoes large and small up the beach, tying them with cedar rope to the polished driftlogs, gazing at the devastation and looking for any remnant of their homes, looking for their friends and relatives.

Fisher and Maranti stood beside Iakinthu. Even Maranti looked exhausted. She wore a boat cloak against the morning's chill. She bent down to pick up a scrap of wood, an elegantly carved and painted claw.

"It's from the doorpost," Paissu said. "The gift to Talishu-Bikulu. Mother Wolf." Her voice trembled.

Maranti gave her the claw. "You may give it back to Talishu-Bikulu."

Fisher gazed up at the devastated beach, the ruined forest.

"Where is he? Where are they all?" he said. He turned to Maranti and grasped her hands. "I have to go find them."

"Look," said one of his new brothers.

Making their way among the fallen trees, climbing down from higher ground, led by Talishu-Bikulu and Lady Kuwayupituchu, old and young villagers returned and embraced the warriors.

"Can I find Red Sea Wolf?" Fisher said, searching for her with his gaze.

Suddenly he laughed with delight.

At the top of the bank, surrounded by little white woolly-dogs, stood Red Sea Wolf. Behind her sat a wolf, red as sunset. The wolf looked at the woolly-dogs, decided they were more wool than meat, blinked, yawned widely, and rose. In the way of wolves, she disappeared.

Fisher ran and climbed to his mother and embraced her.

Too tired to stand, Iakinthu sat on one of the tumbled drift-logs, indifferent to the damp that soaked through her kilt. She bent to pick up a few stones and stacked them large-to-small.

Lord Murusuku sat beside her.

"You use the stones as my sister uses her brush. In the wake of disaster, following the tsunami, beauty."

"The tsunami?" Iakinthu asked. The unfamiliar word sounded Idaean.

"The great waves. They afflict Nipunu."

"They save Idaea. And the Akokulu."

"Yes."

Farther down the beach, Paissu shyly offered the bit of polished wood to Talishu-Bikulu. He accepted it, gazed down at it, and touched her hair gently. Iakinthu felt near to crying again.

"What will happen now?" Murusuku asked.

Iakinthu remained silent for a long moment. She had been trying not to speak on this subject.

"I want..." she whispered. "I want to go home."

"Yes," said Murusuku. "So do I."

Fisher took comfort in the survival of all his people, of the companions of *Flying Fish*. He pushed aside any joy, any satisfaction, at the destruction of the Northerners, who had tried to conquer the sea without understanding it.

Around him people built fires and paddled out in fishing canoes and waded into the water to pick oysters. Everyone was famished. Fisher rowed out to *Flying Fish* and brought back extra blankets and provisions: ship's bread, olives, sweet almonds, even flasks of wine. The Idaeans would want it, even if the Akokulu preferred water. He brought a pottery jug and cups, for all the watertight boxes had been washed away.

All my wealth is gone, he realized, all the wealth of a given child returned and given to his family. Red Sea Wolf and I have nothing.

He glanced across the beach, where Paissu sat beside Red Sea Wolf and scratched the ears of one of the woolly-dogs. Red Sea Wolf had by chance been wearing Murusuku's gift of the kimono, and while it showed the results of flight through the forest, it still glowed with bright color.

And she has the woolly-dogs, as well, Fisher thought. He was glad she had something left.

"Did you bring cacao, my love?" Maranti asked.

He smiled and shrugged. "I forgot. Will I go back and get it?"

She touched his cheek. "When you go back, I'll go with you. So long a day, so long a night."

Carrying the provisions, they walked together to a fire where Iakinthu and Talishu-Bikulu and Kuwayupituchu sat, their backs to the destruction. Fisher made to lay the provisions at Iakinthu's feet, but she made a subtle nod toward his father, who gave a gesture of acceptance. When one of the villagers brought a salvaged plank holding fish smoking from the fire, he accepted that, too, and gave her a share of the Idaean food and a blanket.

They ate the fish, delectable with scorch-marks and crunchy skin. When he finished his share, Fisher wished there was more.

"We may be hungry this winter," Talishu-Bikulu said.

"And cold," said Kuwayupituchu. She glanced briefly, sadly, over her shoulder. "Though we have a great deal of firewood and cedar bark and timber for house planks."

"Our ancestors arrived with less. Yet, here we are."

He patted her hand gently; she squeezed his fingers.

Back on board *Flying Fish*, Iakinthu gathered the companions. She was glad to see Fisher among them, but wondered if that was only because he wanted to spend as much time as possible with Maranti before bidding her farewell.

Or persuading her to stay with him, with the Akokulu.

What will I say, back at Kunusu, if I make away with Eldest Daughter and fail to bring her home?

Fisher had brought Red Sea Wolf to the ship as well, and Iakinthu had the same silent question: Was he spending as much time with her before leaving her again, forever?

Dripping with sea water, Aranthau climbed up the side and onto the deck. "The hull is sound," he said.

Iakinthu gestured her thanks. That answered the important question of her ship's limits.

"What will we do?" Iakinthu asked. "Will we stay here, will we try to help the Akokulu? Will we go home?"

As the sun went down they talked together, drinking wine and cacao. Iakinthu listened. She had the right of command; she would do so if she had to, but she listened to each opinion. When she glanced around to find Kilinkizu, to urge her to speak as she had so often done, a pang of grief took her all over again.

Is this my least successful voyage in all my long life? She said to herself. Then she thought, I have a new given child, Rhenthizu is Fisher, returned to his mother, and if the Northerners send more ships, Kuwayupituchu's young warriors will know them as enemies and delight in vanquishing them.

Maranti, too, listened and kept her own counsel. Iakinthu deliberately skipped over her, for in any discussion among Idaeans, Eldest Daughter was the last to speak. Iakinthu might have the right of command, but Eldest Daughter's opinion carried great weight.

And what will you say, my dear? Iakinthu wondered. Will it bring us into conflict?

"What of Paissu, our new given child, what of our guests?" Iakinthu said when the companions had fallen silent, equally divided between adventure and return. "What of you, Paissu?"

"I want to dance with bulls," Paissu said.

Iakinthu smiled. To dance with bulls was what she had wanted when she was Paissu's age.

"To be sure, you will."

"And I want the People to come and see me, and I want to dance with them on our horses, and I want them to hear of Kilinkizu."

Iakinthu caught her breath. "I'd like that, too." She turned her blurred gaze to Uinthi.

"I promised my mother I'd come home," Uinthi said.

"And I promised I would bring you," Iakinthu said. "Bridges Words. What do you have to say?"

"Tomorrow I may die," he said, "but today I remain with the Idaeans." He frowned. "How would you return?"

She had supposed they would go back the way they had come.

"Lady Jaguar wants your ship, your people, your beautiful islands." His lips quirked with ironic humor. "Would she want me? Or would she kill me as soon as see me?"

"There's another way home," Fisher said. "Far to the north, then east, a passage that leads through cracks in sea-ice, across water too cold to flow."

"Where the whales are trapped when the ice freezes over, and the icebergs crush themselves against each other." Aranthau patted the railing. "A great deal to ask of your ship, which has served you so well for so long."

Iakinthu shivered involuntarily. The frozen sea and Lady Jaguar left very little to choose between.

"There's a third way," Murusuku said.

"Across the Untamable Ocean." Aranthau sounded intrigued more than doubtful, then thoughtful. "A very long voyage."

"Are the Nipunu better sailors than the Idaeans?" Murusuku said.

"Did the Nipunu ship wreck itself on these shores?" Aranthau replied, with an edge in his voice.

"Across the Untamable Ocean, and through the Fantastical Islands, and around Hind, and through Pharaoh's Channel," Iakinthu said. "A *very* long voyage." She smiled at Aranthau. "*Flying Fish* would be the first to achieve it."

"You could refit in Nipunu," said Murusuku.

"You could demand, for me," said Lord Gunjusu, "a very great ransom."

Iakinthu stared at him. He spoke so seldom, except to demand service, that she was used to his silence. He stared back, his impassivity spoiled by the lines crinkling around his eyes.

The possibilities opened out.

Yet she had another responsibility.

"Red Sea Wolf, what of the Akokulu?"

"The Akokulu, I think, have had enough of tsunami, which afflict the Nipunu," she said. "They will stay here at home."

"Will they survive the winter?" The Idaeans would be of help, if they could be of help in an unfamiliar land.

Red Sea Wolf gave her a long and pensive gaze. "If they have only their own people to feed."

A sense of permission, forgiveness, freedom swept over Iakinthu.

"Maranti, Eldest Daughter, what do you have to say to us?"

"I say," she said softly, "that I would like to go home."

Chapter Thirty-Seven

Flying Fish lay at anchor near shore. In only a few days, the Akokulu had begun to construct a temporary village of cedar-branch thatch; they salvaged what they could—very little—from the shore. Iakinthu feared the discovery of bodies, the sight of bright hair tangled in kelp, but that she was spared. She imagined Kilinkizu swimming with the sea people; she imagined Bdarde content at last.

The reconstruction of the longhouses would take more time; the gathering of wealth for a proper potlatch might take even longer. The companions of *Flying Fish* did their best to help, but Red Sea Wolf was right: the Akokulu knew their own land and resources best, and usually they found it easier to do things themselves than to teach the Idaeans.

In their turn, the companions filled the ship's amphorae with fresh water. Iakinthu negotiated with Talishu-Bikulu for the water and for tall fallen trees in case the Untamable Ocean—or a kraken—might take the masts. Better to have seasoned wood, but perhaps the voyage would be so long that seasoning would be complete before the ship needed a new mast.

Uinthi climbed past the fallen forest and searched without success for the right tree to make a small canoe.

And then one morning, at the turn of the tide, the companions and the Akokulu met on the beach to say farewell.

Iakinthu touched her fist to her forehead, saluting Talishu-Bikulu, then Lady Kuwayupituchu. Her companions laid copper ingots at Rhenthizu's feet, and he gave them to the elders, to replace those that had been swept away.

"You will come back," Kuwayupituchu said, "to see what my artists make from Idaean copper."

"I hope I will," Iakinthu said. "I'd like to see Akokulu creatures in Idaean copper."

"And stay for a winter," Talishu-Bikulu said. "To hear our stories and tell your own."

"I hope I will," Iakinthu said again.

Maranti stood at her side, composed. Surely Fisher would join them, to say good-bye to her? Unless she had decided to stay here on the other side of the world...

Fisher and Red Sea Wolf, accompanied by a tide of woolly-dogs, strode along the beach toward them. Red Sea Wolf went to Kuwayupituchu and took her hands.

"I leave you the woolly-dogs," she said. "All but one. I hope...they might survive through the winter, so they can give you warm blankets for next year."

"I hope so, too," Kuwayupituchu said.

Both Fisher and Red Sea Wolf wore Idaean kilts and vests.

Red Sea Wolf faced Iakinthu and touched her fist to her forehead. "Will you take me and my son and my little dog across the Untamable Ocean? Will you show me your Fair Island?"

"With great joy," Iakinthu said, barely able to speak. She embraced Red Sea Wolf. Fisher flung his arms around his mother, and then Maranti, who burst out laughing.

"I may want a new name later," Red Sea Wolf said. "A *new* new name."

"What is your name now?" Iakinthu asked Fisher, for this was an unfamiliar transition.

"I'm Rhenthizu of the Idaeans," he said. He grinned. "For now."

"Aranthau wants us!" Paissu said, always watching, always on lookout. "The tide's turning."

Aranthau gestured to them from the bow of *Flying Fish*. He had continued to respect Talishu-Bikulu's admonition, coming to shore only the once, to warn of the great wave.

In the ship's boat and the small canoes, the companions returned to *Flying Fish* and clambered aboard. Uinthi came last, handing over the carven paddle, resigned to rowing from now on.

Iakinthu welcomed Red Sea Wolf to her new home. She reached down to scratch the woolly-dog's ears.

"Has it a name?"

"Should I name a creature who could so easily be taken from me?"

"You can safely name it now."

It leaned into Iakinthu's hand, then suddenly jumped back and began yapping, the bark so sharp and high it hurt her ears.

"You could name it Bdarde," Rhenthizu said, so softly Iakinthu understood that only Maranti was meant to hear. All three laughed, to the puzzlement of Red Sea Wolf.

Iakinthu wiped away sudden tears, remembering Bdarde-that-is, and his anger; and Bdarde-that-was, and her music.

"Is its bark like a lute?" she said.

"Ah," Maranti said, and stroked Iakinthu's shoulder.

"Kinuku," said Red Sea Wolf. "Her name is Kinuku."

The slide of the anchor rope, the thud of the anchor reaching its place, alerted them all to their duties. Rhenthizu took the steering oar; Aranthau strode to the bow; Paissu scrambled to her lookout post.

"Uinthi!" she cried.

She pointed toward the headland.

Held aloft by the twisted fingers of the last windblown trees, Uinthi's birchbark canoe glowed white against the sky.

Iakinthu hurried to Uinthi's side.

"Shall we go back? Shall we fetch it?"

Uinthi sank to the deck, said, "Kilinkizu might need it," and burst into tears.

Iakinthu and Maranti embraced their friend.

The sails unfurled, snapping full in a sharp gust of wind.

Flanked by Akokulu canoes, paddlers bidding them farewell, *Flying Fish* plunged out into the strait and headed west, toward the Untamable Ocean.

THE END

Acknowledgments

Many thanks to the people who read & commented on early drafts. All errors are my own. Do not try to match the Idaean timeline to ours because your head will explode.

I hope Kate will forgive me the kimonos.

Debbie Notkin
Jane Hawkins
Jay Powell
Kate Schaefer
Kelley Eskridge
Nancy Jane Moore
Nicola Griffith
Paul Preuss
Sasha Rain Dancing Penn-Roco, Chehalis Tribe
Tamara Vining

(To come, next draft:)
Debra Turner
Eileen Gunn
Glenn Hackney
John D. Berry

Books

It would be impossible to list all the books and sources I read over the years that I found immensely helpful, including the websites of the Quileute Nation and the Chinook Nation.

Shake-up-your-brain books include *1491* by Charles C. Mann, and *Amazons* and *The First Fossil Hunters* by Adrienne Mayor.

About the Author

Born in Kentucky in 1948, Vonda Neely McIntyre arrived in the Pacific Northwest as a child of six. She wrote, taught, edited, influenced, nourished, and celebrated science fiction every year of her adulthood. She sold her first short story, "Breaking Point," in 1969, at the age of twenty; in 1971, McIntyre founded the Clarion West Writers Workshop, which instructs and supports emerging science fiction, fantasy, and horror authors. In 1973 she won her first (but not her last) Nebula Award for the novelette "Of Mist and Grass and Sand." In 2019 she died, shortly after completing her last novel's manuscript. A brilliant and audacious author whose complete bibliography is available online courtesy of her website (https://vondanmcintyre.net/biography/), McIntyre also earned a black belt in Aikido, crocheted intricate yet mathematically plausible beaded sea creatures, and baked the fluffiest of scones.